JAMES

CALAMITY JAMES

WILLIAM W. JOHNSTONE

AND J.A. JOHNSTONE

PINNACLE BOOKS
Kensington Publishing Corp.

kensingtonbooks.com

PINNACLE BOOKS are published by

Kensington Publishing Corp.
900 Third Avenue
New York, NY 10022

PUBLISHER'S NOTE: Following the death of William W. Johnstone, the Johnstone family is working with a carefully selected writer to organize and complete Mr. Johnstone's outlines and many unfinished manuscripts to create additional novels in all of his series, like The Last Gunfighter, Mountain Man, and Eagles, among others. This novel was inspired by Mr. Johnstone's superb storytelling.

All Kensington titles, imprints, and distributed lines are available at special quantity discounts for bulk purchases for sales promotion, premiums, fundraising, and educational or institutional use.

Special book excerpts or customized printings can also be created to fit specific needs. For details, write or phone the office of the Kensington Sales Manager: Kensington Publishing Corp., 900 Third Avenue, New York, NY 10022. Attn. Sales Department. Phone: 1-800-221-2647.

PINNACLE BOOKS, the Pinnacle logo, and the WWJ steer head logo Reg. U.S. Pat. & TM Off.

First Printing: July 2025
ISBN-13: 978-0-7860-5150-2
ISBN-13: 978-0-7860-5153-3 (eBook)

10 9 8 7 6 5 4 3 2 1

Printed in the United States of America

The authorized representative in the EU for product safety and compliance is eucomply OU, Parnu mnt 139b-14, Apt 123
Tallinn, Berlin 11317, hello@eucompliancepartner.com.

— PART ONE —

BEING AN INTRODUCTION TO THE PRINCIPAL CHARACTERS IN THIS NARRATION

1842–1851

CHAPTER 1

He was born in the cabin his father's congregation built. It burned down that night.

At least his mother was used to hard luck. Anyone who came to this earth in Kentucky, even those born into money and good stock, knows all too much about misfortune. As a child, Zerelda Cole's father broke his neck in a riding accident, her brother would kill himself in 1895, and between her birth and her brother's demise, she would witness more torment and tragedy, more brutality and beastliness, than a writer of myriad penny dreadfuls could dream up. Giving birth to an illegitimate child fathered by a soon-to-be minister just continued Zerelda's string of foul luck.

This is not to say that Calvin Amadeus James was born out of wedlock. Even those who could not fill a flush at a table or bet on the right horse to win at Kansas City's agricultural fair eventually will see something work out. No, Cal was born on January 28, 1842, one month after Robert James married Zerelda, whose daddy had been dead since she was two years old, and her mama, after remarrying, had left that young but tough girl with her grandpa Cole. And even though the fire that left the new cabin in ashes and just about everything the newlyweds owned was consumed in the blaze, one of the blessings was that Robert James's family Bible was lost, too. The parents of Cal, a pink lad of five pounds, seven ounces, would not realize this at first—indeed, there were many tears and questions to the Lord of why, why, *why?*—but well before Cal reached the age for schooling, both Robert and Zee—Zee being what most folks called Cal's mama—realized that the loss of the cabin, and the family Bible, was a blessing from the Almighty.

That Bible was the only written documentation to prove that Calvin James was ever born into this family. Zee didn't even call for a midwife to birth her first baby. That was all left to Zee and her praying husband, and the baby entered the world bawling and pink and healthy.

Yes, sympathy should be given to Cal, for his father and mother decided, since Robert was about to graduate from Georgetown College and enter the ministry—though he was already practicing his sermoning but not his baptisms at the cabin those settlers had put up—that they would be better off giving up the infant. Robert paid a young couple to take the newborn as their own. It would work out for the best, all parties agreed, because the woman, Charity Marmaduke, just lost her own infant child to an outbreak of diphtheria, and, more important, she and her husband, Obadiah, were headed west.

Robert wiped his eyes and did some serious praying and begging for forgiveness as the Marmadukes rolled down the pike with the sleeping infant in his new mama's lap, but Zerelda was of sterner stock, and she just spit the juice from her snuff into the grass. As fate would have it, Zerelda would get in the family way again and give birth to a strapping young fellow. By then, the Reverend Robert James was preaching the gospel. They named the new baby Alexander Franklin James, who entered this world, on January 10, 1843, on their farm near Centerville, Missouri—which eventually changed its name, as towns were fond of doing in those times (especially when it came time to get a post office), to Kearney.

But we shall come back to the James family in due time.

Obadiah and Charity Marmaduke were, like Cal's true parents, natives of Kentucky. Bluegrass ran through their veins. Their grandparents, if you believe the stories Obadiah told in the taverns and after barn raisings, had traveled to Kentucky with Daniel Boone. And even if the closest the Marmadukes ever got to Daniel Boone was following the trails he had blazed, Obadiah did have a case of the wanderlust that afflicted Dan'l and other explorers of our wondrous western frontier.

The Marmadukes settled in Iowa, and, oh, how Charity doted on that baby boy, even though he had a habit of crying and keeping both new mother and new father awake all night. Charity once confided to a friend that she hardly slept a wink on the journey by wagon from Kentucky. But she was a young woman with a baby boy to hold and she was not one to complain. At least, for the first couple of years.

They kept his name, at least Calvin, which, as most Calvins will tell you, got shortened to Cal. They even told the Jameses they would keep his middle name, Amadeus, and it was penciled into their Bible, too, but the lead faded, and worsened after the roof leaked and soaked that Good Book.

We should point out that by the time the boy was five years old, calamity followed young Cal with such frequency that not only friends of the Marmadukes but the Marmadukes themselves thought there might be some truth to the rumor quickly spreading that a Kickapoo woman had put a curse on the newborn—despite the fact that it's hard to find a Kickapoo in Kentucky. Or Iowa. In fact, after years of investigation, we have never found proof that any Kickapoo ever set foot in the state that has given us Daniel Boone, Jim Bowie, and Kit Carson.

And certainly not Iowa.

Folks started calling young Cal, a tall, good-looking, and fairly smart lad, "Calamity," because bad luck just seemed to follow him, though, more often than not, bystanders—and not that strapping youngster—seemed to get the worse of things.

Like the horseshoe-pitching contest on the Fourth of July when Cal was five or six years old when all the boy had to do was come close and he would have won the fat sow for a prize. Instead, he busted out the windowpane at the Market House—which was behind Cal. The owner of the Market House, a generous sort, shrugged it off, even though glass was right scarce around Flint Hill.

Iowa on the Mississippi River was a fine place to be in the 1840s. The pig market was sound, and cholera was kept in check, at least more than it was down south in St. Louis and New Orleans, where folks boarded steamboats all the time to escape that infernal plague. There were tanners and hunters, coopers and grocers, merchants dealing in dry goods, queensware, boots, nails, iron, stone, steel, nails, Jewett's Patent Carey Ploughs, medicines, dyes, putty, saddles, tin. There were more lawyers than one could shake a stick at. There was a congregational church on Columbia Street, but Partridge often opened up the hall above his store for other religious services. And the *Burlington Hawk-Eye* came out at least once a week, most times. In fact, Mr. Marmaduke read about the war against Mexico in that newspaper, and considered going, but decided against it.

There wasn't a dentist, the nearest one being a steamboat ride down to St. Louis, but you could get a tooth pulled by just about anyone who had a keg of whiskey and a pair of pliers.

"Maybe I should have gone to Mexico," Obadiah was heard to say at Van Dien's groggery in the dreary winter of 1846–47, when Iowa was still celebrating its admittance into the Union. "I could have died a hero at the Alamo."

"That wasn't the Mexican war, feller," the man next to him said.

"Sure, it was," Obadiah said. "Mexicans slaughtered Crockett and Bowie and all them others."

"That was the war for Texas," the stranger said.

"Then Mexico and Santee Annie got riled and that's why we marched to Mexico. To free Texas agin and get all the rest of 'em places. Like Californie."

"You don't know nothin', mister. So quit yer brayin'."

That resulted in Obadiah having to work his way to St. Louis and back as a stevedore to get a busted tooth pulled.

Obadiah could have kept on stevedoring but complained that the work was too hard and that the Mississippi River was a right frightening place to be traveling. And sometimes the river stunk worser than a pig farm.

In short, the Marmadukes had landed in a place that was full of opportunities, for this was the West (at least at that time), and a fellow could make his mark in this wild, new, free country.

Unless your name happened to be Obadiah Marmaduke.

Especially after Obadiah gave up on being a stevedore. Well, that job did require a willingness to sweat for hours, and you ought to be able to carry a fifty-pound keg down the plank and up the bank without dropping it three times.

Speaking of dropping, a pail of nails slipped out of Obadiah's hand and fell on the construction boss's right foot, and so Obadiah was unemployed as soon as Mr. Clavean stopped hopping around and cussing up a storm. The nails didn't weigh anywhere near fifty pounds, but five pounds on your big toe when you're not expecting it hurts just the same.

Old Fullerton gave him a chance at selling dry goods, but Obadiah was color-blind and couldn't tell a bolt of blue gingham from the pink one, and he broke two silk parasols trying to show Mrs. Bettie McDowell how to open one. Those were the five-dollar parasols, mind you, not the fifty-cent ones.

He tried selling bottles of Wistar's Balsam of Wild Cherry, which, he said, reading from the slip of paper he was given and twenty-seven cents in advance, could prevent the consumption killing fifty thousand folks a year and also remedy any liver affections, and asthma and bronchitis, not to mention things like chronic coughs and weak lungs, or even bleeding lungs. Problem was, Obadiah realized he liked the taste of the wild cherry and drunk up three bottles without selling a one. Chillicothe George, who was running that deal, broke one of the empty bottles over Obadiah's head.

Thing was, Obadiah Marmaduke had been quite successful back in Kentucky. That's how come he could afford a wagon and mules to take his family all the way to the Mississippi and cross it into Iowa Territory, which entered the Union on December 28, 1846.

So poor Obadiah took to drink and then, as so often can be the case, he took to cards.

Glory be, for a while he thought his luck had changed.

Obadiah Marmaduke won a sternwheeler in a poker game, and everyone said that the Marmadukes had it made now, for the *Hawkeye* was one of the finest vessels on the Mississippi, a double-engine mastered by the able and fine Christian captain, Silas S. Throckmorton. Two nights later, bound for Oquawka, New Boston, Bloomington, Rock Island, Davenport, Galena, Dubuque, and Potosi, the *Hawkeye* went up in flames just like the

James's cabin. Some folks said they had seen young Cal poking at a fire near the boat landings—though he might have just been warming himself, as it was February and the temperature was well below zero—but most just chalked it up to a stevedore who had been careless with pipe or cigar.

This was about the time that Obadiah began to think about his son who really wasn't his son, and began to believe that the Almighty had turned His back on a poor struggling, kindhearted, and hardworking (at least in his own mind) soul who had had a lovely wife, who had been distraught over losing a young son, then thrived at first with Cal, but now was disheveled, dismayed, and disillusioned.

Once, after Cal had been playing with a dog and one, either canine or kid, had torn up half the butter bean plants, Obadiah had sighed, found the jug of Carmichael's corn liquor, and said, "I swan, Charity, but that boy is a jinx or a curse."

"Hush your mouth, Husband!" Charity barked back, and Obadiah obeyed.

But later—after Charity stepped on a nail and had to find the Indian woman who could cure such injuries, and the Indian woman (who was not Kickapoo, but Otoe) would not treat Charity unless that boy of hers was out of sight, so Charity told Cal to go to the river and fish, and after the nail wound was treated, and though no fish were caught, Grover Denton drowned in the Mississippi that day, albeit his boat capsized a good two hundred yards downstream from where Cal was wetting his line—"Maybe," Charity suggested to

Obadiah, "'taint Cal who's causin' us this mess of bad luck. Maybe it's just Iowa is a curse to us."

Which got them to thinking.

After all, it wasn't like Burlington, Iowa, was some sort of paradise, not after struggling to survive for nigh a dozen years. Charity conceded that she missed Kentucky. She even told her husband she might could settle for Missouri.

Little did she know that Missouri was about to come to their home.

CHAPTER 2

Charity Marmaduke was putting out the fire when, over the towering flames and popping of grease in the skillet in the chimney, she heard a man's voice call out, "Halloooo, the cabin."

She had just screamed at young Cal, because when the skillet got all blazing, she asked for the flour, and the young lad, about eight years old, handed her the sugar by mistake. Fire, in case you are not much at cooking, reacts to sugar a whole lot differently than it does to flour. Much shrieking and some profanity followed as flames leaped toward the roof and smoke caused both mother and child to cough a bit and shriek in alarm a lot more. Charity found the flour herself, thus tragedy was averted.

Strangers were uncommon at the Marmaduke cabin—a little ways out of town—but not unheard of. Still, Charity, fanning herself with a smoky-smelling towel, left the fireplace, which served as the winter and summer kitchen, since the summer setup had been destroyed by an angry cow Cal had been trying to milk.

"Don't open that door, boy!" Charity snapped, when

she realized what her son, her adopted son, was about to do. She dunked the towel into a bucket of water—which Cal had brought in to throw on the fire in the skillet before his mother had screamed, "No!" and later would teach him that oil fires and water do not mix well at all, same as oil fires and sugar, and such an act might could have burned down the entire cabin and, possibly, mother and son, with it.

A muzzle-loading rifle leaned in the corner near the door, but Charity did not go for it. She simply looked through the peephole in the door, pulled back, rubbed her eyes, then tried for a better view.

Recognition was slow to come, but come it did, and Charity stepped back.

"Who is it, Mama?" Cal asked, then coughed, because smoke remained heavy. The fireplace had never drawn worth a fig, even when it was burning oak, not grease.

Well, she needed to open the door anyway to let that rancid smoke out of their home. Rubbing her eyes, she looked at Cal, then peered through the hole again. Maybe she had been seeing things.

She hadn't.

"Stay—" No, she couldn't let the boy stay inside this smoky cabin that stunk of burned grease and scorched bacon.

So she opened the door.

"Come along, Cal," she said. "Leave the door open so the smoke'll go out. And"—she stepped outside—"company's here."

The man held the reins to a good horse. He removed

his black hat and bowed slightly. The wind blew the linen duster.

"Preacher," she said softly. "How are things in—?" She almost said Kentucky, but Robert James had written every Christmas. The letters were always signed by him, not his wife. They were short, simple, usually with a verse or two of Scripture.

"Missouri?" Charity finished.

The Reverend Robert Sallee James bowed, and put his flat black hat atop his head.

"Fine, Missus Marmaduke," the preacher said. His eyes quickly moved from the woman to the boy.

God was good, he thought with a smile. The kid looked more like his daddy than he did his ma. The preacher's wife was a good woman, a fine mother, worked harder in gardens than anyone the preacher had known, and could milk a cow without complaint. And was fat and mean and ugly.

"Cal," Charity said, turning to the tall, strapping handsome kid. "This is— This is . . . a preacher we knew back in Kentucky. The Reverend James."

"Preacher." Cal nodded.

"Calvin," the preacher said. He must have gotten some smoke in his eyes, the boy thought, because he brought a knuckle to his right eye, then his left, and sniffed a bit before his Adam's apple went up and down.

"Why don't you bring your horse to the corral?" Charity suggested. "Cal, go fill a bucket with water from the well, and then get some grain for the preacher's hoss."

Cal did as he was told, and with the horse drinking

and snorting up some grain, he walked over to the
stump that served as a thinking chair in the front yard.
The preacher was sitting, but Cal, without even being
ordered, drug the rocking chair off the porch and brought
it so that his mother could rest. Then he put his hands
behind his back and just stood there like that knot on a
log folks was always talking about.

The stranger, Cal learned, was the minister at New
Hope Baptist Church in Clay County, Missouri. He
had two sons, Frank being the oldest, seven years old,
"just about a year younger than you, Calvin." The man's
clear eyes smiled at young Cal, who thought this
preacher was a real preacher and knowed things better
than anyone who didn't know the gospel from cover to
cover, because most folks thought Cal was a good year
or two older than he actually was.

"A young son—Jesse—he'll be three when September
comes along. And a precious little girl, Susan Lavenia.
She's just a couple of months old now." He looked
around. "Is this strapping young lad your only child?"

"Yes, Reverend," was all Cal's mama said, and she
changed the subject. "What brings you so far from your
congregation—and your family?"

The preacher sipped water Cal had brung him.

"I'm called to preach," he said. "We have a fine new
church at New Hope—made of brick—but I ride the
circuit for the Lord."

He preached on and on about all he had done in Missouri. Luring some Baptist college to the nearby town
of Liberty; it had just opened its doors this year of 1850.
He had married many young couples, saved hundreds

of souls, preached far too many funerals, and shown the unenlightened the Light.

"And my family has a fine cabin on a creek in Clay County. We have a fine farm. Growing hemp for cash. And food to eat. They'll be fine without me. The Lord called me to Missouri, and I've preached and saved many souls. But now,"—he pointed west—"now there is a great migration to California. Gold fever is luring many folks westward. Gold can bring deviltry with it, and I must fight the devil with all my might. So I am bound for California. For how long, I do not know."

"How far away is Californie?" Cal asked.

The preacher smiled. "As far as it takes us to get there."

"You goin' alone?" Charity asked.

"I go with the Lord." Smiling, he pointed south and west. "I'm to join a party in Independence, Missouri."

Charity stared at the reverend for a long while. After glancing at her son, she looked Preacher James in his sparkling clear eyes.

"Ain't this a fer piece out of your way?"

This time, the preacher did not answer.

"Cal," Charity said, "go get that skillet, and take it to the crick and wash it good. We don't want the preacher to think we'll serve him burnt bacon on his journey west to save souls and such."

The boy didn't want to go, but he did.

"Scrub that skillet good," she told him, and then waited for the Reverend James to speak his piece.

Which Charity related to her husband when the worthless oaf came home that evening.

* * *

Obadiah Marmaduke's mouth stayed open.

He was sober, bringing home all of his twelve and a half cents he had earned doing a few odd jobs in town. He scratched the stubble on his cheeks. He was sure he was sober. He didn't recall going into any saloon, and besides, most of the grog shops wouldn't let him inside, anyway.

"Say that agin," he requested of his wife.

"The preacher wants to take Cal with him."

That's what it had sounded like the first time.

The man's sore head shook slowly. He found the cup of coffee, which wasn't really coffee but was all they could afford, and drank about a quarter of it down.

"There's a train—wagon train—they are to join in Independence. A number of Missourians are going."

"We ought to go!" Obadiah sang out.

"We're not going to California," she told him. "I'm too far from Kentucky as it is, and there are wild Indians between here and that gold—if there's any gold left by the time we could get there—and California is full of Mexicans, I hear, who don't speak a word of English."

"Like Kentuckians do!" Laughing at his joke, Obadiah slapped his knee.

Charity's eyes stifled his hilarity and left him groveling and staring at his worn-out boots.

"What's the preacher want with Cal?"

The woman sighed. "Forgiveness," she whispered.

"Huh?"

"He feels he committed a sin. Which"—she shrugged—

"I guess he did. I guess we all did. And he wants to get to know his son. That's the best I could get out of what he was saying. He'd say this, then bawl for thirty or forty seconds, then spout out some Scripture, then cry some more, and then he would talk about that woman he married."

Obadiah leaned forward. This might be something worth hearing.

"Well, between tears and torment," Charity said, "what I taken from his talkin' is that this Zerelda James ain't the most forgivin' and kindly Christian woman you'd expect to be a preacher's wife. She yells and threatens. She don't even like for him to go runnin' off here and there all the time to preach—even if that's what a preacher does."

"Maybe he just wants gold," Obadiah suggested. "I heard on the riverfront that the newspapers say that the gold won't never run out. That it's like pickin' apples off an apple tree. That there's more gold than there is ants in California, and a body can't help but get rich there. Maybe we should—"

"We're not going anywhere," she told him. "Till they run you out of town."

He pouted. She sighed after two minutes and leaned over and patted his hand.

Looking into his wife's eyes, Obadiah whispered, "Do you think he'll tell Cal the truth?"

"Do you think he should?"

He studied his feet, then looked around the cabin, then stared at his wife again. "He's handy to have around, ain't he?"

Charity sighed and shook her head.

"We were young and foolish and heartbroke." Her head bowed, and she sniffled. "But he is a good boy. Handsome. He's just . . ."

"Unlucky."

Her head shook. "To us." Her eyes met his again. "He almost burned down the cabin this morn."

"Did the preacher mention, ummmm . . . you know—maybe offering . . . some money—for getting his son back?"

She would have slapped him, but she recalled the Reverend James's words about forgiveness and charity and love.

The hard part, of course, was telling Cal the truth.

Which is why they lied: California was the land of dreams and gold, and the future—their future—lay in that wondrous place. It would be an adventure. Riding—though from what Charity had heard, it was a whole lot more walking than riding to get to California—across the great West, seeing those never-ending plains and then the greatest spectacles in all of America—the mountains, the glorious Rockies and Sierras, so high they touched the clouds. Waterfalls and rapids. Sunsets with every color on the palette stretching across a never-ending sky. And the Pacific Ocean, blue and calm and wondrous.

Cal's eyes brightened at his future. In California, no one would know how much bad luck he brought with him. He would have friends. And maybe he would keep friends. Maybe his luck would change in California. He probably could find some gold, too. He'd be helpful, for once.

"When do we leave?" he shouted.

"Well,"—his mother reached out and patted his hand—"you're going out with the Reverend James." She waved her hand around the cabin. "We have to sell our place, you see."

He saw—*he saw his mother's eyes.* He said, "I see."

But he told himself that California would be an adventure. And there was something about the preacher that he liked and respected. Cal's ma had taken him to services, maybe not every Sunday, but lots of times, and he had enjoyed the singing. He could belt out "Rock of Ages" like everyone else, and there was much satisfaction in saying amen. And he sure liked that concept of forgiveness.

So he forgave his mother, silently, and asked the Almighty to do the same. Then he climbed up to his bed to pack up his clothes and such, and get ready for the trip west.

CHAPTER 3

Let us take time to dispel those vicious rumors that young Cal traveled west with the unfortunate Donner Party. The Donners, and their fellow travelers, hit the trail in the year 1846—four years before young Cal and the Reverend James departed for that wonderous, glorious gold country—and the Donner tragedy occurred during the winter of 1846–47 in the frigid Sierra Nevada.

That is not to say that the Fernsby–Nuttal party, which departed Independence in the late spring of 1850, crossed our great country without misfortune. Kaynesville on the bluffs in Iowa was closer, but the Reverend James said he wanted to travel west with men from his country, Missouri, so they rode and walked down the Missouri River's banks past St. Joseph in Missouri. It was there that young Cal stopped suddenly in the street, feeling a strange coldness from his eyeballs down to his toes.

It's what his mother often called a premonition, which, since his mother did not explain the meaning of, Cal took it as something along the lines of pneumonia.

"What is it, Son?" the preacher asked.

"I'm c-c-c-cold," Cal stuttered.

"It'll warm up," the preacher said.

Cal looked slowly up and down the streets, seeing houses scattered about. No cemeteries. No ghouls. No Angel of Death. And the chill vanished almost as quickly as it had latched onto his body.

The horse was stolen that night while the Reverend James was preaching at a tent revival, but the good man just sighed and said it was "God's will."

"Come, laddie," the preacher said. "Let us see about passage to Independence. I dare not risk arriving there late. Captain Shufflebottom is expecting us, but he is not one to wait. We do not want to be stuck in the High Sierras of California during the winter."

They joined a wagon train that was bringing supplies to Springfield but had to stop in Independence to pick up a load of hemp. The Reverend James was preaching every night for his passage. Cal had to help tend oxen. But he had always liked animals.

Two busted axles and one poisoned water hole slowed them down, and Captain Raskopf said he had never had such cursèd luck on a short trip like that one, but they reached Independence just two days late, and one day before Captain Shufflebottom's scheduled departure for Hangtown.

Captain Shufflebottom stared at Cal, while shifting the corncob pipe from one side of his mouth to the other. "Preacher," he said, when he finally said something after studying the pair for a good two or three minutes. "I'll put you with the Magees. The boy can walk with the Bartlesons. I thought you had a hoss."

"Stolen," the preacher said. "St. Joseph."

The captain nodded. "That place attracts devils, demons, and dunces. Well, no matter."

"I'd rather ride in a wagon than on the back of a horse for three months," said Reverend James, with a smile.

"Preacher,"—now Captain Shufflebottom pulled the pipe from his mouth and tapped it against his thigh— "nobody rides in a wagon lessen they be sick or with child. You walk. Wagons is loaded with food and things needed. The Nuttals is bringing lots of chickens. Sheep, goats, cows, pigs can walk. Luckily we ain't got no pigs bound for the promised land on this trek. Mr. Magee, he has peach saplings. But I've told him that any watering of those trees comes out of his allotment when we're in dry country. And trust me, boys, there will be lots of dry country."

He returned the pipe to his mouth and stared at Cal. "What can you do, sonny?"

Cal gave that some serious thought. Finally, he said, "I can read. Except for the big words I don't know. But I can usually mouth those out so that they're close, though I can't tell you what they mean."

To the preacher's surprise, the captain nodded.

"Well, that'll come in handy, I reckon, when someone wants to chisel his name at Chimney Rock. Or when we have to scratch in a rock that we're using as a gravestone. Can ya shoot?"

"He is but a mere boy, captain," the Reverend James protested.

"Tall for his age. And buffalo meat is good eating. And ain't nothing better than tongue. And in case you ain't figgered something out, preacher, there's a passel of Injuns we's like to run across. Most of 'em be friendly, or just plumb curious, but some of 'em can be particular about who they wants to let through their country."

He walked to his sorrel horse and pulled a big revolver out of a saddle holster, then barked out a name that Cal couldn't quite catch. Cal saw a skinny, bearded fellow run twenty yards to the wagon master.

"Give that long gun to the boy there, Vincenzo. Let's see how he can shoot."

The swarthy man, who wore a red sash and floppy hat, ambled over to Cal carrying a long rifle in his hands. The man smiled and held out the long gun, which Cal took, and almost dropped.

Everyone, even the Reverend James, chuckled a bit.

"This here, *ragazzino*, is a Hawken," Vincenzo said. "Fifty-three caliber." The man's voice was musical, with an accent Cal had never heard, and those dark eyes danced. "Have you ever fired a long gun before?"

Cal's head shook. He remembered his manners, especially with a preacher just five yards from him, and said, "No, sir."

"Well, first, see if you can lift it to your shoulder. It weighs nigh eleven pounds."

"It is heavy," Cal agreed, and slowly brought the stock to his shoulder.

"Made to last. Though some of that weight is because of the butt plate and trimmings. Iron. But it's a rifle that will put just about anything down, and when it's down, it won't get back up."

Cal studied the long gun and slowly started to slip his finger inside the trigger guard, but stopped.

"There's two triggers," he said, in surprise. "But only one barrel."

Both the boss of the train and the dark man named Vincenzo smiled, while a few other men chuckled. Cal turned to see that a crowd was beginning to gather, boys younger and older than Cal, grown men, some of them sporting long white whiskers, women and children, and a few right pretty girls in bonnets. Cal swallowed down whatever was rising up his throat.

"The rear one's a set trigger," Vincenzo said. "Pull it first. That'll set the front trigger. And it'll be a hair trigger. One soft touch and that cannon's firing, so don't touch that one till you're ready to shoot. And brace yourself. She'll kick like a stallion with *un temperamento focoso*."

Cal figured out what the man meant.

"What do you want me to shoot?" he asked.

He was aiming out toward the prairie—nothing in the way that he could see—but trash and plenty of furniture and trunks and dishes that families were abandoning here because their wagons couldn't haul everything from Independence to California's gold country.

Captain Shufflebottom had come up to Cal's left. "See that cherry chifforobe on its side next to the overturned water barrel without a bottom?" The boss of the wagon train used the barrel of that giant six-shooter in his hand as a pointer.

Cal found it easily. "Yes, sir."

"Off to the left, then beyond that, is a clay pot."

That took Cal longer to find.

After Cal said, "I see it," he realized he was sweating.

"That's your target, sonny. Think you can hit it?"

Cal didn't answer. He glanced toward the preacher and saw the man's head bowed, and lips moving at a right steady clip. And the minister from Missouri appeared to be sweating more than Cal, and that man of the cloth wasn't trying not to drop a rifle that weighed almost eleven pounds and felt like fifty.

"Don't close both eyes," Vincenzo whispered. "That is the way some men shoot, but two eyes see better than one. Line up the target, breathe out, stay steady, and just touch the trigger."

Staring, Cal saw the patch of reddish clay, and suddenly felt at ease. This was a whole lot easier than shucking corn or dragging his unconscious pa out of a riverfront saloon.

Now, Cal was average size for an eight-year-old boy, but the Hawken weighed aplenty, and steadying that proved downright impossible. Folks were laughing as the rifle moved in a circle, round and round, round and round, but Cal kept both eyes open, and his target kept coming into the sights and out again as the rifle went round and round.

Round and round.

Round and round.

He figured out the timing. The rifle kept moving. He touched the set trigger. There was the pot. There it was again. The laughter got louder. There was the pot. The Hawken came around again.

He touched the trigger, and wondered if he would ever hear again or get his right shoulder put back in its socket.

Vincenzo took the rifle, and smiled. Cal couldn't hear much for a moment because of the ringing in his ears, and then laughter exploded and someone sang out a huzzah!

"You missed," Captain Shufflebottom said.

Cal felt like he had been punched in the stomach. He whirled and stared, breathing in the smell of burned gunpowder.

"No," he heard himself saying. "I saw the pot shatter."

"Boy," Mr. Nuttal said. "You couldn't even keep that Hawken steady. I thought you was gonna drop it. You missed by a mile!"

More laughter came hard and furious. He felt tears start to well, and turned to find the preacher, who came over and took the Hawken from the boy's hands.

"It's all right," the reverend said. "You tried your best."

"But I hit that pot!"

He didn't mean to shout that loudly, and felt the tense quiet that came to the campground.

"Boy," Shufflebottom said, "I was gonna see if you might be better with this Walker .44 than a Hawken. Give you a chance to see how good you might be with a short gun. Masterin' a Hawken takes time. But now that you're bein' disrespectful—"

"I hit that pot."

That time, Cal had meant to whisper, but everyone in camp could hear him, even those whose ears were still ringing from the report of the long gun.

"Mr. Fernsby," the captain said, his voice cold but clear, and the potbellied man stepped forward.

"Yes, cap'n?"

"Would you be so kind as to go pick up that pot, sir? See if even a piece is missin'?"

The fat man did not answer and set off to the chifforobe, then walked past the worthless water barrel and stopped, bent over, and picked up a small clay pot.

"It's like it just came out of Wilder's store," the man shouted.

"Bring it back for the boy to see for hisself," the captain shouted.

Cal blinked, shook his head, saw Vincenzo staring at him with sad eyes, and then butted the Hawken on the dirt. "But that's not the pot I shot!" he yelled.

The Reverend James came up to Cal and put his hand on the boy's shoulder and started to whisper, "Exodus, chapter twenty—"

"I ain't lying, reverend." Cal jerked away and pointed. "Turn around." He waved his right hand at Mr. Fernsby. "You're too close."

The fat man turned toward the captain.

But it was Vincenzo who moved, and the lithe man ran fast, leaping over the clay pot that had not been Cal's target, pushed the busted barrel a bit just to see how far it might roll, which was twenty yards.

Cal waved his right arm. "Farther!" He pointed vaguely. "Near that butter churn."

"What butter churn?" a white-bearded man asked.

"The one by that other chifforobe," Cal said.

Vincenzo sprinted off, stopped, turned. Sure enough, he found another abandoned chifforobe, but this one was in a lot sorrier state than closer one.

Cal motioned to his right. Vincenzo stepped off a few paces, then stopped, knelt, and rose.

The captain and the preacher shielded their eyes with their left hands. Vincenzo held something up, then let a few pieces fall. He knelt again, rose, and came sprinting back.

He was breathing hard and sweating when he stopped. His hands opened, and shards of clay fell out of his hands.

"Well," the captain said, "it was probably busted to begin with."

Cal felt the preacher's hand on his shoulder.

"Then put that first pot where that one was," the minister said, "and Cal will do it again."

He wasn't sure if the Reverend James meant that— believed that—but it sure made Cal feel better.

The white-bearded man grunted and said, "That boy hadn't even been near that heap of trash."

"Yeah," a woman agreed.

"Scratch shot," Captain Shufflebottom said. "You couldn't even hold that rifle steady for half a second."

"It was timing," Cal said.

"Timing." Mr. Nuttall harrumphed.

"Let him shoot again," someone suggested. "At that first pot."

The captain laughed, but Cal said, "I'll do that."

And he did. The same Hawken, moving round and round, touching the set trigger on one pass, and the front trigger on the next, and that clay pot disintegrated like the first—but, well, it was a wee bit closer.

"How long you been shootin'?" asked another man, who extended his hand after the commotion and swearing and hurrahing died down, and as the bets were being paid off. Cal accepted, and they shook. Which made his throbbing shoulder hurt worse.

"That's the first time I ever fired a rifle," he said, and then he reached over and winced when he touched his right shoulder.

"Golly, I bet I'll have a bruise for a month."

Captain Shufflebottom shook his head and stared at the big revolver he held. "I was gonna give you a chance at shootin' a short gun, but I think you'll do just fine with a long gun, sonny."

He moved the Colt to his left hand. "One day you might even be able to hold that long gun steady." He moved the Colt to his left hand, stepped closer to Cal, and extended his right toward Cal.

"Shake?"

Cal smiled, and accepted the big hand.

CHAPTER 4

One wagon axle broke. The Nuttals' lead ox roamed off. Clyde Totten chopped off his little finger on his left hand while trying to turn his wife's rocking chair into kindling. Mrs. Totten told him she wished he had cut off his whole hand since that chair had been her grandmother's, but Captain Shufflebottom explained that Mr. Totten was right, and that old as that chair was, it wouldn't have lasted halfway out of Kansas anyway. Mrs. Totten spit snuff juice between the captain's boots.

But no one other than Mrs. Totten complained. The captain said those first few days on the trail were as good as any he had seen on his trains taking settlers to the Oregon country.

After about a week, the routine on the wagon train became something almost regular. Before the second week started, the Bartlesons gave up, turned their wagon around, and said they were going back to Ohio. Captain Shufflebottom called them quitters and he didn't want quitters in his train. After they had left, the captain said he'd shoot the next quitters. He didn't tell Cal who he was to walk with now that the Bartlesons were gone, so Cal just walked by himself, and slept—when he was allowed to sleep—with the Reverend James.

Long before the sun made its appearance, Veronica Louise Fernsby, who was about Cal's age, started wailing on the harmonica. That was the signal to get up and get ready to move out. Most outfits, Captain Shufflebottom told Cal and the preacher, had a trumpet to blare, but the captain said he got his fill of trumpets while fighting the Mexicans with General Winfield Scott, and while other wagon bosses had someone fire a shot, the captain was not a man who wasted powder or lead.

"There's a passel of Indians between here and the promised land, and we might need every chunk of lead and every grain of powder we can muster."

On the first couple of days, Cal was assigned to help gather the cattle, which grazed throughout the night. But Cal realized that cattle did not like him, and he ran more off than he ran back to where they were supposed to be, so his duties soon became keeping the Hawken the captain loaned him—it was only .50 caliber, not as long, nowhere near as heavy as Vincenzo's big booming cannon—and Cal never had any call to fire it during that first month out of Independence.

He couldn't hold the .50 caliber any steadier than he had the larger rifle.

Breakfast, cooked by the women and kids, was always bacon and corn pone, though sometimes johnnycakes, with steaming hot coffee, and by then the skies were showing some light off to the east. The Reverend James always led the folks in prayer before they ate, but Cal heard some of the men and even womenfolk say he kept his prayer short and sweet, unlike many Baptists. At least in the mornings. Evening time, he could be on the windy side of things, but he had a fine voice and could belt out "Amazing Grace" like he belonged to an opera.

While women and young'uns washed the dishes and gathered up the beddings, the men took down the tents—those that had them—and stored them in the big wagons. The sun was rising, the oxen were hitched and ready, and three hours after that harmonica reveille, Captain Shufflebottom hollered out a "*Wagons, ho!*" and the train moved west.

Cal never forgot to thank the Reverend James for buying all those thick heavy socks—two pairs for the preacher but four for Cal—because they walked from right around seven in the morning and typically did not stop, unless some kind of trouble presented itself, till noon.

And that rest period lasted less than an hour most times. Just long enough to drink some water and eat some bread and bacon again—maybe coffee, but the coffee never had any sugar or milk.

Four more hours of walking, walking, walking, wiping dust out of your eyes, hearing just the turning of wheels, the clopping of hooves, cattle, horses, and mules snorting, chickens in their cages clucking, sheep bleating, and lots of cussing from the menfolk, which the preacher pretended not to hear.

When the sun hit the five o'clock position, the wagons would be parked in a circle, sort of like a corral, and the womenfolk would start fixing supper, and duties would be assigned to certain men and the older boys, including Cal. Usually Cal was sent to the highest spot near the campground and told to keep an eye out for anything suspicious.

But the only thing there was to see out in that country was more of that endless country.

He came in around seven, according to those with pocket watches that still kept good time, and ate supper with a couple of other guards. Then the captain would figure out the guard rotation for that evening. He was fair.

After that, songs might be sung, and a few men and women who were bold enough might dance, which the Reverend James ignored, though sometimes his Sunday sermons or evening prayer would mention that dancing was vulgar.

By eight o'clock, about the only noise heard above the animals and the wind, were snores.

Three families, including the Nuttals, had mules pulling their wagons, and the captain had no objections, but those families always "make up the hind end of our train," as Shufflebottom liked to say.

Vincenzo explained to Cal. "Mules are faster than oxen, and the captain does not wish for wagons to pull too far ahead. Oxen are slow, but tough and steady, and a mule can be—how do you say?—contrary. Mules aren't as strong as oxen, either."

Cal nodded his head.

"But"—the young man lowered his voice and stepped closer—"if we run into an Indian party that is not friendly, take your position near the mules."

"To keep the Indians from stealing them?" Cal asked.

Vincenzo chuckled, and slapped the boy's left shoulder. "You are strong and capable, *paisan*, but very green. The mule is fast. You have a better chance of keeping your scalp if you steal a mule and escape."

"I don't like it," Captain Shufflebottom said, after the first week.

"Not like it?" Mr. Fernsby almost spilled his coffee. "We haven't had one single problem since leaving Independence."

The captain's face hardened. "Usually, some fool has gotten gored or trampled or tossed from his horse. Or some kid has gotten run over by a wagon wheel."

"My goodness!" a woman gasped.

"It ain't goodness, ma'am," the captain said. "It's just life on the trail."

"We ain't seen no Indians," Mrs. Nuttal said.

"Too close to civilization," the captain explained. "But we will see them, whenever they decide they want to be seen."

The first Indians they saw were Pottawatomi, but those were just kids at St. Mary's Mission. The preacher had a fine talk with one of the Jesuits, and some of the women traded with the Indian women. After that, they moved northwest to Scotts Springs, where the captain told them to fill their barrels and anything that could hold water, because this was about the best water they'd find this side of the High Sierras. But he said the same thing when they reached Alcove Springs two days later—and when they crossed the Blue River the following day.

And the next eleven days were disastrous.

Gloria Coleman, just eleven years old, got bitten by a rattlesnake, and her right arm swelled to about the size of her thigh. LeRoy Hall had some doctoring skills and sucked the poison out of the arm, and the Reverend James prayed, and the girl recovered.

Mrs. Totten caught a fever the next morning and was dead that night, but the preacher gave her a fine funeral, and everyone smiled at the thought of her rocking in her rocking chair up in heaven, though there were tears in many eyes, too.

Finally, they pulled into Fort Kearny, twenty-three days since leaving Independence.

Mr. Totten decided he was fine spending the rest of his days in the saloons near the military post. Captain Shufflebottom said he signed on to go to California. Mr. Totten said California had lost its luster with the passing of his wife. The captain said a contract was a contract and they needed every man, mule, and ox to make it to the gold country. Mr. Totten reminded him that the Bartlesons had quit. Captain Shufflebottom reminded Mr. Totten that he said he'd shoot the next quitter. Mr. Totten said they could take his wagon and his oxen if they wanted, because all he wanted was his bed and the daguerreotype of his beloved wife. The Reverend James intervened, and the captain listened and sighed, then told Mr. Totten they would miss him and he could keep his wagon and oxen, and they left Fort Kearny the following morning.

Twelve days later, they arrived at Ash Hollow.

The country changed. Courthouse and Jail Rocks were visible on the south side of the sprawling Platte, though Cal couldn't figure out which one was the courthouse and which one was the jail. They just looked like sandstone buttes to him. At least Chimney Rock, which popped up the next day, looked sort of like a chimney. Mr. Nuttal said the sight of such a monument made by God's hand made him feel like an insect. Captain Shufflebottom said they would see a whole lot more before their journey had ended. The preacher led them in prayer, and then everyone sang a hymn.

By the time they reached Scottsbluff, they were sick of rocks. Sick of the trail. Sick of the food. Some were actually sick. But westward they continued.

A little more than four days later, they reached Fort Laramie.

A man with two silver-plated pistols—he said; Captain Shufflebottom later pointed out that they were nickel—calling himself Sean Clean rode into the camp and invited them to his establishment where honest games of faro, twenty-one, and poker could be played. The Reverend James invited Cal to come to the Army post with him and visit with the chaplain, and see if he needed any help preaching the gospel. But Cal said he had already told Vincenzo that he would go exploring with him.

To Cal's surprise, the preacher said that was fine, but not to stay out late and, above all, to avoid intoxicating spirits and women of the night.

Cal didn't know what women of the night were. But Vincenzo explained it quite quickly.

"For money?" Cal asked. "I thought you only did that for love."

Vincenzo smiled. "It is for love. The love of money."

But Vincenzo decided not to get Cal in trouble with Preacher James, and they went to Sean Clean's Cards and Roulette.

"You watch," Vincenzo told the boy. "I'll play. You watch. And don't say a word to anyone."

At the bar, Vincenzo ordered rum for himself and asked about a sarsaparilla for Cal, but the bartender said it was liquor or coffee or go back to your mama. Cal said coffee was fine, but the coffee was anything but fine. So Cal stopped drinking after two sips and watched Vincenzo try his hand at faro.

The game, as best as Cal could figure out, was pretty simple. Vincenzo won four hands in a row and when the dealer suggested raising the stakes, that maybe "Vinnie"—which is what the mustached dealer called Vincenzo—would like to raise the ante, maybe bet that Hawken rifle he was carrying, Vincenzo smiled, and said, "No, I've had enough."

The gambler frowned and slid back his chair. "What do you mean you've had enough? You've just played four hands."

"Yeah. I figure that's the limit I can win. So we're leaving."

The gambler stood before Vincenzo could.

"I think you're calling me a cheat," the gambler said, and Cal realized that nobody was talking now, except the gambler and Vincenzo. The clicking of the roulette wheel had stopped, too.

Mr. Miller from the wagon train got up and left in a hurry. Cal saw no one else from the train in this place, but there wasn't much light.

Vincenzo stood, still holding his Hawken.

"You heard him, didn't you, Sean?" the faro man called out to the fellow behind the bar who had invited them to this cabin. "He called me a liar and a cheat. And called me a dirty name."

"He didn't say—" Cal started, but Vincenzo waved him to silence.

"I heard him," Mr. Clean said.

"Well, no man can insult me."

"Why not?"

Cal turned to the voice that came from the door. There stood Captain Shufflebottom, and he was holding a Walker Colt in his right hand.

The faro dealer slowly turned.

"After all," Captain Shufflebottom said, "you are a cheat and a crook and a liar. And you're ugly. And your mama couldn't cook."

The faro dealer might have done something. Cal wasn't sure. But the .44 in the captain's hand roared and spat out fire and smoke. And the faro dealer spun around, groaned, and dropped to the dirt floor dead. And Captain Shufflebottom then shot Mr. Clean. And then he said if anyone else wanted to die, they should stay inside this coffin because he had four more shots and was ready to use them.

No one, except Vincenzo and Cal and two dead men, plus the captain, was there ten seconds later.

CHAPTER 5

Vincenzo and Cal felt as though they had been turned into stone. For what seemed like an eternity, they could not move. The smoke from the captain's Walker Colt drifted toward the ceiling. Muffled voices came from outside, and Cal slowly turned and saw Vincenzo kicking the gambler's boots, then moving toward Mr. Clean but stopping at Shufflebottom's command.

"No need to check on him, either. I wasn't shootin' to wound."

Cal blinked. The nausea would come later. Somehow, realization of what he had just witnessed struck him and he turned to Shufflebottom and said, "Captain, you didn't give those men a chance."

The captain looked at Cal as if the boy were loco.

"They was armed. That's all the chance they was gettin'. And they woulda shot the both of you as quick as they could."

Two soldiers came through the door and stopped. The captain turned and nodded at them and said, "These two cheats and killers won't be troublin' you no more."

The soldiers looked about as white as Cal felt.

Then a man with a lot of gold on his dark blouse entered, puffing on a cigar, and looking like the boss of the whole United States Army.

"What happened here?" the man demanded.

"Couple of tinhorns and killers. The roulette wheel was rigged. So were the faro boxes. I called them on it. They didn't care for my call, so they called me. And I killed them."

The Army leader walked over to Mr. Clean and kicked his boot, then moved over to the gambler and nodded.

"If you hadn't done it, sir, one of my soldiers most likely would have—or would have gotten killed—and then we would have had to go through the dullness of a trial. I thank you, sir. I thank all of you." He looked at the first soldiers that had entered the building.

"Form a detail. Have these two men buried. Confiscate the liquor and have all of it removed to the post hospital. Except"—he pointed at a bottle behind the bar—"that. Bring the brandy to my office." He looked at Captain Shufflebottom. "And, sir, you may take your choice." The gray eyes darted to Vincenzo and then Cal. "Those look too young to be imbibing. But they can take whatever they find on the bodies of the deceased. Except for five dollars. I am told you have a preacher with you."

"That's right, major," Shufflebottom said.

"Five dollars will go to your preacher for speaking a few words over the graves of those two rapscallions. Not that it'll do them any good."

* * *

"This country does not end," the Reverend James said, some days after Fort Laramie was mostly forgotten.

"Goes a right fer piece," Captain Shufflebottom said, with a nod. "And it don't get no easier. That flat country is mostly behind us now. It'll be hard goin', but as long as we are at Independence Rock by early July, we should be all right."

Cal killed a buffalo with the Hawken two days later, and some men went to work butchering it. He was proud of the kill, thinking they would eat well for the following days, and they did. Except for Herman Grayson, who choked to death while eating some buffalo tongue.

Everyone—or at least Vincenzo, the captain, the preacher, and some of the fine Christian women—told Cal he wasn't to blame. It was Grayson's own fault, and he always ate like a pig.

A few days later, they reached Red Buttes Crossing on the North Platte.

"This is the last time we'll see this river, folks," the captain said.

"It's more lake than river," Mr. Fernsby said.

The captain's head bobbed. "It's wider than usual. That's a fact." He turned in the saddle and found Cal and Vincenzo. "Ride out, and let's get our bearings. See if there's any quicksand or anything that'll be dangersome for the wagons. We'll cross the livestock first, then the wagons."

He pushed the brim of his hat up and wiped his face as though contemplating. "Must be five hundred yards wide and a foot deeper than normal." He sighed. "Must have rained a lot upstream. Usually it ain't more than three hundred yards across. But let's get 'er done—and quick." He pointed upstream. "Them clouds could be sending more water our way right quick."

All the cattle and sheep made it across with no losses, while the lambs and the goats were loaded in the wagons or carried as the river wasn't more than chest-deep for most folks at its deepest, and usually not more than thigh deep.

In midstream on the upstream side stood Vincenzo, keeping an eye on the wagons as they trudged along. Cal stayed on the downstream point, waving like a flag to keep the wagons moving. Neither had found any quicksand, and the first wagons crossed easily. The Reverend James, who had forded the river while carrying one of the Carter family's lambs, returned and stood alongside Cal.

"You ought to let your pants, shoes, and socks dry out some," Cal told him. "The captain won't let us rest." Shielding his eyes, he found the sun. "We'll have two more hours at least of travel after the last of the wagons get 'cross."

"Sometimes I wish Frank and Jesse came with me."

Cal wasn't paying the preacher much attention. He saw the mule-driven wagons were about to get started. That would be the last of them.

"Frank and who?" The words finally registered. "Oh, your sons."

"Yes," the preacher said softly. "Two of my sons."

Those words went through Cal's head. But as he waved at the first mule-drawn wagon, the man—whose name Cal could never get straight and remember—nodded, and the preacher called out, "God be with you, brother."

Usually, no one rode in the wagon, unless they were sick or bad hurt, but crossing a river—especially one this wide—required a man with a good touch on the leather lines. The second wagon passed.

Just one more, he thought. And Captain Shufflebottom called out, "Get movin', Nuttal. I want to get a few more miles before we camp."

"You were right, Son." The preacher spoke in a whisper.

Cal was only half paying attention. Starting into the Platte, the mules balked almost immediately. Mr. Nuttal rose to his feet, trying to hold the lines in his left hand, while his right worked a whip. The big sorrel in front on the driver's side was the problem, acting like it had never seen a river, even after crossing many of them with nary a problem.

Cal waded toward the Conestoga, though he wasn't sure what he could do to calm down that raucous mule. He remembered Captain Shufflebottom's complaint about mules. They were temperamental. Oxen just did the job; they were bred for it. Mules were not oxen.

The brown mule next to the sorrel began acting up, too. Out of the corner of his eye, Cal saw the captain moving his horse toward the wagon, yelling something, but Cal couldn't make out the words because of all the splashing and yelling and the popping of Nuttal's whip. He didn't notice the preacher. In fact, Cal forgot all about him. He just waded toward that wagon and those wild-eyed mules.

"No! No! No-no-nooo!"

Cal heard that, and the profanity that followed. He saw the Rawlings wagon coming up on the other side of the Nuttal Conestoga. The Rawlings wagon wasn't as big as the Nuttals', and its mules weren't throwing a conniption. They were moving at a fast clip, but that just made all of the beasts pulling the Nuttal Conestoga turn as testy and temperamental as the sorrel.

Mr. Nuttal's whip lashed at the newly frightened mule. Likely because the Rawlings wagon got too close, the leaders in the Nuttal harness turned hard and fast toward Cal. The front wheel must have hit a drop-off in the river. Suddenly the Conestoga was tipping over. Nuttal dropped the rope. The Rawlings wagon moved ahead.

Nuttal shouted, dropped his whip, and disappeared.

The Conestoga turned onto its side, and the mules lurched away.

Captain Shufflebottom said some blasphemy and followed that with profanity Cal had never heard.

Cal lunged forward toward the wagon and where he had last seen Mr. Nuttal.

Captain Shufflebottom leaped out of the saddle and came that way, too.

The wagon was on its side. The current sent some blankets and bedrolls and one coffee cup downstream.

Cal got there first. He looked around, then sucked in

as much air as his lungs could hold and dropped to his knees and ducked his head under the water. His eyes opened. He saw nothing. He groped and felt nothing. He moved closer, looking left and right. But the water was too muddy from all the commotion of the mules and the wagon. It wasn't that deep. Three feet maybe. A foot or two deeper in the hole the wagon had found. But he couldn't see or feel anything that resembled Mr. Nuttal.

He rose up quickly, sucking in fresh air and blinking the water out of his eyes. His vision cleared, and he could make out the captain and Vincenzo and the preacher.

"Found him!" the minister said, and he dropped beneath the water's surface.

Cal started to slog over. More men and even several women in the bonnets and summer dresses came into the water from both banks. The preacher went down again and came up almost instantly.

"He's pinned underneath the wheel," he said. "I'll grab him. You men lift the wagon."

The minister disappeared again.

Cal moved past where the reverend had submerged. He and Vincenzo came to the side of the wagon. Shufflebottom grabbed hold. The preacher's head came up.

"Hurry!" he pleaded, sucked in more oxygen, and dropped beneath the frothing water again.

A woman stood next to Cal.

"Lift!" the captain yelled.

The wagon barely budged.

"Again!"

Someone shoved Cal. It was Mr. Fernsby, but Cal

figured he was stronger than that merchant. They lifted again on the captain's order.

This time, with more hands and muscles working, the wagon budged and came up, but not for long. It dropped before it had been lifted maybe six or eight inches. The preacher broke the surface, spit out water, sucked in air. "Higher!" he yelled. "Lift it higher for the love of God!"

"You try—" someone started, but shut up quickly.

Hands found holds again. More men and women crowded against the heavy wagon.

"Give it all you got, folks!" Shufflebottom yelled. "Lift!"

Cal didn't think his muscles had ever worked this hard. He strained. He prayed. He almost cried. But the Conestoga moved.

"I have him!" That was the preacher's voice. "Keep it up. Hold just a little longer."

Cal felt as if his arms were going to be pulled out of their sockets.

"Got him!" the preacher shouted.

"Let it go!" the captain ordered.

The wagon splashed back into the North Platte.

Cal turned quickly, his lungs burning, his arms already feeling cramped.

The head and shoulders of Mr. Nuttal were above the water's surface.

"Hurrah!" someone yelled.

The preacher kept moving toward the riverbank. The man who had driven the wagon that had caused this wreck waded into the water to help.

"Praise God!" a woman on the far bank yelled.

Two men on horseback had stopped the runaway team.

"Hurrah!" came another cry.

"Some of you see if you can't get this wagon righted," Captain Shufflebottom said, as he moved away from the Conestoga. "You might have to move beds and furniture out first, but get to work. We're burnin' daylight. Vincenzo, catch up my horse."

The captain made for the other bank where the Reverend James was dragging Mr. Nuttal toward a shade tree. "Don't worry about Nuttal," Captain Shufflebottom said, without looking back as he waded toward the bank. "We'll take care of him."

But Cal knew better. He had seen Nuttal's face as the preacher dragged him toward the far bank.

Mr. Nuttal was dead.

CHAPTER 6

The long journey from Red Buttes Crossing to Independence Rock was mostly silent. Cal took over leading what was now the Widow Nuttal's wagon, and the poor lady hardly got through one night without sobbing, lamenting the loss of her grandma's china, and the likeness Mr. Nuttal and she had had made after they got married.

They sang some songs at the campground near Independence Rock, but Cal just mumbled the words. He helped get a fire started before the dancing started, then wandered away. Vincenzo was a mighty fine dancer, and all the young girls blushed when he asked their favor. So did the married women. But that was Vincenzo, and Cal wasn't Vincenzo. Besides, Cal wasn't in the mood to dance—and well, it wasn't like any of the girls would want to take a whirl with him anyway. Staring at outcropping of granite, he wondered how it came to be called Independence Rock. It didn't look like a flag or George Washington or Thomas Jefferson. If it looked like anything, it was a whale. At least from the pictures of whales that Cal had seen. And from what he had heard on the trail, it was called Independence Rock long before folks started heading for Oregon and California.

It was big, though.

The clearing of a throat startled him, and he spun around, mouth open, but relaxed at the sight of the preacher.

"You going to carve your name in the rock like all those others?" the reverend asked.

"Huh?"

The preacher held up his hands. One held a chisel. The other a hammer.

"Come on," the Reverend James said, and he started up the path to the rock. Cal followed. He had seen lots of men, women, and some children walking to the rock, but he hadn't paid attention or even considered what they were doing here. But as he walked, he began to see the names, the initials, the dates, some of them already wearing thin.

"My goodness," the preacher said, as he stopped to catch his breath. "I did not realize how many folks have traveled this way." He pointed at a name and read it, then the year, '48.

They played a game. Who could spot the earliest date before they found a good spot to mark their passage. Cal found one from '41, but the preacher had good eyes, and he saw one all the way back in 1837.

When they found a spot not covered with letters and numbers, Cal and the Reverend James went to work.

CAL

"No year?" the preacher asked.

"I don't reckon nobody will care what year I come through."

The preacher smiled. "But they might think that C-a-l stands for California, not Calvin."

"Well, I don't reckon nobody'll wanna know where I hailed from, neither. And wanted to leave room for you."

"Thanks, son." The preacher, with a groan, dropped to his knees, coughed, and held the chisel next to the capital L. He grabbed the hammer, and the clanging began. When he was finished, he laid the tools on the hard ground, and held out both hands toward Cal, who pulled Mr. James to his feet.

Cal looked at the reverend's markings.

CAL AND REV. JAMES, Jul 50

"Yours is a lot prettier than mine," Cal said.

"I don't know about that."

Cal shrugged, then frowned. "Well, they might think that you and me was related."

An odd light danced in the man's eyes, and he stepped closer to Cal, then peered into the rock. "Well," he said, at last, "I reckon they might at that." He turned back and studied the lad. "Do you want me to make a correction?"

Chuckling, Cal shook his head. "I don't reckon that is necessary. Don't think many folks will pay attention to me and you with all these other names here."

The preacher coughed.

"You all right, reverend?" Cal asked.

The coughs continued for a few seconds but the preacher wiped his mouth with a rag he pulled from his pants pocket and nodded. "I'm fine, Calvin. Just fine. It's just that I reckon I swallowed half the water in the North Platte back at that crossing. Let's get back to the party. Serpents will start coming out directly."

They crossed Rush Creek with no difficulties, then waded through the Sweetwater as it cut its way through Devil's Gate. Onward they moved, westward, long days, quiet nights except for the howling of wolves. The sea was made of sagebrush. They had seen no other living human being except those in their wagon train for better than a month now. There were signs of trains that had come before them, even some crosses on the sides of the trail, most of which had been blown down, or pushed down by buffalo or maybe an Indian.

About two days before Split Rock, Widow Nuttal stepped into a prairie dog hole and twisted her ankle. Cal and the widow had been talking while they walked, and he was feeling pretty good, thinking that she might be getting over the sorrow of seeing her husband get drowned and all, but there she lay on the ground, letting out pitiful moans, and Cal had pulled the mules to a stop and hurried over to the poor lady.

He cupped both hands to his mouth and called out, "Hallooo, Mis-terrr Maaarley!"

Mr. Marley and his family—a wife, grandmother, and two boys—were in the wagon just ahead. The redheaded man heard, and stepped away from the wagon, saw the woman on the ground, and yelled at his oldest boy, maybe four years' Cal's senior, to stop the wagon. Then he yelled up ahead, and one by one, the wagons stopped.

By then, Cal was kneeling over the sobbing woman. He didn't have the nerve to touch the woman's ankle, but he tried to tell her everything would be all right, and he asked if she thought it was broken.

"It's as broken as my heart," she said, between sobs. "We never should have left home. Never. Never. Never. Never. Never."

There might have been a few more *never*s, but Cal stopped counting when he saw Vincenzo riding back toward him.

He tossed Cal the Hawken before swinging off his horse, wrapped the reins around a clump of sagebrush, and walked over to the widow and knelt.

She let out a shriek when Vincenzo touched her ankle. By then, Mr. Marley was there, and his wife was running toward them, lifting the hems of her dirty dress, her bonnet falling askew.

"What happened?" Vincenzo asked.

Cal shrugged. "We was just talking and walking. She stepped into a hole." He pointed, but Vincenzo did not look.

Mrs. Marley arrived and started taking off the widow's boot, and Mr. Marley held the woman's shoulders as she shrieked and sobbed.

A moment later, Captain Shufflebottom reined up and stared down.

"Broken?" he asked.

"No," Mrs. Marley answered. "I don't think so. But it's a bad sprain for sure."

"Well, pour some turpentine over it and wrap it up." He looked at Vincenzo, then Cal. "You two get her into the back. We need to make four more miles before we stop, and this is Injun country."

"We haven't seen any Indians," Mr. Marley pointed out.

"Yep." Shufflebottom spat in the dirt. "That's what bothers me."

Mrs. Nuttal rode in the back of the wagon that day and the next, but after that she rode up front, with Cal walking alongside, keeping her company.

And at Split Rock, they saw their first Indians.

The first one was atop a ridge off to the northwest, holding either a lance or a rifle in one hand, sitting on a pinto pony.

Widow Nuttal gasped when she saw him. Cal had spotted the lone rider ten minutes earlier, but kept his mouth shut, though he kept leaning out and looking back, hoping that either Vincenzo or the captain would come riding up.

"It's all right, ma'am," Cal said. "He's friendly."

Cal was glad the Reverend James wasn't nearby. He might wash his mouth out with a dishrag for telling a fib. Well, it might be a fib. The Indian could be friendly—maybe. Possibly. Cal sure hoped so.

He certainly wasn't doing anything mean-like. Just watching. Cal started looking at the other ridgetops but didn't see any other human being.

"Is he Cherokee?" the widow asked.

Cal gave that some thought. "I don't think so, ma'am," he answered, after several seconds. He had heard about Sioux and Shoshone and some other tribes out this way, but the Cherokees, as far as he knew, weren't this far west.

He breathed easier when he saw the captain trotting his horse down the line, saying something to those walking next to the wagon two up from the Nuttal Conestoga, and the same to the wagon just in front. When Shufflebottom reached them, he swung his horse around and slowed it to a walk and came up next to Cal.

"You see him, I take it," he said. The captain held the reins in his left hand. His right dangled near the pommel holster that held his .44-caliber Walker.

"Yes, sir."

"Is he a Cherokee?" Widow Nuttal asked.

The captain gave her a glance, then shook his head. "I don't reckon. Too far away to tell."

"Is he alone?" Cal caught the fear in the widow's voice.

"I doubt it. He could be scoutin'. Could ride down and meet us, try to trade for somethin'. Or he could ride down with a bunch of his pals, demand we pay a toll. Just keep the right distance. When we make camp, we'll bring in all the animals inside our wagon corral. Injuns like to steal. Not because they're crooks and thieves. It's just a way to gain status in the tribe. And to them, it's fun."

He shot Cal a frown. "Where's that Hawken I loaned you?"

Cal shrugged toward the wagon box where Widow Nuttal was riding.

"Up there." He decided not to tell the captain that it was heavy to carry and he figured it would be fine up there.

"You think Widow Nuttal shoots better than you, bub?"

"No, sir," Cal said, and he veered toward the wagon and asked the widow to hand him the long rifle, which she did.

The captain nodded. "Keep your eyes open," he said, and kicked the horse down the line to tell the Rawlings family what to do. "Most Injuns that I know prefer mule meat over ox meat," he whispered to Cal before he rode away.

Every step now felt like eternity. Captain Shuffle-bottom, having finished with the Rawlings family, stopped on his way back toward the leaders. He slowed the horse to a walk.

Cal said, "That Indian rode down the north side of the hill. Reckon he's gone?"

"I wouldn't bet on it. Keep your eyes sharp, sonny."

He spurred the horse into a lope.

The sky was endless, but hardly blue, more opaque, white from the sun that looked twice its normal size. Cal told himself that this was just because of the dust the animals were kicking up, and Cal realized they were walking faster than normal, and the mules and oxen were being urged forward. It wasn't anywhere close to a stampede, but it was faster than they had traveled since that first day or two out of Independence, when Captain Shufflebottom had said to go at a good clip to get the animals trail broke—and too tired to skedaddle during the night.

A figure had stopped up ahead, letting wagon after wagon, man, woman, and child, plod on past.

Cal kept glancing at hilltops, but no rider showed himself.

He now recognized Reverend James and felt good, though still nervous. The reverend smiled, removed his hat, and bowed toward the widow, then returned the hat and joined Cal.

"Did you see the Indian?" Cal asked.

"I saw him. I daresay everyone in our party saw him. He wanted to be seen."

"Ain't you scairt?" Cal asked.

The preacher smiled. "The Almighty shall look over us all. He shall even look over that Indian—if an Indian he was."

Cal jerked his head toward the minister.

"What do you mean? Didn't you see those feathers in his bonnet."

That pleasant smile widened. "Were those feathers? Could you see him clearly—uphill, what?—four hundred yards away?"

"Well, who else would be here other than an Indian?"

"Only the Lord knows, Son."

Cal thought about that Indian on that horse sitting there, holding a lance or something—well, maybe it could have been a rifle, though the sun would have likely reflected off the metal.

"What makes you think—?"

"I have made no final decision, Calvin," the minister said. "God created the Indian. God created you and me. God created bad and good, good and bad, and those who try to be good but are bad and the bad who have some good in them."

They walked about fifty yards in silence.

"He looked like an Indian," Cal said, to make himself believe it.

"At New Hope Baptist Church, we have a pageant every Fourth of July—we have one at Christmas, too, of course, but that is when our children tell the story of Joseph, Mary, the shepherds, the three wise men, and the baby Jesus. But on the anniversary of our Independence, we tell the story of the founding of our country. One boy plays Christopher Columbus. A girl plays Pocahontas. Last year, my son, Frank, just about a year younger than you, was John Smith. And several of our youth dress up as Indians. Then, of course, we have John Adams and Thomas Jefferson and George Washington and Ben Franklin, and then we all sing and praise God."

It took Cal a while to figure out all that, but by then, the reverend had moved to another story.

"There were many Indians gathered at Fort Laramie and at Fort Kearny. Don't you remember them, Cal?" the preacher asked.

"I saw 'em. Like ever'body else."

"I saw them, too. And I saw them on horseback. How they sat. How they rode. In the seminary, they teach you to see with your eyes and your head and your heart. So maybe I see things different, maybe a bit clearer, than you do, or even Captain Shufflebottom does. I saw that rider on that ridgetop turn his pony and ride out of our sight."

Cal waited.

"He didn't ride like those Indians in Kansas and back at Fort Laramie. I'm a pretty good judge of horseflesh. You live in Kentucky and you live in Missouri, and you learn quick about horses. So I'm guessing—and it's just a guess, and Captain Shufflebottom may have a different opinion—but I'm guessing that that man was white. At least, partly white. A half-breed, perhaps."

Cal thought on that, but couldn't find anything to offer to the conversation.

"White or red, I know one thing," the preacher said.

"What's that?" Cal asked.

"If he was friendly, he would have ridden down to greet us, even if he wanted to just trade for food—or foul, treacherous, and demeaning ardent spirits."

That, Cal realized, was about as wise a statement as he had heard this day.

The preacher pointed. "Looks like the captain is stopping our train," he said.

Cal saw that the preacher was right again.

"It's early in the day to stop, ain't it?" Cal asked.

Then he saw the dust rising from the hilltops to the north and south of the trail.

CHAPTER 7

Mr. Fernsby called it "bedlam." Cal hadn't heard that word before, and the only dictionary on the train had been lost when the Nuttal wagon got wrecked at that crossing, but Cal didn't have to ask for a definition. Dust practically blinded everyone as the wagons turned into a giant oval. The men turned the oxen and mules into the compound and quickly worked on unhitching the teams, and all of the livestock were pushed into the center.

"Hobble your leaders!" someone cried. "We don't want them boltin'!"

Behind Cal, Mr. Rawlings swore. "Hobble them! How will any of us make our escape if we hobble our mules? No, sir. I shan't do it. Hobble them? That's insanity."

"Put the children inside your wagons with their mothers!" Vincenzo was yelling those orders on the far side.

"Get in." The Widow Nuttal leaned over the side of the Conestoga, extending her arms toward Cal.

"No."

Captain Shufflebottom happened to be riding his

horse past them. He pulled his horse, already lathered, to a stop and nodded at Cal. "I want you and that Hawken up front. Think you're up for it?"

"He's just a boy!" the widow argued.

"And if he is gonna grow into a man, I'll need him up front," the captain barked.

"I'm up for it," Cal said.

The captain nodded. "Grab your powder horn and a pouch of leaden balls, and get up there."

"Are they attacking?" Widow Nuttal cried out.

"Not yet. But they will be soon. Get down, ma'am, and pray for all of us, if you will."

The captain started to kick his horse forward, but almost instantly jerked back the reins. "Mrs. Nuttal!" he called out, and waited for her to turn around. She leaned out of the opening in the canvas. "You've got the biggest wagon. Could you take a lot of the children, ma'am?" He wet his lips. "I think they'd be safer in your wagon than anywhere else."

"Of course," she said.

The big head nodded in thanks. "I'll send as many as the mamas will let me, ma'am," he said, and nodded at Cal. "Second thought, you stick here. And keep all 'em kids safe if you can."

"Yes, sir," Cal said.

After he twisted in the saddle, the captain sent a flurry of oaths at Mr. Rawlings. "Hobble those mules, sir! Hobble them good and tight."

"No, sir. If we have to make a run—"

"If we have to make a run, sir, we'll all be killed. And if those mules bolt when this war starts—and that'll be soon—this fort that we're making will fall apart and we'll all be dead." He held his Walker Colt high. "Do as you're told, sir, or I will shoot you as a coward."

The first children arrived, a boy and two girls, and Cal turned his attention away from the captain and Mr. Rawlings. Cal couldn't remember the names of these kids. One of the girls held a cat. Cal leaned the Hawken against the rear wheel, and lifted who he figured to be the cat holder's sister. He spun around and walked to the rear of the Nuttal wagon, which was butted up close to the front of the Rawlings wagon. Widow Nuttal was there to take the girl and swing her inside. Cal just got a glimpse of the interior and realized another reason the captain had suggested the kids be put in the Conestoga. The Nuttals had lost a lot of their furniture back at the river crossing where Mr. Nuttal had drowned.

He swung the boy in next, then took the cat from the girl's hand, choking down the cuss word that wanted to explode and refraining from throwing the cat out into the sagebrush after it scratched his left forearm. Widow Nuttal tossed the cat onto a bedroll, then helped the girl in.

By then, more children were waiting in line, most of them crying, some of them pale as the sky.

The cat screeched.

The widow kept saying, "Children, keep your heads down. Keep your heads down, and pray."

He remembered one of the fires back in Iowa. A house was burning. And how men lined up—they wouldn't let Cal help, said he was too little—and passed buckets of water from a horse trough down the line to the orange flames. This was something like that. Instead of buckets, Cal was lifting children into a Conestoga. One after another. One after another.

The dust became worse. A goat almost rammed him. Horses whinnied, cows moaned, oxen bellowed, mules snorted. By now he could hardly see through the dust. But the children kept coming, and he kept lifting. The sweat coming out of him soaked his shirt, but that cooled him. But his eyes burned like they had been doused with coal oil. Still he lifted and swung.

He held a boy in a plaid shirt and straw hat, and felt the weight disappear when the widow took him.

"Calvin!" she yelled as he turned to take another kid, this one a boy maybe five years old holding a wooden gun in his left hand.

Cal grabbed the boy and held him up.

"There's no more room, Cal. There's just no more room."

Cal couldn't see her. He just heard the words.

"I'm sorry."

Cal stepped back, turned, and started to lower the boy, but Mrs. Rawlings yelled, "Bring him here, son! Bring him here. We've got some room. Some room."

The mules hitched to the Rawlings wagon, Cal noticed, had been hobbled. He didn't see Mr. Rawlings.

Staggered, accidentally kicking a baby goat, Cal moved as fast as he could, still trying to blink the sweat out of his eyes.

Mrs. Rawlings took the boy, thanking Cal, then

saying, "No more than two more. We just don't have room."

So Cal took the next two kids, and practically shoveled them toward the rear of the Rawlings wagon. He could see, though his eyes stung, and saw five more kids standing, waiting, and crying.

He swallowed, which felt like sand going down his throat.

"Lordy," someone screamed, "there must be a thousand heathen Injuns out there!"

A woman's shriek followed, and then came: "We're all going to die!"

"Lord, save us!"

Suddenly, another voice thundered.

> *Hallelujah, praise Jehovah,*
> *From the heavens praise His name;*
> *Praise Jehovah in the highest,*
> *All His angels praise proclaim.*

The noise from the animals drowned out the voice, but only for a few seconds.

> *Let them praises give Jehovah,*
> *For His name alone is high,*
> *And His glory is exalted,*
> *And His glory is exalted,*
> *And His glory is exalted,*
> *Far above the earth and sky.*

Cal watched the Reverend James march by, still singing like he was leading the choir at the New Hope Baptist Church.

Vincenzo suddenly appeared, holding his Hawken, sweating and his eyes wide.

"Cal—" He tried to catch his breath.

"You all right?" Cal asked.

Vincenzo nodded, and sighed. Inside the Conestoga, Widow Nuttal was reading from the Bible to the children. The cat screeched.

One of the Thompson twin boys came running, and almost got gored by an ox. He slid to a stop in front of the mules still hitched to the Nuttal team. "The cap—" He had to catch his breath. "Cap'n—he wants—needs—one of you—" He nodded at Vincenzo, then Cal, and afterward still struggled to catch his breath. His face was as white as the bonnet Mrs. Griggs was always wearing. "Up front—"

Cal turned to his friend.

"Just one of us?" Vincenzo asked.

The boy's mouth opened, but he appeared to have lost his voice. He raised a trembling right fist, then let the pointer finger rise.

"One—" His voice was raw. "Need—"

Vincenzo had a water pouch hanging over his shoulder. He started to pull it off for the boy, but the kid shook his head. "Cap'n said—someone—needs to—watch—" His head tilted. "Back—door." Vincenzo still pulled the pouch over his shoulder and handed it to the kid.

"Drink some," he said, in a dry whisper. "But best save some for later." Then he looked at Cal.

Cal shrugged.

"You best go," Vincenzo said.

"I dunno," he said. "You're—"

"You're the better shot, Cal," he said. A smile creased his bronzed face. "Better'n me, anyway. Better'n the captain, too." He moved his Hawken around. "I'll keep the back door closed to any uninvited guests."

Cal nodded, then took off in a hard run, moving around sacks, bags, animals, people; leaping over legs of men lying prone, with their long guns ready; almost kicking a dog of multiple breeds that was barking up a storm; past two women tearing up undergarments that might be needed as bandages; sideswiping a braying ram; then slowing down and coming to a halt where Captain Shufflebottom and Mr. Fernsby, with a spyglass, stared onto the rolling plains between two wagons, the oxen pulling the one on Cal's right, staring complacently, probably glad that they weren't pulling a heavy wagon across this rolling country that never wanted to end.

Shufflebottom turned around and nodded. "Glad to have you up here, boy."

Cal couldn't find any words, so he just nodded his head.

"Here comes the big chief," Mr. Fernsby said.

The captain turned and moved closer. "Come here," he said, without turning his head but motioning with his free hand—the right one held the Walker—at Cal, who stepped between the two men.

A tall man, shirtless, his skin dark, the arms painted— right one black, up to the elbow, left white, up to the shoulder, and the hands appeared red, a breastplate covering his chest, and the rest of his body, even his face painted white, black or red. He wore a buffalo headdress, and feathers flapped in the breeze on his buckskin trousers. The face was covered with warpaint. Cal couldn't make out any features, but the hair hung in braids, wrapped with colorful ribbons.

"Fernsby," Shufflebottom said. "May I borrow your spyglass."

Fernsby nodded and extended his left hand. His right held a muzzleloading musket.

After shaking out the long lens, and shoving the .44 into his waistband, the captain stared, twisting till he found the right depth and focus. "Uh-huh." He held the telescope toward Cal, and it took Cal a moment to realize that the captain wanted him to look at the Indian, not Fernsby.

Cal stepped forward, and leaned the Hawken against the wagon wheel, then took the long brass instrument and looked. It took him a lot longer to figure out how to look through that thing, and longer to focus. He even had trouble getting a line on the Indian who was maybe twenty-five yards in front of the others. The others, Cal had realized before he even looked for the painted leader, numbered far too many to count.

"What do you see?" Shufflebottom asked.

"An Indian. Painted all over. Buckskin trousers. Good-looking horse."

"Uh-huh." The captain spit in the dust. "What else?"

"Good saddle. Some silver on the bridle. Or something shiny."

The captain turned and held out his hand for the

telescope, which he took and delivered back to Fernsby, but he kept his eyes on Cal.

"So what you saw . . . What did that tell you about these Injuns?"

Cal shrugged. "I don't know enough about Indians—yet, sir. I've just seen the tame ones at Fort Laramie and that other fort—umm, Kearny."

"Dogs are tame. Indians ain't. Nor are white outlaws."

Suddenly, Cal stood a bit straighter now, and looked without the spyglass at that Indian. Two other riders came up alongside him.

"That saddle," Cal whispered. "That—bridle."

The captain looked back at the boy. His head nodded slowly.

"He's not . . . an Indian."

The captain's face brightened. Mr. Fernsby turned around. "You mean he's a white man gone Injun?"

"I mean they're all white men. Playing Injun. So when the next train comes by here, they'll figure Injuns done this."

The preacher was right. Cal smiled at that thought.

"Well—" Mr. Fernsby struggled for a moment. "I just—white men—it . . ."

"Welcome to the West, Fernsby." Shufflebottom looked at Cal. "Can you shoot that fella, son?"

Cal blinked. "You mean—?"

"I mean off his horse. That'll let the rest of 'em know what we think, might take the starch out of some of 'em. And it'll be one less of them to kill us."

"But he's not—doin' nothin'." Cal hardly heard his own words.

"He's blockin' our path. Tryin' to scare us. Whilst half his men is sneakin' 'round that bluff yonder to hit us from behind." He turned around and barked at three men with long rifles. "You fellas. Get to the back of the train. Tell Vincenzo that they'll hit us in a minute or two from that way." He whirled to Fernsby. "Cock your piece, sir. And shoot to kill."

Then he faced Cal again.

Cal found himself looking for the preacher, but couldn't see that familiar face.

"Let me have your Hawken, boy." Captain Shufflebottom held out his hands.

Trembling, Cal handed him the long gun. Shufflebottom nodded at the Walker still in his waistband.

"Take my .44," the captain ordered. "Let's see if you're as good with a short gun as a long rifle. I'll take your pouch, too." He took the Hawken firmly, and Cal slowly pulled the heavy revolver from the captain's waistband.

"Cock and fire. Six rounds. When it's empty, it hits harder than a blacksmith's hammer, so use it as a club."

Cal was stepping back when the captain, without word or pause, turned around, braced the stock against his right shoulder, pulled back the hammer. The click of the set trigger sounded, then an explosion almost rocked Cal off his feet, but the smoke blew the other way, and Cal had a clear view of the man Shufflebottom said was a white man painted up as an Indian somersaulted off the back of the pony, which took off toward California.

The echo of the Hawken's report was drowned out by furious screams and gunshots. Every animal in camp began making noises, but a minute later, Cal heard nothing but his own heart racing.

He tried to find a good spot. The oxen were struggling with their braced feet, whining. A woman was bandaging the arm of that red-mustached fellow with the big belly whose name Cal never could recall. Out of the corner of his eye, Cal saw an Indian—no, a white man disguised as an Indian—leap his horse through an opening. The Walker raised in Cal's right hand. The man was no longer in the saddle. The horse somersaulted, and Cal barely stepped out of the way. He didn't know if he had shot the rider, or if someone else had, or if the fool had just fallen off the back of his horse. But he was no longer there, so Cal moved to a spot between two wagons. He saw another rider, aimed, then lowered the .44.

Out of range.

The Walker Colt wasn't as heavy as the Hawken, but it sure wasn't light. And Cal shot it the same way he did the long gun. Unsteadily. Moving in circles. Around and around. But at least there was only one trigger to pull on a revolver.

The next rider was closer, but someone else blew him out of the saddle.

Then Cal heard a battery of gunshots, and he made his way to the rear of the camp. A pinto pony came through an opening. This man had not bothered dressing up in buckskins, feathers, and paint. He held a saber in his left hand and a smaller pistol in his right. One eye was covered with a brown patch. He whirled, away from Cal, aiming at a man's back. Then he straightened the moment something slammed into his back. Both saber and pistol fell. His right hand reached for the handle of the hatchet, but couldn't find it. The skewbald bolted. The man toppled to the ground, tried to push himself up, then fell back.

Grandma Holland put her boot on the small of the man's back, bent over, and pulled the hatchet out, then turned, wailed some crazy cry, and rushed past Cal.

The fighting was furious in the back. Cal ran. Something whistled past his cheek. He tripped over a goat, almost dropped the Walker, and felt his head strike something solid. He dropped to his knees.

When he could breathe, he raised his head and the Walker. But Mr. Holland was stepping on the slim man in moccasins and a breechclout, but sporting a thick gray beard—*Indians don't have beards*—and aiming his shotgun at the man's head.

The man started to scream, but the shotgun drowned it out.

Cal made it to the Rawlings wagon. He wanted to look for Widow Nuttal and Vincenzo, but men were firing, and Cal squeezed in between two of them.

He had to wipe dust and sweat off his face. His eyes burned. He aimed the Walker, his arm moving in circles, and pulled the trigger.

Nothing happened.

Cock first. Cock first. Cock the darn hammer!

Feeling like an idiot, he eared back the heavy hammer, unable to hear the clicks. He saw a rider and did not have time to let the Colt spin around. He squeezed the trigger. His arm rocketed forward and almost out of socket. The ringing in his ears sounded like it wouldn't end in a month of Sundays.

He decided to use two hands now. That kept the Colt from shaking and spinning too much, but he could hardly see through dust and gunsmoke.

A kid goat peed on his trouser leg.

He found a target, aimed, pulled the trigger, but this time was prepared for the massive kick and deafening roar. There was just a pop and a fizzle.

Misfire.

The hammer was pulled back again, and he saw the back of a man galloping away. Probably out of range, Cal thought, but he was about to press the trigger when he suddenly could hear again.

"They're licked! They're licked! Look at them run! Just look at 'em!"

Cal wondered if this was a trick, but more whoops reached his ears. And turning, he saw Grandma Holland smiling. The Widow Nuttal began praising God and telling the children in the back of the Conestoga that it was over, that they had won, that the Indians—she would be corrected later that those attackers were mean white villains—were fleeing.

Cal sighed. He looked at the smoking Walker that felt even heavier now. Stepping to his left, he almost tripped over something. He stared into the face of a man with blue eyes that neither blinked nor saw. He was wearing a black wig that had been pulled off the right side of his head. The buckskin shirt he wore had been peppered with a tidy placement of buckshot—though not too much blood.

He turned, tried to find the Nuttal Conestoga.

The ringing left his ears, and he heard a cacophony of noises. Shrieks. Prayers. Brags. Moans—horrible moans. Wailing animals of multiple breeds.

Suddenly, he felt weak. And he almost dropped the Colt and fell to his knees, but someone grabbed him from behind and pulled him against his own body.

"Easy, Calvin. Easy. Are you all right, Son?"

Cal recognized the voice. It felt reassuring. The ringing had left his ears. He turned his head slightly.

"I'm all right . . . preacher."

"Good." The Reverend James released his hold. "I'll take the Colt."

Cal's right arm did not move, but the minister moved quick and fast, and took the gun. He checked the cylinder as though he had handled revolvers all his life, nodded, and turned the cylinder a few clicks and lowered the hammer, which he shoved in his trousers.

"I have work to do, Cal—grim work. Can you help me?"

"Is it over?" he asked, in a whisper he didn't think anyone could hear.

But God gave the Reverend James excellent hearing.

"It is over. The Philistines won't return today." He stared down with determined eyes.

"There are wounded, Cal. And dead. Not just these rogues and demons, but among our fellow travelers. We must now help those in need. And prepare a few, I fear, for their final journey. Are you up for it?"

"I guess."

But he wasn't. Not really.

Because the first dead man they found was Vincenzo.

CHAPTER 8

They buried Vincenzo and five other members of the Fernsby–Nuttal train, putting crosses at the heads of the graves. The outlaws were dragged into a cut in an arroyo, covered with lime, and then with about a foot or two of shoveled sand.

"It's more than they deserve," Captain Shufflebottom said, but the Reverend James read over their graves, too. The preacher found Cal still standing over Vincenzo's grave.

Cal felt the minister's hand on his left shoulder.

"He was a good man," the preacher said. "But good men die, too. The difference is that the Lord will have mercy on a man like Vincenzo." The hand came off the shoulder. "I don't know about those we just buried in that ditch. But that is for Him to decide. We must live the best we can."

"I shoulda stayed," Cal said. "With the wagons."

"No, my son. You were needed up front. You have a talent. God gave you that keen eye. If not for you, it might be us lying with the sagebrush, coyotes picking over our bones. For I do not think those mercenaries would have covered our bodies as we have done theirs."

"We didn't bury 'em six feet deep," Cal said.

"For we had neither strength nor time." He coughed, then said, "Take your time. The grief will subside, and you will always remember the good times you had with your friend. You won't forget this, but this day will pass from your cherished memories. Remember the good."

"I'm just a jinx," he said. "Bring nobody nothing but bad luck."

"There's no such thing as a jinx. And a man makes his own luck. We'll be leaving soon. I'd better go help Widow Nuttal."

Westward they continued, with few songs at camp those next two weeks, following the trail that slightly paralleled the Ice Slough—Cal wondered how the stream or river or creek or whatever it was got its name, there being no ice to be seen in the summer—then crossing it with ease.

In this remote, never-ending land, the buttes, the creeks, the campgrounds were nameless, and by now, the travelers were typically too tired to sing and dance on the evenings. They ate because they had to, but the food had no taste.

On they went west, then southwest, the captain choosing the forks to take in the trail until they finally reached the Oregon Buttes and South Pass.

"Are we in California now?" Cal asked, at the camping ground.

The preacher laughed and squeezed Cal's shoulder.

"We have a long way yet to go, my son. But I am told that we are entering the Oregon Territory."

Cal didn't correct the reverend. Captain Shuffle-bottom had told him this used to be part of Oregon Territory, but now it was Utah Territory.

The country surrounding them was red in color—from all the stories Cal had heard about Oregon, he had thought it was all green—but the buttes beckoned them, and onward they traveled. Past Rock Creek. Then Willow Creek. And crossed the Sweetwater again—someone said they had crossed it six times already, but the Widow Nuttal said by her count it was nine.

"It's the last time," Captain Shufflebottom said.

"Good riddance," the widow remarked.

The country grew rougher. And somewhere east of the Green River, they ran into Indians that were not white men disguised as Indians, but real Indians.

"What do they want?" Mr. Fernsby asked.

Captain Shufflebottom shrugged. "A toll, I guess."

"I don't think we need to pay any red heathen a toll," Fernsby said.

"It's their land," the preacher said.

Cal just stood there silent, wetting his lips. The Hawken felt heavier all of a sudden.

"It's our land. Land is for the white man," Fernsby said.

"Listen." That was an order from Shufflebottom. "Let me and Cal ride out and have a parley. If they offer us a fair price for a toll, we'll pay it. If they get greedy, I'll let them see how good Cal can shoot."

It is unknown what tribe these Indians were, but let it be known they were not Kickapoos, either.

Cal could not make out the hand signs or the words both a strong, tall, and handsome Indian with three feathers hanging off the left side of his head said, or anything even Captain Shufflebottom said, with fingers, hands, and something that sounded more like grunts than words.

The tall Indian shook his head. Captain Shufflebottom sighed.

"Cal," he whispered. "We might have to shoot our way out of this."

But then another Indian rode up. He was ancient, his red face withered with wrinkles, his eyes glassy, but he sure had a lot more feathers on his head than that handsome one. He spoke, first at the tall, straight, strong Indian who had been doing the bartering, and that Indian turned and looked at the old man as if he were crazy, then twisted until he sat staring right at Cal. He looked him up and down twice, then glared at the old man and said one word angrily and jerked his right hand, holding a lance, at Cal.

Captain Shufflebottom seemed perplexed.

The old Indian spoke. The younger one shook his head. The old Indian gave a long speech, maybe ten or twelve words. The young Indian's shoulders slouched, and he glanced at Cal, looked back at the old man, who nodded, and the young Indian sighed, turned his pony around, and rode off. Most of the men followed. The old man studied Cal.

The wind blew. Cal found himself sweating.

The old man spoke with his hands and his grunts to Captain Shufflebottom, turned his horse around, and kicked it into a gallop. For a grandfather, he rode like a young man.

Captain Shufflebottom then turned to Cal.

"What?" Cal asked, when the captain did not look away.

"Boy," Shufflebottom said. "You earned your keep today—maybe for the whole journey to California. That young buck was ready to fight. But the old man told him we'd best not, that the tribe wanted no part of us. But he pointed at you. He said you are 'bad medicine.'"

"Bad medicine?" Cal almost dropped the Hawken. "I ain't even a doctor."

"I know that. And I don't know what you got about you, but if Injuns is scared of you, that might get us through this country in one piece."

Days later, they reached Fort Bridger, but it wasn't a fort like the ones Cal had seen at Laramie and Kearny. It consisted of two cabins—double-logged, for protection, Cal figured—and a giant corral, and several tents. The Indians there were tame, Captain Shufflebottom said, and they would stay for a few days, letting the animals rest for the climbing ahead, and men could patch their wagons, and women could bathe, and the captain could talk to Jim Bridger.

It was, after all, Bridger's fort.

"Come along, Calvin—you too, preacher—I'd like

y'all to meet the greatest mountain man livin'. Bring
your Hawken, son."

Cal had never heard of Jim Bridger, but the preacher
whispered a few stories as they walked to the corral.
Cal asked why he needed to bring his rifle. "Ain't Mr.
Bridger friendly?" he asked.

"Maybe it needs fixing," the preacher suggested.

"It shot that antelope fine three evenings back," Cal
explained.

"Maybe the captain wishes to trade the musket for
supplies."

Cal didn't like that idea. He had gotten used to the
Hawken—which wasn't a musket, but he wasn't going
to embarrass the preacher—and he pretty much considered it *his* rifle now.

A man in buckskins and a wild animal hat came past,
nodding. He carried a long rifle, too, but Cal didn't think
it was a Hawken. He also carried a hatchet and one of the
longest knives Cal had ever seen, and the fellow's beard
came down to about where his ribs ended.

"Cap'n," the lean man said, stopping but not offering
a hand to shake. "You ain't done nursemaidin' green-
horns to the Oregon Country yet?"

"These are after all the gold in California," the captain said.

The man's pale eyes focused on Cal. "Who's that
hombre totin' that fine Hawken?"

"Calvin James," Shufflebottom said.

"Marmaduke," Cal corrected.

The reverend cleared his throat.

"Beg pardon, son. You and the preacher resemble

each other so much, I forgot. Calvin Marmaduke, this here is—?" He waited.

"Wolfer," the man said. "For the time bein'."

"My pleasure," Cal said.

"And this is the Reverend Robert James. He's bringing the Word from Missouri to the gold seekers in California."

"Uh-huh." Mr. Wolfer nodded and walked past. The captain shrugged, and they rounded the second cabin and went around back, where a small man, in buckskins and a flat-brimmed hat that might once have been white but now was covered with grease, blood, and mud, sat on an empty whiskey keg, whittling.

He hadn't shaved in maybe a month or so, and from his smell, he hadn't bathed since the last time he had shaved—maybe even longer—but he looked up with pale eyes that recognized the captain immediately but then bore through Cal.

"Who's the pup with ya?" Bridger asked.

"Calvin . . . Marmaduke."

"Big rifle for a small boy," Bridger said.

"He handled it well when some renegade whites attacked our train," the preacher said.

Now Bridger's eyes moved toward the minister.

"Is that a fact?"

"It is," Captain Shufflebottom said.

"Crow Eyes," Bridger said, and a tall Indian came from the corral carrying a long rifle. "Hand me Mrs. Matilda." The Indian moved toward the nearest cabin, disappearing around the side, but returning in an instant with another long rifle. That one he handed to Bridger, who rose before taking the gun.

Holding the long rifle in his left hand, Bridger plucked two feathers off his fringed shirt and gave them to the Indian. "You know where to put 'em, Crow Eyes," he said, and the Indian started walking.

"Not that way, Crow Eyes," Bridger called out. "The sun'll be in my eyes. *Our* eyes. Head toward the smithy's."

The Indian stared.

"You heard me. In front of the smithy's. Hurry—afore the wind starts blowin'."

To Cal, the wind was about a gale right then.

But the Indian moved away, toward a blacksmith's shed about a hundred yards away, turned around, and extending his arms till he looked like a cross, the feathers dangling in the never-ending wind in his hands, one facing up, one facing down.

Cal glanced at the preacher, who shrugged, then saw Jim Bridger loading the rifle Crow Eyes had brought him. The thin man talked as he poured powder down the barrel.

"You get to pick, sonny. Left feather or right feather. We'll take aim. The cap'n'll count three. We shoot. Shoot the feather out of the Injun's hand. You gotta clip it in half. And not hit Crow Eyes."

"But—"

"Don't worry 'bout Crow Eyes. I've won thirty-three dollars this year already and I ain't hit him, and ain't none of the losers who tried to best me hit him, neither."

"What are we betting?" the captain asked.

"Nothing," the preacher said. "Gambling is a sin in the eyes of the Lord."

Bridger was putting the rod back into place.

"Even if I give him odds?" Bridger said. "By thunder, his Hawken'll shoot faster than my old flintlock. Three-to-one. He wins I owe him three dollars. If I win, he just pays me one."

The preacher frowned.

"But I don't want—" Cal said.

"By golly, boy, is you yeller?" Bridger laughed. "I don't think you'll come close to that feather. Your ball will wind up in the dirt forty yards away."

"He's not ten years old yet," the preacher said. "And you're—"

"Tryin' to have some fun. Runnin' this tradin' post is 'bout as fun as waitin' out the winter in the high country back when beavers was prime and the rendezvous was a-goin' strong. You got somethin' agin fun, preacher. What is you preachin'?"

"I'm Baptist, sir."

"Well, Rev'ren', we ain't dancin'. We's just shootin' for fun. And I'll give ya a tithin' oncet I win."

Shufflebottom cleared his throat. "It's just for fun, gentlemen. And I've been tryin' for three years to best Jim."

Bridger let out a wild animal scream. "Taken ten dollars off you back in '47 when you was headin' Oregon way!"

"And five in '48, and ten more last year," Shufflebottom reminded him.

"What's our side bet, Cap'n."

"Twenty-five, Jim. So I'll be even."

The mountain man's eyes sparkled. "You'll be busted." He turned toward Cal. "What do you say, boy?"

Before Cal could look at the preacher, he heard him say, "'There is treasure to be desired, and oil in the dwelling of the wise; but a foolish man spendeth it up.'"

Cal was looking at the reverend then and saw his face change when Bridger spoke:

"Proverbs, chapter twenty-one, verse twenty. But let me remind you of the same book, but chapter thirteen, verse sixteen: 'Every prudent man dealeth with knowledge: but a fool layeth open his folly.'" He chuckled. "I know I can best a kid shootin' anything. But iffen I'm wrong, I'll laugh at my folly."

The minister nodded at Cal.

Cal butted the Hawken against his shoulder.

"On three," Captain Shufflebottom said. "One. Two." Cal had to hurry this time, because he would only get one spin of his Hawken. A glance revealed Bridger's smirk at the weaving Hawken. Cal pressed the set trigger. "Three."

Both guns roared. Cal couldn't see for the smoke. He heard a ping, then Jim Bridger crying out in pain, and turned to see him fall to his knees and start shaking his left hand.

"What in tarnation?" the minister cried out, and he and Shufflebottom ran to Bridger. Cal glanced at the Indian, but Crow Eyes was walking toward them, not running like the preacher and Shufflebottom, and Cal couldn't see any feathers in the man's hand. He shifted the Hawken and moved toward the three men.

The preacher must have stuffed his ears because he was ignoring all the cusswords Jim Bridger was bellowing.

"It's hardly a scratch," Captain Shufflebottom was saying when Cal stood over the men.

"What the devil happened?" Bridger asked.

"I heard a *ping*," Cal told them.

The minister nodded. "Ricochet." He held out a handkerchief. "Wrap it with that. Anyone have any whiskey?"

"That's all there is to drink here," Shufflebottom said.

"Well, what about 'em feathers?" Bridger demanded.

Crow Eyes had reached them. He held both feathers up. Both had been clipped.

"Which one hit first?" Bridger said.

"His." The Indian nodded at Cal. "Hawken shoot faster than old gun you got."

"Well, who the devil shot me?" Bridger roared.

"Boy. Ball hit anvil. Fly back." He nodded at the boy. "Good shooting. Two targets, one ball."

Bridger shook his hand. It was bleeding. But not much.

"The dern kid tried to shoot my hand off," Bridger said. "All right. You won your dollar."

"Three dollars," the preacher reminded him.

"Minus two for the doctorin' this hand'll take," Bridger said.

"That's fine," Cal said. He looked at the preacher. "Is a dollar a good tithe?"

"It is," the preacher said.

The captain helped pull Bridger to his feet.

Shufflebottom smiled. "And you owe *me* twenty-five dollars."

The hand was bathed in whiskey, but just once, and wrapped with the preacher's handkerchief and a rag Crow Eyes had. They didn't see Bridger the rest of their stay before they pulled out two days later.

Onward they moved, traveling southwest, into the Wasatch Mountains and through Echo Canyon—a long passage that took them two days. Eventually, they stared in awe at the Great Salt Lake country at the top of Big Mountain Pass, and camped in Salt Lake City, past Black Rock, where they gazed at the vast lake of salt water, then on to and Horseshoe Springs, climbing into the Cedar Mountains. Two of the Rawlings mules died, and the family had to abandon their wagon and ride with Widow Nuttal.

Freezing cold in the mountains, though it was only late August—at least, according to Captain Shufflebottom—and blistering hot in the desert. And into the land of El-dorado. California. And the wildest town Cal had ever seen.

Hangtown. They were greeted by two men swinging from the limb of a tree, ropes still around their necks, some wild dogs sitting with watering mouths, waiting for someone, it seemed, to cut them down so they could eat. The dogs looked as though they hadn't been fed in a month. But they growled as the Fernsby–Nuttal train, or what was left of it, passed.

Captain Shufflebottom collected the last of his

payment from Mr. Fernsby, shook the reverend's hand, and when Cal handed him back the Hawken, Shufflebottom shook his head.

"You earned it," he said. Then he laughed. "She's all yours, lad. Just be careful what you aim at. One day you might even hold it steady—when you grow into it."

Widow Nuttal came over and gave Cal a hug. She said she had found a job washing dishes at a place called Eating Place. She asked the preacher to pray for her, and he said he would.

The Fernsbys said they were pushing on. They'd heard that San Francisco was the place to be.

The reverend said he would be staying here. He wanted to see if he could find his brother, Drury. Cal figured the preacher likely had another reason for staying. Of all the sites Cal had seen on the California Trail, Hangtown seemed to be most in need of a good preacher. But it would likely take a thousand preachers to save this place from the fiery pit the Reverend James kept warning folks about in his sermons.

Most folks were hung from tree limbs. Though one person got special treatment and was hanging from a post sticking out of a cabin. There was talk, Cal heard on the streets, about making one tree the official hanging tree, but that hadn't become law yet—as far as Cal could see.

Bodies found with bullet holes in their backs (and sometimes in their shirtfronts), or with throats cut, or just beaten into a bloody pulp with a shovel or something—those were buried. The Reverend James preached short sermons over as many graves as he could, but he didn't get paid for a one.

Sermons did bring in some money, though, but prices in Hangtown weren't like what Cal was used to seeing back on the Mississippi in Iowa. The reverend said they were higher than what he was used to in Clay County, too. But he had been called here to preach, and preaching he would do.

Three men offered Cal money for his Hawken, but Cal shook his head—even when the last man, who looked as if he couldn't even afford Captain Shuffle-bottom's Walker Colt, much less a Hawken, offered him fifty dollars.

"Best take my gold, bub," the man said, after Cal declined. "Somebody'll just cut your throat whilst you's sleepin' and take it anyhow."

He wandered about Hangtown, wishing he was back with his ma and pa in Iowa. He thought about writing them a letter, but decided he would need a job before he could pay for paper and something to write with. The preacher found him the next morning, said he had bought a tent and had set up camp in the woods, asked Cal if he would like to share it with him.

"I ain't got no money to pay you, but I'm looking for a job."

"That's fine, Son. That's fine."

A week later, they moved to a camp called Rough and Ready. The preacher said, "It is rough, but I'm not sure it's ready." The tent was stolen while the preacher was preaching and Cal was hunting for their supper. But a fellow Missourian offered them a room, which wasn't much of a room, but it wasn't raining then, so they didn't know how bad the roof leaked.

Cal tried to find gold, but he couldn't hardly find a place clear to stick a pan in the creeks, and when he did, he was chased off by a man waving a paper and saying that this was his claim, by grab, and he'd kill anyone who tried to steal from him. That very same man was hanging from a limb the next morning. Turns out, somebody else had a claim to that part of that particular creek. At least, that's what Cal heard.

The Reverend James preached that Hangtown was not a Christian name for a town, and since he had heard that the camp had been called Old Dry Diggins, that was at least not morbid.

To which a miner said, "I don't want nothin' dry"— and fired three shots at the preacher's feet, causing him to do a sort of jumping dance. Folks liked that show, though, and the money in the preacher's hat was good for a spell.

But then the preacher moved to sermons about temperance. And after that, the tithes weren't as generous at all. Fact is, the money stopped coming.

Two weeks later, the preacher got sick.

CHAPTER 9

Cal and the preacher had taken a bed in the fairly large cabin built by one Mr. Wright—"It's spelled with a W, but I'm still right," he was fond of saying—another Missouri fellow. The reverend had been preaching up and down the American River to miners who rarely tithed and seemed annoyed because they were busy in the rough country, surrounded by towering mountains, panning for gold.

Well, Cal had figured out that most of those miners could scarcely afford anything, let alone an offering to a preacher with a cough. Even Mr. Wright allowed that a miner who panned eight dollars a day might be able to pocket just three bucks after all expenses had been paid. And the prices of whiskey, women, grub, and gear had boomed, too. Everything was going up in price, but the gold wasn't coming out of the streams as willingly as it had been back in May, Mr. Wright told Cal, when folks had been panning from fifty to a hundred bucks a day. These days, a take of fifteen dollars was considered excellent.

The landlord, after the preacher asked for another

extension in paying his rent, suggested they might try Dodgertown, Ducktown, or even Hard Scrabble, but Robert James said he was called to Hangtown. He didn't know why. He hadn't found his brother or anyone from Clay County in Hangtown, but he hadn't met everybody yet—and people kept flocking in.

The minister and Cal finally got lucky when a mine owner offered Cal five dollars to dig a grave and the preacher ten to give the fellow a good funeral. He led the two to the body, which was still strapped to a hitch post in front of a bawdy house.

The corpse's shirt hung on in threads, bloodstained and blackening. He been whipped to death.

"What did this poor soul do?" the preacher asked.

"Stole," the man said. "Ten dollars. Said he hadn't et in six days."

The preacher looked up with hard eyes. "I thought the penalty of death was sentenced only for stealing more than five hundred dollars."

"He wasn't hung. He was whipped. Ain't our fault he couldn't take a whipping. Besides, ain't you heard of those cutthroats robbin' wagon trains betwixt here and Sacramento?"

Everyone had heard of that, but most figured it to be more "big windies" than the truth. The breath the preacher let out of his lungs sounded like something out of Scripture.

"How many lashes?"

"Hundred and fifty. Do you want the job or don't you?"

"We'll take it."

And that would have satisfied Mr. Wright, if the money had made it back to that cabin. But a shoe fell off while they were dragging him to a sandy spot where the digging was easier, and inside was a woman's name and an address in Kentucky. Maybe if the address had been in some town in Ohio or New Jersey or a place like that, the preacher might have felt differently. And maybe if the mine owner had not paid in scrip, but in gold, the preacher would not have thought to be generous. But it was Kentucky, his home state, and the scrip was light. He wrote a letter addressed to the woman's name found on the stained paper in the dead man's shoe. And sent it out to Sacramento that evening.

Cal tried helping out the landlord to be deducted from their rent, but he wasn't much good at carpentry or digging a well. So he tried panning, but he had to walk and climb a long way to find a place that hadn't been claimed, or wasn't guarded by men with big revolvers and fierce dogs. He came back with enough color to buy two cups of coffee and some stale bread, which the preacher and Cal had to soak in the coffee so it wouldn't break off their teeth.

The next day, when Cal got off earlier and found his place, three bearded men said this was their claim now. Cal said, "Good luck to you," and walked away. He spent what was left of the day after climbing back down to Hangtown cleaning out two liveries, and took home three dollars for his blistered hands.

So when he came back to the cabin and saw Mr. Wright frowning, he knew something was wrong.

"Your pa's sicker than a dog, boy," the Missourian said.

"He ain't my pa," Cal told him.

"Well, in his delirium, he thinks you're his son."

Cal sighed, figuring that the landlord was stretching the truth. He hadn't seen anyone sick in Hangtown. Just bloodied from beatings, hanged, stabbed, shot, or carved up with ax or hatchet.

When he saw how pale the Reverend James was, though, he knew the man was sick. Bad sick. His eyes opened when Cal sat on the bed and touched his hot forehead, and the preacher smiled, then closed his eyes and stayed asleep. He was asleep even with the doctor, a haggard-looking, bony and pale gent named Newman, came in and opened his satchel.

After probing and using his stethoscope and a little file to hold down the tongue, he shook his head, and put away his instruments and turned to Cal.

"How long has he been like this?"

"Mr. Wright said he come in this mornin'," Cal answered. "I was out, trying to earn some gold."

The man's long head nodded.

"He had a cough for a while."

"He ain't consumptive," the doc said. "Where was he preachin' today?"

"Last night, he said he might try the South Fork."

The doctor shrugged. "Well, my guess is dysentery. Drunk bad water. I get a lot of them cases."

"Will he be all right?"

The doctor had packed his bag and was walking toward the door. "It's possible. Him being a man of God an' all. But I'd get myself prepared to see him die, iffen I was you."

Cal thought he hadn't heard right. He watched the doc put on a miserable hat and leave.

"But he's a preacher!" he called out.

"Preachers die like the rest of us, kid. I'll be back in the morning. Let me know if he dies before then, though. It's a long walk up these infernal hills."

The Reverend Robert Sallee James—Cal found the middle name in the preacher's Bible—lingered for two weeks. He knew that because Mr. Wright let him know how much rent was due. The doctor kept coming by, checking, but saying there was no sign of improvement. For that first week, that seemed good news. He wasn't failing, after all.

But the next week, the preacher sank fast.

"I don't know how this man's held out as long as he has," the doc said.

"I wish he'd hurry up and die," Mr. Wright snarled. "So I can rent this to a man who ain't sick. And ain't a preacher trying to get tithin's from the riffraff that populate this abysmal place."

Robert Sallee James lasted three more days.

On the third day, his eyes opened and he saw Cal, sitting on the bed, holding the parson's right hand.

"Son." His voice was just a whisper.

"Preacher." Cal felt a wetness in his eyes that he had not expected. "Are you feeling better?"

"I'm going home." Cal had to lean closer to hear, and the reverend repeated it.

"Let me fetch you some water," Cal said, but he

latched onto his wrist like a badger, and Cal was pulled back to the bed.

"You"—the preacher fought for breath and strength, which the Lord provided—"are—my—son . . ."

He relaxed then, his hand slipped off Cal, and the eyes closed. Cal did not move.

Then the preacher's piercing eyes opened, and he smiled.

"Do not blame your mother. Zerelda is strong-willed and stubborn—and ugly as sin—but this was my doing. My sin. God will forgive her."

Cal decided that the Reverend Robert James was out of his mind with fever and sickness and a lack of water.

"My mama is—"

But the preacher finished the sentence: "not—Mrs.— Charity—Marmaduke."

Cal felt numb all over.

"But she raised you as her own. She is a fine woman. And Obadiah is a good man."

The story came clearly now, as if he was preaching a sermon. A sermon to one. Or two. It struck Cal that maybe this was the preacher's way of asking for forgiveness.

The Marmadukes' newborn son taken from them by the hand of the Lord. That desperate sin of Zerelda and the preacher. "Not a day has passed that I did not think of you, pray for you, and plead to the Almighty for His forgiveness," the preacher whispered.

He was silent for a long while. If the eyes had not

blinked, Cal would have thought that the preacher had died.

Cal felt the tears dropping onto his shirtfront. He yanked off the bandanna around his neck and wiped his face.

"When I am called away," the preacher said, "you will still have a family—the Marmadukes."

But Cal had been thinking about them since he had started to understand that the Reverend James was not delusional and he was not lying. And he was thinking that if the Marmadukes—he couldn't even think of them as Ma and Pa now—had cared so much for him, had loved him as their son by blood, they certainly would not have let him take off to the goldfields of California with this preacher.

"You have brothers, too, Cal. Frank is tall and intelligent. Jesse, well, he's a bit of a terror when he's angry, but, Lord bless him, young as he is, he pulled on my trousers furiously, begging me not to go to California. And a sister—Susan Lavenia—if our Father has not called her away during my journey here. She is not a year old yet. Born the twenty-fifth of November last."

The preacher let out a long breath.

So did Cal.

"I wish I could lead you back to Clay County, Missouri. But I must say in Hangtown. Till the Judgment Day."

Cal was thinking that he would rather be back in Iowa. With the parents he knew.

He shook his head. "I ain't nine years old yet." The

words came out like a sob, and then he realized that was because he was sobbing like his sister, Susan La-something-like-that, might be somewhere in Clay County, Missouri.

"And well on your way to manhood. But, yes, be a boy. For a while."

He couldn't see the preacher because of the tears in his eyes.

"And I ain't nothing but a jinx. I bring ca-la-mi-ty ever'where I go, to ever'one I see. Ma and Pa—the Marma—" He shook his head. It was too confusing now. "Vincenzo. Jim Bridger, though he brung most of that on hisself. And now—*you*."

The preacher grabbed Cal's wrist and squeezed it hard.

"Calvin Amadeus James," he whispered. "There is no such thing as luck. No such thing as good luck. No such thing as bad luck." He smiled. "It's all just—part of—life . . ." The eyes froze. And the hand released its hold on Cal and fell limply to the cot.

And Cal couldn't look away from the eyes. It was like he was staring into his own eyes. They were practically identical. But his could still see. Maybe the preacher's could, too, but he was in another world now. A better world, Cal figured.

A widow donated a lice-infested blanket, and four rough miners used it to wrap the body of the Reverend James—he was wearing just socks, Cal noticed, not his boots—and carry him to a sandy spot not far from where Cal had buried that thief who'd been whipped to death. Then they dug a grave, dumped the body in the hole, which they covered, and nodded at Cal before they took their leave.

"Amen," one of them said.

And that was the funeral of the Reverend Robert James.

Cal stayed there for a few hours. Had he recalled any hymns he would have sung one. Had he learned any of those Bible verses that the reverend had been fond of, he would had recited one. But there was nothing for him to do but sob a few tears, then rise off the sand, and make his way back to the Wright cabin.

"You're in luck, son," Mr. Wright said. "I sold that horse of the preacher, and his valise, those boots—the soles were worn down to a nubbin—and he had been holdin' out on me. Found ten dollars and fifty cents in one of his boots. Now that don't come close to coverin' all the debt he owed me and the doc, but the doc and me agreed that we can split it right down the middle. Now, I want you to pack up whatever you want. I've rented this room—and not to no preacher. I ain't goin' through that verse and song ever agin."

Cal shook his head. "I reckon I'll just take the preacher's Bible and—"

Mr. Wright snapped his fingers. "The Bible, yeah. I sold that to the Widow Cain. You found yourself a job?"

Cal's head moved again, and he turned around and walked out the front door.

He wandered to one of the big warehouses, where he

found a train of wagons lined up on the road. It wasn't Captain Shufflebottom, but there was a man asking burly men to make their marks or sign their names. Cal anchored the line, and when he reached the boss of the outfit, the man leaned back and tugged on his long red mustache.

"You ain't big enough to be a muleskinner, sonny."

"I know that."

"How old are you?"

"Twelve," Cal lied. "Small for my age."

"And too small for my outfit. I got enough men with me as it is. Don't need no puny kid—"

"You've heard about the bandits robbing trains, I reckon."

The captain laughed. "Yeah. Are you a bandit—or a guard?"

Cal nodded at the Hawken leaning against a cut-down tree behind the wagonmaster. "Want me to prove what I'm worth?" he asked.

That got the skinners who hadn't wandered far off to laugh and gather around. So did a merchant, a woman who had been talking to the merchant, two Mexicans, and a Chinese cook to join the party.

"This is a fifty-caliber Hawken, boy. It weighs more than you."

Nodding, Cal pointed to a jug atop a boulder about fifty yards away.

"One shot," he said. "I hit it, you hire me. I miss—well, all y'all will have a good laugh."

Every man jack among them howled with delight the way Cal could not keep that long gun steady in his not-yet-nine-year-old arms. But nary a one was laughing—most were speechless, but one or two managed to let out a whistle, and one a loud blasphemy—before the smoke from that long gun had cleared.

"Name's Gilmore," the captain said. "And you got yourself a job."

CHAPTER 10

Sacramento had grown in the short while that had passed since the late Reverend Robert James, Cal, and all those others had crossed the American River and continued their quest for gold. When the Fernsby–Nuttal party had passed through, the town had been rebuilding after a January flood that had practically leveled the town, wiping out homes and businesses, drowning livestock and citizens. Men were working on levees on the Sacramento and American Rivers when the captain's train forded the American and entered the bustling city.

The saloons remained overcrowded, and some still pulled out revolvers or single-shot weapons and fired in the air.

"What's this ruckus about?" Captain Gilmore asked a man who had fingers stuck in both ears.

The gent waited for the latest shot to die down, stared at the Hawken Cal carried, then withdrew his fingers, checking the tips for wax, and told the captain: "Celebratin'."

"This ain't the Fourth of July. What's the cause for all this merriment?"

"California has joined the Union. We're a state now. The thirty-first."

"When did all that happen?"

"The ninth of September."

"And you're still celebrating?"

Cal didn't know what the date was, but it had to be pushing late September.

"Well,"—the man looked at Cal—"what's your name, kid?"

"Calvin," he said. "Folks call me Cal. Cal . . . James." He tried that out for the first time.

The man smiled. "Then we're celebratin' the arrival of Calvin—call him Cal—James."

Even Cal had to smile at that.

Captain Gilmore ordered the train to keep moving.

Unlike Hangtown, this city had been laid out, with plenty of public squares and the streets running north–south given letters and the those heading east–west numbers, so it was hard to get lost—if you knew your numbers and your letters. Cal was glad he did. Eventually, the wagons and carts reached the Sacramento River, where ships were lined up along the bank, some of them two-deep. Cal's boss found the captain of a bark that had sailed from the eastern coast of these United States and made it all the way to Sacramento.

Captain Gilmore sold the supplies to a peg-legged man, paid off the crew, and handed Cal some coins.

"What's your plan now, kid?" Captain Gilmore asked.

"Reckon I'll try to get back home," Cal said.

"Good thing to do." The captain turned and walked away, and Cal watched him go.

For a moment, Cal had thought the man might offer him a job to haul supplies back to Hangtown or another one of the mining camps, but now he realized how ridiculous that would have been.

They had arrived a week late. One flooded stream. Two busted axles. One teamster broke his leg. Even Captain Gilmore had sprained his left wrist. And then that rabid skunk had run through the camp two nights back, sent some draft animals skedaddling, and poor Harry Griggs got skunked and it was hard to even breathe around him.

But Cal had some money, though money didn't last long in Sacramento. Not when beef cost fifty cents a pound, cheese a dollar, bread forty cents, milk a dollar a quart—and it might be soured—and butter three bucks a pound. Some of the men complained about paying a dollar for one shot of whiskey.

"A fella can't even get drunk at those prices," one of the men said.

He wandered along the banks. The Sacramento didn't smell like the Mississippi, and found himself standing in front of one of Sacramento's many saloons. His right hand reached deep into his pocket and felt the coins. He had never gotten drunk. Never even tasted whiskey, even when Pig's Foot Van Dorn had found that bottle of rum—Pig's Foot said it was rum—back home.

"Howdy, Cal," a voice called behind him.

Cal turned—and felt his mouth drop open at the sight of Captain Shufflebottom, holding the batwing doors open, then letting them bang as he stepped off the small wooden porch and down to the dirt where Cal stood.

"What brings you here?"

Cal gave him the grim news, and the captain put his right hand on Cal's shoulder and gave it a hard squeeze.

"The preacher was a good man. I am sorry to learn of his passing."

Cal thanked him.

"What are your plans?"

He shrugged. "I guess I'll try to find a way back east."

Captain Shufflebottom shook his head. "The West is the future, son. Were I you, I'd stay out here."

Cal shook his head.

Shufflebottom's smile changed his entire face. "I know that feeling. I'm bound for Independence myself."

Cal waited for an invitation that didn't come.

Shufflebottom pointed at all those ships along the riverbanks. "Likely you can hire on as a deckhand."

Cal figured the captain was joking, so he laughed.

"I'm serious," Shufflebottom said. Cal smelled the rum on the captain's breath, so maybe the liquor was doing all that talking. "I was giving it some thought, myself."

Now Cal was certain that the captain was in his cups.

But pointing at one of the boats that was being overrun by men and women, Shufflebottom said, "Look at that. Captains, most of them, have a full crew when they make it here, but as soon as those sailors see that they are in Sacramento, they abandon ship—desert—swim to shore and make a beeline for Hangtown or some other mining camp. Gold fever. And before the captain knows what's happening, his ship is being taken apart. That one will be turned into a hotel, maybe, or perhaps a store. Home. Warehouse. Grocery. Barbershop. Firewood. Gallows. You name it. You, son, are a fast learner. And that Hawken—where did you get that long gun, son?"

Cal told him, and Shufflebottom laughed hard.

"By grab, Cal, you are a wonder. What caliber?"

"Fifty," Cal told him.

"Can you hold it steady?"

"Not yet. But I will someday."

Shufflebottom gave a nod of respect. "I know you will, son."

The captain went on talking, but Cal found himself studying the ships and those shirtless men hauling heavy sacks, crates, and barrels. Most of them had forearms the size of Cal's thighs. And they were covered with tattoos. A few even had rings hanging from their earlobes, and they weren't women, either, but men— because many had thick beards, and Cal didn't think they were like that bearded lady that came to the Bluffs one time in a carnival that Cal's pa—the pa he knew before he found out that his real pa was a preacher now buried in Hangtown.

"Cal. You want to be a sailor? A deckhand?"

The words reached the boy, and he turned and smiled.

"Don't know that I want to be on water."

Captain Shufflebottom smiled. "I know what you mean. These days, fording a river is enough for me. Well, there ain't no pay in going home, but you're welcome to tag along with me. I'm bound for Independence, and I'd like to get there before the worst of winter roars in."

"It took us four months to get here," Cal told him.

Shufflebottom's big head shook. "We shan't be traveling with Conestogas and oxen. Let's head to Petrone's livery. He has the best horseflesh to be found in this city."

"You sure you want me with you, Cap'n?"

The wagonmaster shrugged. "Well, to be honest with you, the notion might not have hit me if you didn't have that Hawken rifle."

Two days later—after sleeping in one of the city's parks to avoid paying obscene rates at hotels and well provisioned with supplies, powder, lead, percussion caps, and two fine geldings, Cal's black, the captain's gray—the pair put those horses to a trot and found their way on the California Trail again.

After three days on the trail, they had met few travelers. When they climbed into the mountains, the captain let Cal kill a big deer, then showed him how to butcher it. Captain Shufflebottom only cut himself twice during the instructions, but only one of those went deep enough that some rum was needed for medicinal purposes. While the westbound wagon train had made fifteen miles on a good day, Cal and the captain usually covered thirty, sometimes forty. They were blessed, and soaked, by some rain, and at night, the captain talked about the boats they had seen on the riverbanks in Sacramento.

"How come you know so much about sailing, captain?" Cal asked, when they were camping at the Hot Hole, a group of hot springs near the Humboldt River. Cal was perplexed how a country as dry as this one could leave a man spouting story after story of high seas and whales and blown boilers and Mississippi River sinkings and such. Or maybe the desert just brought that out in a man, though Cal hadn't given much thought about those ships since he had left the Sacramento and American Rivers.

"Well, lad, before I was a wagonmaster, I was a ship's master. Yes, sir, laddie, you are looking at a man of the river, born in St. Louis, served as a deckhand on many a ship on the Mississippi and the Missouri. Twice on ships with crews of twenty-five. That's a big ship, lad. Stoked many a boiler as a fireman. Hauling cotton, hauling sugar, hauling people. One day I shall return to the rivers—but not as a fireman—too hot for me. Nay, my dream is to be captain—or first mate, at least. I can read the depths of the Mississippi around St. Louis better'n some mates on the best known ships on that long muddy ditch."

"Why'd you ever leave?"

He sighed. "Your pard Jim Bridger led me astray. In St. Louey. Lured me to the mountains."

Jim Bridger. Cal's face paled. He would have to see that little feller with the giant temper when they reached that trading post.

But they had to get through this never-ending basin of dust and wind first, and the captain broke his leg the next morning.

They were walking their horses through a particularly windy day, Cal on the southeaster side, Shufflebottom on the northwest. His left foot went into a hole, he cursed, the gelding jerked away from him, and he fell awkwardly. The snap sounded almost like the report of a Hawken, and the captain cursed as he fell. But when the gelding started off in a panic, Shufflebottom still had the presence of mind to call: "Stop that hoss!"

Holding the reins of his own horse in his left hand, Cal bolted, leaned and—for once, having some good fortune—managed to grab one rein.

He pulled the gray to a stop, whispered some lullaby his ma—who, he frowned at the thought, wasn't his real ma—used to sing to him after he'd been awakened by a bad dream or the rumble of thunder when he was really little.

"Easy, boy," he whispered, and kept whispering, then led the horses and hobbled them both—since the captain was whispering orders and oaths, oaths and orders—while lying on his back.

Horses secured, Cal knelt by the captain, who stared up at the cloudless pale sky.

"Ankle?" Shufflebottom said, through clenched teeth.

Cal nodded. "And your leg's ain't exactly whole no more."

The captain's sigh sounded like a death rattle in his throat.

"You know how to set it?"

"No, sir."

The captain swore. "Time you learnt."

Despite all the screaming and cussing, Cal thought that didn't go too badly. Good thing he had hobbled the geldings, though, else they both would have been goners in this country.

But there was little wood to be found, and certainly nothing strong enough to use to make a travois. But they used just about every extra stitching of clothing they had between them to wrap the ankle and the middle of the lower leg, and then, by covering the gray's head with Cal's saddle blanket, got the captain into the saddle the next morning.

Cal had met some tough men in his life, but from that moment on, he declared that Captain Shufflebottom was the bravest, strongest, toughest son of the seas (or rivers) and deserts that Cal had ever known—or likely would ever know.

"You sure you can ride like this, captain?" Cal asked.

"Ain't no place for me to stay—without being buried—betwixt here and Bridger's layout, boy," the captain said. "Let's start moving. No need to burn anymore daylight than we already have."

"But it's a long way to Bridger's post, sir."

The captain snorted. "Shucks, boy, what's three hundred, three-fifty miles?"

They didn't make thirty or forty miles that first day. Or the second. Or the third.

But twenty-one days after Captain Shufflebottom's misfortunes, they pulled into the post. They had ridden the last four miles in a snowstorm that the captain kept saying would blow itself out in ten or twenty minutes. It wound up snowing for three whole days, but by the time it quit, the captain was quite drunk, thanks to Jim Bridger, and three Indian women had done a much better job of setting and doctoring and covering with poultices and such.

"Lost another bet," Bridger told Shufflebottom on the fourth day. "I'd even sent a Shoshone out to find a short tree we could use for a pegleg."

The captain grunted. He wasn't in a jovial mood now that the liquor was wearing off and he saw how ugly his leg was.

"You're gonna have to winter here," Bridger said, and that tone didn't come across as something even Captain Shufflebottom could argue against.

"I can make it," the captain said, but his voice lacked its usual confidence.

"*I* can make it," Bridger said. "The kid might make it. But you sure can't. You couldn't make it forty miles."

The captain pouted in silence.

Shaking his head while sighing, Bridger shot Cal a glance, then turned back to Captain Shufflebottom.

"Tell you what," the old frontiersman said. "I'll get the boy back to—where the devil is you goin' kid?"

Cal started to answer, then stopped. Iowa? Or should he try—where was it—Clay County, Missouri? At least to deliver word of the preacher's death. Any family deserved to know that.

"His folks are in Iowa on the river," the captain said, speaking to Jim Bridger, but looking at Cal with that hardness in his eyes.

Cal tried to hold that stare, but couldn't, but Jim Bridger picked up on those looks.

"Seems that the boy has some notions contrary to yourn, Cap'n."

"The preacher—the one with us when we came through with the train—took sick in the gold camps and died of fever," Shufflebottom said.

"I'm right saddened to hear of that." Bridger sounded serious. He cocked his head and looked at Cal's Hawken leaning against the wall. "That ain't the same rifle you had back when you was westering."

"Mine got stole," Cal said. "I won this one in a bet."

"What'd you bet?"

Cal shrugged. "That I could hit a target."

Bridger grinned, and turned back to Shufflebottom.

"Cap'n," he said. "I'll make you a deal. You winter here"—he nodded at the Indian women—"winter as long as you wants to. They'll take care of you. Good cooks iffen you can et what I et, and I know you can 'cause you et with me when you was this boy's age."

"You are not going all the way to Independence, Missouri, on my account, Jim." The captain tried to push himself up, but he wasn't that far healed right yet.

"It ain't fer you, you ornery cuss," Bridger said.

Both Cal and the captain waited for an explanation.

Bridger saw that and sighed. He stood, went to pick up a jug one of the Indian women had brought in, pulled out the cork, and took a long pull. Once he was seated again, he took another long swallow, and stared at Captain Shufflebottom.

"I got me some young'uns in Missouri. Reckon I ought to pay them a visit." He nodded at one of the Shoshone women, said something in her language, and she rose and walked outside, not saying anything. "I'll take her with me. Besides, I've been in this country too long. Time for me to see something else. Maybe I'll buy myself a farm—iffen the land's got some trees on it—so I can hide in the woods if I takes that notion." He drank more, then held out the jug for another one of the Indian women to rise and take the container. She handed it to Cal.

"Not the kid," Bridger barked, and switched to that strange language. The woman brought the jug to the captain, but Shufflebottom, though he took the jug, did not partake.

Bridger, the Shoshone woman, and Cal left the next morning. The captain, still lying on a cot, held out his right hand.

"Guess I'll see you sometime down the trail, captain," Cal said.

Shufflebottom grinned. "Not if I see you first." Then he laughed. "I'm just joshing you, Cal. Don't let anybody call you a jinx. I'd be feeding ants and buzzards if not for you. Don't let that mountain man steal your Hawken."

"He can't even hold it," Cal said, and he walked out of the door before anyone could see the tears in his eyes.

So they traveled, and with Jim Bridger, Cal learned how to make fifty miles a day. That man could move like the wind. So could the woman. Several times, Bridger showed Cal how to hide from Indian parties. He taught Cal how to lose a trail when someone was following you. He taught him how to follow a trail when someone didn't want to be followed.

The Shoshone woman taught Cal some things, too. Sewing leather. Even reading sign. Throwing rocks.

Cal traded with some Indians for a buffalo robe. The leader wanted Cal's Hawken, then the Shoshone girl, till he saw Cal shoot, then said they would take a skillet, tobacco, and a scalp Bridger had lifted from an Indian those Indians did not like at all.

Bridger taught Cal a few words in Shoshone that might prove useful but never did. The Shoshone woman taught Cal the right words that she said Bridger never got right. Bridger taught Cal some Comanche sign language which he said could prove helpful unless the

Comanches decided to cut off his fingers and hands and feet and stuff them down Cal's throat.

Cal was sorry when they rode into Independence, Missouri. Bridger stopped and paid a boy a penny for a newspaper, which he handed to Cal.

"That thing got a date on it, Cal?" Bridger asked.

Cal unfolded the paper and saw the day and date.

"December fourth," Cal said, "Eighteen and Fifty."

Bridger nodded. "Feels like December."

Cal thought it felt colder, but it sure hadn't taken them long, grueling months to travel from California halfway across the continent.

"I'm bound for Little Santa Fe," Bridger said, and gestured. "Get me that farm. See my kids. Where you be bound fer?"

Cal thought about asking for directions to Clay County—for all he knew, they were in Clay County—but after all those long months, he really wanted to see the ma and pa he knew, he remembered, he loved.

"Iowa," he said.

The old man nodded. "Sell that hoss. Tell 'em it's a bonafide Injun pony, that Jim Bridger oncet owned. That'll get you fare on one of them foul-smellin' big ol' ships." He pointed. "You'll take the Missouri all the way to St. Louey. Then get yourself aboard another one of them barges and goes north up the Mississippi. That'll take you where you want to be."

Cal laughed. "Mr. Brid—"

"What's my name, boy?"

"Jim."

"That's right. Have I ever lied to you?"

"Yes, sir."

Bridger grinned. "And I will some more, most like. But do as I tell you. You've become a man—the West makes folks grow up quick—but you're still just a kid. Take that boat home. Get yerself an edgy-cation. You can amount to somethin'. That's my last lesson to teach you, Cal. You'll learn the rest on your own."

They both smiled, but Bridger's face paled.

For a moment, Cal thought the old scout might drop dead, but the man just shook his head, breathed in deeply, and let it out like a cough.

"All these folks," he said, with a sigh. "I been away from civilization fer a long time."

Cal had that same feeling.

The Indian woman came up and gave Cal a hug. She whispered something in her native tongue, then turned, nodded at Cal, and turned, reached up, grabbed Bridger's ear, and she led him, screaming and cussing in his language and hers, away.

Cal worked his way on a ship called the *Examiner* and earned extra money by shooting at targets on the riverbanks with his Hawken. In St. Louis, captain asked Cal to stay with them as they continued up the Mississippi—not only was he a good worker, the captain had won a fair amount betting against the fools who would bet against Cal.

Cal sadly accepted, but let the captain know he

would have to get off in Burlington, and not keep going north, and the captain agreed.

Cal remembered the way to the Marmaduke home, and after a final handshake with the captain, started toward that place, wondering if Charity and Obadiah still lived there. The *Examiner* made it ten miles upstream before catching fire and landing on the western banks. No passengers or crew members were killed, but the ship was a total loss.

Cal found the house, and waited ten or fifteen minutes before he had enough nerve to walk to the door and knock.

Charity answered.

"Oh, Lordy," she said. "It's you."

CHAPTER 11

We depart Iowa, dear reader—but worry none, for we shall return to the Marmadukes in due time—for a brief history of what had happened to the true parents of young Calvin Marmaduke, who you might remember as being born as Calvin Amadeus James on the twenty-eighth of January in the Year of Our Lord 18 and 42.

Cal asked the doctor who had looked after the dying preacher to write a letter to the Mrs. Reverend Robert James, Clay County, Missouri, since he figured, having heard all sorts of things the preacher said about his wife when the delirium set in while the good, but human, man was dying, that Cal's birth mother probably did not want to be burdened with a letter from her oldest child.

Thus, the letter arrived—mail traveling fast even before the Pony Express—and before even the newspaper in Liberty (Centerville had no paper at that time) printed an announcement that the reverend had died in the goldfields of California the week after Mrs. James got the letter.

Ma James did not waste time. She told the neighbor who had been plowing the fields, chopping the wood, and harvesting the hemp that she would continue to pay him since her man was dead in California. Oldest boy Frank, a year younger than Cal, wasn't big enough to do more than pick beans and potatoes and haul some corn to the livestock. Jesse wasn't good for much other than crying and squawking and demanding his mother's attention, and his ma was plenty busy with that baby girl of hers.

The preacher had left her a nice farm with good buildings and a three-room house, and Mrs. Zerelda James was a big woman—six feet tall, some claimed—and folks living in Kentucky and Missouri come tougher than cobs. She could handle a spade, she could knock some sense into her children—and even that fellow who done most of the man's work for her, if he got uppity or out of line.

She wore black, and in November of '50, when she went to the probate court, she saw red, because that fool preacher she had married had not left a will, and Missouri law—she read what the blackhearted lawyer showed her in one of those thick, boring books—said that the children got the inheritance. Zerelda got nothing. And with Frank being only seven years old, and the oldest, that meant an adult man needed to handle the estate.

Things got even tougher because preachers don't make much money to begin with, and once they're dead and gone, those folks owed money by the reverend had to collect. So while the Marmadukes up in Iowa were having their own problems, financially and otherwise, the same could be said for the Widow James and her brood. Stuff had got auctioned off to pay debts, though she managed to make sure Frank at least got himself an education, and soon he could read better than just about any boy in the county. So, while Cal Marmaduke was going through those McGuffey Readers, Frank was learning the works of Shakespeare.

That first year as a widow was all it took. When 1852 rolled around, the Widow James started looking for a new husband, and her eyes landed on a neighbor with some good farmland, named Mr. Simms. He looked a good bit older than Zerelda, and he would age a lot faster once they got married.

By most accounts, he was a good farmer. But he could be one ornery cuss. He had a thick mop of hair on his head and a thick mustache that was well kept and a long goatee that wasn't. That's one way of looking at it. The other is that, well, young boys who are old enough to recall their original pas often aren't so inclined to treat their new pas with respect, and Frank and little Jesse doted on their ma. But Daddy Simms wasn't no preacher. Instead of the Good Book, he ruled with the backhand and didn't need a paddle when anything handy would do—fireplace poker, shovel, firewood, skillet, reins, lariat.

But as the late Reverend James had so eloquently and softly told his congregation at New Hope Baptist Church, "The Lord works in mysterious ways."

And Mr. Benjamin Simms learned the secret to the Great Mystery when he died on the second of January in the Year of Our Lord 18 and 54.

Nobody quite figured out how Simms died. Apoplexy.

Hit in the head by a mule. Sunstroke—in January in western Missouri when ice covered the ground. Pneumonia. Heart failure. Slipping on ice and hitting his head. Froze to death. He wasn't stabbed or shot or choked to death. The final ruling was that he had been thrown from his horse and just never recovered. Lots of good horsemen have been killed by horses, and it seemed to be as good a cause as anything else.

He got buried quick. And was forgotten, especially by Frank and Jesse, just as quick.

Once again, the kids—Frank, Jesse, and Susan—got the inheritance, but Zerelda James was happy for her children. And herself.

But she didn't care much for another city man handling things, especially money, for her boys. So she got herself hitched one more time.

This husband, who said "I do" or maybe "I will," was a doctor, and folks in Clay County agreed that was a good thing for Zerelda Cole James Simms Samuel since her husbands kept dying on her. But Doc Reuben Samuel was a Kentuckian by birth and had gone to a doctoring school in Cincinnati, which was in Ohio, because of a river, but Kentuckians considered Cincinnati their own town just the same. And unlike the most recent late spouse of Mrs. Zerelda, Doc Samuel was respected, and he could handle a scalpel and hoe and plow and amputation saw and could stitch up a knife wound so that it hardly even left a big scar. Mrs. Jeanne Alice Myers said Doc Samuel was the best bleeder she had ever known—didn't even hurt when he cut her arms. He was also about as kind as the Reverend James had been. And he was three years younger than his new wife.

Zerelda liked him because the good doctor did like she told him to do.

He signed an oath, all legal and everything, that the farm, if he preceded her in death, would go to her—and that took a lot of gumption, folks whispered at New Hope Baptist Church and pretty much throughout Clay County, seeing what had happened to her first two husbands, even if one had died in California—a right far piece from western Missouri.

The boys and Susan got along with their ma's new husband, who for most of his life had figured that he would live out his days as a bachelor. And in the years to come, Doc Reuben Samuel most likely came to wish that he had.

— PART TWO —

THE WAY TO BLEEDING KANSAS, A MISSOURI FAMILY REUNION, AND ONE MIGHTILY UN-CIVIL WAR

1851–1865

CHAPTER 12

The Marmadukes tried. Honest, they did.

When Cal turned nine years old that January of '51, they baked him a cake with candles, but the curtain that caught fire not only was quickly put out, and, fortunately, it turned out that Obadiah only burned two of his fingers, not his whole hand (as was reported by gossips and drunks), but not badly.

The year 1851 passed with minimal damage. People admired Cal's Hawken rifle, laughing at the way he held it unsteadily, moving around in that circle like he was about to drop it till he hit the set trigger and, on the next pass, the real trigger and hit that target, eight times out of ten, plumb center. The year that followed turned out a bit tougher, but Cal wasn't kicked out of school the way he had been the previous year when he brought his Hawken to class and shot the wind gauge off the roof. He blamed Archie Clarke for daring him. Obadiah took away the rifle and sold it to Joey Wilkes for three quarts of bourbon—which wasn't really bourbon, as it contained no corn whatsoever, and got Obadiah so sick that he thought he was going to die—and a lame horse, which wandered off and was never seen or heard of again. But that was Obadiah's fault, as he did not shut the corral gate properly, because he had consumed too much of that bourbon that wasn't real bourbon but *was* atrociously wretched.

Joey Wilkes later turned to holding up wayfarers but wayfared the wrong person and was wounded and brought to jail, which was raided by vigilantes who took Wilkes to the woods and promptly hanged him till he was dead, dead, dead. Archie Clarke got a bad case of the chickenpox. The Hawken disappeared. Well, no one in the state of Iowa ever saw it again. Cal's right shoulder didn't miss the Hawken too much, and Cal wasn't too heartbroken, and remembered that the constable had threatened to take the rifle away from him after that wind gauge incident at the schoolhouse.

The year 1853 went somewhat better, as accidents in the Marmaduke family were probably cut in half. The new schoolmaster did stab himself in his thigh with a pair of scissors and didn't treat the wound good enough, so they had to cut off his left leg, but Cal figured that wasn't his fault; that mean old man had been told to go to a doctor, but he hadn't done it. And he wasn't scolding Cal when he jammed the scissors five inches into his thigh, but lambasting Rebecca Ann Courtney. However, the schoolmaster was standing next to Cal's desk. Miss Burdette came in to finish the schooling, and nothing bad happened to her, though her beau broke four ribs and his right wrist when he fell off a ladder while, finally, putting on a new wind gauge on the roof.

The Marmadukes' luck, on the other hand, remained

sour seven ways from Sunday. Obadiah lost three jobs that year. Two windows were broken. They were evicted twice, from a hotel room and a cabin. One mule got taken away in lieu of money owed to the mercantile owner. And a bad hangnail tormented Obadiah for three weeks in July, so bad that he didn't even go to the Fourth of July celebration, during which three horses bolted out of the Swede's livery stable after some boys got ahold of some firecrackers and knocked the mayor into a water trough—which caused the crowd to roar with laughter. But they reelected the mayor the next year—before running him out of town on a rail the following April. Charity got sick from bad eggs and thought she was going to die, but she got better—and it was Cal who nursed his raising ma (as he secretly called her) while Obadiah was working at a lumberyard but not getting paid, as this was the judge's sentence for breaking those two windows after consuming too much demon rum.

Thus, when Kansas Territory got itself organized in the spring of 1854, the Marmadukes, who had worn out their welcome in Burlington, went south and settled near Lawrence, where Obadiah planted corn and Charity fixed up tasty meals, nickel a plate, to abolitionists and slavers alike. The Marmadukes arrived, as fate would dictate, on May 30, 1854, the very day that the Kansas–Nebraska Act created the sovereign territories of Kansas and Nebraska. That bit of legislation got rid of the old Missouri Compromise. And things got ugly in a hurry.

It wasn't "Bleeding Kansas" yet, but it would soon earn that name.

Obadiah and Charity liked Kansas, and so did young Cal, now a dozen years old, tall, and stronger than he had been and able to work a plow or drop seeds or milk the cow or chop wood, then studying his letters and figures most every evening in the cabin they had built a few miles outside of Lawrence.

It was not a well-built cabin. The roof leaked. Dust blew through the cracks between those unchinked logs, but, Obadiah said, that was on purpose to allow the breeze in during the summer. And during the winter, Obadiah said, that was on purpose to keep sickness out of the cabin. The fireplace didn't draw too good, but Cal didn't mind his clothes smelling like woodsmoke, though more often than not, it smelled of the smoke of dried buffalo dung, which was a lot easier to find in those parts than wood, unless you were on a creek or river— and the Marmadukes were a long way from the river. A long way from water, in fact.

Their well was eighty-five feet deep. But it tasted no worse than the water Cal recalled slurping up in Hang-town. And he could recall when, crossing that grim country on the way to California and back, about the only water to be found was a person's or a horse's sweat, so Cal, unlike Charity and Obadiah, did not complain.

The Kansas and the Wakarusa Rivers put together wouldn't make the Mississippi, but it didn't stink like that big dark water, either. Cal liked that. He liked the way the sun set over the Kansas plains, too. He liked the heat of Kansas, a different kind of heat than the mugginess and stickiness and stinkyness of Burlington and Iowa and that big, wide river.

Well, the country was pretty dull. Of course, so was Iowa, but that was a different kind of unexciting. Besides, nothing would ever look as beautiful as a lot of that country Cal had seen on the California Trail.

Those spacious skies. Those purple mountains—practically majesties. Somebody, Cal thought, should write a song or poem about that country. Even here, with those amber grain sprouts shooting up thick and lush from the Kansas sod and looking like millions of folks just waving, and waving, and waving.

But the romance of Kansas ended right quick.

There were abolitionists from the Emigrant Aid Company. Cal smiled at how those folks talked. Hailed from New England, they said, and gave him a pamphlet to read about why slavery was a sin. But Cal didn't read much of it because, not only were New Englanders hard for him to understand, but when the man said "sin," it reminded Cal of his birthing pa, and that just left him sad.

Missourians came, too. They didn't sound like New Englanders, but they got their point across with lead balls fired from their revolvers, or the broadside of a knife with a fourteen-inch blade and six-inch handle. Sometimes, they just rammed the blade into a belly or a back.

For a while, Cal thought this was a fine adventure. But his mother started crying a lot and praying harder than she ever had.

Despite all the horrors of anarchy and murder and villainy going around in Kansas and Missouri, everyone, for the most part, left the Marmadukes alone. There were other things to worry about than answering the door to the wrong person or saying the wrong thing in Lawrence or to a stranger on the pike to Lawrence.

Hail beat the corn to ruin, about the way abolitionists and slavers tried to do to each other. And though neither Iowa nor Kentucky was immune to bad weather, Kansas weather could be particularly nasty. Terrible tornadoes pulled up trees—if the trees were around—as if they were toothpicks and turned log cabins *into* toothpicks. The sod huts were sometimes returned to the Kansas sod.

When Obadiah saw an advertisement in the Lawrence newspaper, he thought he had found an answer to all his woes. The Paxton & Hunt, Attorneys at Law, formerly the Ruck–Davies firm, of Manhattan, K.T., advertised that they were looking for capable salespersons to sell insurance of all kinds. The firm allowed that it was willing to "hazard the perils" by offering "insurance policies of all kinds on properties in this grand Territory." It bragged that it had paid off on claims over the past two years—paid promptly, indeed; none of the insured ever had to hire a solicitor or pay any litigation fees because Paxton & Hunt was a fine, legitimate firm—and based in Manhattan, "we know the risks of black clouds and black fortune."

AGENTS WANTED IN
ALL
K.T. Localities
Please address communications
To Leech Goodenow,
P & H
Manhattan, K.T.

That was enough for Obadiah.

"You never sold anything in Burlington," Charity pointed out.

Not even when you were selling things—or trying to sell stuff, anyhow, Cal thought, but, wiser than his twelve years, kept his mouth closed.

"Never had the chance," Obadiah informed his lovely wife.

Because you got sent packing before you could open your mouth, Cal thought.

Need we remind you, dear reader, of how twelve-year-olds think at that cockily know-it-all youthful age?

Yes, Obadiah was hired by the firm, paperwork and forms and file folders and a receipt booklet came by post, and the eager new insurance salesman started walking—the mule having been stolen, as Cal's father claimed, or sold to pay off a debt, his mother said—and, for a while, bounty reined in the Marmaduke cottage. Which rained dirt daily, centipedes and spiders every other day, in season, and snakes, including two rattlers, that Charity chopped to bits with a hoe, then cooked for supper—from the roof.

Obadiah sold insurance policies almost daily. Honest to a fault—let us praise the good upbringings parents swore by in those golden Kentucky years—Obadiah sent his coins and paper money—to the Manhattan, K.T., office, and almost immediately, his commission was paid.

There was talk of moving off the farm and into Lawrence.

Till Jules Demmet came to the house with a claim.

Demmet was one of those abolitionists, and Obadiah had heard about some trouble he had had with some slavers from Missouri, but the New Englander didn't bring up how he got that scar over his right eyebrow. He just mentioned that wicked thunderstorm that had passed through a week ago.

"Ripped off the roof of the barn, killed my milk cow, and spooked the horses so much they busted out of the corral. Been looking for them three days. Reckon some Pawnees found them and taken them for their own."

"Tough luck," Obadiah told him.

"Yep." He pulled out his policy. "But thanks to you, Obadiah, I am insured."

Cal's dad was silent for a moment, but then smiled and nodded and told him that Paxton & Hunt was a fine, honest firm and paid promptly on claims. "Like you and me," Obadiah said, with a smile, "they know the risks of black clouds and black fortune."

It took Obadiah a while to figure out what all Demmet needed to put down to get his money, but two hours later, the two men shook hands, and Obadiah walked to Lawrence and went to the post office to mail his first claim to his bosses in Manhattan, K.T.

That storm, that had just poured rain on the Marmaduke place, surely did some damage to Obadiah's customers.

Eight claims were filed by Obadiah, who gave them the same friendly "Like you and me, Paxton and Hunt know the risks of black clouds and black fortune. They pay promptly, too."

But no one, not even Obadiah, heard anything for

two weeks. All those letters that Obadiah had mailed and paid for himself came back. Seems that the Paxton & Hunt office in Manhattan, K.T., had closed its doors. "Been gone for 'bout month and a half," stagecoach driver Chance Hazzard told Obadiah, who, remembering that his employer was a fine, legitimate firm, refused to believe. So he rode the next morning's stage to Manhattan, which meant he had to get a room and pay for that, too—he wound up sleeping in a jail cell after a much-needed, he said, bender.

The town marshal felt sorry for Obadiah when he heard his woeful story and just turned him loose—after making him clean up the mess he'd made in the cell—and Obadiah hired on as a muleskinner for an outfit that was heading to the southeastern corner of the state, Lawrence being on the way.

It took them about a week to cover the eighty-something miles, but at a dollar a day, that was money Obadiah thought he would need. And unlike Paxton & Hunt, the burly boss of the outfit paid in silver coins. Promptly. Obadiah did bite into a coin, just to make sure it was real.

Which chipped a tooth, but at least there was a dentist in Lawrence, so he wouldn't have to go to that ruffian in St. Louis again.

When he got home and told Charity all about the woes, she gave him a hug. Then Cal opened the door—he had been feeding the chickens and mule—and told them they had company. Then the boy turned around and said, "Pa's here. Why don't y'all come on in?"

They took all of Obadiah's silver coins, and his

mules—no one wanted the noisy, skinny chickens, especially since the hens weren't that steady of layers—and they even rode off with Buck's Celebrated Cooking Stove, which Obadiah had purchased, back when he was flush, from an outfit in Topeka.

"What was that fuss all about, Pa?" Cal asked, after the wagon—which had belonged to the Marmadukes—was on its way back to Lawrence with Buck's Celebrated Cooking Stove.

Cal's mother said, "Go fetch your papa's jug. You know the one. Hidden in that pile of hay next to the ladder in the barn."

"I ain't never had a snort, Ma," Cal let his Ma know.

"I know that. Just fetch it for your daddy. It's medicinal."

"Yes'm."

When the door had closed, and Charity had counted off enough seconds so that her boy—that wasn't really hers—was halfway to the barn, she looked at her husband and asked: "Obadiah, have you ever noticed that we haven't had any peace or pleasantries—except on a few rare occasions—since you talked me into letting us take the James's infant all them years ago?"

CHAPTER 13

Charity Marmaduke took to educating Cal as best she could while Obadiah took whatever job he could get, and often those jobs were with freighting companies, and things got better. And one day Obadiah came home all excited and said they were moving to Pawnee.

Lowering the Bible she had been reading to Cal, she stared at her husband, thinking—the same as Cal—that he had found some whiskey somewhere and was well in his cups. But there was nothing on his breath but tobacco.

"Where is Pawnee?" Cal asked.

"It's near Fort Riley," Obadiah said.

Cal exchanged glances with his mother.

"Where is Fort Riley?" Charity asked.

"It's the old Camp Center," Obadiah said.

Charity shot her son a glance, and Cal responded with a shrug.

"A hundred miles west of here!" Obadiah exclaimed.

Cal saw his mother's face pale. She had heard Cal's tales of the Indian attack on the wagon train, and despite all of Cal's reassurances, she thought anything *west* meant Indian attacks and all sorts of butchery and devilment.

"We are not moving west," she said. "No. Never."

The assurances of Pawnee's safety and the proximity of the Fort Center or Camp Riley or whatever they were called could not alleviate her fears.

But Obadiah put his foot down—too hard, and he got to hopping and cussing and had to sit down, and Charity allowed him one sip of the rheumatism medicine a peddler had sold her three months earlier, but just one sip. And once her husband had finished what she allowed him and was feeling somewhat better, he explained, as best he could, the reasons they needed to move to Pawnee, Kansas.

"I have it on good authority—you have to believe me—that, first, this new city is safer than Lawrence." He lowered his voice. "The owner of that outfit that I just worked for is a cousin to Andrew Reeder—and you know who Andrew Reeder is."

"Who's Andrew Reeder?" Charity asked, before Cal could.

Obadiah started to reach for the bottle of medicine, but he saw his wife's eyes turn to slits, and rested his palm on his thigh and wet his lips. "He's the governor of the territory of Kansas."

Charity gave Cal a look, but Cal just shrugged.

Obadiah sighed. "We can get to Pawnee before most folks settle there, but we have to make this quick. Once Governor Reeder announces this, the prices of lots will jump to the moon, and we'll be too late. I've got enough money to buy us several lots."

"Why?" Charity asked.

"Because Governor Reeder is making Pawnee the new territorial capital of Kansas!"

Which caused Cal to ask, "Where's the capital now?"

"Leavenworth," Charity answered.

"No," Obadiah corrected. "It was. But the governor moved it to Shawnee Mission."

"Why?" Cal asked.

"I don't know!" Obadiah snapped.

"You're buying lots?" The words her husband had spoken earlier must have finally reached Charity's brain. "Where'd you get enough money to buy several lots anywhere?" she demanded.

"From working!" he barked, and Cal glanced at his mother, who gave him a slight nod, which meant that they both knew working did not mean freighting for the Kansas governor's cousin or the late John Jacob Astor's heirs. He had been stealing again. Or maybe Obadiah still had some of the money he had earned back in March during the territorial elections. By Obadiah's account, he had voted twenty-nine times and had been paid a dollar for each ballot—though given how long Obadiah had been gone, Charity had told Cal one night before saying prayers with him, she thought Cal's daddy had voted twice that number.

"Is it worth staying here?" Obadiah bellowed, when he saw the dubious looks on the two faces staring at him.

He had a point.

They sold the place to Samuel S. Snyder, a minister with the United Brethren Church. He thought the place would be part of Lawrence in no time, the way that

town was growing. Then Obadiah rushed off to Pawnee.
Cal and Charity bought a wagon and mule, and loaded
up everything, which wasn't much—Cal thought they
didn't need a wagon or a horse, but a hundred miles was
a long way to walk—and they found the military road
that led to Fort Riley, unless the government had
changed the name already.

It took Cal and Charity right around a week to make
it to Pawnee, and they found out that word had already
spread across the territory. Obadiah had snagged up two
lots instead of twenty—because that was about all that
was left, but he was confident that it would work out
fine. After all, Pawnee was going to be the new capital
of Kansas Territory.

The biggest building, as might be expected, was the
territorial Capitol, two stories of Kansas limestone,
about forty feet wide and eighty feet long, chimneys on
each side, and a slanted roof.

It was a lot bigger and better built than the tent Obadiah had pitched, but he wasn't worried. He said they
would build a new home after the legislature met. He
was in a hurry, though, and showed Cal the stable he
had built. Charity at least thought her husband would
help her down from the wagon box, but Obadiah had
been selected as the gravedigger for this day, and a
Free-Soiler had killed a pro-slavery "Border Ruffian"
that morning, and one of Governor Reeder's assistants
wanted him buried before the pro-slavers found out.

That would be hard to do, since the pro-slavers had
run away with the election. At least that's what a lot of

well-dressed men were yelling on the streets of the territorial capital.

"I am a duly elected representative from Leaven-worth!" yelled a man with a Missouri twang, and brace of revolvers on a belt around his waist.

"You are a demon from Missouri," said a man with only one revolver, but he was holding it, though the barrel for the moment was pointed at the dusty street. "And this is a bogus legislature."

"You be callin' me a liar?" the man with the twang twanged.

"More people voted in Leavenworth than live in Leavenworth!" the man said.

"Three, four, five times as many," another gent with a tall stovepipe hat agreed.

"I demand satisfaction," the twanger said, and reached for one of his revolvers.

He was dead before he could even cock his piece, and the Free-Soiler turned and saw Cal and Charity and their wagon.

"Put that Missouri dog in that wagon," the man said. "You, boy. Isn't your pa doin' today's buryin's?"

Cal didn't know how to answer, but a woman yelled that what the man who had just killed the Missourian said was gospel.

"But," Charity said, "we haven't even unloaded it yet."

Later that night, outside the tent, Charity said, "The Lord works in mysterious ways," as they cooked their supper. All those Free-Soilers, especially after hearing that they came from the town of Lawrence and, before that, the free state of Iowa, had unloaded the wagon, and a young man maybe two or three years Cal's senior jumped on the wagon that now carried the unwrapped dead body of the Missourian who had been elected to the Bogus Legislature, and guided him to Pawnee's cemetery.

Of course, later, Cal had time to check out the new Capitol Building and realized that the tent he had for a home wasn't so bad after all. Carpenters were busy trying to put doors on the hinges, and when Cal peeked through a window that did not have a window yet, he saw more men working inside trying to put a floor onto the second story of the building. And maybe finish the roof.

Governor Reeder and other legislators, those from the sovereign state of Kansas and those who said they were Kansans but actually lived in Missouri, crowded the streets on the morning of July 2, 1855, when they went into that limestone building—most of them armed to the teeth.

Cal tried to make some friends, but the boys around his age asked him where he was from, Missouri or Kansas, and which side was he taking, slavery or freedom, and Cal just hung his head and said, "Iowa."

The Missourians and the Kansans all laughed at him, then ran off to torment some of the girls walking to a patch of tallgrass that hadn't been chopped down yet.

Not that Cal would ever be a student of political

history—as if anyone with any common sense can understand anything politicians do—the way he understood things that happened those few days in the new town of Pawnee, Kansas, was that Governor Reeder had a bevy of problems with those who had been elected to the legislature.

Now, even if most of the members of that august party of men were pro-slavers from Missouri, they did have a point that Pawnee was a long way from civilization, not that any God-fearing Kansan would call Missouri civilized. The legislature voted to move the capital from Pawnee to a place more reasonable and easier to get to.

Governor Reeder said there was an entire army post to offer protection.

A Missourian said, "A lot of good that did Colonel Hugh Peterson."

A Lawrence man Cal remembered seeing in a barbershop once said, "He shan't be the last Missouri sidewinder to be covered with Kansas sod."

The Missourian responded, "You'll be buried long before another Missourian is."

The gentlemen of that body, most of them from Missouri but some of them Kansas who felt the blade of an Arkansas Toothpick or a Navy Colt pressed against belly, back, or side, voted to move the territorial legislature to a closer and more convenient place.

Governor Reeder vetoed that bill.

The members of that quickly deteriorating body of politicians, many of them remembering the feel of a steel blade or a cold, hard gun barrel pressed against their sides, backs, or bellies, but most of them still pro-slavers from Missouri overrode the governor's veto.

Pawnee, Kansas, which became territorial capital officially on July 2, and did get to have a nice celebration of the Fourth of July, became the former territorial capital of Kansas on the Sixth of July in the Year of Our Lord 18 and 55.

Cal didn't know what he should feel. After all, he wasn't a native of Kansas and had only moved here a while back from Iowa. But his birthing parents, if a Baptist minister is to be believed, had been living in Missouri, though they weren't natives of Missouri but—where was that?—

"Kentucky!" he said aloud.

"What?" his mother and father asked, at the same time.

"Nothing," Cal said.

"I wish we'd never left Kentucky," Charity said.

Anyway, the Territorial Legislature of Kansas moved from Pawnee back to Shawnee Mission and held court, or whatever it was called, at a Methodist mission there.

Pawnee became a ghost town, but Obadiah refused to leave. Someone had suggested that he move to Lecompton, that he had heard the legislature was going to move there, since there were dang few prostitutes in Shawnee, but Obadiah said he knew that Pawnee would become a great town, one of the greatest in Kansas, and his lots would make his pile here.

He might could have done just that, too, but soldiers

from Fort Riley rode in one day and ordered them off. This land now belonged to the United States Army.

They came back to Lawrence, pitched that tent on some patch of ground nobody had yet to claim, and Charity went back to teaching Cal his letters and numbers.

Cal had gone fishing early one morning in May 1856 and was coming back home to do some chores before getting to his lessons when a party of well-mounted and better-armed men rode up to him. The man riding on a black horse in front of the others removed a feathered military-style hat and gave Cal a friendly nod.

The nod was the only thing friendly about him—and all the others. He had four revolvers on his person, under his armpits, and on his hips. There was a nasty scar across his left cheek, and he held a shotgun that was butted against his thigh.

But he also had a badge pinned onto the lapel of his coat, and Cal's mama had always told him to be nice to peace officers—though, in Kansas, Cal had rarely seen any peace officer who was fond of keeping the peace.

"Son," the man said, "I'm sheriff of Douglas County." That meant as much to Cal as if the man had said he was from the moon. "How far away are we from Lawrence."

Cal made a slight gesture. "You're practically in it. Just follow the trail and you'll be there right quick."

The sheriff nodded. "There's a hotel there. The Free State. You know it?"

"I know where it is. Never been inside it, though."

"Where exactly is it?"

Cal told him.

The sheriff looked at those rough-looking, gun-heavy

deputies—well, Cal figured they were deputies—riding behind the lawman.

"There's a couple of newspapers, too. *The Free State* and the . . ."

One of the bearded men behind him spat out the name: "*The Kansas Herald of Freedom.*"

Sure. Cal knew of both papers. His parents couldn't afford either, since the *Herald of Freedom* wanted two dollars in advance for a subscription—his pa had told his mother that's why they couldn't get that one. But Cal told the sheriff where those papers were located, generally, but they should be able to find both easy enough. Or if they didn't, most folks in town could direct them straight to the place.

They rode off. And then some more riders came loping after them, none nodding at Cal or hailing him or anything friendly. And while math was never Cal's best subject in school—back when he went to school; now that his mama was teaching him he did a lot better learning her math—he tried counting.

Whew. That was some posse. Cal couldn't see all the men, but he counted just about a hundred. Maybe not quite, but possibly even more. Then he stopped counting. That posse was bigger than anything he had seen before. Cal's mouth dropped open when he saw the cannons.

Anyway, the sheriff and his followers found all those places just fine.

Instead of arresting outlaws, Cal learned, the sheriff arrested Lawrence's leaders. According to Cal's daddy, the cannon was put atop Mount Oread, which hardly was a mountain, but folks could see it. They dragged the presses out of the *Herald of Freedom* and the *Free State* and to the river, and threw them in. They forced everyone out of the Free State Hotel, then brought in some kegs of black powder and blew the hotel up.

Cal heard the explosion. He thought it was thunder, though the clouds hadn't yet appeared in the Kansas sky.

Then they burned the hotel down.

One fellow died—got hit in the head with a Free State Hotel brick—but he was for slavery, and the sheriff hauled his body back when they left.

All that did was just fire up this mean-looking gent Cal had seen a time or two, named John Brown.

A few days after Lawrence got sacked—meaning that first time, not when it got sacked a whole lot worse some years later—John Brown, who hated pro-slavers more than just about anyone in the world, and some of his pards rode to Pottawatomie Creek and killed five fellows.

Cal couldn't figure it all out, just from hearing his father and mother talk. Or listening to what the parson said in one sermon before he fled back to Springfield— Cal wasn't sure if it was the Springfield in Missouri or that one in Indiana or Iowa or whatever that state was where that Abraham Lincoln fellow was politicking.

Turned out, Cal figured, that maybe they never should have left Lawrence after all. Sure, a constitutional convention was scheduled to be held in Lecompton in 1857, but the Free-Staters this time outvoted the Missourians and won with minimal bloodletting and only a handful of deaths. On December 7, the Free-Staters led the first meeting under Freedom's Flag in Lecompton, quickly adjourned, and sent the whole congress to Lawrence.

Obadiah took more to drink, and he had been drinking more than his fill for quite some time.

CHAPTER 14

Lawrence was rebuilt. The "sacking" by that mean sheriff did nothing but get the anti-slavery folks mad.

Old John Brown attacked and defeated some pro-slavers at a place called Black Jack shortly after the Lawrence sacking and that nastiness at Pottawatomie Creek.

Cal was sent to buy some flour—well, not actually buy with money but put it on the Marmadukes' account—and Cal was surprised to find so many men carrying firearms. Even the Widow Clay shouldered a blunderbuss, but that just made Cal miss his Hawken rifle.

Before Cal made it to the mercantile, a man in an alley whispered, "Boy," as Cal passed him.

Cal stopped and turned. The man didn't look like Obadiah Marmaduke or any of the beggars Cal recollected from Iowa and, mostly, Hangtown and Sacramento, but Lawrence didn't have many poor and homeless and bums. And this fellow was wearing a tailor-made coat. Sure, his cravat was askew and his paper collar all mussed up, but his boots were shiny black and he had a really nice watch chain that likely was attached to a really nice timepiece.

And he reached inside one of that fancy coat's inside pockets and pulled out some paper money.

"I want you to do something for me, kid. Can you do that?"

Charity had raised Cal better than to jump into something like that.

"Depends on what you need, mister."

"See that office across the street." The man's chin did the pointing.

Cal turned quickly, then looked back at the stranger.

"The stagecoach office?"

"That's right."

Cal saw that bill in the man's trembling fingers.

"What do you need?"

"I want you to buy me a ticket."

Cal straightened. "Why don't you buy it yourself?"

"Because I don't want anyone to know I'm leaving this miserable, lawless place that belongs on the eight hundredth level of Hades." The man slipped back toward the shadows and wall when the boards creaked along the walking path, but Cal turned to see some fat man go into a barbershop.

The man realized he wasn't in danger of being seen and wiped his brow.

"Son, I just have to get out of this town before I am killed."

That, Cal decided, didn't make him feel any better about this job.

"I am not a criminal. I am not wanted. I, as God is

my witness, have done nothing wrong in the eyes of the Lord or in the books of the law. But if I do not get out of Lawrence, I shall be killed. Or driven to taking my own life. You must believe me, boy. I am at my wit's end!"

Cal had just about decided to run across the street and hide till that man got someone else to do his trickery, but those last words—and the look in the fellow's eyes, and the cracking and authenticity of his voice—made him stay.

"Where do you want to go?"

"Anywhere," he said. "East. Just get me out of Kansas and, preferably, nowhere close to Missouri. I'll find my way from wherever that ticket takes me."

The man waited, then said: "I'll pay you twenty dollars—once that ticket is in my hand." He pulled another note from his hand. "And here's twenty more."

Well, his father and even his mother would not mind Cal helping out with a fortune like that. The man gave him some bills for the ticket and a twenty-dollar gold piece for Cal before he crossed the street. Now, Cal thought, if he were like Obadiah, he could just run off and keep that money for himself and leave that well-dressed gent to whatever peril he had gotten himself into. But Cal was not like Obadiah, and he checked the schedule and asked the pockmarked man who was half in his cups about places that stage could go, and eventually he decided that the fare to Denver, Colorado Territory, would do just fine. That town had been booming a few years back, and it was far from Missouri if that map on the wall was mostly accurate.

The man thanked Cal profusely and, true to his word, gave him another twenty dollars.

The stranger took his ticket, put it in his coat pocket, and pulled up his collar and pulled down his hat. Then he found some paper money and gave Cal two bills.

"Keep one for yourself, son. And do me one more favor. Will you?"

"Sure." Cal liked this kind of work. He figured his ma would like it, too.

"See the jehu, over there, getting that coach ready?"

Cal turned and saw the slim, bearded man with the dirtiest mouth Cal had ever heard barking orders as some fellows hitched a six-up of mules to the mud wagon.

"Yes, sir."

"Give him one of those notes—the other is for you— and tell him that a man in a Prince Albert and fine hat will be waiting at the edge of town. Give him the ticket you bought for me. Tell him that's my ticket. And that there's twenty dollars for him if he stops and picks me up. Tell him I have no bags."

Cal didn't think the driver of the mud wagon would believe him. And even if he did, the jehu wouldn't likely stop to pick up this man who was half frightened to death already. But Cal did as he was told. When he turned around, the man was gone, but Cal picked him out a half minute later, as he made his way toward that rendezvous point.

So Cal forgot all about his errands, and watched the jehu climb up to the driver's box with another gent carrying a shotgun, and saw the jehu and the shotgun jawing, and some folks piling into the wagon, then heard the whips barking and the jehu shouting out some pretty salty words for a civilized town like Lawrence, and then saw the wagon lope down the street and stop just where the man was waiting. The man climbed up and rode atop the rig, and Cal watched him till the dust swallowed the mules and the jehu and the shotgun and the mud wagon and that strange man.

"Did you hear the news?" Obadiah called out the next evening when he got home from doing some odd jobs for twenty-seven cents.

"My goodness!" Charity exclaimed. "What has happened?"

"The governor. Governor Shannon. Governor Wilson Shannon. He has fled Kansas. No one has seen hide nor hair of him since yesterday. He disappeared in Lecompton, but someone said they thought they saw him here—in Lawrence—yesterday."

Blood still flowed. So much that Kansas became known as "Bleeding Kansas." Word came that Missourians were marching toward Lawrence and Topeka, but they were stopped by Brown and his boys. Osawatomie was burned. In September, John Brown came to Lawrence when word was that thousands of liver-eating, merciless Missourians were coming again to sack the town, but the latest idiot who had been fool enough to take the job as governor of Kansas negotiated a truce, and Lawrence was saved. The Missourians returned to their state.

Cal was fourteen years old. No longer a boy, but—in Kansas during those wild and bloodstained years—a man. And this was a time when Kansas needed men. This was a time when men had to make choices.

Obadiah Marmaduke made one choice. Like one former, cowardly governor of the territory of Kansas, he fled Kansas. He left no note for Charity or Cal, both of whom looked for him for two full days before someone said they had seen him talking to a man who was taking some supplies to Santa Fe way down in New Mexico Territory.

That was the year that Lawrence held a shooting contest for its Fourth of July celebration.

Cal and Charity walked through the tents that had been set up. The band played all kinds of tunes. Folks were eating cakes and pies. Red, white, and blue bunting flapped in the strong wind. The flags whipped hard high up on their poles.

And booms echoed across the prairie.

"Is that thunder?" Charity asked.

"No, Mother," Cal said. "It's a shooting contest."

"Oh." His mother surprised him. "Can we watch?"

Cal watched. His fingers twitched. He recalled those glorious days when he was just a little boy holding a heavy Hawken rifle. He smiled at most of the memories of Captain Shufflebottom and even the Reverend James. He sighed when he thought about poor Vincenzo. But mostly, he thought of the good times. Jim Bridger, folks like that. And the smell of black powder in the nostrils after you knew you had hit your mark plumb center.

"How about you, young man!" the barker called out. "You're tall enough and heavy enough. Two bits. Hit the target, you can win a ribbon for yourself and a china plate for your lovely wife."

"He's my son!" Charity said, with delight.

"I do not believe that for one second, miss," the barker said.

She laughed. Then she handed Cal a quarter. "Go on. You've told me so many stories about shooting, and the only thing I ever knew you to hit was a wind gauge."

Cal joined her in that moment of merriment. But his ma grabbed him by the hand and practically pulled him to the table.

"Your choice of weapons, my good boy. I have a Henry. A Springfield. And an Enfield."

Cal saw another rifle, and he pointed at that.

"Boy." The barker tugged on his mustache and shook his head. "Son, that's a Hawken. Fifty-four caliber. What mountain men used back in the day. I just have that to show off. Nobody wants to shoot a relic like that anymore."

"I do."

Their eyes met, and the barker turned to a freedman who was his assistant.

"Joe. Did you clean that Hawken?"

"Yes, sir. But it ain't loaded."

"We got a ball that'll fit it?" the barker asked.

"Yes, sir. Molded some myself the other day, just for the fun of it."

"Show the kid how it's loaded," the barker said.

"I'll load it myself," Cal told him.

A crowd gathered. The target was a paper plate a hundred yards away. The bull's eye was a blue star in the center—not that anyone could make out a star—just the dark color—at that distance.

Side bets were made by just about everyone. The barker and his assistant laughed.

And everyone howled when Cal hefted the Hawken to his shoulder and did just the way he had done as a youngster on the California Trail. Round and round the Hawken went. Men and women and even Cal's mother laughed.

Then he hit the set trigger.

Then he touched the front trigger.

Then nobody was laughing at all.

"Did he come close?" Charity asked.

A man standing a good bit to the right of the target moved to the plate, pulled it down, and put his right forefinger through the hole in the center of the star.

"Bull's-eye!" the man said, after a few choice words of profanity.

CHAPTER 15

Some citizens pitched in and bought that Hawken for Cal. It really wasn't for Cal, of course, but since Cal's raising, not birthing, daddy had run off and his raising mama was struggling, some Kansans—despite all that bloodshed staining the territory—had kind hearts and Christian spirit. With the .54-caliber beauty, Cal became busy, and his mother, eternally grateful: For when the citizens of Lawrence rebuilt the Free State Hotel, the owners wanted meat, Cal and that Hawken rifle were kept busy hunting, and Charity sure was kept happy, having someone bringing cash home and putting fresh meat on her own table come suppertime.

The story of Cal's keen eye and that Hawken spread across Kansas Territory, and one morning, a United States Army officer and two enlisted men rode up to the cabin the Marmadukes rented.

Now the acting man of the house, Cal stepped outside. Back in Iowa, he would have done so with a smile on his face, but these days, this being Kansas, Cal came out with the Hawken cocked and ready.

The officer nodded. Cal saw the revolver belted,

but the flap closed on the holster, and the two soldier
boys kept their carbines in the saddle sheaths. The officer had a red sash around his waist, with the belt over
that. Neither of the privates carried a revolver. That
made Cal feel better, but he waited for the soldiers to
state their business. He knew that sometimes those
Missouri Bushwhackers came dressed in blue but with
deviltry in their hearts.

Their brass buttons reflected the sunlight, their collars
were pulled up high, and those hats looked silly to Cal.

"You'd be Calvin Marmaduke," the officer said, "I
take it?" He pointed at the Hawken. "That rifle and its
owner have become legendary."

Cal studied the country around them. The last sentence had him doubting that these men were real soldiers. From all those newspapers Cal and his mama had
been reading lately, these men could definitely be some
mean ol' Missourians.

"State your business," Cal said.

The enlisted man with the scruffy red beard chuckled. "He's a bit young to sound so tough."

"Downright uppity," said the other bluecoat.

The officer turned and stared hard at the soldiers. "I
don't believe I gave you permission to speak, soldiers."

Both men frowned.

"But I will give you permission now. Apologize to
Mr. Marmaduke."

"Mister?" The red-bearded soldier tried to stop
that sarcastic statement but was too late. He drew in a
deep breath and quickly released it. The other man
had apologized immediately, and Redbeard hurriedly

muttered, "No offense meant, mister. I was just funnin' ya is all."

Cal nodded, but did not lower the hammer on the Hawken.

"Calvin?" came the voice of his mother from inside the cabin.

Cringing, Cal said, "It's just three soldiers, Ma."

All three of the troopers smiled, but before Cal could do anything, out came Charity Marmaduke, and those soldiers quickly straightened and removed their hats. The officer even gave a slight bow and said, "Ma'am, I am Second Lieutenant Alvin Johnson and these are"— nodding at the one with the red beard—"Private Aitken, and"—turning to the other—"Private Drabowski."

Cal had not looked at his mother, but kept his focus on the three strangers. When he heard his mother offer the three coffee and some breakfast, Cal stiffened and ground his teeth, but that lieutenant shook his head and returned the hat to his head.

"Thank you, ma'am, but no. We had breakfast at camp this morning—though not as fine as what you had." He cleared his throat. "Captain Jackson ordered me to come here to discuss a possible job for your son."

"Cal," Charity said, turning so quickly Cal could feel that hard stare she was giving him even though he would not take his eyes off the three strangers. "You didn't tell me you were joining the Army."

"I haven't," Cal said. The Hawken was feeling heavier than a mountain howitzer all of a sudden.

That lieutenant tried hard not to laugh. "We were not sent here to enlist soldiers or offer commissions,

Mrs. Marmaduke—even though someone with your son's reputation and legend would be most welcome during these dark days for our territory and our nation."

Cal thought: *Reputation?*

His mother said: "Why don't you young men get out of this sun and wind?"

"Ma . . ." Cal whispered.

"Oh, hush, Son. It's so nice to see men in uniform, serving our country, protecting us settlers. Lord knows it has gotten mighty tiresome with strangers asking, 'Are you Free-Soiler or Slaver?' Happens all the time. Sometimes I've wondered why I ever left Iowa."

The lieutenant smiled. "You're from Iowa?"

"Not Iowa-born," Charity said, with a warming smile. "I was born in Kentucky. But my late husband wanted to settle in Iowa, so we were there for a number of years, then moved here."

"I was born at Fort Armstrong," the officer said.

Charity's smile widened. "We lived in Burlington," she said. "You were just upriver from us."

"Well, we were gone by '42. My father was transferred to Jefferson Barracks."

"And you followed in your father's boot prints." Charity sighed, and then whispered, "I'm glad you didn't do that very thing, Cal." She motioned the soldiers to dismount and come over.

Cal started grinding his teeth.

"Put your horses in the corral," Charity said, with enthusiasm.

The two privates stared at the lieutenant, who nodded and all three men dismounted. They led their horses to the corral, hitching them to the rail instead of putting them in with the mule. The red-bearded one stayed with the animals. The lieutenant must have ordered him to that duty, and when the one with the strange last name reached for the long gun in the scabbard, the lieutenant whispered, "Leave it, Drabowski," but the wind carried the words to the Marmadukes.

The two soldiers sipped coffee, and Charity filled a third cup and handed it to Cal with the instructions to "Take it to that nice-looking soldier with the flaming hair."

Reluctantly, Cal obeyed. No words—not even a "Here" from Cal or a "Thanks" from Private Aitken.

When Cal returned to his mother and the two troopers whose names Cal had already forgotten, the lieutenant was telling Charity, "We come from Fort Scott."

Cal shifted the Hawken and put his thumb on the hammer that he had only moments ago lowered.

"Fort Scott closed some years back," he said, and stared hard at the lieutenant. He had caught them in a lie. They must have thought he was dumb as a rotted stump.

"Yes, Mr. Marmaduke, our government closed the fort in '55. The buildings were auctioned off, and have become part of the city of Fort Scott. We were at Fort Leavenworth when the captain ordered me to take twenty men to the city of Fort Scott for protection against Missourians." He shook his head. "It is a shame that our country is coming so dreadfully close to a civil war." He started to spit, but saw Cal's mother, and swallowed it instead.

"If you will forgive me, I must ask you first—"

Cal and his mother knew what was coming.

"Where do you stand? Pro-slavery, Free-Stater, or abolitionist?"

Charity glanced at Cal, who just stood there wishing these three soldiers would take their leave and leave them alone.

"I am a woman," Charity said, with a laugh. "No one cares what women think."

"That is one reason," the lieutenant said, "of how this entire situation has gotten completely out of hand. If we listened to women, we would be much better off."

What a charming scoundrel! That was the thought that flashed through Cal's brain, but he bit his bottom lip to keep from vocalizing his opinion. But Cal knew where his mother—well, this mother, his second ma— stood. She was a Kentuckian by birth, had grown up around slaves. Charity Marmaduke might not be an abolitionist, but she certainly was not pro-slavery. Which meant she was a Free-Stater. Let Kansans be free. Let slaveowners live in peace. Let those who found slavery a sin live in peace.

Cal thought: *That ain't never happening.*

"I guess that's our business," Cal said. He waited till the lieutenant's and the private's eyes met his. "We don't rightly care what you think. So you don't need to know what we think."

The lieutenant smiled, sipped his coffee, and said, "That kind of thinking can get a man killed, son. In these uncivil times."

Cal nodded. "So can asking those kinds of questions."

That got the bluecoat with the red sash to laugh.

"You are indeed Calamity James, aren't you?" the lieutenant said.

"What? Who?"

The officer removed that strange hat and slapped it against his thigh, lifting dust that the wind swept away.

The private, still drinking coffee, nodded.

Cal and his mother stared at each other for a moment, then Cal turned back to the lieutenant.

"Listen," the soldier said. "I'm not asking you, Mr. Marmaduke, to choose sides. The captain did not send me all this way to talk you into joining the Army of the United States of America or to join any of those Jayhawkers or Border Ruffians. What he wants is someone who can shoot game to feed our company and scouts and any prisoners—mostly ruffians from Missouri—that we capture."

Cal ran his tongue over his left molars, trying to size up that offer. "You're in the United States Army," he said, at length. "Can't y'all kill a rabbit or buffalo yourself?"

Both soldiers laughed. The lieutenant rattled his saber. "You think any one of us could kill anything with this old wrist-breaker? We have Hall's carbines, but they aren't reliable. We lose half the charges just carrying the cumbersome things." He pointed at Cal's rifle. "That long gun is what we call a real weapon. I bet that rifle's twenty years old, maybe older, and it shoots as true as it did in the days of the free trappers." He nodded at the horses. "A Hall carbine is many things, but what it is mostly is *fickle*. It'll let you down when you need it most." He laughed while shaking his head. "It'll let you down even when you expect it to let you down."

Cal just stared at the officer, who smiled, and tossed out the dregs from his cup.

"Tell you what, son," the lieutenant said. "Why don't you and your mother talk it over? The captain will pay you fifteen dollars a month, paid—like us—every two months. We'll furnish you lead and powder—and even better—all you have to do is bring in what you kill. Our cooks will handle the butchering—or oversee whoever is in the guardhouse who is assigned that duty. Which is much better than getting duty in the priv—" He stopped quickly and cleared his throat. "Well, it's good pay."

Cal didn't know what to think. He glanced at his mother, but she looked as astonished as he did.

The officer put on his hat. He said, "We'll camp just off the Lawrence road. Sleep on it. Talk it over. But we have to leave tomorrow early. It's more than a hundred miles from here to Fort Scott."

The other soldier took the lieutenant's coffee cup and his own and handed them to Cal's mother, who took a moment before she realized what the dragoon was doing. Then she took the cups, and whispered, "You're welcome," even though the soldier had not thanked her.

The lieutenant did, though.

Charity Marmaduke regained her faculties and lowered the cups. "You boys come by for breakfast in the morning," she said.

"We cann—"

But Cal's mother cut the lieutenant off. "I won't take

no for an answer," she said. "It is a long ride, as you say, to Fort Scott, and I won't have anyone leaving my house without a good meal."

Though Cal knew that his mother wasn't all that good of a cook. Still, they had bacon, and the hen was laying again—or had been, Charity had said, while Cal had been out hunting for the new Free State Hotel and some of the other eateries in the town.

Cal had been rendered mute for a moment, then he started to say something, but his mother started yapping at the lieutenant, so Cal had to bide his time.

When the officer called at the red-bearded dragoon to bring their horses—and his coffee cup—to the cabin, Cal glanced at his smiling mother. His mouth opened, but still he couldn't think of what he wanted to say.

The horses arrived. The cinches were tightened. The sabers rattled as the three men pulled themselves onto the backs of their mounts, and the lieutenant raised his right hand and started to give a command.

Finally, Cal found his voice. "Mister."

The officer stopped and looked down. "Yes, lad?"

"Well, sir." Cal ran his tongue over his lips. "Well, captain—I mean, lieutenant. But, sir, how come you know about me and this here rifle of mine?" He didn't re-member leaning the Hawken against the cabin, but when he turned around he saw it next to the open door. He looked back at the three soldiers. "I mean. Like you said, it's better'n a hundred miles from here to Fort Scott."

The dragoon with the red beard chuckled, the other one stared blankly ahead, and the lieutenant grinned. "Are you joshing me, son?" the officer asked.

Cal shook his head, then remembered his vocal chords. "No, sir. I'm serious."

The lieutenant's face became unreadable. Then, without a word, he twisted in the saddle and worked on the straps on one of his saddlebags—the one on the opposite side of the horse. He came out with a flimsy book of paper. The wind almost took it away from him, but he hadn't put his gloves back on so he caught it, turned around and leaning down, extended the book.

"Take it, Cal," the officer said. "Read it."

Charity came forward and stared at the book. Her eyes widened, and her jaw fell a bit, and she stared at the lieutenant, who had straightened back in the saddle and was pulling on one of his gloves, then the other.

Grabbing the reins again, he looked back at Cal and his mother.

"I reckon just about everybody in our United States and her territories know about you, son," he said. "See you tomorrow morning."

He tipped the brim of his silly hat, waved his right hand, and spurred his horse into a trot. The two privates nodded and thanked the Marmadukes for their hospitality and followed the young lieutenant.

Cal and his mother stared at the book's cover, then at each other, then back at the cover, then at the soldiers till the dust swallowed them. Then they looked at each other. Then at the book. And how long they stood there with that flimsy paperback book they could not say.

CHAPTER 16

*THE AMAZING
BUT AUTHENTIC AND TRUE STORY
OF A KID CALLED CALAMITY—
AND HIS DUEL WITH DEATH;
OR, BORDER RUFFIANS
ON THE OREGON TRAIL.*

By Colonel Horatio L. Delmont

*Who Heard the Amazing
Yet Authenticated & True Story
From That Hero of America's
Wild Western Territories,
That Saint and Savior,
Captain Malachi J. Shufflebottom,
A Witness to These Extraordinary Events*

That was the book's title, which struck Cal almost as outrageous as the illustration that depicted a young fellow with a curled mustache and underlip beard, holding a light-haired woman in a fine dress behind him with his left hand, while his right held a smoking blunderbuss, and three pirates—at least, they were dressed like the pirates in the stories Charity had read to Cal when he was just a little boy—charged toward them. There were some covered wagons in the background, along with towering mountains and a few dead or dying folks here and there, and maybe fifty or fifteen hundred wild Indians and machete-holding Mexicans—well, they looked like some of the Mexicans Cal had seen in California—and maybe a pirate or two.

It was hard to take all of that in.

"Cal?"

When his mother's voice finally registered, Cal made himself look away from the gaudy cover. "Yes, ma'am?"

She pointed a trembling finger at the book. "Who is that girl?"

"I don't know, Ma."

She leaned closer before looking up at Cal. "You didn't tell me about this," she said.

Cal couldn't figure out what his other mother meant by *this*. So he just shook his head.

"I thought the Reverend James said he was going to California."

"Yes'm."

"But you went to Oregon instead?"

"Yes'm." He shook his head. "I mean, no ma'am. We went to California. We passed through what once was part of Oregon, but was—still is—Utah Territory."

"Are you sure?"

"Yes'm. Well, the captain said, and so did others, including Jim Bridger, that he—meaning, the captain—had taken folks to the Oregon Territory. But we went to California. Hangtown. That's where the preacher died."

"And this Captain . . . ?"

"Shufflebottom. Yes'm. He was the leader of the wagon train." Cal studied the name. He realized he had never heard anyone call Shufflebottom anything except Captain. Funny, he never would have pinned the name *Malachi* on the captain.

"And this, um, Colonel Delmont?"

"I never met the man," Cal said.

Charity sighed. "Maybe he's that nice young lieutenant's commanding officer."

Cal nodded. "Maybe."

"Well,"—his mother took the book into her hands—"if you're not going to read it, I'll read it to you. Just the way I did when you were just a little bitty baby. You never talked too much about your journey west, and I'm curious."

He heard his mother's footsteps as she stepped inside the cabin. He looked up and searched the prairie for that dragoon lieutenant and those two privates, but the tall-grass had swallowed them and there was no sign of dust.

"Calvin!" Charity called.

Cal sighed, and went inside.

The old salt stops at the batwing doors, and his right eye—the left one is gone, plucked out by a stiletto on the Barbary Coast years before—searches through the smoke and vileness of the roughest saloon at Natchez Under-the-Hill. Captain Malachi J. Shufflebottom recognizes me and pushes through the squawking doors.

His entrance causes the hussies to look up with admiration and want, and the men to sink in their chairs or turn toward the bar and stare into their steins and glasses—and pray that Shufflebottom is not coming to mete out justice.

But the old salt comes not for vengeance or justice. He comes to seek me.

Only when he stands at the table and I rise and extend my right hand, which he clasps stronger than ever, and that one eye smiles, does quiet conversation—almost church-like when one compares it to the bawdiness and profanity that had filled this hovel just moments before—return to his den of drunkenness and debauchery.

But the captain had suggested it as a meeting place, and I have come with reams of paper and plenty of sharpened pencils. Because when Captain Shufflebottom says he has a story to tell, any writer with ink in his veins, knows to be at the anointed place at the anointed time, ready to hear a tale for the ages.

"You never told me that Captain Shufflebottom had only one eye, Cal," Charity said.

"He didn't," Cal said. "He had both eyes—at least when I last saw him."

"Oh, that poor man. To be maimed like that." She

sighed, then tested the first name. "Malachi. You never told me that was his first name."

"I never knew him by any name other than Captain Shufflebottom," Cal said.

"Malachi. I had an uncle named Malachi. He had a beard to his belt. And knew Daniel Boone when he was but a boy."

When your uncle or Daniel Boone was a boy? Cal thought, but did not say a word.

"Well, how did you meet this colonel, this man Delmont, and how come you never told me he was writing a book about you?"

Cal shook his head. His voice was barely a whisper. "I never met the man. I never knew anyone wrote a book about me."

"Well, let me read some more," Charity said. "I want to read about my baby boy, not about ugly saloons and such filth."

"What," asks I, "amazing tale have you to tell me, Captain?"

"It is about a daring youth I met on the way west," answers the old salt. "He was but a boy, not twelve years old—this being in the year of Eighteen and Fifty—but he proved to be a better man than Bridger, Crockett, Hercules, and Boone combined."

"That cannot be true!" I start to say, but stop myself, for to call Captain Malachi Shufflebottom a liar is a quick way to leave this Earth until the final Day of Judgment. Instead, I whisper, "Go on, Captain," and

wet the lead of my pencil tip with my tongue before turning to the next clean page in my tablet.

"Mind ye," says the Captain, "that the boy was just that—a boy. Twelve years old when me eyes first laid on that youngster, slight of build, but when ye put a fifty-caliber Hawken rifle in his hands, no one could shoot better than this boy—and I seen that with me very own eyes when I was gatherin' all these pilgrims who wanted to light out west—leavin' their homes in Ohio and Illinois and Iowa and places that had turned civilized and crowded, leavin' behind the churches and barns, and be willin' to travel with all their worldly possessions in a Conny Stoga wagon, pulled by a team of oxen or maybe even mules. Bound for the West, because that was the new country. Oregon beckoned. I was to lead them, and lead them I would. But when I saw the boy, the first thing I asked of him was, 'What can you do, boy?'

"For the boy traveled with a man of the cloth, a preacher who knew—as every preacher I've ever met knew—the Good Book from cover to cover. And while I figured we would have need of a parson quite often on such a long, arduous journey, I didn't know what we could do with a runt of a kid like this one."

"Well, I don't know about this Captain Shufflebottom," Charity Marmaduke said. "He sounds rude and vile."

"He didn't say all of that, Mama. This writer is making things up."

"Well,"—she shook her head—"I don't know."

"Do you want me to read it?"

"No. You shouldn't read. If you read, your eyes won't be able to draw a bead on a buffalo or antelope."

Cal studied the mother who wasn't his birthing mother but was the only mother he knew and smiled. He really loved her.

"Ever held a Hawken rifle?" I am asked.

"Nay," laments I, and brandish the pencil I hold. "This, though, in the right hand, is more powerful than any firearm."

The captain grunts. "A brace of Walter Colts and a Mississippi Rifle I would rather hold while facing whooping Blackfeet and Comanches—and we would face their entire nations on the vast prairies along the aptly named Savage River country."

"Where is the Savage River, Cal?" his mother asked.

"I've never heard of it, Mother," he replied.

"Are you sure?"

"Yes, ma'am." Cal wanted her to keep reading, so he said, "They might have renamed it. I mean, 1850 was some years ago."

She smiled. "You were just a little boy then. Now look at you. All grown up and handsome."

She turned the page.

* * *

"The boy was like none I ever seen afore," says the Captain. "But all me eyes can see—before I saw him with a Hawken—was a kid who wanted to come west with a preacher. I needed a man who could shoot and hit what he aimed, and when he aimed he aimed to kill. Wounded men, white or red or any color, can still kill you. That's one thing I've preached, and will continue to preach till I meet my better."

"And this kid was that good?" queries I.

The Captain snorts, bangs his fist on the table, and calls out for more ale. Then he says:

"'Boy,' I say to the lad, 'I don't think you have the makin's as a skinner of mules or a man who can make an ox move like a jackrabbit. But let's see how you can shoot.' And I reach for the Walker .44 on my right hip, but the kid says, 'Nay.' And that leaves me thinkin' that he is ready to give up and run back to his mama and papa. But, nay, he points to the one rifle leaning against the nearest Conny Stoga.

"'How 'bout if I try that fancy long gun?' the runt asks."

"You are not a runt?" Charity shouted.

"But I sure am not a giant," Cal says, and pleaded: "Keep reading."

Reluctantly, she did.

"Now, Col'nel," the Captain says, "I give a nod to a farmer from Iowa, and he grabs me Hawken, brings

it—all nineteen and one-half pounds of walnut and iron and brass—and gives it to me, and I hold it out for the boy. I expect him to drop it when I put it in his puny hands, but he pulls it close to his chest.

"'What do you want for a target?' my segundo inquires.

"'See that cherry chifforobe on its side next to the overturned water barrel without a bottom?' asks I, and point the boy in the right direction by aiming my .44 at that spot.

"The boy replies in the affirmative almost immediately, fast I mean, as though his eyes are as sharp as mine.

"But a chifforobe is much too easy to hit. I smile. And point again. This time I point at a clay pot. And I say, 'Hit that clay pot, boy, if you can.'"

"This man is making all this up," Charity said, and looked at Cal. "Isn't he?"

Cal shook his head. "He got most of that just the way I remember it happening."

"The lad is puny even for his age, and that age," Captain Shufflebottom tells me, "is right around eight. So holding a twenty-five-pound Hawken steady is impossible for a boy that size."

* * *

"It didn't weigh no twenty-five pounds, Ma," Cal conceded. "But it was as heavy as the one I got now."

Charity nodded and turned the page.

"That Hawken's barrel moved like a whiskey barrel rolling downhill," the Captain says. "Round and round. Round and round.

"BOOM! roars the long gun, knocking the kid to his buttocks, and my segundo hands me a spyglass, and I check the target and announce, to nobody's surprise: 'A miss.'

"But the boy becomes adamant, angry, and says that I, Captain Malachi J. Shufflebottom, am mistaken. The preacher that is his father tries to console the youth, but that boy will hear nothing. Thusly, I send one of our most honest members of our wagon train to find the clay pot I had pointed out. And he does, and announces that, just as I had said, the boy missed the target."

Now, dear reader, understand that by this point I am at a loss as to why Captain Shufflebottom thinks this is a story worth writing. But the captain continues, and I resume taking notes.

Relates the Captain: "Thus, mainly to silence the whining little boy, I dispatch a loyal servant—and a fine marksman himself—to see if he can find this mysterious clay pot the boy says he has hit.

"It takes a while," continues the Captain, "but not only is there another chifforobe, but near it is a clay pot." The captain reaches for his stein and finishes a drink. "Or . . . was."

He reaches inside a vest pocket and pulls out a reddish chard of clay. "I carry this for luck. Have ever since that spring day in Independence, Missouri. But at that time, I did not believe my eyes, and said, 'It was probably busted to begin with.'

"Emigrants bound west with me agreed. The kid could not keep that Hawken steady for an instant, but the preacher said, as though he were delivering a sermon: 'Put that first pot where that one was and Cal will do it again.'

"So the pot was placed near the other, farther away, chifforobe. And again the boy, with a reloaded Hawken, did the same round and round and round, touched the set trigger and the trigger, and blew that other pot to pieces."

I look at Captain Shufflebottom. He nods, and when that old salt nods, it means it is final, it is true, it is not legend, but fact.

My head shakes in amazement. "What is this lad's name, Captain. And tell me more of this amazing story."

Says that grand old master of rivers and oceans: "You will hear the lad's name for many years to come. This was but his first taste of his destiny. Remember this name, my good friend. It will be impossible to forget in the years to come—this keen-eyed marksman, who later outshot not only I but Jim Bridger himself; this young- ster who is as good and true as Crockett and Boone and all those I have mentioned—it will be hailed and remembered long after you and I and our great-great- great grandchildren are looking down from Heaven. His name is" . . .

CHAPTER 17

"'Calamity James,'" Charity read, almost inaudible, and let the book fall from her hands to the cabin's floor.

"Ma." It took Cal four more tries before she heard his whisper, and by then he really couldn't see her too well because of the tears in his eyes, but he could hear her soft sobs. He came to her on his knees, and took her trembling hands in his own, and kissed them.

"Oh, Cal, oh, my baby boy."

"That's right," he said. "I'm still your baby." For most of his life that he could remember, he had frowned whenever his mother—well, his raising ma, but the only mother he had ever known—called him her baby. He would inform her, even when he was only five or six years old, and whoever was visiting—or more than likely, just to Charity Marmaduke, as visitors were scarce for as long as Cal could remember—that he was not a baby anymore.

But now he sobbed like one. "I—didn't—know . . ." And he cursed that book, and he cursed Captain Shufflebottom for telling that Colonel Horatio L. Delmont all that had happened. Then his voice rose: "I'll whip that dastardly captain for blabbing all that stuff. I'll cane him worse that that Carolina fellow clubbed that Yankee last spring."

(They had all read about that caning. Every newspaper in Kansas Territory has printed what had happened in the Senate chamber in Washington City. A congressman from one of those Carolinas had stormed into the Senate—Cal still couldn't figure out the difference between a senator and a congressman—and clubbed the senator, some gent from Maryland—no, it might have been Massachusetts, as Cal was equally confused with all those tiny states up in the Northeast. The senator had been an abolitionist and, well, nobody in either of those Carolinas cared for any abolitionist, so the congressman beat that poor fool unconscious for speaking out against bringing Kansas into the United States as a slave state.)

His mother stopped sobbing. "You will do no such thing, young man." Her voice was stern, sharp, and when Cal looked up, he saw no more tears except those dripping off her chin.

Cal's head dropped. "Yes'm," he whispered.

They waited some time for that anger to subside, and then he felt his mother's hand on his chin, and she lifted his head.

He stared at her. Charity Marmaduke smiled.

"There, there," she whispered. Her eyes slowly turned away and found the book that she had dropped. Cal couldn't look at it. If he saw it, he figured, he'd fly off the handle like his mother always warned him not to do. That had been Obadiah's problem—well, one of his problems, like cursing, and chicanery, and laziness, and drunkenness—and on went that long, long list.

"The preacher, your daddy, told you?" she asked.

His heart felt like it was going to beat so hard it would come through his ribcage. At first his head shook, his eyes closed, and then he felt Charity's hand underneath his chin, lifting it.

He heard the preacher, sick and dying, but speaking in a suddenly Baptist-strong voice:

You—are—my—son. . . .

Cal forced his eyelids to open, and he saw Charity smiling. "He was out of his head with fever," Cal whispered.

"But you knew he was telling you the truth," Charity said.

"Not at first." He sniffled but stopped any more tears from flowing.

"Did he tell you everything?"

He shrugged. "Bits and pieces." The sigh felt like it was his last breath. But he was still alive, and Charity was still there, her face not hard, but filled with love.

"He said you are my mother," Cal said, or rather choked. "Honest. He said you're a fine woman, too." He had to wipe his nose, then rub that on his trousers. "He said you raised—he said you raised me as your own. Called you a good—no a fine, yeah—a fine woman. He even said that pa—I mean, Obadiah—he called—called him—a good man."

Charity coughed slightly. "Well, he was right about me, anyhow."

They both laughed, but it was a brief respite.

The only mother he had ever known sighed, but she was still smiling at Cal when the tears finally stopped stinging and he could see her wonderful face.

"The good Lord took our baby—Obadiah's and mine—and we were heartbroken. The midwife I had said, after it was all over, that I just couldn't have another child. That practically killed me—and maybe I even feared that Obadiah would have left me and found some woman who could give him babies. I guess that was the Lord's way of blessin' me—blessin' us—because I bet any son of Obadiah Marmaduke would be as cussedly worthless as his daddy—"

She stopped, but just long enough to let out a long sigh before looking at the cabin's ceiling. "Lord forgive me for that mean remark, but you know as well as I do that it's the gospel truth."

Smiling, she looked down at Cal. "Well, I'm glad you know. And you mustn't be too hard on the preacher, God rest his soul, or his widow. They were young—we were all young—and they were foolish and, well, the Lord works in mysterious ways, and I reckon he had a reason for the Jameses. Because they blessed me, and even Obadiah, with the greatest and handsomest and now *famous* baby boy." She let out another long breath. "But I reckon he's not a baby anymore. I reckon you haven't been my baby for a long, long time. You're a man, full growed."

He had to think of the year—1857. Then he said, "I'm just fifteen years old, Ma."

"You were a man when you were eight years old, Cal. The Oregon—I mean, the California Trail—that growed you up faster than you should have." There came another one of those long, ragged sighs, followed by a cough that Charity couldn't quite stop. She cleared her throat, patted Cal's right arm, and shook her head. "Kansas has growed you up considerable, too. Had Obadiah and me knowed just how hard Kansas would be, maybe we would have stayed in Iowa. Well, not Burlington, but Iowa. Or gone back to Kentucky. But fate, the Good Lord—or something, the stars— whatever . . , Anyway, we came here. And you growed up good and strong, and the Good Lord gave you that keen eye, and I don't know how you manage to shoot that big rifle the way you do—because I tell you, having seen my daddy shoot a flintlock, and his daddy and my grandpa on my mama's side, and they wouldn't know what to make of you and all that moving around."

When she brought up her arms and imitated the circling, weaving, straining way Cal made that Hawken move around, then whispering, "Boom," and moving back and upward just the way Cal shot the Hawken, he had to laugh.

"But rarely have I seen you miss." She looked at the closed door. "Maybe the Lord had His reasons for bringing you to Kansas. I guess we'll have to see what He has in mind."

"You're my mother," he said, and the words of the Reverend James came to him clearly, not the weak whispers when the preacher was dying in that dirty room in Hangtown but full of vigor like when he was holding a stump meeting or gathering around the camp-fires on a Sunday with Captain Shufflebottom's train.

When I am called away, you will still have a family—
the Marmadukes.

"Why don't you come with us to Fort Scott?" he
asked his mother.

"No," she said, and sighed heavily again. "Your fa—
Obadiah might come home again when he's broke and
worn out his welcome wherever he has got to this time.
And I know folks here. I'd be a stranger in Fort Scott.
Besides, that town, from what I gather, is a lot closer to
Missouri than Lawrence is. But you promise to write
me and I'll write you."

Somehow, he found enough strength to give her a
smile. "I promise."

She nodded. "You best pack some stuff," she told
him, then motioned at the floor. "Hand me that book by
that Colonel what's-his-name?"

Cal cocked his head, uncertain. "You sure?" His
voice was barely a whisper.

"'Course I'm sure. Getting you to tell me any stories about your adventures was like pulling up some
weed with a long, strong root. A weed with thorns, mind
you. I want to hear about what all you done—or what
that Cap'n Shufflerotten or that Col'nel Harold Dull-
mont says you done on that trail to wherever they've
put you on."

Packing was easy. He was wearing his warm weather
duds. All he had to pack were the extra pairs of socks
and his cold weather clothes, and a good pair of gloves,

likely stolen or won on a bet, that Obadiah had left behind.

He took the Hawken out and walked to the creek bed that evening, and waited till a pronghorn came by. Again, he raised the heavy long gun to his shoulder and let the barrel move around in those circles. Set trigger. Back around and . . .

The buck was butchered there. They would have fresh backstrap for supper tonight, and he had shown his mother how to dry the meat. She could take some of the rest of the meat in to town to sell, the way Cal had been doing, and keep enough in the small cave Cal had dug where they kept ice from the winter for as long as it would last. Charity would have some food to tide her over for a while. After that, well, Cal would be sending her money regular every couple of months. And he would write. Once a week.

She told him all about his adventures, according to Colonel Horatio L. Delmont, as related to him by Captain Malachi J. Shufflebottom in *The Amazing but Authentic and True Story of a Kid Called Calamity— and His Duel With Death; or, Border Ruffians on the Oregon Trail.*

Little of it sounded like anything that Cal had witnessed, as far as he could remember. The Indian attack was real Indians, not white renegades, and Cal had dispatched practically every one of those with Hawken, bowie knife, club, tomahawk, Apache lance—his mother could not remember where Cal had gotten hold of an

Apache lance—and they had made it to California, and Captain Shufflebottom had found the richest strike of diamonds in California history, but then the captain's daughter had been kidnapped by a Californio bandit, and the captain had sought out Cal to help him get the girl back.

That tale was to be concluded in the next book from Colonel Delmont, which Charity promised to read, if she could ever find it. Cal said if he came across a copy, he would mail it to her from Fort Scott.

The dragoons arrived a little after dawn. The private, Drabowski, was leading a black gelding behind his mount this time. Cal had seen that horse at Bagley's livery stable the last time he had been by it. But Cal didn't ask any questions, though he looked at his mule and realized he wouldn't be bringing it to Fort Scott. Which wasn't a bad deal at all.

Charity had gotten up early and cooked some antelope steaks with bacon and eggs. She had baked a corn bread the night before for Cal's last supper here for a spell, and warmed that over for the men. Cal had fashioned a table outside using some planks and one old keg, which the lieutenant graciously took for his own, and the three chairs from the cabin.

"The United States Dragoons furnish enlisted men, officers, and paid employees—especially those who keep us fed." He winked at Cal. "This horse is yours, Mr. Marmaduke, as long as you are assisting the service of the United States Army."

"My goodness," Charity whispered.

Cal simply nodded.

For once, the wind became a gentle breeze, the sun was neither baking nor nonexistent, and the two privates seemed pleasant. Everyone had manners. Aitken, the bigger one with the red beard, talked about his home in Scotland and traveling on a ship when he was but thirteen years old across the Atlantic. Drabowski said his parents had left the Poland in 1849. They had settled in the state of New York, but he took a notion to join the Army and ran away from home, enlisted in St. Louis, and had to learn to ride a horse, which he found fun.

The two privates insisted on washing the dishes, so Charity pointed to the tub she used, which Cal had filled with water from the creek just that morning, and both men went to work.

That's when Lieutenant Johnson pulled out an envelope and slid it across the plank to Cal.

"The United States Army always advances its hired men one month's salary, so my captain gave me this, Mr. Marmaduke."

Cal wasn't sure what to think about that "mister" stuff, but he did like the look on his mother's face when Lieutenant Johnson said "Marmaduke."

He felt a mix of coin and scrip in the envelope, and looked inside since the envelope had not been sealed with wax.

There were a couple of Liberty dollars, both from 1850, and one that, if Cal was making out the year right, was marked 1798. A halfpenny from the Bank of Montreal, wherever that was. An 1844 half-cent piece.

An 1840 dollar. A five-dollar note from some bank in Hagerstown and another, crumpled like it had been traveling across the Europe and the Atlantic with Private Drabowski that came from, if Cal read it right, the Mechanic's Bank. Cal guessed that with the rest of the coins he didn't count, the total might amount to the fifteen bucks he had been promised a month.

Cal returned the paper money and coins to the envelope and handed it to his mother.

"No," Charity protested. "You will need that."

Lieutenant Johnson said, "Your son will have credit, and the Army will feed him at no charge. Nor will he be charged rent. We all have rooms in what everyone calls the Free State Hotel."

"Take the money, Ma," Cal whispered. "You know how unreliable the mail is out here. I'll be fine. Like the lieutenant said."

His mother sighed, and brought the envelope to her lap. She fought back the tears.

"You soldiers are very nice," she said. The next words caught in her throat. "You'll—take care—of my—baby?"

"Yes, ma'am," Lieutenant Johnson said. "You have our word."

A few moments later, the two privates were coming back from the tub, holding the relatively clean dishes and trying not to drop them, as though tin and pewter would break.

The lieutenant looked at Cal. "I guess we should be getting along. It's a long ride to Fort Scott."

CHAPTER 18

Since Fort Scott had once been a military fort, the town lived up to its name. What had been the officers' quarters was, according to the sign, the Fort Scott Hotel.

"Everybody calls it the Free State Hotel," Lieutenant Johnson told Cal, "because that's where most of the Free-Soilers hold their meetings. But the owners won't change the name because they remember what happened to your Free State Hotel when those border men from Missouri rode in."

"I wouldn't call it my hotel," Cal said.

The officer looked at him. "Meaning you hold with slavery?"

The shock had Cal straightening in the saddle. "No," he said, and shook his head. "No. I—well, no— Just that all I did was hunt game for their cooks to serve to the guests."

"Boy don't know where he stands," Aitken said, with a rough chuckle.

Drabowski said something that Cal figured meant yes since the dragoon was nodding his head.

"Like I said back at your place, we stay at the Free

State—the *Fort Scott*—Hotel. So most folks in town figure us, as soldiers in the Army of the United States of America, as abolitionists. And I reckon that's where I stand, but that's going to be up to each man—sooner, the way things are looking, than later."

He pointed. "That park was the parade ground." His arm moved and stopped at a building on the opposite side of the Free State, or Fort Scott, Hotel. "That's the Western Hotel, but most folks call it the Pro-Slavery Hotel. So that's where—well, you're pretty smart for a fifteen-year-old. I guess you know who hangs out there."

Cal nodded his head. The Pro-Slavery Hotel seemed to do a lot more business, at least on this day, than the Fort Scott Hotel.

To Cal's surprise, the lieutenant led the men to the park, reined up, and held up his right hand, and they stopped in the center. The grass was well trampled, and not many people were in the park. The town seemed crowded, but certainly not as crowded as Lawrence could be on a nice day like this one.

Lieutenant Johnson turned to Cal. "Most of the people who live in town are fine with slavery. Some of them even own one or two themselves. And for the moment, the president and plenty of senators and representatives agree, even though England and even Mexico have outlawed the practice."

"Mexico abolished slaveholdin'?" Aitken asked.

Johnson nodded. "Twice. First in twenty-nine. Till Texas settlers had conniptions over it when they started moving into Mexico." He turned to Cal. "Texas was part of Mexico at that time, before the Alamo."

Cal knew that, but he just let his head bob.

"Then after the Mexicans got whupped by the Texans for what they did at the Alamo, Mexico abolished slavery again in thirty-seven."

The history lesson made Cal think. Maybe that's what Lieutenant Johnson wanted him to do. But Cal was just thinking that he sure didn't know a whole lot about anything.

"So while slaveholders have the majority in the town of Fort Scott"—the lieutenant waved his arm in a circling motion—"most folks who live around here, but not in town, are either ardent abolitionists or solid Free-Soilers."

Lieutenant Johnson stopped talking for a long while. He let his horse graze on the park's grass, so the other horses, Cal's included, decided to follow suit.

Cal looked at the Fort Scott Hotel. It was wooden, not brick like the new Free State Hotel in Lawrence. Plenty of floor-to-ceiling windows, white columns in the center with porches on bottom and top floors with white picket balustrades, and stairs on either side. Some ladies in white dresses were sitting at a table on the bottom porch, sipping coffee or maybe tea, while a woman in a black dress was talking to a priest—since he had a white collar, Cal figured him as a priest—on one side of the upper porch, while on the far end stood a man smoking a cigar. Cal wondered where the soldiers stayed.

The man on the balcony tossed his cigar to the ground, grabbed a hat that must have been setting on a table or chair, and rounded the corner and practically ran down those steps. Nobody else in the town seemed to be in a hurry, and Cal turned to study the Western Hotel. It was busy, but it wasn't as nice-looking as where Cal would be staying. He wondered where the other dragoons were. Out on patrol. He wondered when he should start hunting. And where he should go hunting. This country was new to him.

"Here comes trouble," Aitken mumbled.

"I see him," Lieutenant Johnson said.

Cal turned to see the nice-looking man from the balcony making a beeline toward the park. He thought that maybe this guy was the mayor of the town and didn't want the citizens, and especially the children, of Fort Scott to have to avoid horse apples in the park. That thought caused Cal to look around. He didn't see any children anywhere. And it was late in the afternoon for them to still be in school.

The man stopped in front of the dragoons and Cal. He put his hands on his hips.

"Lieutenant Johnson," he said, but did not nod or wave or anything like that. And he hadn't said those two words in what Cal would have called a friendly way. He had a funny way of speaking, but probably nobody who had heard it enough found it amusing.

"Montgomery," the lieutenant said. Alvin Johnson didn't sound sociable himself.

"Is this what you call protecting the rights of American citizens?" This man Montgomery spoke in an accusing tone.

Lieutenant Johnson looked toward the Western Hotel, then straight ahead, then at the Fort Scott Hotel, and then twisted in the saddle and looked that way, too. Finally, he pushed up his hat and turned to face the newcomer. "Who needs protecting?"

The man didn't answer. Suddenly he was looking straight at Cal.

"Is that a Hawken?"

Cal wasn't expecting the question. He wasn't expecting to be asked anything.

"Well, yes, sir."

Montgomery looked back at the lieutenant.

"Are you recruiting children for your army?"

"Hired him as a hunter," Johnson said.

"A hunter?" Montgomery studied Cal so hard and for so long he started sweating.

"Where are you from, kid?"

Cal swallowed. "I—"

"He came from Lawrence," the lieutenant interrupted. "Does that suit you?"

The man's face changed suddenly. His mouth formed what looked like the word Lawrence, but no sound came from the man.

He had dark hair and a thick mustache and beard that needed some attention. Cal couldn't guess at the man's age. He certainly had some wealth from the cut of his clothes and how those black boots practically reflected sunlight. What struck Cal most, though, were the man's eyes. Almost translucent—a word he had learned reading *The Amazing but Authentic and True Story of a Kid Called Calamity—and His Duel With Death; or, Border Ruffians on the Oregon Trail*, and his mother had told him what it meant after he had asked.

"Calvin Marmaduke." Cal was thankful the lieutenant was talking again. "Meet James Montgomery. Lives in Mound City." Johnson pointed north. "Little less than a good day's ride from here. Born in Missouri."

"Ohio," Montgomery corrected.

"My apologies. Ohio."

"I lived in Missouri, but the slavery and bigotry and treachery and avarice and everything that is abysmal in the eyes of the Lord drove me away. Destiny has brought me here. Kansas will be—must be—free!"

"In a pig's eye."

Everyone turned to look at another man, with a brass-framed revolver stuck in his waistband, and holding a beer bottle in his left. His clothes weren't near as fancy as Mr. Montgomery's, but his eyes were just as hard and cold.

"Kansas is gonna be a slave state, pardner." The man laughed.

"Not if I have any say in it." Montgomery spoke in a whisper, but it certainly didn't sound soft to Cal.

The man laughed. "You voted, didn't ya?" The man laughed again. "So did I. Fifteen, twenty times. And I'll vote a hunnert more iffen I have to. So you jus' keep beggin' these here bluecoats to run us bona fide Kansans out of the ter'tory. It won't matter in the long run. In the long run, you'll be a-workin' fer me."

He turned and walked back toward the Western Hotel.

Cal watched him go into that building, where men waiting and watching patted him on his back, and then followed him into the hotel's saloon. When Cal turned around, he saw James Montgomery walking toward the Fort Scott Hotel. Then he realized that Lieutenant Johnson was staring right at him.

"You know why I brought you here?" Johnson asked.

"To hunt." Cal's voice cracked.

Both Aitken and Drabowski laughed. The lieutenant just smiled. "Yes. To hunt. But I meant"—he pointed at the ground—"right here. This spot in town."

Cal thought for a long while, then slowly shook his head.

"Just to give you fair warning, Cal. Fair warning. If you want to go back to your mother, now's the time."

Cal's heart started pounding, and he took in a deep breath and exhaled, hoping that would steady his heartbeat, but it didn't. "I'll stay." His mother would need that money he'd be sending her.

Lieutenant Johnson nodded. "All right." He pointed toward the Western Hotel. "Like I said, Cal. That's where the pro-slavers hold court." Then he nodded toward the Fort Scott Hotel. "And that's where the Free-Soilers and abolitionists stay." Then he nodded at Drabowski, Aitken, and finally, at Cal. "And here we are. Right in the middle."

But for the most part, 1857 passed quietly. There was a lot of shouting in the Fort Scott Hotel about what they called an illegal constitutional convention in Lecompton, and later Cal heard people in town and the soldiers either cursing or praising and shrugging over the actions James Buchanan was taking on the matter of Kansas.

That's when Drabowski told Cal that James Buchanan was president of the United States.

And those at the Fort Scott Hotel said something about "popular sovereignty." Drabowski didn't know what popular sovereignty meant, and Cal didn't want to trouble Lieutenant Johnson. He wrote his mother asking if she knew, but her reply didn't answer that question but went on and on about the sunflowers.

That was fine with Cal. He'd rather think about sunflowers than sovereignty, whatever it was, anyway. Besides, he spent most of his mornings and evenings away from Fort Scott. The hunting here was pretty good, a lot better than around Lawrence, though not nearly as many buffalo.

Winter came in quick and cold, but Cal had enough money to buy some thick gloves and a warm mackinaw and some scarves to cover his mouth and nose. The soldiers weren't particular about what they ate, and the captain and Lieutenant Johnson were pleased.

Not all the soldiers stayed at the Fort Scott Hotel, Cal found out. Most of them were camped about a mile north of town. That's generally where Drabowski and Aitken stayed, and Cal was feeding those at that camp, too. The Fort Scott Hotel was for the officers, including a first lieutenant whose name was too long for Cal to remember or pronounce. Sometimes Drabowski and Aitken stayed there, too (when Lieutenant Johnson needed them), as did two sergeants, one called Little—though he certainly wasn't small—and the other O'Shaughnessy. Two other sergeants, one Irish like O'Shaughnessy and the other a German with a mighty long name, stayed at the camp, along with two buglers and forty or more privates. There was also a farrier and a blacksmith. Cal hunted for all of them.

Nothing came between James Montgomery and the other gent (Cal later learning that fellow's name was Ross), but the dragoons stayed busy at the camp—at least whenever Cal was bringing in some antelope or rabbits or turkeys and such—but mostly they practiced their riding and sometimes fighting with each other and sometimes fighting for what one of the Irish sergeants said was for the honor and the glory of the company.

Finally, the Year of Our Lord 1857 passed, and 1858 came in blustery and even colder than December had been. Some dragoons were supposed to be in charge of lighting some Roman candles, but they got drunk and fired all of them at each other, for which they were punished by having to dig a new latrine ditch, and when the temperature is three degrees below zero and the ground was already frozen pretty solid, Cal decided that he had no plans to enlist in the United States Army—at least not in the Dragoons.

He walked into the Fort Scott Hotel one cold afternoon, and into the room he shared with Lieutenant Johnson but liked to have dropped his Hawken on the floor when he saw that room filled with Drabowski and Aitken and Captain Jackson and Sergeant O'Shaughnessy.

"Happy birthday, Calamity!" they yelled, and cheered, and then the Irish sergeant began singing an Irish song about a boy and whiskey and a girl, and Cal was mighty glad his mother—though he would have loved to have seen her—wasn't there to hear most of the lyrics of that song.

But the soldiers laughed and Cal stopped blushing, and the hotel's baker brought in a cake, and Sergeant O'Shaughnessy pulled out a bowie knife from his boot top and sliced off a good-size piece and picked it up with his fingers—on the left hand; the right still held the big knife—and shoved it in front of Cal.

There were no candles, but Cal didn't mind.

The cake tasted mighty good, but the hotel's baker came from New Orleans, which meant, the way everyone talked, that he was a top soldier.

And that's what they all called Cal, even though he was just a hunter, not a dragoon.

"You still think you're a jinx, Cal?" Lieutenant Johnson asked.

Cal had forgotten when he and the lieutenant had talked about that, but he couldn't answer because his mouth was full, and by the time he had swallowed, Captain Jackson had pulled Johnson away and they appeared to be in a serious conversation. Then Drabowski came with a jug and said that, seeing Cal was sixteen years old, that day—actually, his birthday was the next day—he was old enough to enjoy a taste of "vodka."

But Cal didn't enjoy that at all, though most of those in the room laughed hard.

"That was nice of you," Cal told Lieutenant Johnson when everyone was gone, including Captain Jackson, who was sweet on a girl who worked at one of the mercantiles.

"I don't think I heard your answer to my question

earlier," the lieutenant said, as he sat on the edge of his bed and began tugging off his boots.

"Oh." Cal sat on his bed. "Well, I don't know. I reckon—"

But Lieutenant Johnson had given up on his boots and had fallen onto the bed and was already snoring, since he had drunk a lot of whatever Drabowski had in that jug.

And Cal sighed and started pulling off his own boots. Lieutenant Johnson never asked that question again, so Cal never got to answer. Which turned out to be for the better, he would later reckon.

Because 1858 was just about ready to blow Kansas Territory apart.

CHAPTER 19

Folks in Fort Scott kept talking about all the shenanigans going on in Lecompton, but Cal still wasn't sure where Lecompton was, though he did know it was currently the capital of Kansas Territory. But he had had his fill of territorial capitals after what happened to Obadiah's get-rich scheme. He also sort of figured that Obadiah deserved what he got, since he had never been much of a businessman and proved to be a worthless husband to Charity and pa to Cal.

Winter passed, and with spring the grasses grew tall, and Cal found himself being used not just for hunting. Captain Jackson realized that the boy was a good horseman, so Cal started carrying dispatches for the dragoon company. There were a lot of messages being sent from here to there and there to here, because the weather wasn't the only thing heating up in that spring of '58. That James Montgomery fellow, with lots of other abolitionists, rode across Linn County while Captain Jackson's company happened to be patrolling everywhere else and drove some men, all pro-slavery fellows, out of their homes. Cal had met one of those fellows—when he was walking past the Western Hotel—and, well, Cal wasn't sorry at all that he no longer had to see that mean cuss, since he had a mean temper and a foul mouth, and slung all sorts of insults at Cal.

So one May day found Cal, having brought in a fine antelope to the cook that morning, being sent loping up north, when a fellow just seemed to pop up out of the prairie like a sunflower and started waving his hands over his head.

Cal reined up.

The man ran toward him, causing Cal's horse to buck for a couple of seconds, and that made the man stop.

"Sorry," he said, after Cal got the black gelding settled down. The stranger focused on Cal's Hawken that he was carrying in his right hand. He had had to use the left to control his horse. Cal didn't see any firearm, nor even a knife, on the stranger, who had a big bruise on his right forearm and a cut that had stopped bleeding on the left side of his face.

"Sorry," the man said again.

"It's all right."

"My horse threw me. I was bound for Trading Post."

Cal pointed north.

"Yeah," the man said. "I know. But it's on the other side of the river and, well, I can't swim."

Cal sighed. This time of year, the Marais des Cygnes—Cal hadn't ever heard that name pronounced the same way twice—would be running dark and deep.

Trading Post had been established by a Missouri trader long before Cal was born. Lieutenant Johnson had told Cal that the post had been named after the founder, but nobody could recollect the fellow's name, so they just called the place Trading Post. But it wasn't that far out of the way for Cal, so he kicked his boot out of the stirrup, and, holding the Hawken and reins in his right hand, helped the fellow climb onto the back of the black.

That was the easy part. What scared Cal, and probably the stranger, was getting across that river, but they did it since the black was a great swimming horse, and the man said, "This is turning out to be my lucky day," when they were on the other side.

Glad to have the river behind them, Cal kicked the horse into a walk and found what passed for the trail to Trading Post.

Five minutes later, they were staring down musket and revolver barrels. Cal didn't recognize any of those, but the man riding behind him did.

"Hamilton," he said.

One of the gents, holding a Navy Colt, stepped in front of the others. He didn't grin. He didn't frown. He just aimed his revolver.

"You missed the ruckus," that Hamilton fellow told the guy riding behind Cal. "Your zealot, that scoundrel Montgomery—Satan's right-hand archangel—has already been to Trading Post."

"Poured out ever' last drop of whiskey there was," one of the ruffians behind Hamilton said.

"Griggs," Hamilton said. "Relieve that relic from the boy who hunts for those dragoons."

A thick-bearded fellow with a big potbelly and bigger straw hat came forward, giving the black gelding plenty of room, and took the Hawken from Cal, who was smart enough not to resist. There wasn't much use in putting up a fight or even protesting. He stopped counting the men when he got to twelve, and knew he wasn't quite halfway through.

Cal and the fellow he shouldn't have picked up were told to dismount, and they were led toward Trading Post, where five men sat along a palisade fence, hands tied in front of them. Cal and the stranger got their hands tied and were shoved to the ground.

"What's going on?" the fellow who Cal had helped asked.

An older gentleman whispered, "They came upon me as I was walking to my cornfield shortly after dawn." He nodded at the man next to him with the busted nose and bloodied face. "Ripped ol' Jimmy here out of his cabin. Ain't that right, Jimmy?"

Jimmy's lips were smashed so much and his nose so crooked, he just nodded.

For about an hour, Cal and the others just sat there, while Hamilton's men waited around. Two more men were brought in, hands bound, but neither one of those badly beaten, about twenty minutes later. Then another, who was limping badly. And five minutes after that— making the total, counting Cal, eleven—one more, but he just had a busted lip, though he kept holding his left arm because the hand fell limp and dangling like it had been separated from whatever held a hand to an arm.

"You are all under arrest," the fellow Hamilton said, "for the crime of drivin' us out of our homes. You zealots told us to 'quit the territory,' but as you can see, us being Missourians, we don't quit that easy. Now—"

Hooves sounded in the woods, and Hamilton and the others turned, their guns ready, but relaxed when one rider came in, pulling a horse behind him. The relaxation disappeared when they could see a body draped over the saddle of the second horse.

"That's Bell," one of the Missourians whispered.

Several harsh curses followed.

Cal thought: *This ain't gonna turn out good for none of us.*

"What the devil happened?" Hamilton roared.

"Snyder put up a fight," the rider said. "Shot Jimmy here deader than dirt."

That set off Hamilton and, after a string of profanity, he was booming: "Get those prisoners to their feet!"

"Ernest can't stand on his own," one fellow shouted. "You busted his leg."

"Then you carry him!"

"With my hands tied tighter than—"

That fellow got his teeth knocked down his throat with the stock of Cal's Hawken. And that made Cal mad, though there wasn't anything he could do about it, because he was being pulled up to his feet.

"To the ravine!" Hamilton bellowed. "Get them to the ravine."

Cal was shoved forward. He almost tripped and fell, but made himself stand because he figured if he hit the dirt, those ten men behind him would just walk right over him, and then someone would likely put a ball in the back of his head. They stumbled down a deer trail into the ravine, and walked just far enough toward the river before that Hamilton yelled at them to stop.

They stopped. Then they were turned around, facing east, but the sun wasn't in their eyes this late in the morning, and Cal saw the Missourians lining up. He looked at a red-bearded fellow standing in front of him about twenty yards away. The fellow sort of reminded Cal of Private Aitken, but this guy wasn't a dragoon.

"Are you going to give us time to pray?" someone down the line from Cal asked.

"No," Hamilton roared.

Another Missourian ran over and shoved the fellow who had been facing Cal down the line a bit. There were complaints and curses, but the man now standing in front of Cal said, "I want to shoot that abolitionist with his own rifle."

Some men laughed. One spit out tobacco juice and said, "Careful that ol' Hawken don't knock you on your hindquarters."

That's when Cal realized that he was about to die.

"I never got around to thanking you for the ride here."

Cal realized that the man standing next to him was the fellow he had picked up on the other side of the Marais des Cygnes.

He was about to say, "No need to thank me now," or something like that, but Hamilton yelled, "Shoot those dirty sons of—"

Rifles, muskets and revolvers boomed.

Cal saw the smoke from the Hawken, and saw the man holding Cal's rifle fall back on his back and the Hawken sail behind him into the side of the ravine, and then Cal saw the sky, a nice blue, and he closed his eyes.

He also held his breath.

Silently, he thanked the Almighty. And he prayed that this murdering crazy Missourian named Hamilton wouldn't walk over and shoot all eleven of these men in their heads with his Navy Colt.

Hoofbeats sounded, followed by the noise Cal would never forget for the rest of his days. That sound of firearms being cocked by men who did not shy away from murder. The sound of the horses stopped as though the riders had heard those deadly metallic clicks.

"Charles!" Cal detected that western Missouri twang. "It's Von Barfus and me, Black Hill."

"Come ahead," Hamilton said, and the riders must have ridden their horses slowly into the ravine.

The next voice was a whisper: "*Mein Gott.*"

"Well, 'em abolitionists won't be botherin' us no more," someone said.

"We best hightail it out of Kansas," another Missourian recommended. "White's got that store near the bridge. And even though that bridge got washed out, the folks from Bloomin' Grove mighta heard our firin' squad. They'll be comin' here directly."

"Let them come," Hamilton said. But then he said: "All right, mount up. We've made our point."

Horses snorted. Men spat. Weapons were reloaded. Saddles squeaked as men swung into the saddles. Corks were pulled. And the pro-slavers rode away.

But Cal did not move until he heard birds singing

again in the timber, and frogs croaking along the Marais des Cygnes.

After a short prayer, he pushed himself up and saw the man he had picked up on the other side of the river. He was dead, eyes open, a bit of blood at one corner of his mouth.

You are Calamity James. Bad luck is just always gonna follow you.

He figured all the others were dead, too, but he heard a moan, and moved to an old man.

"You're gonna be all right, sir," Cal told him when the fellow's eyes opened. He had been hit in the left shoulder and was bleeding like a stuck pig, but Cal found some wet leaves and pressed that against and into the wound, then lifted the old-timer's right hand and pushed it over Cal's doctoring job. "Hold down on that, mister," Cal told him and moved to the man on the wounded gent's right.

He was alive, too, with a big hole in his right side. Breathing, but not groaning, certainly not conscious, so Cal plugged those holes, front and back, too.

The next man in line was dead.

Cal was at the last on this side of the line when he heard voices.

"Horse tracks are all over here."

"There's blood here."

"Well, where's everybody got to?"

He didn't recognize anyone, but he didn't know anyone in Trading Post or the little settlement nearby, Blooming Grove. Then one man, who had been standing a couple folks past Cal, cried out. So Cal figured that he might as well get some help.

"Down here!" he yelled. "Down here. In the ravine! We got wounded men down here." He took a gamble. "Wounded Free-Soilers. We got dead men, too."

The Blooming Grove men questioned Cal, asking how he came away without a scratch when about half of the others were wounded and the others shot down dead like rabid dogs.

Cal had no answer for that, but the Missourians had left in a hurry and hadn't even bothered to take Cal's horse.

"They might be Bushwhackers," one of the Free-Soilers said, "but I reckon they ain't horse thieves."

Some of the men rode after Hamilton's Missourians, but they didn't let Cal go, still suspicioning him as a Ruffian.

Since Cal's horse had a U.S. Army saddle and bridle, they took his word that he had been one of those the Missourians had tried to murder. He wrote a note to Lieutenant Johnson, explaining what had happened, and one of the men said he might as well ride down to Fort Scott, let some government-paid men—paid by the United States of America, not that worthless mess of folks up in Lecompton—know what had happened up here.

"But I—" Cal had started, but one of the Kansans gave him an explanation.

"You say you're with the Dragoons. But maybe you

are a Missourian who killed a soldier and got this horse. So we'll just see what the Army has to say about you."

It turned out that one man who arrived later was James Montgomery, who now called himself Colonel.

"He's with the Dragoons in Fort Scott," Montgomery said. "But keep him here till the soldiers from down south get up here. I'll be riding after Hamilton's marauders. Who'll ride with me?"

So Cal waited at Blooming Creek for another day before Captain Jackson and maybe half his men showed up. And Cal was still there a week later, helping tend to the wounded, when John Brown arrived, and had his men build a log fort, two stories tall. Brown had a lot of men with him.

And, green as he was, Cal knew that neither Kansas nor Missouri would ever be the same again.

CHAPTER 20

Back in Linn County and Fort Scott, Cal wrote Charity and said that all was fine, that he was doing well, eating regular, and having a grand time hunting and fishing, and that, yes, while there was a lot of bad things happening in this part of Kansas, and across the territorial line into the state of Missouri, everything was peaceful where he was.

He found a minister at the Free State Hotel—things had gotten so bad, the owner had the Fort Scott Hotel sign taken down.

"Might as well go whole hog," Lieutenant Johnson said he'd heard the man say.

The Western Hotel kept its sign up, but that was probably because it sounded a lot better than the Pro-Slavery Hotel.

Spring gave way to summer, and that summer was a hot one. Cal was still hunting but now also carrying dispatches, and still sending money to Charity back in Lawrence. He couldn't say that things had settled down in Kansas, though. By that summer, John Brown was a wanted man. Kansas Territory offered a $250 reward for his capture. Missouri had put up a reward of $3,000.

Montgomery rode into Fort Scott with plenty of men, firing bullets through the Western Hotel and even houses nearby. They brought a wagon with them, filled with hay, and Montgomery himself tossed a torch into the back of the wagon, as men freed the mules pulling it, and then, with some fellows holding the horses, pushed the burning wagon up against the building. Shooting weapons into the air or at some men holding shotguns or pistols, those Free-Soilers galloped out of Fort Scott, but pro-slavers and even some of the Free-Soilers who lived in the town joined together to put out the fire and the hotel was saved.

"It's not that the Free-Soilers care for that hotel," a deputy U.S. marshal told Cal. "It's just that, well, if you live in a town long enough, you know that fire ain't got no prejudices or likes. It just burns down anything it can. I've seen whole towns go up in one night."

It wasn't long after that that Lieutenant Johnson came with grim news for Cal.

"The governor's asked us to leave," he said, "and the colonel has agreed."

"Huh?"

The officer explained: "The state of things being the way they are, the governor thinks the only way to bring peace to Kansas is to let the people sort things out for themselves. Having the army around just makes the Missourians think that Kansas wants to be free of slavery."

"Don't we?" Cal asked.

"Well, I'd like to say that everyone thinks like that. But even in our Army of the United States, I can't say that's true." He shook his head and sighed. "War's coming, Cal. I hate to see it but war's coming. And I don't think it'll be a quick war."

He withdrew an envelope from inside his blouse and handed it to Cal. "This is from Captain Jackson. It's payment for you. Now, don't say anything about it. The captain passed around a hat and just about everyone—even the bugler—put in something. Then the captain counted it all out and, to make it easier for you, since mailing paper money to your ma would be easier than a bunch of halfpennies and dollar coins, he just got some paper money for you."

Cal took the envelope but just stared at the lieutenant.

"I've talked to John Little—he's the deputy marshal here. You know him."

Sure, Cal knew him, but not by name till right then. That was the lawman who had told Cal all about fire and towns.

"Well, deputies and jailers and prisoners have to eat. He might not pay as much as the Army paid you, but he'll keep you busy. If you want the job."

Cal wasn't sure about the job, but he knew he had to keep mailing money back to his mother, but he couldn't find the words. His head just bobbed a bit, and Lieutenant Johnson held out his hand, and they shook.

"We're pulling out in an hour. I reckon this—well,

let's hope it's not a goodbye, Calvin Marmaduke. Just till we see each other again—during better days."

Summer passed, fall came and went, and winter arrived early. Cal was writing a letter to Charity when Deputy Little came in with a fellow wearing shackles on his wrists.

"Where's Henry?" the deputy asked.

"I don't rightly know," Cal said, as he slid the paper away and stood. He was sitting at the deputy's desk.

"Well, grab the keys to the cell—the good cell, not the one for drunks and brawlers—and come along." He shoved the shackled man ahead. "This is Benjamin Rice. He's a Jayhawker with a robbery charge against him."

The good cell was the one on the top floor of the Free State Hotel. Not that Cal found anything good about it. Cal had seen closets bigger than that cell, but that was a whole lot safer than the other jail the deputy used, though Cal wondered how wise it would be to lock up a Jayhawker, which was what folks were calling Free-Soilers these days, in a hotel that cottoned to Free-Soilers and abolitionists mostly.

Deputy Little asked Cal to keep his eye open for John Brown and James Montgomery, but Cal saw neither hide nor hair of either of those two. He was hunting on a frigid December morning and had managed to kill two fair-size turkeys and was bringing them back to town, when he was surprised to find the street in front of the Free State Hotel filled with those opposed to slavery and those for it.

"What happened?" Cal asked.

A maid at the hotel stopped sobbing long enough to whisper, "Montgomery and his Jayhawkers."

"Oh."

"They—" She sniffled. "They broke Mr. Rice out of jail."

Now, Cal didn't think the woman would be upset that Montgomery had been broken out of jail. Then she whispered, "They shot down Deputy Little. He's— d-dead."

He went to Deputy Little's funeral, of course, but he figured he was out of a job with the deputy's demise. The new deputy told Cal to stay on if he wouldn't mind, and although he wasn't as nice as Deputy Little and didn't pay as much money, it was still more money than he figured he could make in Lawrence. And his Ma said she would miss not seeing her son for Christmas, but that was all right, that it was practically 1859 already and Cal would be seventeen years old.

So 1859 came, and Cal kept writing Charity, and Charity—usually, but not always—scribbled a note that typically said, "Thank you, Son. Keep sending money when you can." But she had stopped writing about things happening at home and was not even thanking Cal for sending the money.

The good news, Cal thought, was that nobody had seen John Brown in Kansas for some time. But there was a reason for that, which the citizens of Fort Scott learned when word reached the town that John Brown and others had raided a place in Virginia called Harpers Ferry. He remembered ferries on some of the rivers, and wondered what kind of idiot would keep rifles, muskets, and lead balls and gunpowder on a river ferry. Apparently, Brown and his followers, including some kinfolk, had struck the ferry to get a bunch of rifles and ammunition to supply the slaves in Virginia for a revolt. Or something like that. Which struck Cal as foolishness.

Old John Brown was hanged by the neck till he was dead, dead, dead before the year was out. But he was still alive when Cal found that he was out of a job.

The deputy was sad about letting Cal go, but just said things were getting ticklisher—that's what he said, *ticklisher*—all the time, and that the United States marshal had told him they needed to save money because war was coming sure as the turning of the earth. But the deputy suggested to go up to Leavenworth, that a fellow with Cal's skill with a long gun could easily find work in that country, and he even wrote a letter of recommendation for Cal to show to folks who had need of a good hunter.

Cal was in Leavenworth before the year was out. There he saw a tall—really tall—fellow who looked even taller with that stovepipe hat on his head and asked him if he knew if anyone might be hiring in this city.

The man, Cal realized, was maybe the ugliest fellow he had ever seen.

"Well, son," he said, "we are both seeking employment."

"Oh," Cal said, and figured the man wasn't about to

give Cal any advice since he might be looking for the same kind of work.

"How old are you?" the man asked.

"I'll be eighteen next month," Cal told him.

The man smiled. He wasn't quite as ugly when he smiled. "You can't help me find the job I'm seeking, then, son."

Cal didn't know what to say to that.

"Because you are too young to vote."

That got Cal to laugh. "Mister," he said, "you don't know how folks run elections in this territory."

The man wasn't even ugly at all when he laughed. He had to wipe his eyes, then put a bony but strong hand on Cal's left shoulder.

"Son, I might be able to use you to help me write speeches. You see. I am running for the office of president of our United States. My name is Lincoln, son. Abraham Lincoln."

"Oh." Cal remembered hearing about Lincoln, but decided that this gent was too tall and too ugly to be anything other than some kind of owlhoot.

The tall fellow was about to say something else, but that's when a man ran out of a building screaming, "John Brown has been hung! John Brown has been hung!"

And folks ran into the street. The man was waving a little sheet of yellow paper in his right hand, and folks were running to see that paper and make sure he wasn't drunk. But Cal figured he was drunk or just a grafter when the man yelled, "He was hanged on December second in Charles Town, Virginia!"

The tall, ugly gent was wetting his lips. Most folks kept running to hear that news, but the man was deep in pondering, and Cal just shook his head, and said, "How can that fella know John Brown got hung when it just happened in Virginia yesterday."

"The telegraph," the man said, and Cal looked up at the man.

"The what?"

"The telegraph. Surely you know about the telegraph."

Cal shook his head, but the man was now looking up in the sky. When he looked back down, he said, "How does this sound to you, my good man? 'Old John Brown has just been hanged for treason against a state. We cannot object, even though he agreed with us in thinking slavery was wrong. That cannot excuse violence, bloodshed, and treason.'" He nodded. "What do you think?"

And the man might be ugly, but he could put together an argument that was hard to reject as a good thought.

Cal's head bobbed, but stopped after two nods, and then he said, "Maybe . . . *executed*."

That Lincoln fellow stared down at Cal, but the eyes weren't friendly. The man seemed to be pondering Cal's suggestion.

"Executed." He nodded. "Yes. Hanged is too grisly a picture." He smiled and extended that rough, callused hand.

"Thank you, my good man. Thank you. Executed. If you will excuse me, Master—?"

"Cal. Cal Marmaduke."

"Thank you, Cal Marmaduke." He began to walk away, then turned and looked back at Cal.

"Can you ride a horse, Cal Marmaduke?"

"Yes, sir." Who couldn't ride a horse in Kansas Territory?

"I mean ride. Ride long and hard and fast."

"I can ride a horse." That's one thing those dragoons had taught him well.

"I thought so. You have that look about you, young man. I rode mules—still do. But I cannot say that I am fond of that way of travel."

Cal nodded. The tall, ugly fellow looked again across the street, and then back at Cal.

"Well, there's an outfit forming, young fellow, and you might be just the type that enterprise is seeking." He chuckled. "They sure wouldn't want me to ride a pony—ponies, actually—as far as they want their riders to go. At least, according to what they have told me. They haven't started yet, but by spring they should be running—I should say galloping—at a right good clip. I don't know if the business will succeed—that telegraph that just brought us news about the fate of John Brown could be proof of a new day and age in our great country. But for the moment, these entrepreneurs— Mr. Russell, Mr. Majors, and Mr. Waddell—might be looking for young men to carry the mail across our great country, to link Leavenworth with California. And they will have to pay riders handsomely, because it will be dangerous for daring young men."

He looked down again at Cal.

"Son, not to sound rude, but are you an orphan, by chance?"

Cal lowered his head, and thought about that question. Then he stuck his right hand inside the deep pocket on his trousers and nodded, and whispered that lie. "Yes, sir, I am."

"Well, son, go see Mr. Majors. Alexander Majors. Tell him that I suggested that you seek him out." He nodded down the street. "The sign reads Russell, Majors and Waddell. Just look for that sign."

And that's how Cal wound up later in St. Joseph, Missouri, and then Rock Creek Station in Nebraska. Riding for an outfit called the Pony Express.

CHAPTER 21

"*You're just the kind of lad we are seeking, Master Marmaduke. I think fortune has shone on our enterprise, thanks to Mister—and perhaps President—Lincoln.*" Those words from Alexander Majors kept ringing in Cal's mind for about eighteen months.

Cal started out at the Marysville home station in Kansas, where he would ride at full gallop on one horse all the way to Cottonwood, where the boys and men working there would have a horse ready for him, and he'd jump off the mount, grabbing the mail pouch—that folks called a mochila—and slapping it on the fresh mount a couple of workers were holding for him. That horse would be running and Cal would have to swing himself into the saddle, and keep that horse moving to Rock House Station and do the same thing again there. Then Rock Creek. Then Whiskey Run. And finally, with his innards rattled so much his stomach felt like it was in his left lung and his right lung felt like it was pressing through his bowels, he'd reach Big Sandy Station, and then some other dang fool of a kid would take his mochila—and, thankfully, Cal's place on a fresh horse—and head west so that Cal could rest a bit. But only until the eastbound rider came racing in. That meant it was Cal's turn to ride all the way back at breakneck speed to Marysville.

He carried only that mochila. No revolver. Certainly no Hawken—since his had been stolen by those Missourians, he hadn't seen an old rifle like that, so Cal was going around undressed, as folks in Nebraska and Kansas liked to call it.

But the food was regular. And the bunks comfortable.

Cal had barely gotten the job. Mr. Majors said they wanted boys—orphans preferred—not yet eighteen years old. And being that it was still 1859 when Cal had talked to Mr. Majors, he hadn't turned eighteen yet, and when Mr. Majors asked if Cal were an orphan, he had been hanging around soldiers long enough down in Fort Scott that he had learned how to tell a lie.

Besides, Obadiah might be dead, making Cal a half-orphan. Sometimes, when Cal was feeling angry, he sort of wished that lazy, ignorant cur had died. Maybe run over by a team of mules. Or scalped and left staked out on the prairie by Comanches or Kiowas. Then he'd feel bad, because he knew Charity wouldn't want to ever hear Cal saying something like that, and he'd sigh and tell God that he really didn't mean it.

Cal, however, was exactly what Russell, Majors and—shucks, he'd already forgotten the other fellow's name—wanted, though. He was young. He was skinny, weighing right at one hundred and nineteen pounds, six under the maximum weight this outfit was hiring. And Cal was wiry.

"Are you willing to risk death daily?" Mr. Majors had asked him, back in Leavenworth.

"Mister," Cal had said, "I've been living in Lawrence and Fort Scott the past few years."

And Mr. Majors, knowing all about the roughness going on in those places between the Missourians and Kansans, simple nodded his head in complete understanding.

Now Cal was drawing one hundred dollars a month. He felt richer than a king.

But this sure was a hard way to make that kind of money, and he always sent ninety of those dollars back to Charity in Lawrence, Kansas, with a dumb note saying that he was all right and seeing lots of country. And he *was* all right, mostly, and was seeing lots of country. Just the same country westbound or eastbound, but it wasn't like he had time to notice much about the countryside.

The Pony Express, which had officially started in April of 1860, wasn't the only business Russell, Majors, and that other fellow owned. The company also owned a freighting outfit and some stagecoach lines. What the company didn't own was the Pony Express station at Rock Creek. The fellow who owned that was a mean cuss named Dave McCanles, and Cal would later learn to keep his mouth shut and mind his own business whenever McCanles came around.

Cal learned lots of things riding for the Pony Express. That November of 1860, he heard it from Mr.

Wellman—Horace Wellman being the station manager at Rock Creek—that Abraham Lincoln had been elected president of our United States! A couple months later, he heard that Kansas, not a territory any longer, had become a state, and he thought maybe that would end all of those raids and such. But a few months after that, they all learned—and most of the folks when they heard the news were silent for the longest while—that a bunch of the Southern states had left the United States and formed their own country, something called the Confederate States of America, and then some fellows in South Carolina fired on Fort Sumter, which was still commanded by the United States, and war had begun.

"Brother against brother," Mr. Wellman said.

For more than a year, Cal had ridden with hardly any injuries. Of course, anybody riding horses that often and at those speeds was sure to get bruises and cuts. Mounts Cal had been riding had stumbled, buckled, slipped on the creek bottoms, and every now and then, gotten spooked by a snake or some critter than popped out of the brush.

But Cal didn't think much of those bruises and cuts and rattled innards. After all, one hundred dollars a month cured a lot of discomfort.

In May of 1861, though, Cal was changing horses at Rock Creek station when the holder let go too quick of the pony Cal was trying to climb aboard, and Dave McCanles decided that this was a good time to shoot the whiskey bottle out of Horace Wellman's hand, and that really spooked the dun Cal was trying to mount, and the horse rolled over Cal, cracking four ribs and breaking his left wrist.

The ribs were just cracked—not broken—so no lungs or other organs that a body needed to live got a hole punched in them, but Cal wouldn't be riding a horse for a while. Slim Mosby, a stableboy, got the horse up as someone dragged Cal away, and Slim leaped into the saddle and took off west.

But the company of Russell, Majors and that other guy was good to its riders, especially its top riders, so Mr. Wellman said Cal would continue to draw his regular pay, which caused Cal to softly ask about that pay, seeing that he had not seen even a dollar, and never all hundred of them, in the past two months.

Which caused Dave McCanles to crack, "Boy, I ain't seen a penny on the rent you folks owe me in four months."

Wellman and McCanles walked out arguing, but Halderman, another of the station hands, told Cal not to worry, and brought him some soup that he said he had added some of McCanles's whiskey to, because whiskey was good medicine.

When Cal woke up, he had company.

He was a tall, slender fellow who had been mauled by a bear somewhere in New Mexico Territory while freighting for Russell, Majors and that other gent, and Cal realized having an eight-hundred-pound gelding roll over you wasn't anywhere near as bad as having a bear attack you.

But the fellow laying in the cot next to Cal didn't seem to mind, especially when a gal named Kate Shell came over from one of the other cabins and started doctoring both Cal and the other gent, who had long hair, a scraggly mustache and goatee and the clearest eyes Cal—and Kate Shell—had ever seen.

That fellow's name was Jim Hickok.

Dave McCanles would come over, too, most times just to yell at Mr. Wellman about getting paid his rent money, and then maybe play cards with Jim Hickok, but whenever Kate Shell got too close to Hickok, McCanles would get mean.

It wasn't long after that that Jim Hickok opened one of his saddlebags and pulled out a revolver. "Ever shoot one of these Navies, Cal?" Hickok asked.

Cal walked over—he was walking pretty good by this time—and stared at the pistol.

"Ain't that a Navy Colt?" Cal asked.

"It is," Hickok said. "Thirty-six caliber."

Cal nodded. "Shot a Walker a few times. But mostly I fired a Hawken."

Hickok's sharp eyes looked hard at Cal. "A Hawken?" he said.

Cal nodded.

Then Hickok withdrew another one of those slender, brassy revolvers.

"What say we take us some target practice?"

That suited Cal. It being summer, the cabin was getting stuffy, and Mr. Wellman kept telling Cal and Hickok that they'd get better sooner and ready to work a lot faster if they would start moving around some.

So Cal and Hickok moseyed over away from the corral of horses and behind the barn, and Hickok picked up a few of the empty whiskey bottles McCanles had been tossing into the grass near the barn, and walked to an empty round pen and set the four bottles atop four posts.

When he was back, he capped the chambers of his revolver.

"You go first, Cal," Hickok told him. "How about the closest bottle."

Cal nodded, then eared back the hammer and raised the Navy—which felt like a feather in his hand compared to those big pistols he had been shooting during his California Trail days.

He held his arm out straight and then started moving it in circles, even though he was pretty strong for a skinny kid—now nineteen years old—but that's the way he had always been shooting. The .36 popped and the bottle busted clean in half, the top falling to the dirt, and the bottom just setting on that post.

After Cal lowered the Navy, he turned to see Hickok rubbing his eyes and shaking his head.

"Smoke bother you?" Cal asked.

Hickok shook his head and looked up at Cal with those eyes of his wide.

"What was all that—?" He couldn't think of any words to describe what he had seen, so he just made a circling motion with his arm.

"Oh." Cal shrugged. "Well, when I was just a button—eight years old—and on the California Trail, that Hawken rifle I shot was too heavy for me to hold steady. So I just learned how to shoot at the right time. And a Walker Colt, even a Dragoon, felt just as heavy. So I shot it the same way. Like I just did."

"But that Navy—it's nowhere near as heavy as a Hawken or Dragoon Colt."

Cal smiled. "Old habits, I reckon."

Hickok nodded, cocked the second Navy Colt, which he held in his right hand, aimed, his arm steady, the barrel not moving an eighth of an inch, drew a deep breath, and pulled the trigger.

Staring at the bottle reflecting sunlight atop that post, Hickok swore softly.

Cal walked over, sliding the other .36 into his pants pocket, and took Hickok's revolver. Once again his arm started moving in that circular pattern, but this time he didn't cock the hammer till his arm was moving. And on the next pass, he squeezed the trigger and the bottle Hickok had missed shattered.

When the white smoke was gone, Cal flipped the Colt, letting his middle finger catch the front of the hammer and the two other fingers right at the barrel and his thumb circling around to land between the two fingers on the barrel. Hickok saw the butt of the Navy and took it.

Cal drew the Colt Hickok had let him borrow.

"The key," Cal said, "is that little pimple near the end of the barrel."

"Pimple," Hickok whispered. "You mean the sight."

Cal nodded. "That's all you got to look at. Then you get the feeling. You ain't got to hold the gun and wave it around like you're about to drop it the way I do. I ain't seen nobody around—and let me tell you that in the parts of Kansas were I grew up—I seen a lot of folks shooting Navies and Remingtons and Starrs and pistols and rifles I ain't never heard of before. They all do it their own way. My way's just a little different. But that *sight*, as you call it. That's what you got to look at. Feel it. Get a feel for that gun. Try it again, Jim."

He did. And missed again.

"Oh, yeah," Cal said. "I forgot to tell you. *That* Navy pulls a mite to the left."

"Left," Hickok whispered.

Cal checked his own two hands, just to make sure. "Yeah. Left. So keep that in mind this time."

And that time, Hickok broke the bottle in half.

Cal whistled. "That's some shooting, Jim."

They practiced another ten minutes, but then that pretty gal came over and asked what they were doing, but Cal could tell that Kate wasn't all too particular about what he was doing—just Jim Hickok—so he excused himself and walked back to the cabin.

But after that, Cal Marmaduke and Jim Hickok practiced a lot with those two .36-caliber revolvers. Till Mr. Waddell told them to stop it, that all that "cannonfire"— Mr. Waddell's word—was spooking the horses and Mr. Waddell himself.

And when Pony Bill brought in the mail in July, he pulled a letter from inside his buckskin shirt and handed it to Cal before he rode off. It was a letter sent all the way from Lawrence, Kansas.

Cal read it right away. Then he went to see Mr. Wellman, but Wellman swore a bit and said, "Cal, I don't know when any of us is getting paid." Cal just handed him the letter. And Mr. Wellman stared up at the young man and then at the letter. "I thought you knew how to read, Cal," he said.

Cal couldn't form a sentence. He just nodded.

And Mr. Wellman took the letter and the envelope underneath it, and read it. It was a short letter, and Mr. Wellman was a real fast reader, but he held the letter up and read it again, then sighed, shook his head, and set the letter and the envelope atop the table that served as his desk when folks weren't eating. "Cal,"—he sighed again—"I am sorry for your loss."

Cal just nodded. His mouth couldn't find any words.

"You'll be wanting to go back home," he said, "take care of everything."

Cal sighed. His head somehow managed to move up and down again.

Mr. Wellman sighed again, too. This was a day for much sighing. "Cut out a horse. That'll be partial payment for what Russell, Majors and Waddell owes you. Take the saddle, too." He stood and extended his hand.

After shaking the hand, Cal found some words. "I hate to leave you short—"

But Mr. Wellman shook his head. "Cal, there's a war going on. A bad war. And that telegraph line will be connecting California with New York in a few months. And Russell, Majors and Waddell are practically broke. The Pony Express is going to be deader than Simon Cameron's brother. So, son . . ." He stopped again.

Cal didn't know who Simon Cameron was, let alone his brother.

"Cal," Mr. Wellman said, "I wouldn't come back here after you've settled your dearly departed mother's estate. There probably won't be anything to come back to."

They shook hands again. "Good luck to you."

So Cal picked out a pretty good buckskin gelding— not the horse that had rolled over him and left him stove up for a right long time—and Jim Hickok helped him saddle him, and then they shook hands.

"Thanks for all the shooting lessons, pardner," Hickok said. "Anything I can do for you?"

Cal's head shook.

"Maybe our paths will cross again," Hickok said.

"Maybe so."

Hickok turned toward the cabin, then back to Cal. "I'd ride a ways with you but, ummm . . ."

Well, Cal had seen Kate entering the cabin, and he knew he couldn't compete with that pretty gal. He just smiled, and they shook hands, and Cal swung into the saddle.

"Good luck to you, ol' hoss."

Cal nodded. "Keep practicing with those Navy Colts. I might read about you someday."

Jim Hickok laughed. "Maybe so, pardner. Maybe so."

Turning the horse, Cal rode toward the road. He stopped when he saw some men riding, and a few others walking, but saw that it was Dave McCanles and some of his pards. He didn't want to have to talk to him, but they all stopped in the middle of the road, so Cal did, too.

"Where's your playmate, boy?" McCanles said.

There was whiskey on that bully's breath. But Cal just shrugged and tilted his head toward the station.

"You seen Kate?"

This time Cal didn't answer.

"What I figured." McCanles spit tobacco juice onto the ground. "Come on, boys," he said, and they rode around Cal.

Cal glanced over his shoulder, then put the horse into a walk.

Funny, he started thinking. For better than a year, he had ridden for the Pony Express, but hadn't seen more than a short stretch from Kansas into Nebraska. He figured he could get someone at the Marysville home station to tell him the best road to take to get to Lawrence, and he'd also have to tell the boys there goodbye. And then maybe he'd shed tears over Charity Marmaduke and let the Kansas wind dry his face.

She wasn't his real ma. But she had been the only mother he had ever known—and loved.

About a quarter mile later, he heard some faint reports of gunfire back west, and turning in the saddle, he looked back down the trail, and laughed.

That Jim Hickok. He sure loved practicing shooting those Navy Colts.

The horse whickered, and Cal patted its neck, then let it move into a trot.

"Wonder what Jim was shooting at this time," he told the horse, then kicked the buckskin into a gallop.

CHAPTER 22

"Have you enlisted yet, Calvin?" the preacher asked.

Kneeling at his mother's grave, his hat in his hand, Cal sniffled, wiped his eyes, and shook his head. Not to answer the reverend's question—and it had been mighty nice of him to send him that letter—but he just couldn't quite understand the date carved onto the stone.

Charity Marmaduke
B: 1824
D: Feb. 3, 1861

Five months ago.

Rising, Cal reached into his pocket and pulled out the letter the preacher had written him. Sure enough, the man had written the date before he started with "Dear Cal," and that date was June 9, 1861. Granted, the letter had not been delivered by the Pony Express, but it had reached him in what Cal figured was right good time.

He double-checked. Yep. That was June 9, all right.

"How come you didn't write me till just last month, reverend?" he asked.

The minister had told him his full name, but Cal's brain really wasn't holding much information right then and there. His mind was whirling, and now he was confused.

The black-bearded man sighed heavily.

"Her husband—your pa—he said he would send you word." The man bowed his head as if in prayer. "When he left, without a word, I took it upon myself, fearing the worst, that he—well . . ."

"Obadiah." Cal tested that name. "Obadiah was here?"

"Your fa—"

This time, Cal barked: "He ain't my pa."

The preacher stopped, stared, but quickly looked away and sighed. Cal waited, but the man said nothing, though his lips were moving as though he were praying.

"I was sending Ma money," Cal said.

The reverend finished his prayer, lifted his head, and nodded. "Yes, your mother told me. She kept bragging on you. We all did. You riding for that valiant enterprise, the Pony Express. And sending her a good deal of money. They paid you well."

"I earned it," he said. He pointed at the gravestone. "So did my mama."

The man nodded. "When Obadiah left, I feared the worst. That's why I wrote you."

Some of the boys Cal had ridden with the Pony Express were salty talkers, and Cal felt like letting loose with a string of cusswords, and he wouldn't care what that preacher said or thought or sermoned about. But

his mama—maybe not his birthing ma, but the girl—
she was hardly a woman when she took Cal in—was the
woman who had brought him up. Charity was Cal's
raising ma. She made him who he was now. And she
wouldn't want to hear him swearing like—well, Obadiah
when he was in his cups.

"You know where Obadiah went?" Cal asked.

The preacher's face paled.

"Don't worry," Cal told him. "I ain't going after him.
He ain't worth it. And as much money as I sent Ma,
well, he's probably already done spent it or lost it."

The preacher nodded.

"Which way?" Cal asked again.

The parson pointed west.

So Cal rode east.

Not with any purpose. He rode like he was lost.
When he saw the sign pointing toward Fort Scott, he
realized where he was riding, and quickly turned
northerly, not wanting to return to Fort Scott. He saw a
sign pointing to Independence, and that suited him, just
for a little bit. That's where he had lit out with Captain
Shufflebottom and the Reverend James. Where he had
returned with old Jim Bridger. The captain and the
preacher might have been the closest thing to real fathers
that Cal ever had.

Then it struck him. Well, the reverend *had* been his
real daddy.

In Independence, Cal saw a minister walking on the
boardwalk and turned his horse toward him.

"Excuse me," he said, and the preacher stopped,

turned, and gave Cal a slight nod. He didn't say anything, though. In fact, he looked pretty scared, though Cal didn't think he was doing anything threatening. Cal saw the white collar, and the crucifix, and figured him to be Catholic.

"Can you tell me how to get to Centerville?" He thought after he had said the town's name, then nodded, sure that was the name of the town.

The priest let out a sigh of relief. He pointed at a street. "That'll take you to the crossroads. Turn right. There's a fork about two miles up, and if the signs are up, don't pay attention to them. They might be right. But someone might have turned them around. So take the trail that leads northeast. It's the Liberty Pike." The man chuckled. "Liberty. What a misnomer."

Cal told himself to remember that word and find out what it means sometime. Mis-no-mer. Mis-no-mer.

"Go straight through Liberty. Keep bearing northeast. Centerville is about ten miles up that trail."

Cal nodded. "I appreciate your kindness and time, preacher—I mean rev—I mean—"

"James suits me fine, lad."

Cal smiled. So did the priest.

"James." He tested the name, and nodded. "My name's Cal."

"Good to know you, Cal." The man seemed to relax, but as Cal turned the horse toward the direction he needed to go, the priest cleared his throat, and when Cal looked back, he asked. "Cal, are you for the Union or are you for the Confederacy?"

Cal shrugged. "I don't rightly know."

The preacher was frowning. Cal studied him.

"Son," the man said, "that answer can get you killed in Missouri."

Cal blinked. "So what am I supposed to say in Missouri?"

The priest made the sign of the cross. "It depends, my boy, on who's asking that question." Head bowed, praying again, he walked away.

He got scared in Liberty. Not about the war going on, but about where he kept thinking about going. Maybe he would stop at Mount Hope Baptist Church. Maybe he would go see the Reverend James's family. That petrified him, so he wound up working at a livery. He got free room—well, a free stall with clean hay to sleep on every night. And he had always like working with horses.

To him, what he had read in the newspapers, this war between the states was being fought way over in the east, in places like Virginia and, well, Virginia. The only fighting going on in Liberty was typically between pro-Union men and Southern sympathizers in saloons and in the streets.

Cal got asked the question all the time whenever men came in to board their horses: "Are you for the South or are you for the Union?"

And Cal had learned to answer: "I am for Missouri." He sure wasn't going to let them know that he had ridden with a bunch of Yankee dragoons and that Kansas had been his home for a long time.

The pro-Union folks in Liberty were putting on the shooting match, and the prize was an Enfield rifle. Cal had enough money to enter but had to borrow a big planter's rifle. The big man stared at Cal, then smiled. "Cost you a nickel. You got a nickel, boy?"

Cal showed him a dime.

The man smiled. "I owe you a nickel, then. But tell you what, why don't you bet that nickel with me. I win this contest, which I aim to, I keep the whole dime. You win, I give you back the dime and add a nickel."

"Suits me," Cal said.

He had never fired an Enfield. The pro-Union folks said it had been carried gallantly by a St. Louis man who used it at Boonville. The Confederate supporters said it had been taken off a dead Yankee at Boonville.

Missourians, as a whole, were much better shots than Kansans, Cal learned. That big hoss who had bet Cal on the contest turned out to be one of the best, and Cal had never used this man's rifle, but it sure shot true.

Of course, every man jack among them howled like rabid wolves when Cal started spinning that rifle the way he always did.

"He's gonna drop your rifle!" one yelled.

"Look out, boy," another yelled back, "old Janie's gonna buck you off."

The gun roared. The men fell silent.

Cal walked away with a new Enfield and fifteen cents.

That display got Cal a job hunting, though he kept the livery job since he had gotten used to sleeping in a stall and he had always liked horses.

Word came about a fight between Union and Confederate troops at a place called Wilson's Creek, which was somewhere near a town called Springfield, a far piece south of Liberty.

Coming back from a hunting trip, he saw a tall man in ragged butternuts walking down the pike. The man pushed back a raggedy hat and watched Cal as he rode toward him. Cal's saddle had no scabbard, so he held the Enfield in his right hand and the reins in his left. The fellow didn't appear to have any firearm—rare in this country for these hard days—but Cal gave him a friendly nod and reined up a few yards in front of him.

"Howdy," Cal said.

The man coughed, then nodded. He had the most piercing eyes Cal had seen since his Pony Express time with Jim Hickok. And those eyes just locked on Cal so hard it made him uncomfortable.

"Soldier?" Cal asked.

The man kept staring. "Was. Paroled. Got caught after Wilson's Creek." He didn't blink at all, and Cal found himself sweating, but it was August.

"Sorry." The man chuckled slightly. "Didn't mean to stare. You just—well, you remind me of my brother."

Cal nodded. "Oh." Then he smiled. "Never had a brother. Or a sister."

"Lucky."

"Where you bound, if you don't mind telling me?"

The man nodded up the trail. "Back home. Farm outside of Centerville."

That stopped Cal for a moment, but then he hadn't had much luck at hunting today, and he probably ought to just go see Centerville. What it looked like. That didn't mean he had to go to—well . . . Cal shook his head and said, "I've been hunting for an eating place in Liberty. But all I got is two scrawny squirrels, and there ain't much left of them after a .577-caliber ball tore through them. But I'd gladly share them with you."

"I wouldn't turn down even an Enfield ball. I have not had a bite to eat in two days."

Cal swung off his horse and nodded. "There's a clearing. Looks like that farm hasn't been worked in some time. Think you can walk fifty yards."

"I've gotten real good at walking."

"How far you reckon it is to Centerville?"

"Just five miles," the man said.

Cal made his decision. "All right. And after we eat, I'll let you ride behind me."

The man's head tilted in suspicion.

"The war has hardly gotten started, and everybody's stopped being neighborly," Cal said. "My ma wouldn't have none of that. Besides, the hunting might be better around Centerville. It's mostly played out down here."

The man relaxed. Then he laughed. "My mama has never been known for being neighborly."

Cal laughed with him. He held out his right hand. "My name's Calvin—Cal for short. Cal Marmaduke."

The man had a firm handshake. "Glad to make your acquaintance you, Cal," he said. "Call me Frank. Frank James."

Chapter 23

Cal's mouth hadn't felt this dry since those long days walking across the Utah drylands on the California Trail. Frank James cocked his head.

"You all right?" the tall man asked.

Cal tried to nod his head, but wasn't sure he had managed that.

"You look white as a sheet," Frank said.

Cal wet his lips. Then he smiled, though making those lips turn upward took about every muscle he had. "Nothin' that a good meal wouldn't fix. Even if it's squirrel meat. How 'bout you?"

"All right," Frank said, with a grin.

After eating and wiping their fingers on their trousers, Cal unhobbled his horse, tightened the cinch, and swung into the saddle, kicked one foot free of the stirrup, and reached down to help Frank James. But Frank seemed like he was born in the saddle. He came up easily.

"'Preciate this, pardner," the tall man said. "Ma will repay you when we get home with a meal."

Cal had to make some kind of conversation. "Your ma's a good cook, I bet," he said.

Frank chuckled. "No. I'm hoping my sister will grow up to be one. But Ma makes food that'll fill your belly and keep you working in those fields."

The miles went by mighty fast. The one time it didn't was when they passed a patrol, where a Confederate officer raised his right hand and called for them to stop.

"Where y'all be headin'?" the thick-mustached lieutenant asked.

"The James farm," Frank answered. "Outside of Centerville."

"Why ain't you boys fightin' to keep Missouri free from Abe Lincoln and his vermin?"

Cal heard Frank digging in his pockets, then paper crinkling, and he saw the long arm extend and the hand flap the document open.

"Captured near Wilson's Creek," Frank eventually explained as the officer started glancing over the paper. "Was with the Missouri State Guard."

That got the men's attention. From the looks of their uniforms, these men—including the lieutenant—had seen nothing of combat.

"Wounded?" the officer asked.

Frank snorted. "Measles."

The lieutenant's hand jerked and almost dropped the paper as if it were a hot iron, and the man didn't even ask Cal about what outfit he was with. His arm shot forward and Frank took the paper, and all those Confederate boys put their horses into a trot, giving Cal and Frank a wide berth, and there wasn't nothing left of them but some horse apples and dust.

Frank laughed when they were gone. "If that's what those Confederates are calling an army, we Missourians are in big trouble."

"Measles," Cal said, and tried to chuckle.

Frank folded the paper, and stuck it in his pocket. "I wasn't lying about the measles," he said. "But the doc said nobody could catch it from me. Said wasn't that bad of a case, I mean." He sighed. "Sure will be glad to see our farm."

Cal kicked the horse into a walk. He wasn't all that certain he would be happy to see the James farm, but yet, deep inside him, he did want to see it. He wanted to see his birthing ma. And his other brother—Jesse—and his sister, Susan Lavenia. What a musical name she had.

Besides, from all Frank talked about as they got closer to Centerville, the James farm was quite successful. Cal loved his late raising ma, and sometimes didn't really feel like he would grind his molars to nothing but roots when he started thinking of that scoundrel of a raising pa of his, Obadiah Marmaduke.

He thought of Zerelda James asking to hear about the Reverend James's final hours, or about his adventures—or whatever they were—on that long, hard trek to California. He could see the whole family sitting at the table, clinging to every word. He could smell squirrel stew simmering, maybe neighbors coming to hear the story, maybe Cal being invited to talk to the congregation at the New Hope Baptist Church.

And then he thought: *Or they might just shoot me dead.*

They reached Centerville, which had nothing in common with Lawrence, Kansas. It might have reminded Cal of Bridger's Fort, but Jim Bridger's trading post had a lot more activity. Frank chuckled when they rode into the town. "Grown some since I went off to war," he said, and laughed hard.

There hadn't been a Centerville when Frank was born, he told Cal. A couple of gents, Mr. Duncan and Mr. Cave, laid out the town in 1856. Frank and Jesse liked to torment those two men and the surveyors by sneaking into the settlement at dark and moving all the surveyor's stakes or at least cutting off the cotton flagging from the pins that had been hammered into the ground to make them harder to find.

"Probably wouldn't have done that had our pa been around," Frank said, with a chuckle. "But he'd gone—" He stopped to lean a bit toward his left and yell at a big man stepping out of one of the few stores in Centerville. "Cole Younger," Frank James called out, "what brings you to this metropolis?"

Cal felt a nudge from behind. "Ride to that fellow by Wade's store over yonder," his brother told him.

Cal couldn't make out any store. In Lawrence, stores had signs, but he did see a big strong man tightening the cinch to the saddle on his big dun horse. The man was looking up over the saddle, then pushed up the brim of his hat.

"Frank James, I figured you were dead." Cole Younger

laughed and waited for Cal to get his horse to the store. If it was a store, it sure didn't have much in stock.

"What happened to Mr. Wade?" Frank said, seeing exactly what Cal had noted.

"Folks found out he was from Ohio," Cole explained. "Well, we had known that for some time. But being from Ohio ain't the same today as it was before all the shooting started." He nodded at Cal. "You from Ohio?" He laughed to let Cal know he was joking.

Cal sure wasn't going to tell him he was from Iowa, though. "Been hunting for some hotels and restaurants in Liberty," Cal said. "Name's Cal." He started to give his last name, but voted against that.

Younger nodded. "You give up the fight?"

"Measles," Frank said. "Then I got captured by the Yankees. They paroled me."

Cole laughed. "So the Yankees didn't want you, either. Well, I can't blame them for that."

"Me, neither. Those boys—Yank and Reb alike— they have not one single good idea when it comes to fighting a war."

"That's how come I plan on staying out of it," Cole said. He shook Frank's hand, then Cal's, then went back to his horse and swung into the saddle. "Give your mother and stepfather my best."

"Same to your folks."

They watched him swing into the saddle and ride out of town, which Cal still didn't think of as a town. A few cabins, this one abandoned store and another that remained open; the one that was still open was run by a Kentuckian, a state that, well, just like Missouri, had not quite decided if it went for the Union or for the Confederacy. But Cal could see that Centerville only needed one store for as few citizens as it had.

"Ride straight ahead to the crossroads," Frank told Cal. He pointed out the schoolhouse.

Cal didn't see any church, but then the Reverend James had never said New Hope Baptist Church was in Centerville.

It was nice country. Good woodlands. And the cleared pastures were already green with high corn. They rode past that farm. And another one. "That's not corn," Cal said, when they reached another farm.

Behind him, Frank snorted. "You've never seen tobacco before, Cal?"

"Not green tobacco, no, sir," Cal said, and thought up a joke. "I've seen some boys green after they smoked some or swallowed the juice."

Frank laughed at that, too. He pointed to another pasture. "That's hemp. That's what we've been growing here since I can recall. For cash. We eat what we grow, and we cure some of the tobacco for ourselves. Some hemp, too." He nodded. "Turn at that lane. We're just about home."

And the word *home* caused Cal to shiver.

A boy who looked to be in his teens walked out of the barn holding a rifle, and a younger girl was sitting on a stool, milking a cow in a pen next to the barn.

Cal guessed the boy to be Jesse and the girl Susan Lavenia.

A family reunion, Cal thought, but it wasn't.

"Ma!" Jesse yelled. "We got—" The rifle almost dropped to the ground. "By thunder, it's Frank! Ma! It's Frank! Frank's home, Ma! Ma! Come quick!"

He let the rifle fall to the dirt and ran forward. The girl stopped milking the cow and ran to the fence. Stepping out of a woodshed was a dark-haired man with a thick mustache and beard.

A short, solid, homely dressed woman stepped out of the cabin, but she held an infant in her left hand. Her right came up to shield her eyes from the sun that wasn't quite behind the trees yet, and a girl—Cal guessed her to be two or three years old—tugged hard on Mrs. James's apron, till the woman barked something at her, and the girl's head dropped and she looked at her shoes and wrung her hands.

Jesse stopped a few feet from the horse, which Cal reined up.

Frank swung down, and slapped his right hand hard on his brother's left shoulder.

"How many Yankees did you kill?" Susan Lavenia called out.

"None," Frank said. "But they didn't kill me, either." He turned to his mother. "Ma."

"We heard you were captured," the bearded man said.

Frank nodded. "Sure was, doc. But they let me go. After I promised I'd sign an oath of allegiance."

"Susan Lavenia," the hard woman said. "Come take John Thomas. And watch after Sallie."

The girl wasted no time, and once Mrs. James was free from the burden of an infant boy and a toddler, she strode toward her sons.

"Light down," Frank told Cal, who obeyed, but held firm to the reins.

Frank made the introductions. The bearded man was Doc Samuel. He had married Frank's ma in '55. Cal didn't need any introduction to Jesse. He knew that had to be him. His eyes were just like the Reverend James's. Just like Cal's. And he was right about Susan Lavenia, too.

The new kids were Sarah Louise, who everyone called Sallie, born in '58, and John Thomas Samuel, born just this May. Doc Samuel was their daddy.

"This fellow picked me up on the road," Frank said, pointing at Cal. "Named Cal. Cal Marmaduke."

"Cal." His mother lowered the right hand that had been blocking part of the sun's rays. "Cal. Short for Calvin."

"Yes, ma'am."

She nodded, and looked at her oldest son—no, her second son. Cal was her oldest. "Well, if this young man give you a ride home, least you could do, Frank, is take care of his hoss. And you, Jesse, give him a hand." She turned back to let those hard eyes bore through Cal some more. "You'll be stayin' for supper."

He nodded, though Mrs. Zerelda Samuel had not

asked Cal anything. She told him he'd be eating with them.

"Step out of the heat, Cal Marmaduke," Mrs. James—no Samuel—said. "I'll pour you some coffee. We'll chat a mite."

"Want me to help set the table, Mama?" Susan Lavenia asked politely.

"No." The woman was already walking to the cabin, and Cal, in surrender, meekly followed like a church mouse.

He saw her drag a chair out from the table as she moved to the stove where a coffeepot waited. She didn't tell Cal to sit, but he knew the chair was for him. Still, he waited, remembering the manners his raising ma had put in him, and when she turned with a tin cup in one hand and a jug in the other, he still stood.

"Sit, boy. You're a guest. And I'm on my third husband. I can do without manners."

He sat, and she put the steaming cup in front of him and moved around the table, dragged out the chair directly across from him, settled onto it, pulled out the jug's cork with her teeth, spit the cork onto the table, and took a long pull.

After wiping her mouth, she slid the jug toward him. "Have a snort," she said.

His head shook. Well, Cal thought he shook his head. He wasn't sure. He must have, because she pulled the jug back but took no more of what smelled like corn liquor. She found the cork, slammed it back in place, and leaned forward, elbows on the table, chin in her hands.

She stared at him so hard Cal couldn't even think about drinking.

"You got your daddy's eyes, boy," she said. "The eyes of a preacher." She sighed heavily. "Preacher. Or maybe Eros or Dionysus. Bacchus. Cupid. I don't know."

Cal didn't know what she was talking about, other than the eyes. He had seen the same in Frank. And Jesse. They had the same eyes as their father, the Reverend Robert James.

"Did the preacher tell you?" she asked.

Cal had no voice.

"Of course he did." She answered her own question. "Maybe when he was dying. That'd be like him. When he lit out for California, I figured he would try to find you. You haunted him for a long time. So now you've found us. What do you want? Money? Birthday presents for"— she paused and stared at the ceiling, her lips mouthing the numbers—"nineteen years. My goodness. Nineteen."

"Mrs. James," he said. "I just met your son on the road. Gave him a ride home. I was just being neighborly. I didn't even know his name."

She gave a harrumph, started reaching for the jug, but her hand froze, and her head turned sharply. "What are you two boys doin'?"

And Cal turned to see Frank and Jesse, who had come into their home, quiet as church mice. They were staring hard—at him, Calvin Amadeus James, their oldest brother.

CHAPTER 24

They let Cal stay. But Cal explained that he had a job in Liberty, and ought to at least finish the month. Zerelda, Cal's birthing ma, had no problem with that. Cash money could be hard to come by before the hemp and tobacco were sold, and she promised to have a bed for him—in the barn. There wasn't room for him in the house. That put a smile on Frank's face, but Cal couldn't blame his brother.

Frank James had had a run of bad luck. Measles. Captured by the Union. Paroled. He didn't even have a bullet hole in his Home Guard uniform. And now he was no longer the oldest brother anymore. But at least he had a bed in the house and not a cot in the barn.

Cal finished out the month, and the merchants in Liberty were sad to see him go—and that was a shock for Cal to hear because most folks were glad to see Cal go away. But one of the cooks asked Cal if he could do something for him—and he'd be paid well in gold— just ride over to the town of Osceola and deliver a wedding dress to his cousin Arabella.

Well, a five-dollar gold piece was hard to turn

down—Ma James would sure appreciate it—so Cal accepted and the merchant drew up a map, pointing out that the sign to Osceola always got knocked down, and told him what street his cousin lived on and what the house looked like and even wrote out her name: A-r-a-b-e-l-l-l-a. Cal wasn't sure about three *l*'s, but he nodded and thanked the man, strapped the box that held the dress atop the bedroll behind the saddle, then draped the box with his black rain poncho just in case there came a storm, because you could never tell about Missouri weather.

The dress was delivered without any problem, and Arabella/Arabellla was so happy to see the box that she squealed with delight and gave Cal a big hug, and her daddy gave Cal a cigar and a quarter for his troubles, even though Cal said he wasn't partial to the weed and that he didn't need the quarter. But the father was too happy and just shook Cal's hand and left Cal on the porch and closed the door behind him.

So Cal mounted his horse and rode away, and it wasn't long before he saw the dust over the treetops down the road, and he reached down and touched the Enfield's stock that was sticking in the scabbard of the saddle Frank James had loaned him but did not pull the rifle out, because, as Cal kept telling himself, he didn't have any opinion when it came to anything about the war that was raging—although that wasn't close to the truth.

But people kept telling him—and this was especially true for anyone living in Missouri—that answering the wrong way could get a body killed.

Besides, Cal understood a single-shot Enfield wasn't much of a match against an entire army. And when he reined up, that was what came out of the woods heading up the trail toward him.

They were a colorful bunch. The top of their boots were wrapped with red sashes. Red legs. Jim Lane's bunch.

Ten riders galloped toward him while the rest of the army of Kansas marauders kept coming at a slow clip. Cal could make out some wagons that didn't appear to have any supplies or men in the back, but most of the men were riding horses—and they were armed, as the expression went, to the teeth.

One wild-eyed man bolted ahead from the rest, drew a revolver, and Cal lowered the reins, and held up both hands. He wasn't sure if that would stop the rider from killing him, but he didn't see much reason to give that rider a reason.

The horse slid to a stop, and Cal had to take the reins with his left hand—keeping his right one held high and away from the Enfield—and steady his gelding.

A man back with the rest of the army yelled out, "Don't kill him unless he fights or runs."

Don't fight, Cal thought. *Don't run.*

"Who are you, boy?" the rider said. Cal didn't pay much attention to the horseman. The cocked Navy Colt took all of his attention.

"Cal . . . Marmaduke." The men might have been coming from Liberty, he thought. And maybe they had heard of the young hunter. No one, not even Cal, had been calling him Cal James. Cal still wasn't used to that handle. "I hunt for some businesses—cafés and hotels—in Liberty."

Four more riders came loping forward. They pretty much formed a semicircle, and as the dust from the horses started settling, the fellow who had reached Cal first said, "Says he's a hunter for hotels and such in Liberty. Says his name is—"

"Cal," one of the men said. "Cal Marmaduke."

Looking at the man who had spoken, Cal breathed in deeply. He wore a long black cravat loose over a high white collar, woolen vest, and long blue coat. A saber rattled on his side, causing his horse to snort and sway till the man popped the horse between its ears and barked an oath. When he removed his Abe Lincoln hat, Cal saw the receding hairline and the wild hair. Light stubble covered his face. His lips were thin, his eyes blazing.

"Senator." Cal nodded at Jim Lane of Kansas.

"It's General Lane now, son." The man made a motion to the army behind him. "Why aren't you back home with your mother?"

Cal frowned. His lips parted, then closed, then he breathed in and out and finally whispered. "She passed a while back, sen—general."

The man nodded. "It's hard on boys when their mothers are called to Glory. I am sorry for your loss. She was a fine, God-fearing woman." The sympathy disappeared. "Why are you not wearing the uniform of your country?"

Cal sighed. Then he thought of a lie. "I am not of age."

Some of the men laughed.

Cal put on an act, letting his brow wrinkle and tightening his grip on the reins. "I turn eighteen next year, and then I'll out-soldier all of you."

That led to more laughter and a soft smile on Lane's lips.

"You were at Fort Scott during some of the troubles there, if I recall correctly," Lane said.

Cal nodded. "Yes, sir."

The general relaxed and turned back to the men behind him. "He's all right. A Kansan. Parents came from Iowa. And if the stories I've heard are true, you don't want to bet against him in a shooting match."

He leaned forward in the saddle, letting the reins fall across his mount's neck. Then he brought up his arms, mimicking as though he were holding a rifle that swung around and around. "But"—Lane said, as he kept his arms moving, and his men smiled—"*but* the way he holds a rifle, you wouldn't want him in your army, either." He stopped the playacting, and gathered the reins in his hands. "You have to shoot fast in war, Master Marmaduke," Lane said. "You'd be dead after the first volley."

The men laughed. "Come ahead," one of the riders yelled back to the rest of Lane's command.

"Which way to Osceola?" asked the rider who had, more or less, captured Cal.

Cal turned and pointed. His mouth opened, but he quickly shut it, kept pointing, then turned around.

The flag that flew on the pole in Osceola was bonny

blue, not the American flag. "Down that way," he said,
"I dunno, three miles, four." It was nearer one mile,
maybe two. "Wasn't paying much attention."

Jim Lane smiled as if he understood completely.
"Bates, just follow the horse's tracks. That'll take us
all to Osceola." He raised his hand, and brought it down
fast, pointing down the lane. The riders moved out first,
and Lane tightened his gauntlets, and turned around
to make sure the rest of the command was coming forward.

Lane then kicked his horse into a walk.

"If I were you, Cal Marmaduke," he said, as he
walked past, "I'd return to Kansas. A land of patriots and
not rebels, trash, and traitors. You might live longer.
Again, my condolences for the loss of your mother."

There wasn't much left of Osceola when Lane's red
legs left. At least, that's what everyone around Centerville heard. Cal sure hoped that Arabella/Arabellla had
been spared. That her betrothed wasn't one of the nine
that had been shot to death by Lane's firing squad. And
if he had survived, that he had not joined up with
Quantrill's Missourians—as so many Osceola survivors had.

Frank James left the farm early in 1862. Jesse tried
to join up, too, but all he did was take off the tip of a
finger trying to load a heavy Colt revolver, and Quantrill
sent him back home. Cole Younger, whom Cal had met

in Centerville when he first came to the town with Frank James, joined Quantrill, too.

At the James farm, they read of battles far, far away—Seven Pines . . . bloody Antietam . . . Fredericksburg . . .

And 1862 passed, but the next year seemed even grimmer. Chancellorsville in May and Stonewall Jackson's death . . . the waste of Gettysburg . . . and the fall of Vicksburg on Independence Day.

Cal would read the letters from Frank to his mother and siblings and—was the good doctor Cal's stepfather? And then they would all watch her throw the letters into the fireplace, because Yankee patrols often came by unannounced, wanting to know Frank's whereabouts. The bluecoats reminded them that Frank had sworn an oath not to take up arms against the Union.

"He isn't fighting the Union," Zerelda would fire back. "He's fighting red legs and ruffians and murderous felons who spit on women and children and plunder and beat mothers and dogs and babies." She could keep going, and would keep going, till the bluecoats and detectives would flee. She was as fire-and-brimstone as the Reverend James had been compassionate and uplifting.

And then a Union patrol came to the farm. They were dragging Jesse behind them.

Cal took the shotgun from his mother's hands when she ran out of the house, prepared to do battle. The good doctor was already kneeling over Jesse.

"Don't start anything, Ma Zerelda," Cal whispered.

Turning he saw a dozen muskets and four revolvers aimed at him, and he lowered the hammer on the single-shot ten-gauge and walked to the well, leaned the weapon against it, and started toward Jesse.

"Hold it!" a lieutenant barked and punctuated his command by cocking his .44-caliber Remington revolver.

"He's all right, sir," a man said. The accent was foreign yet familiar, and Cal turned to a man in blue with sergeant's stripes on his sleeves.

His mouth moved, but he did not speak the name, just mouthed it. Drabowski.

His old pal from the Dragoons back during those Bleeding Kansas years. Now the entire country was bleeding.

"He's a James!" the lieutenant said.

"No, sir. He's a Marmaduke. Hunted and scouted for us at Fort Scott. And you don't want him shooting at you, lieutenant. Trust me on that account. He can trim your thumbnail at four hundred yards and not leave a scratch."

The officer looked at Cal's birthing ma.

"Where is Frank?"

"Why did you hurt my son?" Ma James demanded.

"Because he wouldn't tell us where Frank is? Now where is he?"

Ma James spit, and shook her fist at the officer.

"Search the premises!" the officer barked. "Drabowski. Keep a sharp eye on that one. If he moves, kill him."

The officer swung out of the saddle and moved toward the barn.

The rest of the soldiers scoured the place. The baby cried. So did Sallie. Susan Lavenia tried to comfort both. Cal started toward his mother, but Drabowski cocked his .44 and stopped a few feet from him.

"This'll be over, peacefully," Drabowski said, before adding in a whisper: "I hope."

Cal heard furniture being overturned and dishes smashed inside the cabin.

"What the devil are you doing here—working for these Bushwhackers?" Drabowski asked.

Cal turned, sighed, and shook his head. He didn't feel like explaining.

The lieutenant came out, started for Cal, but then Doc Samuel rose from Jesse's body and shook his fist. "You have no right to do this! We aren't soldiers. We are farmers."

The officer spun immediately, then yelled. "Grierson. Throw a rope over that tree limb. Maybe this rebel will tell us where we can find that traitorous Frank James."

Cal held his breath. He thought they meant Jesse, but it was Doc Samuel.

Cal exhaled. He took a step forward, past Drabowski, and then he started to yell, but the pressure of a Remington barrel against his spine stopped him.

"Don't say a word," Drabowski whispered. "You want them to hang everyone here on this farm? That martinet of a madman lieutenant, he isn't Lieutenant Johnson, Cal. He's as crazy as everyone else in this horrible state."

They jerked Doc Samuel up countless times, but he never told them anything. The lieutenant called him all types of names, kept threatening to leave him up the next time—that they had left one stubborn farmer hanging in his tobacco-curing barn.

"He doesn't know where Frank is," Cal whispered. "None of us knows. Frank hasn't written us once."

Only the last sentence was a lie. But there was no proof of any letters except the ashes in the fireplace.

Ma James yelled and screamed and begged God to strike down these vermin, but, as the phrase went in Missouri in those days, "There's no God in Missouri."

CHAPTER 25

The federals took Doc Samuel to Liberty, where he was jailed. When he finally came back to the James farm—with a neighbor who let him ride in the buckboard the last three miles—he was frail and pale, and spoke with a voice so hoarse he was hard to understand. And he took to wearing silk scarves around his neck to hide the rope burns.

They had taken Ma James, too, and she didn't return until a couple of weeks later. She said they had made her take the Oath of Allegiance, but she told her family that giving an oath to ruffians and murdering swine wasn't like swearing with your right hand on the Good Book.

"I bring bad luck wherever I am," Cal told his birthing ma. "To whomever I'm with. That's my name. Cal—short for Calamity. I'm Calamity James."

She stared at him as she stirred a pot of stew on the stove, but said nothing. Jesse was walking around by then, ready to kill. But Ma James kept telling him that he, and Cal, were needed on the farm. The good doctor wouldn't be much help for the rest of the summer, and with Frank riding with Quantrill and killing as many Yankee vermin as possible, she couldn't spare any more sons to fight for the right cause.

But in August, after supper but before the moon rose, riders came to the James farm. Jesse held a big Dragoon. Ma stepped out with the single-shot, and Cal held the Enfield rifle. The only light shining came from behind them from the candles burning, and only Ma James stood in the door. Cal found a spot behind a post. Jesse was on the other side, maybe near the woodpile.

"It's Clell Miller, Mrs. James, ma'am," a voice in the darkness called. "Friend of Frank's."

"Anybody can say that," Ma James called back, "and it ain't just Clell Miller, unless my hearin's plumb gone or you're bringin' me a passel of good mounts that the bluebellies stole from us."

The speaker sounded like he was laughing.

"You're just as ornery as Frank said you are, Mrs. James," Clell Miller called out, and laughter echoed in the darkness. "No offense meant."

"Step into the light," Ma James said, "so I can blow you out of the saddle."

The speaker cleared his throat. "Frank said to tell you, 'Thou art my mother's glass and she in thee/Calls back the lovely April of her prime.'"

"What else did he say?"

"Shakespeare Sonnet Number Three."

Cal heard the click of a hammer being lowered, and then saw the shotgun pointing at the ground.

"You remembered that?" she asked.

The rider chuckled. "Well, Frank recited it so much I couldn't help but recall it all. And he told me that if you asked, I should just say 'Shakespeare Sonnet Number Three.'"

"Light down, Clell Miller, and whoever's riding with you."

Cal could tell that Clell Miller was no bluebelly. He wore the embroidered shirt of a Missouri Bushwhacker, with four revolvers that Cal could see, under both shoulders and on both hips. The hat was straw, the boots high, with the handle of a knife sticking out of the top of his right boot.

Zerelda Samuel nodded at Miller. Jesse and Cal slowly came into the light, Jesse keeping his eyes on Miller's four guns and Cal staring into the darkness.

"Frank wanted to know if you needed anything, ma'am," Miller said.

"We are making out all right. How is Frank?"

Miller shrugged. "Well, we have many supporters in western Missouri. Have some good hiding places that the Yankees don't know about. And we are planning on getting revenge for Osceola."

Cal's stomach almost turned over. He still felt partially responsible for what happened, though he hadn't given Jim Lane's red legs any information, and, undoubtedly, they would have found the right road to Osceola. But still . . .

"And," someone in the darkness added, "getting

retribution for what those coldhearted beasts did to your son, ma'am. And you. And your fine doctorin' husband."

"Where is Doc Samuel, ma'am?" Miller asked.

"In with our little ones," she said. "Do any of you need medical assistance?"

Miller gave a sad smile. "Not at this particular moment, Mrs. Samuel."

She nodded.

"But we do need assistance, just not—well, not of the medical nature, ma'am."

Cal grew suspicious. Jesse started to raise the heavy .44 revolver.

"We aim to sack the city of Lawrence, ma'am," Miller said. "Burn it to the ground."

Cal's heart felt like it would break his ribs, blow a hole through his chest.

Miller turned to Jesse. "You'd be Jesse," he said.

The boy nodded.

"Thought so. Yankees roughed you up, didn't they?"

"Not as much as they done my stepdad."

Miller smiled. "You learned how to handle that Dragoon, Dingus?"

"I can shoot the finger off any man I can see." Jesse then grinned. "Instead of taking off the top of my own finger."

Miller's head went up and down. "And Frank said there's another one here, one of the top shots in this part of the country—and I know a lot of men who can shoot better than most. Most of them are riding with Cap'n Quantrill."

Slowly, Cal stepped into the light.

"So you be the one they call Calamity James?"

Cal tried to make his head move, but it wouldn't co-operate. He stared at those guns on that one rider, a man who spoke with that twang of western Missouri but appeared to have an education. He certainly had a good memory, able to recite Shakespeare, even if it wasn't much of an oration. His mouth started to open, but a voice in the darkness spoke first.

"No. That's Cal Marmaduke."

Everyone turned toward the voice, and once again, saddle leather groaned in the night, a horse snorted and stamped its feet, and spurs chimed. The head was bowed, the large brim of a black hat shielding most of his face, but Cal could see the embroidery on the shirt, the pockets filled with cylinders for any of the revolvers he carried—all .44-caliber Army Colts.

A hand rose, and removed the hat, and Cal saw another face from his past. His Kansas past.

It was Aitken. The other of the dragoons who had befriended him. But the uniform of the United States Army was gone. And Cal knew that Aitken was not a spy for the Yankees. He was a Bushwhacker. Well, he had read about all of those Union officers and enlisted men who had left the American army and joined the Confederates.

"At least, that's the name he was using when he scouted and hunted for the Dragoons," Aitken said. "And he lived in Lawrence. With his mama. A handsome gal from Iowa. He's as Yankee as I've ever seen."

Miller stared at Cal, then turned back to Mrs. James.

"Ma'am? What do you know of this man?"

She turned and stared hard at Cal, then looked back at Miller. "He picked up Frank when he was walking back after my *oldest* son got sick with measles and captured by the Yankees." She made up a lie on the spot. "Said he knew my first husband, the late Reverend James. Said he was with him when poor Robert died. Said lots of things. So I taken him in as my own son." She turned and stared hard at Jesse. "Even called him my son." Then she looked back at Cal and spit in his face.

"But he ain't no relation to me. Or my good first husband, God rest his Christian soul."

For a long while, no one spoke. The wind dried the dribble on Cal's cheek and chin.

"Ma." Jesse broke the silence. Faces turned to the young teenager. "I'm going with them. I'm going to join up with Frank and Captain Quantrill."

Cal's birthing ma nodded. "I'd hoped to keep you, Jesse. But I reckon you've got to do what your heart tells you to do." Then she looked at Miller. "You won't let my baby die. Promise me that."

"Yes'm. You got my word. Jesse'll come back to you when we've driven the tyrants out of Missouri. So will Frank."

"And what about this one?" Aitken asked.

Clell Miller gave Cal a long stare.

"Ma'am," he said. "We'll be taking our leave. If you want to have some words with Jesse, you can do that while he's packing what he needs."

She nodded, and neither looked at Cal as they went

inside, though they left the door open to give them some light.

"We can't leave him," a voice drawled in the darkness. "He'll warn the folks in Lawrence."

"Warn the bluebellies in the whole state," someone said.

"Both states," another added.

Miller's head went up and down, and he turned to Cal.

Thunder rolled. Lightning flashed.

"Aitken," Miller said. "Take this Jayhawker to the neighbor's pasture. Catch up with us at the hideout. Remember where them wild hogs were?"

"Yeah."

Miller nodded again. "Them hogs'll likely take care of that body so that nobody would look for a bullet in his heart."

"Be my pleasure," Aitken said, and the cold eyes reaffirmed Cal that that ex-dragoon wasn't a Yankee spy pretending to be a Missouri Bushwhacker.

"You know the way, I reckon?" Aitken said.

Cal didn't answer. He stepped down and started walking, and heard Aitken's feet as he followed.

He could smell the rain in the air, and feel the electricity, the humidity. And his pounding heart.

When they reached the road to Centerville, he heard the loping horses, but Clell Miller and Jesse James and those other ruffians were not riding toward the neighboring farm and woods on the far side of the pasture.

Where wild hogs ran off most every critter. And had killed one dog, three cats, and countless hens.

Jesse had begged his mother to let him go kill those hogs, but they were on a neighbor's land and the neighbor was one of the few men in Clay County who remained loyal to the Union, and she feared Jesse or even Cal would be murdered.

Cal was walking, sweating, trying to figure out a play. Aitken's heavy breathing was all Cal heard. Cal knew he'd have to try something soon. Not that he would be successful. He just needed—

The flash blinded him, even though it came from behind, and he felt a searing heat that drove him into a ditch in the neighbor's field. He landed in water, rolled over, and—maybe he imagined it or maybe it really happened—but he felt as though he heard and felt hissing steam as the water doused the fire that burned through his shirt.

He thought he should just lay here in the ditch. Thunder—*or was it cannonfire?*—rolled. He reached for the blackness above him and cringed at the pain. His fingers clinched mud, then pulled down more earth that splashed in the water.

The rain had slackened, but still pelted his face. He expected to make out the outline of Aitken and see the flash of a rifle or revolver being fired, and then meet— he hoped—the Reverend James in heaven.

But all he saw was blackness. And then he felt nothing.

Until the dawn started to break.

* * *

He bit back pain when he made himself sit up in the ditch. His clothes were soaking wet. His hair felt like it all should be shorn. His back burned and when he rubbed the back of his head, parts of his hair felt like bristles. Somehow he managed to get to his knees, and then he saw what was left of Aitken.

"Lightning," he whispered, and wondered why the bolt hadn't killed him, just fried part of his back and singed his hair.

Well, that was the way things went with Calamity James. Bad things happened to those around him—he was grateful it had happened to Aitken.

"Traitor to the Union," Cal whispered, then wondered what he was. He answered his own question. "Bad luck."

He could see smoke rising from the James farm, and figured he needed to start making tracks. He didn't make it to Centerville before a Yankee patrol caught him.

And before he could tell the sergeant about Lawrence, someone clubbed him from behind, and he didn't wake up until he was in a cell in Kansas City. Where no one came to him until women were screaming and others cheering and Union soldiers cursing about Quantrill and his Missouri Bushwhackers who had burned Lawrence and killed many patriots.

Four more days passed before he was hauled to a Union major.

"Where are you from?" the major asked.

"Lawrence, Kansas," he said.

The major removed a monocle and frowned.

"This is no time for dark humor, boy. We're building gallows at this very moment."

"My mother is buried in Pioneer Cemetery," Cal said. "Charity Marmaduke."

The major stared, fingering the monocle. "And your father?"

"I don't know where he is."

Their eyes held, and suddenly the major grinned. He stood, reached into his holster, and pulled out an English-made revolver, then carefully removed the caps from the cylinder's nipples.

"Let's see how you handle a revolver, Kansas," the major said. He nodded at the painting of George Washington on the wall. Three armed soldiers stepped forward, one drawing a revolver and aiming it at Cal.

When the major frowned, the soldier with the Remington said, "Just in case he decides to bash your brains in, major, with your own six-shooter."

The major frowned.

Cal turned toward the painting, and aimed the revolver, just as he had been doing all his life. The arm moving in a circle, his thumb cocking the hammer on one pass, and his finger touching the trigger on the next.

No one could believe Cal's marksmanship, but the major decided that Cal was telling the truth—if he would enlist for the cause of the Union.

That was almost the end of September 1863. He joined a Union outfit, but led his squad into an ambush, where they were taken—by regular Confederates, not Bushwhackers—and imprisoned. He took an oath to the Confederacy and put on gray pants and a blouse that didn't fit.

He was captured at Fort Davidson in the fall of 1864, and when someone told the captain how Cal had been aiming a Springfield rifle before he was captured, the captain had Cal demonstrate. And everyone howled—since they wouldn't dare give any enemy soldier a loaded rifle—and the captain figured Cal to be a dunce and told him to take the oath of allegiance and say he'd be loyal to the Union—even though the captain was told by a sergeant that he, the sergeant, didn't think they were allowing oaths of allegiance anymore. But the captain said there was no use in spending money feeding and keeping a dunce in prison for the duration of the war.

Cal enlisted in the Union Army next and was captured less than a month later at Bryam's Ford in Jackson County—even though the Yankees won that affair—and a Confederate detail was sent to take the prisoners to some camp in Texas. But when they got out of Missouri, the Confederates told Cal and his ten fellow prisoners that they were done with this stupid war and were going home, and that the Yankees could go wherever they wanted to.

So Cal joined another Union outfit, but when the surgeon saw the scars on Cal's back from that lightning strike, and then the sergeant-major saw how Cal handled a revolver and a carbine, they both declared Cal was unfit to be a Union soldier and said, in jest, maybe he ought to try to enlist in a Johnny Reb outfit.

And Cal might have done that, but instead he drifted into Springfield, Missouri, near the end of 1864, and landed a job in a livery stable. And that's where he was when he heard the news that the war was over, that Lee had surrendered to Grant, and then all the other Rebel armies were giving up.

Then, when most of the Union supporters were cheering and Cal felt glad that the war was over, came word that President Lincoln had been assassinated, which was just a big word that meant murdered—and Cal felt sad, remembering that tall man who had gotten Cal a job on the Pony Express.

But he kept right on mucking stalls and learning how to shoe horses and feeding animals, and making a bed in hay so that it didn't really feel like you were sleeping in a barn with a bunch of horses owned by other people.

And then one morning a rider came in with long hair and a brace of Navy Colts.

And Cal blinked, stared harder, and asked, "Jim?"

And the man, who was sideways to Cal, turned fast, bringing up a Navy Colt quicker than a rattlesnake could strike. And just as quickly raised the barrel, lowered the hammer, and slid the weapon behind a pretty red sash.

"Cal?" Jim Hickok said, and he came over and squished Cal in a bear hug. And Cal was mightily glad that his back had healed from the heat of that lightning strike that fried Aitken like Ma James—and even Charity, Cal's birthing ma—burned bacon.

‑ PART THREE ‑

A BRIEF INTRODUCTION
TO A WOMAN
WHO WILL BECOME INTEGRAL
TO THIS NARRATIVE IN DUE TIME

CHAPTER 26

Texans would say that the only luck Catherine Eugenia Thorpe was that she was born in San Antonio—many years after the fall of the Alamo, so nobody could pin that on her—but that was the only time luck favored her. Folks who lived in Arkansas and Louisiana and New Mexico Territory and basically anywhere other than Texas would say that being a native Texan was just another piece of bad luck for that poor clumsy gal.

The author and editor and publisher of this narrative take no side in that particular debate.

It wasn't that Cat's luck soured to the point of disaster the way it had for poor Calvin Amadeus James/Marmaduke as a child. She was just, well, on the clumsy side.

She broke practically every dish her great-grandmother had left her mother, and plenty of earthen pots and coffee cups, till the Thorpes replaced all their dinnerware with blue-speckled enamel plates and bowls and tin cups. The cups would eventually be dented, but they still held water, tea, or coffee—and even hard cider or Joey Belgrade's harder spirits—just fine.

October 8, 1849, was not just the day Cat was born in that fine mecca of myriad cultures, the fabled Alamo, and a thriving metropolis with beautiful missions, dirt streets, and the best enchiladas anywhere, but also the very day her father became the second man imprisoned at Texas's new prison down in Huntsville.

There has become some debate over if the imprisonment was bad luck or good luck, but at least Eric Richard Thorpe didn't have the distinction of being the first prisoner in Huntsville.

With her mother frequently suffering from the grippe and other ailments, the de la Rosa twins and their mother usually cared for Catherine, and she soon could speak Spanish as well as the Mexican natives. When she was thirteen years old, she was a grand dancer at *bailes* and fandangos.

She could not cook. Dollars' worth of bacon, steak, eggs, cakes, pies, bread, mutton, cabrito, greens, carrots, tomatoes, grapes, soups, and posole were ruined, and Catherine's mother gave up on even letting Catherine butter bread by the time the girl was ten years old.

She could not sew. It was a wonder that she did not bleed to death as many times as she stuck her fingers and thumbs with needles or pins, and even cut her uncle's left palm so deep it required stitches. But that was her uncle's fault. He had grown fed up and bellowed, "Hand me those scissors, Cat, and I mean now!"

And if readers recall the earlier mention of the time—oh, 1847 or 1848, before Catherine was born—when Calvin Marmaduke was pitching horseshoes in a Fourth of July contest and busted a window pane at the Market House up in Iowa—Cat outdid him when she was pitching in a contest and threw a horseshoe that knocked the San Antonio mayor unconscious, bounded off his head, and caught Antonio Lopez in the ribs, and then landed on those trophy turkey eggs Ophelia Rhinehart was carrying to show Mrs. Milligan.

"That's what I'd call a ringer," said Sergeant Timothy O'Halloran, who could say things like that since he had been decorated by General Winfield Scott himself.

"And would have been a *dead* ringer if ol' Lockwood hadn't turned his noggin," J. M. Beck added.

Not much time passed before Catherine broke Joey Brant's foot while they were playing checkers, but no one should have really blamed that on Catherine because it was Joey who jumped up and said, "I'm gonna double-jump you, you dumb little girl," and landed wrong and on the wrong board, which busted, whereupon Joey turned the wrong way—the snap was mighty loud—and Joey went down screaming. And the schoolmaster came out and slipped on the checkers that had fallen onto the porch boarding at the schoolhouse, and the back of his head caught on one of the hard boards, not the rotten ones like the one that helped put a big cast and splint on the young fellow.

That's when the people in that part of San Antonio started calling Catherine "Clumsy Cat."

Before long, they even had a song they'd join in to sing whenever Catherine did something that was near catastrophic.

> *Who did that?*
> *Clumsy Cat*
> *Was that a prat?*
> *No, just Clumsy Cat*
> *Eggs go splat*
> *Cakes fall flat*
> *She's not a rat*
> *Just Clumsy Cat*

Merchants could be heard humming the tune whenever Catherine came into their stores, and probably crossed fingers behind their backs. Others might just be softly praying. Those were the English-speaking residents of San Antonio.

The Mexicans were much more polite. But they had their own name for Cat. That was *torpe*, which meant clumsy. "Torpe Thorpe" they'd call her, and she didn't mind that. After all, there was a bit of alliteration to it, and the Mexicans spoke everything in such melodic voices. And there was one thing that Catherine Thorpe truly loved: music.

Her mother thought Catherine would grow out of her clumsy period. Her mother said that she had been addle-brained when she was Cat's age, and that all children go through these kinds of awkward periods. Cat's mama recalled all those times when her parents and the mean old schoolmaster would paddle her hands with a yardstick because she couldn't quite make the numeral 4 not look like the numeral 9, but Cat's mama got better. Clumsy Cat's baby *a*'s always turned up backwards. That got to be such a problem that she would make only capital *A*'s, which looked odd when she had to put CAnAdA on the chalkboard when they were learning geography, and if she had to write the year 1859, it would be 1850nine.

But there was one thing Catherine Thorpe specialized in, and that was dancing. And there were *bailes* and fandangos and contests all across San Antonio when Catherine was growing up. Oh, how many Texas boys did Catherine dance with, all of them looking so young but brave in their uniforms of blue, gray, butternut, or rags from their farms or hovels. And she but twelve years old in 1861.

She never stepped on anyone's toes while waltzing. She could even waltz with a visitor from France or Spain or England, and those Europeans always wanted to turn right while Americans and Texans preferred to turn left. But when Catherine danced with a Frenchman, she never forgot to turn right, and when a Texan turned left, she did not misstep—"*¡Qué chiva!*" men and women, girls and boys, would cry out.

While dancing, anyway. Walking back to the table or line, there had been a number of trippings or slippings or running into someone because her partner couldn't take his eyes off Cat or because Cat just tripped on the hem of her dress. Or that time Peter Maloney turned three black cats loose on a dare.

She was taller than most girls her age—even taller than many older boys—and looked older than her true age. People—men *and* women—could not take their eyes off her when she was part of a quadrille. She could do the polka, the mazurka, the *zulma l'orientale*. She learned the schottische simply by watching those two Bohemians in the circus do it just once. Well, it really wasn't anything other than a polka, she explained, just slower.

Yes, she was a wonderful dancer. But dancing was about the only thing she did well—and who has ever heard of a *good* woman making a living dancing?

By 1863, when the war had turned bad for the Confederate states—even Texas, which was so far west it had been spared the bloodshed and horrors seen in Virginia, Tennessee, and, yes, even Missouri and Kansas. Oh, there were battles—Sabine Pass, Galveston, and other places—but most of Texas, and especially San Antonio, was spared.

Yet while those gallant soldiers were winning accolades and medals on the glorious fields like Shiloh, Gettysburg, Elkhorn Tavern, Chickamauga, Glorieta Pass, Wilson's Creek (and on goes that roll call of glory), the citizens of Texas suffered greatly. Prices soared so much, only the wealthy—or the smugglers— could afford coffee. Flour was hard to come by. There was little salt to be added to stews, and if the stews had any meat, it was typically squirrel or maybe ham before it spoiled. Men and women, boys and girls, lived off beans—with no salt for flavoring. Beans for breakfast. Beans for dinner. Beans for supper. Beans. Beans. Beans.

So people got sick. And Catherine's mother was one of those poor, wretched, kind Christian souls who took ill. Her mother passed away in her sleep on

April 9, 1865, the very day—glorious for the Union, horrific for most, but probably not all, who backed the Confederacy—that General Robert E. Lee surrendered to General Ulysses S. Grant, which pretty much ended the Civil War. (Texas would see one more battle, almost a month later, at Palmito Ranch—but that was practically in Mexico, a long way from San Antonio, and not much of a battle, from what Catherine read in the newspapers.)

But the young girl was now without a mother, and she had never known what became of her father, who did not come home after his ten-year sentence was over.

The landlord, a man with a slickened black mustache and long sideburns, took all of Catherine's mother's jewelry and the tinware as payment for rent that was owed, then held the door open and told Catherine he was truly sorry for her loss but he had rented the room to a lawyer.

The end of the war had changed everything in Texas. People feared that Yankees would come in and kill without mercy and without fear of prosecution. And here was a young girl, just fifteen years old and months before she would turn sixteen, with no home, no friends. The schoolmaster said he could not teach her since her mother had not paid the subscription for two years and he had to eat just like everyone else.

So Catherine wandered the streets of San Antonio, listless, hopeless. But then she heard a beckoning . . . and was drawn to the music in a vacant lot where a tent had been set up and men and women were dancing. She read the sign:

10¢ a Twirl

And handwritten below that beautiful script, a much cruder:

Gold, Silver, Union or Mex Money ONLY
ABSOLUTELY NO TEXAS
oR CONFEDERATE SCRIP

She watched Mexicans and Americanos dancing.

The fiddler was a woman who knew how to play. The pianist looked older than Methuselah, but he could tickle the ivories. A man with a wooden leg and one empty sleeve—pinned up, a Confederate shell jacket missing all of its buttons and stained with just about anything a person could imagine—banged a tambourine against his real leg.

The song ended. The women scurried away. The men ran to drop in their money and dance again.

"Missy," a voice breathed behind her, and she turned to look at a man in a black suit, black vest, black pants, a thick black mustache, and very black eyes, who was smiling at her. He tugged on the left end of his mustache. "What brings a pretty lady like you to this side of San Antone?"

"The music," she said.

He nodded. "My band ain't bad."

Now one of the men dancing let out some cusswords that would have made Catherine blush had she not heard the schoolmaster cut loose with many when Jimmy Walsh put a snake in his lunch pail.

"She—stepped—on—my—foot!" he screamed, as he hopped around. The others stopped dancing, except one short guy with a gangly tall woman, and that woman kept swinging him around like they were in a square dance, even though the music had been a waltz.

"Don't you have some good dancers?" another man yelled.

"What do you expect?" someone in the crowd shouted. "He's only takin' Yankee money!"

Catherine started backing up once the revolvers and knives came out of pockets. Most of the women fled. The man in black tried to, but the Texans caught up with him and brought him back. And Catherine saw her first tar-and-feathering.

But she also saw something else. Something she needed.

An opportunity.

That's how Catherine "Torpe" Thorpe got a job with Withersteen's Dancing Emporium. He probably would have hired her anyway, but she was the one who knew how to get tar and feathers off a man without skinning him alive. And she knew the right amount of salve to use because she knew what doctor to ask, and that wasn't the one who had treated her late mother.

Still, Mr. Withersteen wasn't in condition to do much other than moan and beg for whiskey, but the one-legged tambourine player knew how to hitch a team and keep the wagon moving, and the two women that didn't quit after seeing their first tar-and-feathering, kept their distance from Catherine.

They drifted north. Following what was called the Sedalia Trail. Mr. Withersteen decided that towns weren't a good place for this traveling dancing emporium, but cow camps were.

With the war over, some ranchers with not just cow savvy but financial savvy heard that Yankees wanted beef. They couldn't drive to Missouri because Missourians had grown sick of something called Texas fever that left Missouri cattle dead. But somebody had mentioned a town in Kansas, Baxter Springs.

So Withersteen told One-Legged Dirk to take them to Baxter Springs. Then he looked at Catherine.

"Can you dance, girl?"

Before she could answer, he told the fiddler to play "Lorena." "Let's see you waltz."

"I don't have a partner," she told him.

"Pretend you have one."

So she pretended. The fiddler stopped after two verses. "Glory," she whispered. "She's like a goddess."

"You need a job?" Mr. Withersteen asked.

Now Catherine was just about sixteen years old, though she looked twenty-one, and she was a good girl, but she knew things. And in a town like San Antonio, she had heard all types of stories.

"All you have to do is dance," Mr. Withersteen said. "Dance."

Which is all Catherine wanted to do, so she nodded, and Mr. Withersteen seemed to turn twenty years younger.

— PART FOUR —

TRAVELS OF A WANDERING JINX

1865–1882

CHAPTER 27

Jim Hickok's hair was longer now, his mustache thicker, his face darker, but his eyes still bright and full of mischief. Cal couldn't help but sniff. Jim Hickok smelled like—

"Perfume," Hickok said, and brushed his curly locks. "After all that war, I wanted to get the stink of death out of my nostrils. The barber recommended it." He sniffed himself. "Guess it is a mite on the strong side."

He had two Navy Colts stuck in his sash.

"You look to be a man of prosperity," Cal said.

Hickok shrugged. "Sometimes. Been gambling. Come on, pardner, let's have ourselves some grub and chew the fat."

Hickok had been a scout and a spy for the Union during the recent unpleasantness.

"Avoided most of the big fights," he said, as he sipped a whiskey in a saloon on the city square. "Except for one in Arkansas. Elkhorn Tavern, the Rebs called it. Pea Ridge if it's a Union man telling the story." He winked. "Since I was a spy, I can call it both names." The whiskey vanished, and he snapped his fingers. A man hurried and refilled Hickok's glass. Cal had hardly touched his.

"What did you do in the war?" Hickok asked.

Cal chuckled. "I became an expert on getting captured," he said. "Captured. Paroled. Captured. Paroled."

Hickok smiled. He snapped his fingers and started on his third—or it might have been his fourth—whiskey. "What brings you to Springfield?" Hickok asked.

Cal shrugged. "Just drifting."

Hickok nodded. "Lot of ex-soldiers are doing that, North and South. Heading west, most of them. To see the elephant. That's what we said in the war. See the elephant. You know what that meant?"

Cal nodded. "I saw the elephant. Tasted battle. But I didn't see nothing like Pea Ridge."

Hickok finished his whiskey, but this time he turned the glass upside down. "I didn't see anything that could compare to Shiloh—Pittsburg Landing, the Rebs called it. Or Antietam, Gettysburg. Guess we were lucky being in this part of the country."

"Lawrence," Cal said softly.

Hickok frowned. "Yeah. Well, that was a dark, awful day for Kansas."

"Yes, I reckon it was."

"Well, pard, there is no need in getting maudlin. The war's over. We're alive. Living is good. And the cards have been running good. Sure beats working for Russell, Majors and Waddell. And see the elephant now has a new meaning. To see new country. There's always something better over the next hill."

Cal smiled at that notion. Then he snapped his fingers. "That reminds me. What did Dave McCanles want to see you about?"

Hickok's eyes went cold. He turned the whiskey glass right side up and snapped his finger. The sweating barkeep quickly came out to add a splash, but Hickok said, "To the rim. And leave the bottle." The barkeep obeyed. He seemed to sigh with relief when he stood behind the bar.

"McCanles." Hickok's voice was a dry whisper. He sipped half the whiskey from the glass and kept staring at Cal.

"When I had to quit the Pony Express," Cal said. "Dave and some of those ruffians who hung around him asked me if I had seen you. I was riding east to get to the road to Lawrence. You know. After my ma had died. You were back at the station."

"You don't know?"

Cal didn't know what Hickok meant.

"You didn't read about it in the papers? You didn't see that five-penny dreadful?"

Cal's head shook slowly.

Then Hickok's face softened. He killed the remaining whiskey and laughed heartily. Color returned to his cheeks.

"Son of a gun, Cal, you might be the only person west of the Mississippi who hasn't heard of Wild Bill's Duel With Death!"

He swung around and found the bartender. "Jake,"

Hickok cried, and when the bartender reached toward a bottle on the back bar, Hickok shouted. "I've got half a bottle here, Jake. Not whiskey." He snapped his finger. "Bring that half-dime novel over here. And while you're at it, a glass of pilsner for my pard."

THE AMAZING BUT AUTHENTIC
AND TURE STORY
OF
WILD BILL HICKOK'S
DUEL WITH DEATH;
OR, The TERRIBLE
BUT GLORIOUS & JUST END
Of THE MacCANDLASS GANG.

By Colonel Horatio L. Delmont

"Ture?" Cal pointed to the main title on the cover.

Hickok grinned. "Delmont said that was what they call a typographical error. Supposed to read 'True.' But I figure, since their ain't a smidgen of truth to found in this thing, it was done on purpose."

"Well," Cal said. "That Delmont sure is consistent."

"Huh?"

"Nothing," Cal smiled, and picked up the novel for a closer look.

There was a likeness of Hickok on the cover, holding a girl, her bodice ripped off one shoulder, behind her, as he fended off about six men—two others on the floor—

and another woman fleeing a saloon. The men facing Hickok were armed with sabers, bowie knives, shotguns, revolvers, one pitchfork, and one, an Indian with a mohawk and paint on his cheeks, a feathered lance.

Cal looked up. "Bill?"

The handsome man shrugged. "Names don't matter west of the Mississippi, Cal. You know that. I answer to Bill these days. Answer to Jim, too. I've been called worse—but not by the same fellow twice."

Cal looked back at the book. There was that colonel fellow, the same name of that rascal who had made up all sorts of nonsense about Calamity James, once again making up mostly lies. The same scoundrel who couldn't spell *true*. Only this time he didn't have someone, like Captain Shufflebottom, telling him what he recalled (or made up). Cal sure would like to meet that Delmont dude one of these days. He'd give him an earful and then maybe even challenge him to a duel.

Seeing that look on Cal's face, Hickok laughed. He tapped the cover. "That wasn't the first one of these dreadfuls. And this Delmont gent pretty much stole a lot of it from every other crazy gent with pencil and paper, none of whom was in Nebraska at the time, and most who'd never ever heard of Rock Creek Station."

When Cal turned the page, Hickok put his hand on Cal's and shook his head. "Don't waste your eyesight—mine's getting bad enough—reading a mess of lies, Cal."

Cal pulled his hand away from the booklet, which Hickok dragged back and stuck inside his coat pocket.

"I guess I owe it all to you. Teaching me how to shoot."

That left Cal feeling like he had been hit with a pole ax.

"I couldn't do all that spinning stuff." He raised his right arm and let it move around in circles. "But the sighting. Seeing your target. Making it true. That stuck with me. Saved my hide against mean Dave. Saved my hide a few times in the war."

"Well . . ." It was the only word Cal could think of.

They left the saloon and found a restaurant, where Hickok insisted on paying for supper. He said he was having a string of luck playing poker, and after supper would take Cal to his hotel room, where he could sleep and stay as long as he wanted.

"Where will you sleep?" Cal asked.

"I'm off to a gambling parlor. That's how I've been making my money these days, since the Army doesn't have need for any scouts these days. I won't be back till daylight. Then I'll sleep to noon or into the afternoon. It's not like they ever clean these rooms till folks move out."

They walked to the hotel, and Hickok was about to open the door, when a voice called out, "Duck Bill."

Hickok spun fast, and his right hand gripped the butt of one of his Colts. Cal spun, too, and saw a man grinning—a revolver hanging on his right hip—but his hands spread wide.

"Tutt," Hickok said, but kept his hand on the .36. "You call me Duck Bill again, and you'll rue the day."

"Who's your shadow?" the man asked.

"He ain't my shadow. We were pards during my Pony Express days."

Cal cleared his throat. "Name's Cal. Cal—" He paused.

The man laughed again. "That explains it." He raised his hand off the pistol and pointed at Cal. "He's a dummy. No wonder he'd be hanging out with a tinhorn like you."

"Withdraw that comment, Tutt. And apologize to my pard."

The air had turned humid. Cal saw a few people standing on the other side of the street, some frozen, others moving as fast and as far away from the hotel as they could.

"I'm just joking, Bill," Tutt said, but his eyes still danced with merriment and his tone was mocking. Tutt nodded at Cal. "Just funning you, Mr. Cal." He looked back at Hickok. "I'll see you at the poker table later tonight. Bring that watch of yours. I aim to win it off you."

He gave one more nod, then turned. But Hickok did not let his hand move off the Colt's grip until he was on the other side of the square.

"I'm going to have to kill Dave Tutt one of these days." Hickok pulled the door open, and held it for Cal, who moved inside the hotel.

The door closed, and Hickok nodded at the stairs.

"And that day is coming soon."

* * *

"What are your plans?" Hickok asked, two nights later.

Cal had found some work at the hotel, mostly bringing down laundry for the women and two Chinese men to work on and hauling chamber pots and emptying them in the privies behind one of the liveries. He hadn't told Jim, er, Bill Hickok that, but he did pay for their breakfast—or what Wild Bill Hickok called breakfast—one afternoon.

"I don't know." He sighed. "Nobody seems to need a hunter these days. Not in Springfield. I guess I'll mosey along, Bill. But I sure appreciate your friendship."

"Shucks, Cal. I might be tending livery or freighting for some other company if you hadn't sent Dave McCanles over to see me." He chuckled. Cal frowned. "I owe you." He pulled some bills from his vest pocket and slid them over.

"No," Cal said.

"Yes." Hickok's eyes brightened. "It's just a loan, pardner."

Cal noticed something was missing from Wild Bill's vest.

"Where's your fancy watch?" he asked.

The eyes and face hardened and Bill straightened in his chair. "I'll get it back." He shrugged. "Cards didn't go so good last night." After another shrug, he repeated: "I'll get it back."

They sipped coffee, and Bill nodded toward the door. "You want some advice?"

"Sure," Cal said.

"Texas."

Cal blinked.

"Beef. Longhorns."

Cal thought Hickok had lost his mind. Maybe he was still drunk from last night.

"You wouldn't know it, but Springfield here saw a fair amount of Texas beef coming up this way before the war—and a few herds during the war. That was illegal, of course. Texas being a Confederate state and Missouri still in the Union. It's died down some, the cattle business, here, but Baxter Springs"—he pointed east—"just over the border and right on the line separating Kansas from the Indian Territories, that's seeing some cattle. Texas cattle."

Cal laughed. "I don't know anything about cattle."

"You don't have to know a thing. You just have to ride a horse and keep the cattle moving. And I know you can ride a horse. You can ride a horse almost as good as you can shoot the lights out with anything, pistol or long gun. If you put your mind to it, you might even outshoot me."

Cal laughed. "No. I've seen you practice."

"Well, if I were you, I'd stick to cattle. Not gunfighting. That's one thing I regret about having all those stupid stories coming out about Wild Bill Hickok, prince of the pistoleers. I've had to knock two punks over the head with my Navies over the past three days. That or shoot 'em, and I'm particular about who I shoot."

Cal smiled. "Texas," he said.

Hickok nodded. "Just a thought."

"Well, I've never seen Texas."

Both men rose. "You still ain't got enough cash money to get your horse out of that livery." Without waiting, Hickok slid another roll of bills across the table.

"Bill, I can't."

"Sure you can. Pay me back next time our paths cross." He held out his hand. "They will cross again, I hope."

They shook, and Wild Bill Hickok took one of the bills off the table and smiled. "I'll buy our breakfast with this." He walked to the waiter and handed him the bill, then went into the hotel bar.

So Cal went upstairs, gathered his meager belongings—and left a few of Bill's dollars on the dresser. He took just enough to pay his debts and maybe get him down to Texas. The idea of cattle had some appeal to him, and he had heard a lot of stories about Texas.

At the livery, he paid his fee, and mounted his horse, and rode away. He was on the other side of the square, passing a small saloon, when he heard a familiar voice call out, not his name, but "Hey, Wild Bill's pard."

Cal reined up and turned to see Dave Tutt step onto the street.

"Where's your pard, kid?"

Cal noticed the watch. Tutt was checking the time—or maybe just showing off Wild Bill's watch—and he let it slide back into his vest pocket.

"I want to show him something," Tutt added.

Maybe, Cal thought, Tutt had won the watch Hickok had lost gambling and wanted to sell it back to him. Or give it back to him. No. Tutt didn't want to give Hickok anything.

"C'mon, kid. I don't have all day. I'll see him tonight. I just don't want to wait that long."

Cal sighed. He tilted his head. "He's probably in the hotel," Cal said.

"Much obliged." Tutt started walking, but stopped and turned, studying Cal and his horse. "You leavin' Springfield?"

Cal nodded. "Bound for Texas."

The response sounded like a snort. "Too bad. You'll miss the show."

Cal didn't care about any shows. He wanted to see what this Texas was all about.

He was just outside of Springfield when he heard the shots. Which might have been one shot with an echo, they were so close together. It sort of reminded him of the time when he was riding out of Nebraska, and McCanles and some of his pals were headed to Rock Creek Station. Looking back over his shoulder, Cal almost reined around, but the horse resisted, and Cal figured it was just telling him that they were going to Texas.

So he rode southwest.

CHAPTER 28

Cal was disappointed when he rode in. He didn't think Jim—er, Wild Bill Hickok had played a joke on him, but there wasn't much to the settlement. Even calling Baxter Springs a "settlement" was a stretch. "Town" would be an outright lie.

What he remembered about Baxter Springs was during the late war, when Quantrill's raiders—maybe with Frank James, or even Jesse—ambushed Union soldiers near here. The federals had established a post called Fort Blair, but more commonly called Fort Baxter. A hundred Union soldiers had been shot down.

But the war was over, Cal told himself.

There was a man shoveling near the road, so Cal reined up and said, "Howdy."

The man jammed the shovel into some stinking mud and nodded.

"I was looking to hire on to a cattle outfit?" It came out as a question.

The man blinked.

"Cattle?"

Cal nodded. "Yes, sir. Texas cattle. On the Shawnee Trail?"

"Yeah. Cattle come through here. Texas cattle. But they hardly stop except to soak in the springs."

Cal looked perplexed.

"The drovers soak. Not the cattle."

Cal nodded. That would have been something to see. Cattle soaking in springs. Not cowboys.

"None been through yet. Hope they don't. It'll interfere with my mining."

"Mining?"

"Coal."

That was the smell.

"You can just dig it up." He pulled off his gloves and stared at his hands, then looked up at Cal. "Now, if you want to hire on as a coal digger, I might could use some help."

But Cal had smelled enough, and he had seen the blisters—those that had popped and those that were just forming—and he also saw the piddling pile of coal behind the farmer.

"No, but thank you. I guess I just want to see what this cowboying is all about."

The man shrugged. "Well, like I said, the cattle don't stop. Keep right on goin'. Kansas City. Springfield. St. Louey. And all from Texas. Now, folks keep saying that a railroad will come through sometime, and then we'll be livin' in hawg heaven, and Baxter Springs will boom. But you don't want to wait that long, do you, sonny?"

Cal was smiling as his head shook.

"Iffen you want to join a trail herd, I'd suggest you go south. Find some Texan who'll give you a job." He looked around. "We might get a railroad one day. Wouldn't that be something? Wouldn't have to haul my coal to sell in Fort Scott."

"Texas," Cal said.

The man pointed. "Just foller that trail. As long as you see cow dung, you ain't lost."

Cal thanked the man and rode a few yards when the fellow shouted out a string of curses. "I'm snakebit," he yelled. Cal turned the horse around and loped back, pulling the Enfield rifle.

His horse reared, and Cal leaped off. Somehow he landed on his feet, and brought the stock of the rifle to his shoulder.

"Rattler!" the man said. "But he didn't rattle." The man backed away fast, holding his left arm. "Well, shoot that serpent."

The barrel started spinning.

"What the Sam—?"

The rifle roared, and the snake's head vanished. And Cal's horse loped off another two hundred yards.

After laying the rifle in the grass, Cal hurried to the man, who was already cutting the fang marks with a pocket knife, then sucking and spitting, sucking and spitting. Cal pulled off his bandanna and fashioned a sling, and the coal miner thanked him, slapped some chewed tobacco on the bloody marks, and slid his arm into the sling.

Then they walked to the dead snake.

"His head is blowed clean off," the man marveled. He turned to Cal and cocked his head. "You always shoot like that?"

Cal shrugged.

The man shook his head, let out a sigh, and stared at the snake. He pointed with his good hand.

"Ain't got no rattles. That's how come he snuck up on me. No rattles." He sighed. "That's my luck. Get bit because a snake lost its rattles."

"You want me to find you a doctor?" Cal asked.

"In Baxter Springs?" The man laughed. "Good luck findin' a sawbones between Fort Scott and Dallas, pardner." He smiled. "I'll be fine, kid. This is the sixth rattler to bite me, and I ain't dead yet."

So Cal left him, and headed for Texas.

The trail led straight through the Indian Territory, but he saw no cattle herds. He did run into a party of Cherokees, and while he didn't think they would do him any harm, Cherokees being one of the Five Civilized Tribes, he thought they might charge him a toll. And one of them appeared to be doing just that till an old-timer rode up and started speaking to him in what Cal assumed was the Cherokee tongue, pointing hard at Cal, and shaking his head hard. Two of the Cherokees in that bunch turned their horses around and loped up the hill and out of sight. One of them made the sign of the cross—Cal figured he had been converted by some missionary—and backed his horse a good fifty yards behind the rest of the party.

Eventually, the rest of the bunch loped off up that same hill the other two had climbed, leaving only the holy man and the one fifty yards down the trail.

Cal figured he was free, so he told the holy man, "Much obliged, sir," and the holy man did not blink or speak but just stared, while the horse stamped its feet and snorted. And as Cal got closer to the other one, that Cherokee quickly turned his horse and galloped off away from the other Cherokees and toward the Creek Nation.

The skies were threatening as Cal crept down toward McAlester's Store, near one of the Canadian rivers—with Texas still south—and saw a decrepit wagon coming up the trail. And, by golly, if someone in the back of that wagon wasn't playing a banjo and another a jaw harp. Cal hadn't heard much music in a long time.

The driver stopped the wagon and held out his right hand. And Cal waved back, and let his horse walk to the wagon.

"Howdy," said the driver.

Cal stared. People climbed out of the wagon. Cal stared.

"My name's Withersteen. This is my Dancin' Emporium. We're on our way to set up and let the good folks of Baxter Springs dance to their heart's content. Can you tell me how far we are from Baxter Springs?"

Cal stared.

The man waited.

Cal stared.

"I say, son, but how far are we from Baxter Springs?"

A gent with a tambourine sighed and leaned against the side of the wagon, then fanned himself with his tambourine. He only had one leg.

Cal stared. But not at the missing leg. Or the tambourine. Or the woman, a pretty gal, holding the fiddle down in her left hand and the bow down in her right.

"Baxter Springs, son?" the driver said. The driver had a face that looked like it had been torn up with something harsh, and his hair was missing parts above his right ear and on the left side, and he just looked to have been dipped in acid or something.

"Baxter Springs?" the driver asked.

Cal blinked. Nothing had changed.

And then that lovely creature who sat next to the ugly driver, that most beautiful gal that Cal had ever seen, sighed, and leaned forward and said, "How far away are we from Baxter Springs, mister?"

She had spoken to Calamity James.

Cal's heart skipped a few beats. And the woman repeated, "Baxter Springs?" And the woman fiddler, who was handsome in her own right, said, "Maybe he's deaf."

Something snapped in Cal's brain, and he mumbled an apology, turned, and pointed.

"By my reckoning," he said, "I left there, oh, four days ago, I reckon. Baxter Springs. Reckon it'd take you a bit longer, wagon and all, and—"

He forgot what the goddess had asked him.

"Thank you."

He almost toppled out of his saddle. The goddess had spoken to him. Not just spoken to him. She had *thanked* him.

"So," the goddess said. "Five days, six, seven at the most?"

His lips parted, but he could find no voice. He was not worthy. He should not speak to a woman that beautiful. So he looked at the one-legged dude with the tambourine.

"About that. If the rivers aren't flooding."

The driver of the wagon spoke. "And what about these red Indians?"

Cal stared.

The goddess translated for Cal. "And what about these Indians?"

Cal nodded. "You're in the Choctaw Nation now, miss." He waited for her to correct him and say, "Ma'am," but she didn't say "Ma'am." She didn't say anything. Just looked at him.

"They haven't bothered me."

"Thank you," the woman said. "You've been very kind."

And the troupe started climbing back into the wagon.

He opened his mouth, but stopped himself. It would have been glorious to volunteer to escort this beautiful woman and her troupe to Baxter Springs, but he could not speak again. He wanted the last words said to be hers.

You've been very kind.

He smiled. *She thinks I'm kind.* He nodded. *Well, I am kind.*

He felt the sun on his face, and when he looked up, he saw that those dark clouds were gone. The day was sunny. The clouds had moved far to the east.

The wagon crept forward. Cal removed his hat and bowed.

The woman, that marvelous creature, smiled at him.

Cal sat straighter in the saddle. He heard the mules bray and the wagon wheels squeak, and his horse stamped a hoof to let him know he was sick and tired of waiting here. But Cal just pictured that lovely woman, and finally he summoned up enough nerve to turn the horse a bit and look up the Shawnee Trail.

The woman was leaning over the side, looking back, staring at Cal.

He tipped his hat at her.

He imagined that she smiled again, but couldn't be certain, yet she did not jerk back and out of view. She kept looking at him for another ten or twenty seconds. Then she gave him a short wave, and vanished from his view.

Cal whistled pretty much until he reached the ferry at the Red River.

Finding a job on a cattle drive, Cal learned when he stopped in Denison, would be hard this late in the season. Most of the herds were already heading north. The boy selling newspapers in front of the hotel seemed to know what he was talking about.

"But," the boy said, "I know a feller who could probably use you."

That's how Cal hooked up with Slick Willie, who had a wagon with lots of paintings on its side and crates of bottles in the back. Slick Willie sold those bottles for a dollar each, and the elixir inside those bottles was sure to cover ailments, including plenty that Cal had never heard of—and that was because, Slick Willie said, he, William Beaufort Putnam, had created those diseases.

Cal didn't know how, or why, someone would create a disease, but Slick Willie paid him a nickel for every bottle he sold.

By Cal's counting, he had earned thirty-two dollars and fifteen cents by the time they had stopped at Sherman. That's as far as they got because that's where Slick Willie got tarred and feathered. They wanted to tar Cal, too, but didn't have enough, so they just rode him out of town on a rail. And that's when Cal came to expect that that fellow in that wagon with that beautiful girl might have been tarred and feathered himself.

Cal got most of the tar and stuff off Willie, then decided to quit the snake-oil business. So did Slick Willie, now that he had learned how painful hot tar is on one's body. Slick Willie went back to Arkansas to visit his mother. Cal joined a gambler name Perkins who went to Dallas, and taught Cal the ins and outs of poker.

McKinney was where Perkins got caught cheating, and Cal barely escaped that saloon, that town, that county with his life. He feared that Perkins had been lynched, or shot dead and thrown into a garbage heap, but Cal ran into Perkins in 1867 and was glad to see him alive, even if there were a couple of spots on his head where his hair hadn't grown back and one gaping hole in his beard for the same reason: that the McKinney folks used quite a lot of tar and not that many feathers.

Other jobs came and went. Swamping saloons. Clerking in a mercantile. Freighting. Chopping cotton. Swamping saloons again. Serving as a jailer in Dallas. Serving time in a jail in Fort Worth.

Then Cal tried scouting for the Army at Fort Richardson in Jacksboro, but that didn't last long, either.

"Son," the lieutenant in charge of the scouts said, "I've got an eight-year-old daughter who can hold a rifle steadier than you can."

He figured if they had let him at least pull the trigger they would have shut up, but Army officers did not have much patience.

So Cal drifted back to Fort Worth, and that's where a trail boss found Cal breaking horses in a corral. And the trail boss asked Cal, "You want a job workin' for me?"

And Cal said, "What's the job?"

And the trail boss said, "Herdin' twenty-five hunnerd beeves to Kansas."

And Cal asked, "To Baxter Springs?"

And the trail boss said, "Son, ain't much action at Baxter Springs right now. Not for longhorn cattle nohow. How does Abilene suit you?"

And Cal didn't know anything about Abilene, except that Abilene wasn't Baxter Springs. But the only reason he even remembered Baxter Springs was because that's where that fellow with that lovely dancing gal said they were going, and that had been a long while ago. That gal was probably long gone. He'd never see her again. And even if he did, she would probably lose all her teeth, and her hair would fall out. That's how Cal's luck seemed to go. Besides, the trail boss was offering him a cowboying job. So he said, "Suits me fine."

And the trail boss held out his hand and said, "Pay's a dollar a day. Ten dollar bonus if the herd gets more than thirty-five a head. My name's Gus."

And Cal liked the man's handshake. "My name's—"

But the guy whose right wrist had been broken when he wasn't looking where he was going and tripped over Cal's feet when Cal was taking a break and stretching his legs in front of the Green Elephant Saloon shouted out: "His name's Calamity. Calamity James."

There wasn't much to the job. Cal's horses—he had six in his string, and he'd go through two or three a day and night, since he didn't think Gus would ever let him sleep—weren't hard buckers, but they would make him pay attention, especially in the mornings.

He only caused one stampede, and that was the first morning when the sorrel practically jumped to the moon as soon as Cal's butt hit the saddle, and on the fourth jump, Cal went flying onto the chuckwagon, scattering tin plates and cups and forks and spoons all over the place—that was the racket that sent those longhorn steers heading back the way they'd come from.

Gus gave Cal a good chewing out four hours later, saying they would have to drive these cattle over the same trail they'd come up yesterday, and Gus wasn't a man who liked to see the same trail twice.

But the wrangler, a kid maybe fifteen years old with sandy hair and freckles and two missing front teeth, told Gus that it wasn't Cal's fault. That somebody had stuck a cocklebur under the saddle blanket and that's what set that gelding to bucking like there was no tomorrow.

Gus didn't apologize to Cal for blaming him for the stampede, but he drew his pistol and aimed it at all of his cowboys, even the wrangler, and said that if a cocklebur got found under another saddle, he'd shoot everyone till someone confessed.

Which didn't strike Cal as logical or fair or legal, but he wasn't about to tell Gus that.

There were stampedes—seven of them, but that included the one caused by the cocklebur—three of them in the middle of the night, spooked by coyotes once, thunder once, and Ben Whitaker's sneeze—Ben rode drag with Cal, and all that dust that drag riders breathed in, even with bandannas pulled up over the men's mouths and noses, it's a wonder more sneezes and coughs didn't cause more stampedes. A rattlesnake caused another stampede. Nobody knew what caused the rest, but Ben Whitaker suggested that by that time—the herd was already in Kansas—those dogies were just used to running.

It was the worst drive Gus said he'd ever had, and he had driven cattle, before the late unpleasantness, to St. Louis, and during the war, to Confederate troops in Mississippi, to Union troops, also in Mississippi—but that was just because Union money was worth a whole lot more than Confederate scrip by 1865.

Things got ticklish when three Kansas farmers held up the drive because the herd that had gone through there three days earlier killed Karl Potash's milk cow with Texas fever.

But Gus prevented another stampede by clubbing the big-mouthed leader with the barrel of his revolver instead of shooting them all dead. Every other drover, including the wrangler and Ben Whitaker, drew their weapons—the wrangler just had a slingshot—and the other farmers turned and ran away. And the herd reached Abilene in mid-July.

They bedded down the herd south of town, and rode into town the next morning.

"It's growed a lot since last year," Gus said.

It certainly was much bigger than Baxter Springs, the last time Cal had been there.

"Noisier, too," said point rider Cat Ketchum.

Shots rang out as two cowboys came racing their horses right down the street, firing their six-shooters in the air, which caused Cal's horse to start bucking, which caused Gus's horse to buck, and when Gus fell into a pile of mud mixed with horse apples, one of the cowboys slid his horse to a sliding stop, and turned and laughed like a wildcat. The other cowboy slowed his horse, turned it around and rode right back to the fellow he was racing—Cal assumed it was racing—and that was the one Gus shot. But only after the second rider called Gus a dirty name.

Gus only winged the guy, but the bullet went through the flesh part of his arm and smashed a window in a saloon and, if the saloon owner wasn't a liar, busted a whiskey bottle and then smashed into a keg of beer. And the frightened fellow who had to wear a badge this week was scared more of the cowboys in the saloon than he was of Gus, because the cowboys in the saloon were mad about the loss of one keg of beer and one bottle of whiskey. No one cared about the cowboy Gus had shot in the arm, except the cowboy himself, but when Gus said he'd pay for all the damages and buy everyone some drinks, the animosity disappeared, and everyone went into the saloon.

The next day, a buyer came out to the camp to look over Gus's beeves, and they haggled a bit before they agreed on a price, then Cal and the other hands saddled up and drove the longhorns to the Great Western Stockyards—and Cal had never seen that many cattle in one place in all his days.

That evening, Gus paid off all the hands, thanked them, even Cal, for their hard work, and told them he'd be hiring next spring at that gathering spot south of San Antonio.

And Cal stared at those bills and coins in his hands, and quickly shoved them into his pockets before the wind blew the notes all the way to Denver or he dropped the coins into the mud.

And the men asked about the horses, and Gus said he would sell them one from their string for five dollars, and that was fine with them, except for the wrangler and two others, who decided they'd take the train somewhere, and Ben Whitaker, who said he didn't need a horse because some cowboy broke his leg and Ben Whitaker had hired out to take that cowhand's place on account of that trail boss planned to push on to Kansas City.

And Cal not only had to buy a horse, the dun, not the bucking sorrel, but also a saddle, bridle, and saddle blanket, and all the other hands swore and sighed and said one of these days they were going to bring their own horses to the roundup, but Mescal Juan, a swing rider, said, "No, the boss will not allow any horse except those that he provides." Four of the men said they had left their horses at Gus's ranch, and Mescal Juan said they had better save some money, because there would be a bill waiting for them for grass and grain back in Pleasanton.

So nobody was sorry to see Gus go, but Cal was sorry he had not asked Ben Whitaker if that boss driving some steers to Kansas City needed another hand, but then Mescal Juan suggested to Cal and some others who looked to be down in spirit that he knew of a good place to drown their sorrows and shake a leg and give a pretty gal a twirl on the dance floor.

And Cal could not believe his eyes when he saw that goddess from that Withersteen fellow's band of musicians and dancers he had met on the trail in the Creek Nation a few years back. What had that Withersteen called his group. A Dancing Emporium?

Must have changed the name. Because the sign above the awning read: $1 A DANCE.

Which seemed to be a lot of money for a dance, but this was Abilene, and a dollar a dance would be well worth a twirl on the floor with that beautiful gal.

Somebody shoved Cal, who took a few stumbles but didn't fall. "Get out of my way, buster. I see me a filly that I'm gonna show how to dance."

Cal didn't even look at the guy. He straightened and saw the woman who had been going to Baxter Springs. She saw him. Their eyes met. Held. Another pair of hands shoved him forward, and Cal managed to stop before he ran into a cowboy talking to a redheaded dancer, and when Cal turned around to give the fellow who had shoved him a dirty look, he saw the grinning face of Mescal Juan, who held a dark-skinned, black-haired thin little gal in his left arm.

Mescal Juan laughed, but the band started playing, and he and the black-haired dancer went to twirling.

When Cal turned back around, the gal who had been with Mr. Withersteen's Dancing Emporium was right in front of him.

"Indian Territory," she said.

"Yes'm." Cal was surprised he could even get that much out of his throat.

She laughed and shook her head. "I don't see how I remembered that."

"Me, neither," Cal said. "We just talked for a few minutes."

"And you rode south."

His head bobbed once. "And y'all went on to Baxter Springs."

Her head cocked. "You remembered where we were going?"

"Yes'm."

The fiddler hit a bad string.

But neither Cal James nor Catherine Thorpe noticed.

"Where's Mr. Withersteen?" Cal heard himself ask, then almost let a foul word escape his tongue for asking such a fool question. He didn't give a fig about where Mr. Withersteen was.

"Oh, he got hung in Baxter Springs," she said. "That's how come I came up to Abilene."

Cal took a step back. "He got hung?"

"He had a crooked dice game going on the side," she explained.

"Well, they don't hang folks for cheating at dice."

"They do in Baxter Springs."

A gunshot rang out somewhere in the night. Followed by four or five more shots.

The girl said: "They shoot them here. But there were more trees, though not many, around Baxter Springs."

"Because of the water," Cal said.

Said Catherine: "I expect so."

"Get to dancin', Clumsy Cat!" a voice bellowed above the terrible piano. "Or find yourself another job!"

"Want to dance?" Catherine asked Cal.

He reached into his pants pocket for a dollar bill.

But she grabbed his hand and pulled it up and placed it on her shoulder. "Later," she said.

The big voice shouted again: "And if you break his foot like you did the town constable's, you're fired!"

And they danced. And danced.

"I can't believe you broke a fellow's foot dancing," Cal told her. She danced like an angel.

She leaned close to him and whispered, "I didn't appreciate where his hands went."

She did not go back to the dance hall that night. Cal took her to the Drover's Cottage for supper, and there was a band playing in the lobby, and they danced there, too.

"I like the way your spurs jingle," she told him.

He had forgotten he was still wearing spurs.

"They remind me of a tambourine," she said.

And when the band had finished the song, they heard applause. From the clerk. From cattle buyers and railroad men standing in the lobby. From a few folks peering over the batwing doors to the bar. Even from women in dresses on the staircase.

Cal blushed. Cat, being used to dancing and admirers, bowed. Then she took Cal's hand and led him out onto the porch.

The citizens of Abilene turned happy. So did the farmers whose farms surrounded the city. For two weeks, no windows were busted in Abilene. Gunshots rarely sounded in the night. The jail cells remained practically empty. No farm cows died of Texas fever. The rains were welcomed, good rains, that caused no flooding. The nearest tornado was in Nebraska.

Cal and Cat danced practically every night. He took a job mucking stables so that he could afford the dollar a dance, but the man who ran the dance hall eventually

told Cat that she didn't have to take any money from, as
he called Cal, "that saddle tramp." That was because
people came into the dance hall, and drank whiskey or
wine or danced themselves at a buck a twirl, just to see
the couple dance.

But when the cattle season ended, and the cowboys
and cattle buyers left Abilene, and October turned cold,
and many of the cowboy businesses closed up for
winter, Cal knew he would have to drift. He wasn't a
farmer, and the farmers couldn't afford to hire a hand—
not during winter, anyway, and the owner of the dance
hall was renting his place out as a schoolhouse for winter,
but he'd be back in June.

Thus, Cal and Cat had to separate, though he told
her he would be back next year on another drive to
Abilene. And Cat said she would write him, but Cal
said he didn't know where he was going to be, so
Cat said she would write to him care of a sister she
had in Jefferson, Texas. And that her sister would be
instructed to save all the letters for Cal to read. And
Cal said that he would write to Cat at the dance hall in
Kansas City. And Cat said she would read every word
and memorize them.

And Cal asked Cat if it would be all right if he kissed
her.

And Cat answered by kissing Cal first.

And Cal said, "Parting is such sweet sorrow," and
Cat sniffled. The owner of the dance hall said, "It ain't
half as sorrowful as what happened to Romeo and Juliet,"
and Cal gave the owner a nasty look, then kissed Cat

again, and walked out of the dance hall and mounted the horse he had bought from Gus.

He rode south.

Cat and her colleagues and her boss went north to Kansas City.

And Cal was working as a carpenter in Dallas on his way south when he suddenly straightened and knocked a pail of nails off the roof, and it landed on his boss's right foot, just as Cal was realizing the mistake he had made up in Abilene.

"Surely I could have found a job in Kansas City!"

"Well, find one!" his boss shouted as he hopped around on one leg. "'Cause you ain't got one here!"

CHAPTER 29

Cal did not ride to Kansas City. Someone in Dallas told him how to get to Jefferson, but Cal got lost and wound up in Shreveport, Louisiana, where a fellow told him that a steamboat could get Cal to Jefferson in no time, and one was coming in later that day. Cal asked how much would a ticket cost, and the fellow told Cal to ask the ticket seller down on the docks, and Cal did as he was told. When Cal frowned, because carpentry doesn't pay any better than cowboying, especially when a fellow's salary is deducted for three broken bones in his boss's right foot, the man who sold the steamboat tickets, who had a kind heart, leaned forward and whispered, "Look here, youngster. See that big fellow in the blue shirt and black hat?" He pointed toward the river.

Cal saw the man and told the ticket seller that.

"Tell him you're willing to work for your passage to Jefferson." The man looked up at Cal. "You are willing to work, aren't you?"

Cal nodded excitedly. "I'll work."

"You'll be unloading cargo when the boat gets here, and then you'll be loading cargo onto the ship. And while the ship's chugging along to Jefferson, you'll be sweating and wishing you were on land as you keep the boilers boiling and the ship moving toward its destination."

That didn't scare Cal. Cal had been in stampedes.

"Then go see that fellow."

Cal thanked the ticket seller and hurried to the man in the black hat and blue shirt.

The work was hard—Cal thought they would never get all those bales of hay onto that handsome side-wheeler—but Cal knew about hard work.

The *Mittie Stephens* was a good steamboat, one hundred and sixty feet long with an experienced captain and crew. Cal hardly got to sleep, but he didn't care about sleep when he'd soon be near Catherine's sister.

But that was before one of the haybales caught fire on the night of February 12, 1869.

We won't go into the gory details, but suffice it to note that the newspapers called it the worst disaster on the New Orleans–Red River route. It wouldn't have been as bad as it was if the boat had not run aground near Swanson's Landing, where the water was just three feet deep or thereabouts. And it wasn't the fire that killed most of those sailors and passengers. Several drowned. And the paddlewheels did in a score or more.

Cal carried three children to safety, though, and then he and the crew and travelers who survived watched the wreck burn. Another steamboat arrived, picked up the survivors, and brought them in to Jefferson.

After talking to some riverboat officials and the county sheriff and avoiding all the scribblers at the newspapers, Cal tracked down Catherine Thorpe's sister, who burst out crying when Cal introduced himself.

Cal thought she must have heard that he had been aboard the *Mittie Stephens*, but that wasn't it at all, she managed to choke out between sobs. Then she showed him the bowl that contained all of the waterlogged letters that Cat had written for him.

"The roof—ohh—it leaked!" Cat's sister wailed.

Cal couldn't even make out his name on the envelopes, or any of the words in the papers that hadn't stuck together. The envelopes and the papers were still damp.

"The roof—didn't start—leaking—till—three nights back," Cat's sister explained.

He patted Cat's sister's hand and told her not to blame herself. It wasn't her fault. And Cal wondered if that roof that he had been building in Dallas leaked, too. Besides, Cat's sister must know where Cat was living since she had left Kansas City.

But the woman burst out sniveling again.

"No," she said, and sobbed. "Cat said she'd write when she settled down—but [*snort*]—that was [*choking noise*]—three [*wail*]—months [*clasping of hands, as in prayer*]—ago!"

"Miss Thorpe?" Cal whispered to Cat's sister.

She looked up and wiped her eyes with a pink handkerchief. "Do you happen to know where Cat's living these days? She left Kansas City."

"Kearney," she said. "Kearney, Missouri."

Well, he sure was glad she added the state. Otherwise,

Cal might have wound up at Fort Kearney in Nebraska, as he had never heard of Kearney, Missouri.

"Well, Miss Thorpe,"—Cal gave her a reassuring smile—"I'll just ride up to Kearney, Missouri. You might write her and tell her I'm coming. Do you know where she's living?"

She shook her head. "I just write to general delivery."

But that was fine. Cal had a town. It was getting colder now, but he could find her all right. Cat's sister said she would write Cat herself and tell her that Cal James was riding north and would be in Kearney . . .

Cal shrugged. "Sometime. Can't say exactly when."

CHAPTER 30

So Cal rode north. He wanted to gallop the whole way there, but galloping isn't much fun when the weather turns cold, and a horse can't gallop five hundred and fifty miles.

Of course, Cal didn't know it was that far. And he had to stop to work every now and then on his ride north. Most of the jobs proved easy enough, earning him a place to spend the night and a meal or two. Chopping wood. Mending fences. Slopping hogs. Gravedigging.

Well, the carpentry job in Fayetteville, Arkansas, didn't turn out too well, what with that big plate-glass window Cal broke, and the burial of Slim Lancer took Cal more time that he had figured on account that Slim Lancer wasn't slim at all—the fellow weighed better than three hundred and fifty pounds, and Cal had to turn carpenter and put two coffins together before the corpse could fit. The man he had buried in Waldron, Arkansas, had been a puny cuss, and Cal had had two other fellows to help dig that grave, and no hammer and nails and an extra coffin had been needed.

But Cal managed. He helped dig a well in Bentonville,

and that wasn't too rough on his hands since he had three helpers—to begin with. One fellow broke another fellow's foot, and Cal had to haul him up and take him four blocks to a doctor, and when he got back the two fellows he had left digging were talking to a score of folks, including a reporter for the *Traveler*, that town's newspaper, and showing everyone the human skull they had found while Cal had been taking Amos Baxter to that sawbones.

Everyone agreed that the skull looked pretty old—maybe a caveman, some said, but others allowed that was too old; it certainly didn't look to have been hurriedly buried by Yanks or Johnny Rebs during the recent unpleasantness. But it was those two fellows—and not Cal—who got their names in the newspaper, and then the boss man came by and demanded that Cal get to digging that well, said the other boys would join him as soon as the newspaper scribe was done with them.

In Mound City, Missouri, Cal met a horse trader who liked the look of Cal's mount. And Cal was fine with making a trade, and he figured he got the better end of the deal with this fine red mare. Even better was the fact that the man who orchestrated the horse swapping gave Cal the directions to Kearney, and Cal thanked him, and rode on north.

Cal remembered those old days when he had hunted for some businesses in Liberty, and then Cal started thinking that he would be going through Centerville—and that started him reflecting on the late Reverend James and his birthing ma and two of his brothers,

Frank and Jesse—and then Cal realized that he was in Centerville but that Centerville wasn't Centerville anymore.

It was now Kearney.

"You look perplexed, son," a voice called out.

Cal turned and saw Colonel C. E. Kearney himself, at least that's how the old gentleman introduced himself, and Cal said, "What happened to Centerville?"

The man laughed. "It's still here. The old village joined us, or maybe we merged with it. We have a population of four hundred now, a fine steam grist mill"—he gave a vague wave—"and a railroad station being built for travelers on the Hannibal and Joseph Railroad." Then he proudly pointed out the spot where "Alfred Pyle shot down Charles Drake back on the nineteenth of April."

Cal nodded as if those names meant something to him, but then he wet his lips and chanced a question. "Is the James family still farming?" And it was Cal's turn to give a vague wave.

The colonel nodded. "Indeed. A good farm. And two loyal and devoted sons, Frank and Jesse, who served the Lost Cause well."

And then Cal got enough courage to ask if the colonel knew a pretty dancer named Catherine Thorpe, and the colonel's face darkened.

"Young man," he said, "I am a Baptist." But then the gentleman's face softened, for he must have read the disappointment in Cal's face, and he sighed. "There was a dance hall on Battle Row." Again, there was that wave that didn't really point out any particular spot. "But it burned down two—no, three weeks ago, and those women and the whiskey peddler took off for Gallatin."

"Gallatin," Cal said.

This time the main pointed north. "Fifty miles northeast." And he gave Cal directions, which Cal figured would take him right past the James family farm.

He didn't get there. He ran into Frank and Jesse on the road.

"What the devil are you doing here?" Jesse demanded.

"Passing through," Cal said.

"That's a good thing," Jesse said. "You ain't planning on stopping around here are you?"

"Like I said," Cal told him. "I'm just passing through."

His mare snorted, and then Frank spoke, but his tone wasn't menacing. "Nice-looking horse you got there."

Cal thanked him.

Jesse noticed the horse, too. "That is a fine horse." He cocked his head and studied Cal before asking, "How'd you come across a horse like that?"

"Traded for her in Mound City," Cal answered.

Jesse swung off his horse. "We're trading," he said. "You take my horse, and I take yours. Even."

"Jesse," Frank warned, but Jesse's hackles were up. And when he saw that Cal hadn't swung out of the saddle, Jesse put his hand on one of the butts of his revolvers.

"We can do this friendly or not, Brother." His eyes looked like a snake's when he stared up at Cal. "It's your play."

"Make out a bill of sale," Cal said, and he swung off the bay and started uncinching his saddle. Of course,

Jesse found some paper and a pencil and busied himself writing down the information, but Cal figured he was doing that so Cal would have to unsaddle Jesse's horse, too, and that's exactly what happened. The saddles, blankets, saddlebags and bridles were swapped by the time Jesse handed pencil and paper to Frank and told him to witness it and date it. Then Frank handed the pencil and paper to Cal, who looked it over, and saw Jesse now had hands on two of his revolvers in case Cal did any objecting.

But the paper looked to be in order, and Cal signed it: Calvin J—but stopped and heard his raising mama's voice whispering a prayer or a warning, so he put a period after the J. Then signed:

Marmaduke

After that, they copied everything on another sheet of paper except this one was a bill of sale for Jesse's dun to Cal.

"Shake on it," Jesse said, and extended his right hand while keeping his left on a revolver.

Cal shook, Jesse laughed, and swung onto the red horse. "Keep riding, Brother," Jesse told him. "I wouldn't stop to visit nobody in Clay County." He spurred the mare and she took off at a good lope, and Cal had to grab the reins to the dun or else he'd be chasing down that horse the rest of the day.

Jesse's horse wasn't as good as the bay, but the gelding wasn't bad and might not have had the mare's speed, but he also wasn't too skittish. Cal stopped early that evening near a creek and made camp. He could have pushed his way on to Gallatin, but didn't want to get lost and wind up in, oh, Minnesota.

He woke early the next morning, caught another fish—same as he did the night before—and fried it up for breakfast mixed in with some corn pone, and felt satisfied. Then he shaved in cold water, because if he did find Catherine Thorpe in Gallatin, he at least wanted to look presentable.

He decided to bathe in the creek, too, but before long he and the gelding were back on the trail to Gallatin.

Cal figured he would be there soon enough—except that he found himself staring into pistol barrels when he rounded a turn. Two men. The taller of the bunch held the reins to a horse that had been run ragged.

The man who wasn't holding the horse swore, and that's when Cal recognized both men.

They recognized Cal, too, because at least Frank James lowered his revolver.

"You sure slickered me with that mare, Calamity!" Jesse barked. "I ought to plug you just for that."

"Dingus," Frank said, "you made the trade."

"You let me!" Jesse snapped.

"Because you won't listen to anybody."

"I'm taking my horse back," Jesse said.

Cal knew better than to argue with Jesse James when he was holding a cocked .44, so he held out the reins, and Jesse snatched them. "We'll get you a fresh mount when we get back to the farm," Jesse told Frank.

It wasn't until Jesse had swung into the saddle and shoved the revolver into a holster that Cal finally spoke.

"What about my horse—the mare?"

Jesse had already turned the gelding around and spurred it. "We left it in Gallatin. She's all yours."

He laughed, and Frank spit out tobacco juice and moved his horse closer to Cal.

"You didn't see us." Cal recognized the threat and nodded.

Then Frank James kicked his tired horse into as fast of a trot as that horse could go.

It was the seventh of December, 1869, a date that would live in infamy in Missouri.

Cal figured that out when the posse caught up with him.

"You seen two hombres riding double, stranger?" the sheriff—or maybe he was a marshal—asked. He had a star pinned on his vest.

"They took my horse," Cal said.

The lawman swore.

"Did you recognize them?"

Cal thought quickly. "Mister, I'm just coming up from Texas." Which wasn't a lie.

"The James boys are getting away!" a posseman who looked like a farmer said.

"The James boys?" Cal asked timidly.

The sheriff answered. "The shorter one—that'd be Jesse—got throwed after those owlhoots robbed the Daviess County Savings Bank. Killed the cashier. Wounded the clerk. When we opened up on them, he got throwed. That mare was bucking like she was an angry stallion. Those bold, nefarious bandits rode out double."

Cal bit his lips.

The fellow who looked like a farmer said, "And we found a bill of sale signed by Frank and Jesse James. Their ma has a farm down 'round Centerville."

"Kearney," Cal and the lawman said, at the same time, but the peace officer had a booming voice, so nobody heard Cal.

"Well, what am I to do about my horse?" Cal asked.

The leader of the posse was holstering his pistol. "The mare's yours if you can prove it. It's probably still on the streets of Gallatin."

And the sheriff, unless he was a marshal, spurred his horse after Frank and Jesse, and the others followed.

And Cal's feelings were somewhat torn. Frank and Jesse were his brothers, and he would hate to see them get thrown into prison or hung. But that mare, Cal sure did think, was a mighty good horse.

CHAPTER 31

After Cal had walked three miles northwest, a farmer driving a buckboard was nice enough to stop and ask if he needed a ride into town. It was December, the big man in overalls and a Johnny Reb kepi pointed out, and though there wasn't much threat of snow and it wasn't quite freezing, it was cold enough to make a fellow want to get to where he was getting to a whole lot quicker than his feet could take him.

Cal thanked the stranger for his hospitality. He wondered if the farmer would start up a conversation, but they rode into town in silence—so he reckoned the man had used up enough words already—at least till they reached the town square and saw all the commotion going on. By then, practically the whole county had swarmed into Gallatin. What Cal saw, however, was his horse.

"Bank robbery," the farmer whispered, repeating the cries echoing through the various huddles of people. "And cold-blooded murder." He sighed. "Well, at least they didn't rob Beaumont's store." He whispered: "I hope."

The farmer let Cal off, then clicked at the mules, and rode on toward a store that was on the other side of the square.

Cal summoned up enough courage and walked to the deputy and a bunch of men who were looking at Cal's horse.

"Says this hoss was sold to Jesse James by one Calvin Mammyduck," one of the man said, as he passed the bill of sale to another gent.

"The James family," another man said. "They come from good stock. Daddy was a Methodist preacher, if I ain't mistaken."

"Baptist," Cal corrected, and bit his tongue quick. No one had heard him because now they were yacking at each other.

"We ought to give this horse to Captain Sheets's widow!" one person shouted.

But Cal wasn't about to let that happen. "I'm Calvin Marmaduke," he said.

And all that racket of voices stopped, and everyone turned around and stared at him.

The deputy sheriff who had been left in charge of Gallatin while the sheriff and a right good-size posse went after the bandits, moved fast toward Cal, and three lawyers, a newspaperman, the deputy, the town marshal, two ministers, and three hangers-on fenced in Cal suddenly, but only the marshal and deputy were armed.

Cal told the truth—mostly—about trading the mare for Jesse's gelding. Well, after a bank robbery and the murder of an upstanding citizen and the wounding of a teller who ran out of the bank for his life, which was almost ended by a .44-caliber bullet, the citizens were suspicious. But they had that bill of sale and someone gave Cal a pencil and he signed his name which the Methodist preacher agreed was undeniably a match.

"You traded horses?" the deputy asked.

Cal nodded.

"Then what happened to yourn?"

Cal sighed and told them that he had camped by a creek and had fish for supper and breakfast—and Eugene Fountain said, yeah, the fish had been biting down that way, at least according to his cousin Albert, and the Methodist said they sure weren't biting much up this way, and everyone agreed, but then it was practically winter even though they hadn't had a good freeze yet. Then Cal did not stretch or fabricate or anything like that but said that the two men who had made him swap his horse at gunpoint came right down that same trail, and when they saw him, they drew their irons, and made him give them the horse he had been forced to trade.

"They coulda shot you," the Methodist said.

Cal nodded. "I prayed they wouldn't."

The Methodist was pleased. "A God-fearing man."

Cal said yes, he was, and he feared a lot of things, especially when he was looking down the barrel of a deadly Colt's revolver.

The deputy said he preferred a Remington.

The farmer said a Remington was a Yankee gun.

But then the Methodist said that the signatures

matched, and the deputy agreed, and a lawyer happened by and said that Cal could give a statement and then if the judge agreed, he could take his red mare back—as that seemed like justice, and someone agreed that it would serve Jesse James right. Trading for a horse, and then stealing the horse he had traded for was downright treacherous banditry. And Cal said that sounded like the right thing to do all around, and that he sure would like to make a donation if one was going around for the family of that brave Captain Sheets.

And he gave the Methodist minister two nickels and a dime, and that started others contributing, and that led to someone saying that they ought to also get a reward put up for the capture of those two James brothers. And then folks started talking about the other crimes that had been going on in Missouri. And someone asked if anyone recollected the robbery some years back, not even a year after the War for Southern Independence had ended, and someone said, "You mean the war for the preservation of the Union!" But the fistfight was over before anyone got bloodied, and the two instigators were shamed red-faced by the lecturing they got from the bank president, who had lost a good cashier and one of Gallatin's finest, and the Methodist and Baptist and Presbyterian ministers amened that. And then a lawyer brought them back to the robbery of the Clay County Savings Bank in Liberty in 1866.

"Nobody ever thought to rob a bank in broad daylight," the deputy recalled.

"But there was more than two men that pulled that job," a clerk said.

"Dang near an army," said the telegrapher.

"Locked the fellow in the bank in the safe," someone said.

"Woulda died—suffocated—but the fool murdering scoundrels didn't turn the combination thingamajig so the lock didn't catch."

"But they killed that boy as they rode out of town."

"Shootin' like they was whoopin' Injuns."

"Injuns ain't as bad as 'em murderin', thievin' trash."

The Baptist brought up "that robbery in Lexington."

"Same year as the robbery in Liberty," said the telegrapher, who would know such details as that.

"But not near as many gun-firing scoundrels as in Liberty," said the deputy.

"And that might be why they didn't get as much money as they took in Liberty," argued the telegrapher.

"Reckon them James boys did those jobs, too?" the Presbyterian asked.

"Wouldn't surprise me," said the farrier.

"Wasn't there a robbery, oh, two years back in Savannah?" a woman asked.

"No," said the farrier, "the robbery was in Richmond. March of sixty-seven. Three men got shot deader'n dirt."

"No," the telegrapher recalled, "the lady's right, too. The Savannah bank got robbed first. Then Richmond's streets ran crimson with the blood of martyrs a coupla weeks later."

And everybody bowed their heads for those martyrs. And when someone cleared his throat, and nobody brought up any other robberies of banks and savings associations, Cal asked if anyone recalled a troupe of dancers that had come through here by way of Kearney.

But the newspaperman then said that the paper had reprinted part of an article they got from a newspaper, which had come on the stagecoach, from Kentucky— the newspaper, that is, came from Kentucky; the stagecoach had started its run in Springfield—and that in March of '68, a bank had been robbed in Russellville, Kentucky, of $17,000, and everyone looked at the telegrapher for confirmation, but he couldn't confirm or deny that as that news had not filled the telegraphs on account of that Kentucky wasn't likely to think of bold, brazen murdering bank robbers coming all the way from Missouri to rob banks.

"Didn't Frank James ride with Quantrill?" the newspaperman asked.

The Baptist nodded. "Yes, he did. But that was because his daddy had died while bringing the Word to the gold mines of California."

And Cal almost corrected them that the miners in Hangtown were panning for gold and he didn't see too many mines in that country, but Cal stopped himself before he uttered one word, and then saw the Baptist was staring straight at him, and so he pretended that he had something in his eye, and that wasn't too farfetched with practically everyone in this part of Missouri filling the town square and kicking up dust and all.

And the preacher turned away and likely forgot about how Cal's eyes were just like the Reverend James's, and the preacher said he had known the Reverend James and he was a good man. And a man wearing a pistol in his waistband said so were his boys, who were brave enough to fight against them murdering red-legged Kansans.

"Young Jesse, I hear," the newspaperman said, "rode with Quantrill, too, didn't he?"

"And Bloody Bill Anderson," the lady added.

"I rode with Bloody Bill and Quantrill," said a bony cuss, "and the James boys rode with us, though Jess—Dingus, we called him—didn't kill his first man till late in our Lost Cause. Rode with the Younger brothers—Frank and Cole was like brothers."

"And who might you be?" the telegrapher asked.

"Jim Cummins," Jim Cummins said.

"Well, maybe we ought to ride over to the Younger farm and see if Cole might know Jesse's whereabouts," said the deputy.

But then the sheriff came riding back into town, and they were not riding fast, but looked like they had been whipped and flogged and drug through a patch of briars. And everyone ran over to hear what the sheriff had to say, and what he said was that they had ridden to the James farm, and the two brothers had been in the barn, and they started shooting and whooping and hollering, and rode out of that barn like they'd been born in the saddle, and jumped their horses over a high fence, and the posse went after them, but only the sheriff's horse could leap the top rails, and the sheriff wasn't paid enough money to ride after those men alone.

And they all followed the sheriff back to his office, except the telegrapher, who said he had to get back to the telegraph wire in case some important news came in, and that's when Cal asked him about a troupe of dancers and a beautiful girl named Catherine.

And he said they were here, but the Baptists didn't like them, so they went back to St. Joseph, and Cal thanked him and said he reckoned he'd head to St. Joseph, and the telegrapher said he didn't think they would still be there because the man of the bunch said the girls wanted to go see Chicago. And Cal dug his right hand into his trousers pockets and fingered the coins he had and didn't think he had anywhere near enough money to buy a ticket to Chicago by train, and this was December, and he surely wouldn't want to ride his mare all that way north at this time of year and be found frozen stiff come March in a wheatfield.

He had hoped he might find his true love still in St. Joe, but he just saw what was left of the hotel where the troupe was staying. It had burned down a few hours after the dancing emporium had checked in. Nobody was hurt (except the owner of the establishment, moneywise), and some people said it was that Clumsy Cat's fault—Clumsy Cat was what the headman of the outfit and two of the fattest dancers called the blonde beauty—because she opened the door to the room she and six other dancers were sharing and knocked the clerk who was carrying a lantern onto his hindquarters, and his lantern dropped through the railings and smashed on the bar below, and the fire whooshed and caught the curtains, and flames started roaring.

"The clerk shouldn't have been carrying a lantern," was said in Catherine's defense. "It wasn't that dark."

"God's will," someone else said, nodding.

"If they served only beer, instead of that coal oil they call whiskey, this tragedy could have been avoided," said a man with red sleeve garters and a stovepipe hat.

"Was that the same gal who screamed at that scorpion that caused Zeke Wilson's horse to rear and toss him into the street where Ol' Lady Halstead ran over him in her buggy?"

"Yep. Busted Zeke's ankle right good."

"Chalk that up to that—what was that the cap'n of 'em dancers called her?"

"Clumsy," Red Sleeve Garters said. "Clumsy Cat."

"And they were going to Chicago?" Cal just wanted to make sure he was on the right trail.

"Chicago," four folks agreed.

"The Chicago in Illinois?" Cal didn't want to make any mistakes this time.

"Only Chicago we know," two men said, one in a deep bass, the other in a pretty high tenor, and it sounded like they were harmonizing.

"Reckon I'll be going to Chicago come first light."

The blizzard started two hours later.

CHAPTER 32

So Cal spent the winter of 1869–70 shoveling snow off sidewalks in St. Joseph, and sleeping in a stable, where he fed and watered horses and rubbed down the mounts of boarders who paid extra. He also shoveled paths to privies and the town cemetery.

When spring came, he mounted his horse and rode north, working his way as had become second nature to him. Farm work here, swamping saloons there, occasionally finding a job on a ranch. A fellow had to eat. And another year passed.

So did part of 1871. He prayed that Catherine still waited for him. He read the letters Jesse James wrote that declared his innocence in many newspapers, saying that he had been falsely accused, and when he could be assured of a fair trial, he would surrender to the proper authorities. The rewards for Frank and Jesse for the Gallatin robbery and murder of Captain Sheets kept going up. Descriptions of the brothers were posted, and that's what got Cal in trouble when he rode into Davenport, Iowa, where he felt those pangs in his heart when he recalled his Iowa years with sweet, wonderful, loving Charity and that sometimes not so lazy and scheming husband of hers.

He was immediately staring down rifle barrels, shotgun barrels, two hatchets, and a pitchfork held by a one-eyed woman in a black dress.

"Don't he look like an arsonist?" the woman said.

Every head nodded.

Cal had to ask, "What's an arsonist?"

"Admit it," said a man who walked through the crowd, and Cal saw the badge on the fellow's coat. "You set fire to the City Flour Mills."

Cal shook his head. "Never heard of that place."

"It's on the corner of Third and LeClaire," he was told, and Cal said he didn't even know where that was, and explained that he was on his way to Chicago.

But these folks had their dander up, as this was not the first time someone had set fire to a building.

But then a man came running and said they had found a kerosene can in the attic, which must have been used to start the fire, and then Mr. Brown, who owned that burned business along with Mr. Irwin, said that the safe had been opened, and five hundred and six dollars and eighty-five cents had been stolen. So the theory was that the criminal had picked the lock to the safe—which would have been easy enough as everyone knew Mr. Irwin and Mr. Brown were skinflints and too cheap to afford a safe with a good lock and not just a spring lock—and that setting the fire was just a way so that the fire would attract all the attention so that the thief and arsonist could escape.

And Cal started to say something that he was sure would set him free, but before he could even say "Gents," someone waved a newspaper, and said, "By Jove, this here is Jesse James!"

Because there had been descriptions about the James brothers and this stranger sure had the eyes of a killer and the eyes of Jesse James.

"Or maybe," said the person who owned the watch and clock and fine jewelry store on Brady Street, "it's his older brother Frank."

Cal just sighed and slowly shook his head.

"There's one way to find out," said the fellow with the black sleeve garters and waxed, curled mustache.

And everybody, even Cal, stared at the fellow, waiting to hear his secret.

The man didn't speak. He pulled open his coat and that's when folks saw the nickel-plated Colt revolver with the ivory grips, and he pulled out that pistol—one of those fancy Tranters that didn't need to be cocked to fire, you just had to pull the trigger. He removed the caps except for one because this guy wasn't about to give Frank or Jesse James the chance to gun down more than one man.

"Are you crazy?" asked one gent, as he backed his way back toward a saloon.

But the man just grinned and then nodded at a pile of mule dropping in the middle of the street. "See if you can't hit that pile," he instructed Cal, and Cal felt the balance of the revolver, and people's mouths opened and then they all gasped when Cal pulled back the hammer.

"You ain't got to cock that piece, sonny," the owner of the revolver said.

"I do it this way," Cal said, and he raised the revolver, which didn't feel right in his hand, perhaps because of the funny-shaped grips, but he saw the manure and then the Tranter started moving around in quick circles.

And everybody laughed.

"He's doin' that so that he'll miss it a-purpose," the backing-up fellow called out, before his disappeared into the saloon.

"Not if he's one of them James brothers," said the barber.

But the fellow who owned the revolver put his hand atop the barrel before Cal could touch the trigger, and the man shook his head and laughed, and said, "Powder and lead are expensive enough, kid. No need to waste that shot."

And Cal felt sort of torn, because he would have liked to have seen the shock on those Iowans' faces when he scattered that pile of manure all across the street.

A minute later, while folks were arguing over whether Cal could have hit that pile or not, a redheaded woman stepped away from Cal's horse, and she waved a piece of paper in her hand and yelled, "He ain't Frank or Jesse James!" And Cal realized she had his bill of sale. "He's Calvin J. Marmaduke. But he traded for that hoss—and he traded it with Jesse James."

Cal thought he would get strung up right then and there, but newspapers in Iowa had been reprinting all sorts of Missouri newspaper articles about the James boys, and most everyone in Davenport had heard about the Gallatin bank robbery and the mare that had helped identify those murdering scoundrels and Border Ruffians.

Similar events delayed Cal's journey north and east. It was less than two hundred miles from Davenport to Chicago, but it took Cal a long way to get there. The folks in Prophetstown did not mistake him for any notorious Missouri outlaw, but did hold him accountable for knocking over the lantern that burned down the Rock River Boarding House, and made him work with some other miscreants rebuilding the cabin. He was broke when he reached Bradford Township and spent a while felling white pine trees, which didn't suit him, but the money was good, and so was the food—and he just couldn't get to Chicago with no money in his pockets, because what could he offer Catherine Thorpe other than a bill of sale for a horse that most folks wanted to see?

Someone had suggested to Cal that he start charging a nickel a peek for those who wanted to see Frank and Jesse James's signatures. He helped some homesteaders clear land on Blackberry Creek, because they sure looked like they needed some help, and his mare was favoring her right front leg.

The horse, cow, pig, and chicken doctor at Downers Grove told him he ought to let the mare rest for a week, which turned into two, then three weeks, but Cal earned some money for meals, and to pay the horse, cow, pig, and chicken doctor, for the smelly wrappings that the doc kept putting on the mare's right front leg, by shooting targets and hitting them all, and amazing people because no one had ever seen shooting like that. And he liked Downers Grove a lot, because nobody mistook him for a James brother, but Downers Grove was not Chicago, so he moved on to Cicero Township, and just stayed there one day, even though he paid for two days—but only because the barber wouldn't be back from visiting his Aunt Clarice till then and Cal wanted to have his hair all barbered up and his face shaved clean and close because he really wanted to look like a gentleman and not a saddle bum when he met up with Catherine Thorpe. And he would have done just that, except someone gave him a copy of *The Chicago Tribune*, and there was an article on the fourth and final page, under the headline REPORTS FROM THE COURTS, that said a dancer and "Notorious She Scallywag" was being held in the city jail for trying to defraud the son of a minister, and the woman was going by the name of Clumsy Cat.

So Cal mounted up the mare and galloped most of the way to Chicago. He got there late, of course, and not familiar with the city, he did not know the location of a jail, but a grand Irish lady named Catherine said Cal could stay in their barn if he wanted to—as long as he helped do some mucking and pitchforking and watering come first light, and Cal was fine with that, and he enjoyed eating supper with that grand Irish lady and her husband, Mr. O'Leary, and they stayed up in the evening and Cal listened to their stories about the old country. And then Mr. O'Leary gave Cal a lantern so he could see his way to the barn, and Cal did that—but he swore he heard a woman singing, and he set down the lantern and walked to the open barn door, and, yes, that was a woman singing—but the O'Learys had said nothing about a dance troupe or a dance hall or anything of that nature being on DeKoven Street, and Cal was lured out a few yards, then decided that, no, that was not the beautiful voice of Catherine Thorpe (although the singer did a mighty fine version of "Shoo Fly, Don't Bother Me")—

And then he thought: *What's that burning?*

He got the cow out of the barn. The mare didn't need Cal's help. She bolted past Cal as he hurried to the barn, but even with the O'Learys' help, the barn couldn't be saved.

Nor could most of Chicago.

But Cal did his best. He could see those fiery tornadoes, just spinning around and flinging hot embers and chunks of burning wood and millions and maybe billions of sparks. He tried to recollect the last time he had seen rain, but no recent memories came to him. So he fought the flames for a while, and then he found himself helping people carry their children and dogs and invalided grandparents, a rosary or two, some crosses and crucifixes, a wedding dress, a hambone. He was still working, his clothes, his face, his hands and arms blackened, when dawn came.

And yet Cal kept moving through the rubble, the

ruins, and he often tried choking or coughing out Cat's name. No response came.

The next day, the rains finally fell. But by then a great deal of Chicago had been reduced to rubble and ash and smoking ruins. The stockyards had been saved, Cal heard, but not many folks had an appetite. He couldn't find the O'Learys. He didn't even know what side of Chicago he was on now. Or what was even left of Chicago.

People wandered past him as though in a trance. Cal buried his face in his hands and cried for just a bit, and then he raised his face toward the dark clouds and let the misting rain mingle with his tears and he cried out, "Catherine Thorpe—where are you?"

And a voice answered, oh, so meekly. "Cal?"

He had to be dreaming. Or maybe his mind had snapped. But he spread out his fingers and looked ahead through the slits, and there stood a beautiful woman— hair singed on one side, the tan dress far from its original color, and ripped in places, burned here and there, covered with smut and mud, and her hair dripping wet from the rain.

Somehow Cal managed to stand. He rubbed his eyes, but that just made them burn more, and then he shook his head and tried to make out this figure, wondering if she were real or apparition.

And then he saw her smile and heard her say, "Cal, it *is* you. It's you. It's you . . . you . . . you . . . you . . . !" and she ran into his arms.

A few passersby smiled, though neither Catherine nor Cal noticed, and one old prude snorted and turned her head toward the smoking ruins of what had been a beautiful two-story home and spoke ill of any public display of affection, and tripped over an empty water bucket and fell into the street. And some people snorted and said she got what she deserved, but others ran to help her up, and she barked and hissed at them and turned down the street, still complaining about kissing and hugging and twirling in public, but Cal did not notice. He noticed nothing but beautiful Catherine, at least until someone shouted:

"Take your arms off my bride!"

And that stopped everybody, and Cal turned to see a man whose face wasn't covered with grime or soot, and whose clothes might not have been clean enough for some churches, but in Chicago on this day was better than anything anyone had seen since Sunday evening.

"Jasper!" Catherine took a couple of steps toward that fellow. "I told you I'd never marry you, and I meant it. Now you go back to that hussy you've been seeing *for how long?*"

"You're marrying me, and I'll see whoever I feel like seeing!" And he started across the street.

And Cal met him. And Catherine gasped and begged Cal to be careful. And Cal told himself that he wasn't a Marmaduke anymore—at least until he whupped this scoundrel who had bruised Cal's beloved heart. And folks gathered around the street, including one priest and several children—girls and boys—and matrons and two grandmothers.

Cal figured he had that fight won, even though the man who had betrayed Cat's trust put up a good bout, but Cal had been doing all sorts of work since he set out—*how long ago was that?*—to track down Cat. And nobody, except the children, heard the whistles. And then four Chicago policemen ran to the two men rolling in the rubble and at least they just jerked Cal off the top of that mean dude, and didn't club Cal's head like one of the coppers done to Jasper, but the sergeant said, "They'll work till we've rebuilt this great city!"

And Cat begged for them to let Cal be, that it was Jasper's fault, and some of the men and women and especially the grandmother agreed with the sobbing, young, and quite beautiful woman. But the coppers were not in a listening mood, and they hauled Cal and the fiendish ex-almost-groom away.

It was four months, two weeks, and twelve days before the sergeant told Cal that he was free to go. And when Jasper said he was ready to go, too, and they had best let him go if they knew what was good for them, the sergeant punched Jasper in the mouth and said he just got himself another month of tearing down burned-up buildings.

So Cal looked for another week for Catherine, but his beloved was nowhere to be found. No one had seen a woman of that description. But one gent said he had heard of a dancing emporium that had moved out of Chicago two weeks ago and headed down to some city in Missouri.

That's how Cal ran into Frank and Jesse James— again.

CHAPTER 33

One cannot blame poor Calvin Amadeus James/
Marmaduke for the terrible path he took. Broken hearts
can do that to just about anyone and everybody. Thus
began Cal's dark days, that stretched into years, as he
traveled the frontier of our Western states and territories, searching for his true love—and not knowing that
all that while that good and graceful creature of the
heavens sought him. That's why she had left Chicago.
Some miscreant said that Cal had escaped the police
and had fled to Tucson, Arizona Territory. There she
joined another traveling dancing troupe, since the journey to Arizona had taxed her finances, and a girl has to
eat, especially when she's dancing in Arizona's summer
heat and Butte, Montana's, miserable cold.

Descriptions of the James brothers were appearing
throughout the West, published in newspapers, printed
on dodgers that were tacked all over courthouses and
even outhouses, barked out by Pinkerton operatives
and railroad guards, United States marshals, town con-
stables, and county sheriffs.

Cal's eyes always got the curiosity of lawmen, undertakers, wild saloon hussies, and newspaper journalists. He slept in many a jail, but usually not more than a month or two before he was released, because no one could say for certain that he was an outlaw. Indeed, many a time a witness might come by and stare through the iron bars of the cell Cal occupied, then slowly shake his head and tell the peace officer, "I do not think this is that villainous fiend, sir. I do not see death in his eyes—just—just . . . disappointment."

Cal heard similar sentiment often enough.

Which beat being sentenced to a state or territorial prison for twenty-five years or being hanged, legally or illegally.

Fate would take a hand in this game of Cal's life. Fate and Jesse James.

Cal had been stopped on a public road, roughed up a little—which he had grown accustomed to—and then taken to the town of Ste. Genevieve, Missouri, where four men had robbed the savings bank in that town on May 27, 1873. No one had been killed, so the posse wasn't all that angry nor in a hurry to catch up with the James–Younger Gang. (By then Cole Younger and some of his younger Younger brothers had been identified as members of that band of outlaw brothers, since one member of the posse had served under Quantrill and recalled when Cole had a bunch of Yankee soldiers lined up just to see how many bodies one bullet from an Enfield rifle could go through.)

"No," the teller said, when Cal was presented to the

still startled individual. "I do not see death in this man's eyes. And he looks sad, brokenhearted even, so I daresay he is not a notorious bandit and mankiller."

Which was too bad, because one of the deputies said that the food served in the Ste. Genevieve jail beat anything you'd find in any of that town's restaurants.

Having seen in a newspaper a report about a visiting dancing troupe in Adair, Iowa, Cal visited that fine town, but the troupe was gone, and the railroad clerk told Cal that he didn't recall the name of the outfit or how any of the dancers looked or which train they took out of town—or even if they took a train out of town. But he talked about all the other trains and such, what they were carrying, when they left, which were the fast trains, and which ones never ran on time—and it was an hour before Cal got out of the station and was riding west.

That's when he ran into his brothers and the Younger brothers.

That's when Cal started his career as a criminal.

"Hands up!"

Cal had just come up a hill and found himself staring into the barrels of one revolver and one double-barreled shotgun. The two men wore potato sacks for masks and long linen dusters.

"You heard the man," came a voice behind Cal, so he just sighed and did as he was told.

Then one of the highwaymen in front of Cal lowered his revolver, shook his head, and walked toward Cal. He stopped a few feet in front of the horse and rider, and

appeared to be staring at Cal for the longest time. Then
the hammer was lowered, the revolver slipped into its
holster, and the mask was pulled off so that Cal could
stare into eyes that looked just like his own.

"What the devil are you—?" came the voice behind
Cal, but Jesse James shushed that question, and said,
"You won't believe this, Brother, so come see for your-
self."

Frank James, still masked, came around and sighed.
Frank then turned toward the man with the shotgun
and said, "You can lower that scattergun," but Cole
Younger was already pulling off his sack with one
hand, and the shotgun was now pointed at the ground.

"I remember him," Younger said, and gave Cal a
slight nod.

"I'd shoot you," Jesse said. "I ought to shoot you.
But Ma would have a conniption."

Cal said: "You haven't seen a dancing troupe with a
beautiful, golden-haired goddess, have you?"

The outlaws laughed. Cal sighed.

They invited Cal to their camp, and Cal ate corn pone
and bacon and drank bad coffee, which surprised Cal.
He figured that with as much money as the James–
Younger Gang had stolen from honest folks, they'd be
living high on the hog, but Jesse explained that they had
to sell most of the bonds and such they took to a profes-
sional crook who gave them a small percentage—but
that was better than nothing—and Frank said those stories about him giving money to widows and orphans
and pretty girls, and helping pay off mortgages or other
types of loans was nothing but hogwash.

"Widows charge us more than a fancy restaurant in Kansas City," Frank said. "Else, they'll tell the law and try to collect the reward."

"Orphans are just as bad," Jesse said.

"And banks ain't the easy pickings that they used to be," Cole said. "We didn't know we were starting a trend. Seems like everybody's robbing banks these days."

Frank added: "So banks are ready for bold robbers, such as ourselves."

Cal shook his head. "So y'all are robbing from travelers. There can't be much money in that?"

Jesse shrugged. "Man's gotta eat."

"You ever thought about robbing trains?" Cal suggested.

They looked at Cal as if he were loco, and later, Cal figured he must have been just plain crazy. But he said, "Don't y'all recollect the stories of the Reno brothers up in Indiana?"

"What I recollect," Frank said, "was that they got dragged out of jail cells and lynched."

"That's because they got caught," Cal heard himself saying, but it was like someone else was speaking. "And they were in Indiana. We're in Missouri."

"Well, right now we're in Iowa," Cole said.

"But we're close to the Missouri border," Cal said.

"So?" Jesse asked.

"Well, you boys fought for Missouri. You boys got friends all over Missouri."

"We got enemies, too," Frank said.

Cal nodded. "But your friends and those who fought with you would hide you. Lie for you, too."

Cole snapped his fingers. "And we hid enough in the woods and hills to know the good caves and such."

Jesse grinned. "And if we paid our friends, they'd lie to a lawman."

So Cal told them about that talkative railroad clerk, and about the Chicago, Rock Island and Pacific Railroad hauling tons of gold. And Jesse liked the idea, while Cole and Frank shrugged and said they might as well give it a whirl. And Cal said they could put up a barricade so that the train would have to stop, and that's what they did—only Jesse and Clell Miller, who the boys picked up, along with some other Quantrill men, suggested that they loosen some of the rails to make sure the train didn't run through the barricade, and Cal said he didn't think that was such a good idea, but Jesse gave him a mean look, and Cal said, "You don't want to wreck the train." But Jesse said, with a slight grin, "Maybe I do," and Clell Miller whispered to Cal that when Jesse was in one of his moods, it was best not to provoke him.

But Cal knew he was right, and that sure proved the case when the train wrecked and then they couldn't find the big shipment that was supposed to be on that train—probably because they robbed the wrong train—and while they got away with right around $3,000, it sure wasn't the way Cal had thought his first train robbery would go.

That got them through about six months, and Cal realized that the outlaws weren't lying about how costly it was to be an outlaw. And so they had to drift out of Missouri and into Arkansas, and did some soaks to soothe their aching buttocks and bones in Hot Springs, and figured that robbing a stagecoach would be easier than robbing a train, and they got about just as much money and didn't have to derail anything, and nobody got hurt. Cal gave a blonde woman back the broach and ring that Frank had taken, and Frank gave Cal a mean look, but then remembered how heartbroken Cal was over the loss of sweet Catherine, so he didn't plug Cal with his .44.

They had better luck in Gads Hill, Missouri, when they robbed a St. Louis, Iron Mountain and Southern Railway, because this time Frank, Cole, but mostly Cal said they weren't going to derail the train this time, because it just made a mess out of everything. They simply waylaid the fellow in the train station and put up a red lantern, so the train just stopped and everyone stared into gun barrels.

No mess was made. Nobody even got hurt. And they took somewhere around $10,000, though Cal thought it was more and that Jesse might have pocketed some extra, but then everyone was calling Jesse the leader.

And in March of 1874, while Jesse and Frank were off courting their girls—whom they would marry that year—Ma James snorted and pulled out a letter that she had buried in her flour barrel to keep it out of Pinkerton agents' and other lawdogs' hands, because the boys learned that when you rob a train, or more than one train, the Pinkertons are usually called in, and the Pinkertons are a lot more ruthless than county sheriffs and even United States marshals.

And Cal was surprised when his birthing ma handed him the letter. And the letter read:

My beloved:

I have long sought to see you in the dAnce halls & tents and places, but I suppose you have found someone new, & I hope she mAakes you hAppy.

But I felt I must write you in cAse thAt you hAve not forgotten your deArest CAtherine Thorpe. Oh, whAt lousy luck Ive hAd since ChicAgo. But Im in KAnsAs now, A cook—& dAncing instructor for A fAmily's three beAutiful dAughters—& if you visit the JAmes family & if Mrs. JAmes gives you this letter, then you cAn find me still loving you & missing you & hoping to see you At

Lucien CArter's FArm
Ford County, KAnsAs

And joy filled Cal's heart and tears filled his eyes, and Jesse snatched the letter, but Cal was so happy to have heard from his true love that he did not mind. And Jesse read the letter and tears filled his eyes, too, and he handed the letter back to Cal and said: "Well, I reckon you'll be going to Kansas."

And Cal whispered, "I must go."

And Ma James fixed up some vittles for him to take, and Frank saddled Cal's horse, and they all shook hands, and Ma James gave him a hug and said, "You must promise me that you'll never turn to outlawry agin."

And Cal promised her, and when she pulled away, he saw her eyes—and realized that probably what she meant by making him make that promise was that it would keep him from coming back to Clay County, Missouri, and likely would mean Ma would get more money from her two favorite sons.

Cal rode to Atchison, Kansas, and being in such a hurry to reach Catherine, he bought a ticket on the Santa Fe so he'd get to Ford County a lot sooner, and it was a good ride until the train derailed, but that wasn't on account of bold robbers, just bad luck. Nobody was hurt, but Cal was in such a hurry, he didn't want to wait for a crew to come and get the train back on the tracks, so he took his horse and rode west.

Dodge City had been a buffalo town, but when Cal got there the first trail herd was coming through and heading for the stockyards, and cowboys were hollering and hooting, and that got Cal's horse to bucking and he got bucked right through a milliner's door—and Cal tried to explain to a deputy or some sort of lawman what had happened, but the lawman pulled out his pistol and knocked Cal out cold.

"Earp does like to buffalo a feller," said the toothless drunk, who shared the cell with Cal, but the judge who heard Cal's story just fined him $10, which Cal paid with part of his share from the Hot Springs robbery, and he felt kind of bad about that but felt better when the judge pocketed the money and told him he was free to go.

And Cal asked for directions to Lucien Carter's farm, and a merchant gave him directions but the directions were to a bank, and that's where a fellow with a green silk ribbon tie told him that the bank had taken over the farm but would be happy to sell it to Cal for a great price.

But Cal wasn't interested in the farm, just in Catherine Thorpe, and the bank man wasn't interested in Cal after that. Cal rode out to the farm anyway, and it looked like a good farm, and a neighbor was farming it, leasing it from the bank after the Carters and that lovely woman helping them teach their children to dance had taken off to Muncie—not the one in Indiana, but near Kansas City—but he sure could use some help.

And Cal helped him. Well, at least till the swarms of locusts came and ate anything and everything that was green—including, Cal hoped, the banker's green silk ribbon tie.

Irritated is not a strong enough word to describe poor Cal's feelings as he rode, oh, three hundred and more miles back east, because Muncie, was just a wee bit over the Missouri border, and Cal asked about the family and about Catherine, but the locusts had pretty much picked everything clean around Muncie, too.

That's when Cal was told that Mrs. Carter had gone crazy from the locusts, and Mr. Carter had abandoned the farm and taken his children and his insane wife back to Pennsylvania, but, no, the pretty girl who worked for them had not gone with them but somewhere else—and he couldn't come up with the territory or town, but it was right on the tip of his tongue.

And then a neighbor came riding up on a donkey, screaming that the James–Younger Gang had robbed the train. And Cal started feeling like he was sweating, which would not seem normal to farmers in December. And that's when a fellow came out of the remnants of a locust-eaten cornfield, and that's when the neighbor said that one of the robbers had been captured and that that fellow must be another one of them. And it turned out that the fellow was, because when he saw Cal and the two farmers, he turned and ran back toward Missouri, but the farmer picked up the shotgun he had leaned against his cart, and he must have had double-ought buckshot in it because that man was running at a good clip, but the two barrels boomed and the man went falling down, and he was mighty dead when Cal and the two farmers looked down on him.

So a deputy came over a few hours later, right before the sun started to sink, and pulled out some papers and said, "This sure could be Bud McDaniel, and he's one of the James–Younger Gang."

Some say that's why the James–Younger bunch went to West Virginia, where they robbed the Huntington Bank on September 7, 1875.

We cannot verify that, though it is a good guess, but it is beyond doubt that that's why Calvin Amadeus James—no, Marmaduke, right then at that moment—rode to Wyoming Territory.

Because Bud McDaniel reminded the farmer of Daniel Budd, a friend of his from the recent unpleasantness, and Daniel Budd had taken off to Wyoming Territory after the locusts wiped him out in Kansas, and by grab, that's where that girl who had worked so hard for the Carters said she was going, as there was an advertisement in one of the newspapers saying that a new dance hall had opened up in Cheyenne and sought beautiful women who knew the redowa.

CHAPTER 34

Cal reached Cheyenne in the fall of 1875. He knew the Union Pacific went through the territorial capital, but he didn't think the town would be full of people. The hotels were full up. So were the livery stables, and everybody in the streets was talking about nothing else but gold.

Gold.

Gold.

Gold.

Gold had been discovered in the Black Hills, but Cal didn't see any black hills around Cheyenne. There were some purple mountains way off to the west, and lots of hills and lots of sage, and a whole lot of wind that would even put Kansas winds to shame.

But Cal wasn't interested in gold or hills. He wanted to find his dear Catherine Thorpe. She wasn't with the Social Union Club at Recreational Hall. Someone suggested he try the Methodist Sociable, which was at Mrs. Tuttle's house just down from the Continental Oil Company's offices on Eighteenth Street. But Cal couldn't even get to that street because of all the people, and he didn't think they were going to the Methodist Sociable.

There was a dance at the American House, but that was just a banjo and a fiddle, and since men outnumbered females by a hefty majority in Wyoming Territory, the men who had silk or cotton bandannas wrapped around their left arms were serving as the women and letting the fellows in suspenders and gun belts lead them around the dance floor.

Someone sent him to Beno's Brewery on Seventeenth Street, which wasn't nearly as crowded as Eighteenth Street, but Cal knew he wouldn't find Cat playing inside because it was an orchestra—German, it turned out—but even the polkas didn't sound as good as the ones Catherine Thorpe could dance to.

They did have a free lunch, though, and Cal was hungry, and he partook—and accidentally tripped a fellow he didn't see, and that gent went down to the floor and spilled a spittoon, which stained one miner's boots. And the miner drew a knife and threatened to gut the clumsy oaf, meaning the fellow Cal had tripped, and Cal said to leave that fellow alone and went to help the man up. And then the mean cuss with the knife started to bury that blade into Cal's back, but Cal brought his left arm up and stopped the knife from cutting anybody, and then Cal punched the man right in the nose and down he went, tripping over the spilt spittoon, and landed with a thud against the brass foot railing, and that knocked the fellow out. And the tuba player took a break and dragged the ornery cuss through the door and deposited him on the street.

And the man Cal had accidentally tripped thanked Cal, but Cal said he sure was sorry that he had tripped him, and the man just shrugged, and Cal bought him a good German beer—at least the bartender said it was German—and they were chatting, and Cal sighed and told him his sad story, and the man finished the beer and said, "I recall a dancing troupe here a while back, and there was a golden-haired gal dancing with them. She danced like an angel."

"That has to be my Cat!" Cal exclaimed, though calling Catherine his sounded presumptuous.

"Well, sir," the man said. "You might find her at Fort Fetterman."

And Cal drew in a deep breath and held it.

"Where's this Fort Fetterman?" he asked.

And the guy, after Cal bought him another German beer, gave him directions, and it sounded like a desolate and remote place, full of wickedness and soldiers, and when Cal said that, the man nodded in agreement but said it was a good place to start.

"Why would the troupe leave Cheyenne for a place like that?" Cal asked.

"Well," the fellow said, "that's on the way to all that gold in the Black Hills. And that's where the soldier boys take back all those miners who they catch trying to sneak into that country. That's the Sioux's country, you know."

Cal didn't know that particular fact, but he did know that's where he was bound for.

* * *

She wasn't in the stockade at the fort, nor in the town jail, and no one had seen any dancing troupe or nothing like that in Fort Fetterman, but if they were bound for the Black Hills, they would likely have tried to sneak past Fetterman.

"I'd pity her, if she's in that country," said a corporal, who had been a sergeant and was digging a new privy, and when Cal asked him why, the bluecoat said, "Injuns. And winter."

Thus, Cal figured he would have to risk soldiers and Indians and find his way into the Black Hills. And he made it about one day out before the first storm hit, then he slogged his way back to Fort Fetterman and spent the rest of the fall and all that winter there, worrying about Cat in that Black Hills country. And he was there until the late spring and thinking of how he could head for those hills without getting captured when a voice called out, "Hello, Cal Marmaduke, ain't you a sight for sore eyes!"

And Cal turned and saw Jim Hickok, older, taller, even handsomer, and now known across the United States and her territories as Wild Bill Hickok, and wearing the dangest pair of dark eyeglasses that Cal had ever seen.

That's how Cal came to join Wild Bill on a train of wagons and horses bound for the Black Hills in 1876. So let us correct the myth that Calvin Amadeus James told George Armstrong Custer to go to the Little Bighorn River in June of that year, and that led to the demise of the soldier with the golden locks and many a brave soldier with him, because Cal didn't even see Custer, as he was on his way with Wild Bill to the new, glorious, wild mining town called Deadwood.

Well, at least the newspapermen called Deadwood wild and glorious, but to Cal it was just a muddy mess of men and buildings, and he went to every saloon and establishment and found no dancer who was as lovely and as fine as Catherine Thorpe. And Cal was saddened and wondering if he would ever get to see his true love again, and he wasn't watching where he was going—and that made it easy for someone to stick out a leg and trip him. Cal landed with a splat in the mud, and when he rolled over, something hard landed on his chest, and he got the breath knocked out of him and then knees and shins pinned his arms to the thick muck, and the cold steel of a Schofield .45 pressed against his forehead. And Cal's eyes opened as he struggled to catch his breath, knowing his life was almost over, and he saw the ugliest critter he had ever seen.

And the ugly critter said, "Buster, I hear ya call yerself Calamity James, and, buster, I'm here to tell ya that nobody goes around stealin' my name. *I'm* Calamity, do you hear me? I'm Calamity—Calamity Jane. And I don't cotton to you pallin' 'round with my beau. Wild Bill's my man. And you ain't man enough to take my man."

A gun roared. And Cal thought he was dead, but realized that no smoke or hot flame and deadly lead had come out of the gun held by that ugly woman—

who dressed in dirty buckskins and flannel—and then a numbing voice shouted: "He has murdered Wild Bill!"

And Calamity Jane dropped the Schofield into the muck that had practically swallowed Calamity James, and her face lost all color and she sprang off Cal and said, "Oh, no!" And ran away.

So Cal rose slowly, confused, and then his brain started working, and he realized what someone had said.

"Wild Bill," Cal whispered, "murdered?"

And he started to go after Calamity Jane and the voice that had made such a terrible announcement, but then he heard footsteps slogging through the mud in the alley behind him, and he saw a skinny punk running like he was being chased by the entire Sioux Nation, and Cal tried to get out of the fellow's way, but in doing so, he tripped the poor soul, who fell face-first into the gunk that Cal had just gotten himself out of, and he reached down and started to apologize and help the lad to his feet with about half the population of Deadwood that was next to him and jerking the fellow to his feet, and slapping him and scolding him, and wrapping his wrists with rope.

"Who is he?" a voice shouted.

"Calls himself Sutherland," someone answered.

"No. His real handle is Jack McCall."

Then folks were slapping Cal's back and pulling out his hands, left and right, to shake, and stuffing cigars and gold nuggets and pokes and pennies in his pockets, and calling him the hero.

"Here's the man who caught Wild Bill's assassin."

Thus, Cal was there at Wild Bill's funeral, and Calamity Jane bawled her poor grieving head off, and it was a sad day for Cal and for all of Deadwood—but not that sad for Jack McCall, as a miner's court had acquitted him of shooting a man through the back of his head. And after the funeral, Cal was hustled back to a saloon—though not the Number 10 Saloon, where Wild Bill had been assassinated, because you couldn't hardly get inside that place. But Cal found himself pushed into a chair, and folks wanted to thank him, fill him with bad liquor, and then a voice said, "Shake hands with the bullet that killed Wild Bill."

And Cal turned, and saw a man with a bandaged hand and a quick smile.

And a miner said, "This is Cap'n William Massie, riverboat cap'n," and told Cal: "The bullet that killed Wild Bill went right through that grand man's head and went straight into the cap'n's wrist."

Captain William Massie nodded slightly and smiled at Cal again.

"Been a while, Calamity James," Captain William Massie said. Only Cal didn't know any Captain William Massie. But he sure wasn't apt to ever forget Captain Malachi J. Shufflebottom.

CHAPTER 35

Through a drizzling rain, they sank in the mud of Deadwood's main street and pushed their way to Captain Shufflebottom's tent. There, the captain dragged a crate over and handed it to Cal, who, when he saw his old comrade use a crate as a chair or stool, did likewise. The rain pattered on the tent, leaking through in several points but not—at least for that moment—on either occupant's head.

"I'd keep your hat on," Shufflebottom said. "Unless you want a bath."

Cal managed a grin. "I probably could use one."

Shufflebottom nodded. "So could every soul in this nasty little town."

"What brought you here?" Cal asked.

The smile was the same one Cal remembered. Then the old man shrugged. "Gold. Money."

"I thought you were going to return to riverboating," Cal said.

"I did for a few years. Then the wanderlust called me again. No need in asking about me, son. What have you been up to since I last saw you? Gosh . . . I don't think I'll even try to count the years."

Cal's head tilted. He studied the old man's face, one weathered by winds of the rivers and the plains and prairies, one aged by just living in these times and those glorious years of yesteryear when America was young. But she still was young, just a hundred years old.

"Do you remember a man named Colonel Horatio L. Delmont?" Cal asked.

Shufflebottom shook his head.

"He wrote a book, a dime novel they call them now, titled *The Amazing but Authentic and True* (though they misspelled *True*) *Story of a Kid Called Calamity*, and—well, it was a bunch of mostly lies about me on the California Trail. Although this fellow changed it to the Oregon Trail."

"You don't say." The captain grinned. "Well, I'll be. I'd like to read that one. Am I in it?"

Cal's head tilted. "You're in it some—so are lots of folks we knew, but they got those names wrong. In fact, there wasn't hardly a truthful thing written. That colonel said he got all the facts from you. That was on the cover of that book."

The captain's head bobbed. "Oh, I see. A blood-and-thunder tale."

"Yes, sir."

"Well, I'd still fancy seeing it. Seen my name in some newspapers—ships' arrivals and things like that—but never in a book."

Cal didn't know what to think or say, but he repeated.

"But the book's cover allowed that the stories were told to that colonel fellow by you."

"Me?"

"Yes, sir. Captain Malachi J. Shufflebottom. He— that colonel fellow—he called you something like a savior and sainted hero of the West. Says you were a witness to everything in that book."

Shufflebottom leaned forward, right into a dripping spot, but he didn't seem to mind. "And you don't have a copy of that book?"

Cal shook his head again. "Not anymore." He bit his bottom lip, then asked, "Did you ever meet a fellow named Delmont?"

After pushing himself out of the dripping spot, Shufflebottom wiped his head and sighed. "Cal, I've meet hundreds, thousands of folks in my travels. And there's a chance I met this Belmont—"

"Delmont."

"Whatever his name is, or was, or what he made up. And I told some stories about you and me and others I'd known on the trails to the Oregon country and to the California goldfields. Many times. But even when I had far too much John Barleycorn, I don't think I ever stretched the truth—not much, anyhow. But you have to remember one thing, son. The truth often gets twisted up into a lie. And some writers aren't too careful with their facts. And when it's all said and done, it's only how you remember things that counts. It's how you lived your life. Not what some harebrained idiot writes to make a few dollars."

Cal let out a sigh and leaned back, running the captain's words through his head.

"How have you lived your life, son?" Shufflebottom asked.

"Well,"—Cal had to think—"I made my share of mistakes, I reckon. Took some trails I wish I hadn't. But for the most part, I tried to do the right thing."

"You sure? They always say that a preacher's son usually turns out a wild one."

"Well, I ain't—haven't—had enough good luck to be wild, I reckon. Too wild." He thought it best to leave out that train robbery and his brief try at outlawry.

The old sailor laughed and leaned back on his crate. "How old are you, Cal?"

Cal had to think on that, too. This was August and the year was 1876. And he was born on January 28 in— He was shocked.

"I'll be thirty-four come January, almost February."

Shufflebottom blew out air.

"Shucks, son, you're still a young man. Got the best years of your life ahead of you. You got plenty of time to find that gal you're chasing, and no matter if you don't find her for another ten or twenty years, if she's the one, then she's worth chasing."

Cal studied his old mentor, waiting for the funny part of his joke.

But the captain's face had saddened. Maybe it was the lantern light.

But the old man let out a long sigh. "I remember a pretty gal I fancied." His head shook slowly. "But I thought I loved the rivers more. The seas. The feel of a boat. The strength of being in command. That all those lives depended on you. And I was a wanderer. I wasn't fit to fancy any gal, so I fancied several. And now here I am"—he held up one hand—"carrying the bullet that killed one of our most famous heroes in my hand. Joking that you're shaking hands with the bullet that killed Wild Bill. Ol' Bill, he'd get a kick out of that. He was a man who loved to laugh. And now he's gone. The world's a bit darker without Wild Bill."

He cleared his throat, looked at his muddy boots, then back up at Cal. "Did you know that Bill got married?"

"Jim?" Cal asked.

Shufflebottom nodded. "That's right. His real name was Jim. Yes, sir, Cal, Wild Bill—J. B. Hickok—married a theater gal named Agnes. I bet she's brokenhearted—or will be when word reaches her. Bill told me he had found his true love, and Bill had had lots of loves in his life. But Agnes was his true love. And I take it that this Catherine is yours."

Now Cal found himself staring at his muddy shoes. "I don't know—I think—but . . . I just don't know."

When he looked up, Captain Shufflebottom was smiling.

"You never will know, Cal. Till you find her. And if I was you, I wouldn't make the mistake ol' Cap'n Shufflebottom did. I'd find her. If she's the one, it'll be worth the time, no matter how many weeks, months, or years it takes. And if she ain't—well, shucks, ol' boy, at least you'll know. And you'll have stories to tell of all the years you wasted on a fool's errand."

He laughed again, and Cal smiled, though he was trying to decide what the devil Captain Shufflebottom was telling him. It didn't sound like one of his late birthing dad's sermons. It didn't sound like any of the speeches he had heard from politicians.

The captain was speaking again, and Cal looked back up at that wonderful sailor and wagon train boss.

"I do know one thing, Cal."

Cal waited.

"You will not find anyone—especially any woman—worth knowing in a place like Deadwood now that Wild Bill's been called to glory. So, if I were you, I'd set out looking. And I wouldn't stop till I found her."

"But we bring bad luck—both of us—to whoever we meet."

Shufflebottom raised his bandaged hand.

"People make their own luck. Take Wild Bill. He always sat where he could see the door—except when he got killed. He asked Charlie Rich to swap seats, but Charlie wouldn't do it, and that'll be on Charlie's conscience for a while, I reckon. You weren't in the saloon, so you can't say Wild Bill—Jim Hickok—is dead on your account. He died because he didn't insist to Charlie—and I don't think Charlie would have held firm to a man with that reputation. Or Bill could have left and tried his luck at another saloon. Remember that, son. Luck is what you make of it. Good or bad or in between. And love is something you have to work hard for—and look hard for."

The captain stood, and Cal did the same. They shook hands, and then Shufflebottom said it was his bedtime, and Cal thanked him and walked out of the tent. The lantern was blown out, and Cal felt like a bull ox as he moved through the thick muck and to the livery stable.

He was on the trail out of Deadwood the next morning.

Cal rode east, of course. He didn't see any point in riding west, not with the Sioux and Cheyenne angrier than hornets and cocky as a spry rooster after they had wiped out George Armstrong Custer at the Little Bighorn River. And while one newspaperman in Omaha pointed out that the deaths of Hickok and Custer could be attributed to Calamity James because "that's how strong Calamity's medicine was; he just had to be in the vicinity to cause trouble," Cal was trying to keep Captain Shufflebottom's words in his head and heart.

But in Fort Randall, he was shocked to discover that his birthing mother had lost an arm because Pinkerton detectives tried to blow up the James farmhouse and wound up killing Calamity's stepbrother. Cal even found a letter waiting for him in the village of Sioux Falls, Dakota Territory, from Mrs. James, which had traveled across most of the Western states and territories. But she just asked him to join the Pinkertons—that would be her revenge: The Pinkertons would all die horrible deaths because Calamity was one of them.

Cal tossed the letter into a stove, whispering, "There's no way the Pinkertons would ever hire anyone named James." And he was done with riding the owlhoot trail. Besides, he suspected that his birthing ma just wanted him to try robbing and stealing again so he could get himself hung.

He had one purpose in life. And that was to find Catherine Thorpe. Cal kept telling himself that she hadn't found some other beau, that she was still dancing—and maybe, just maybe—waiting for him to take her in his arms and away to some nice place where they would make their own luck.

In Madelia, Minnesota, Cal worked for a while helping a farmer bring in his wheat, but it was new wheat, and the fellow in charge of the elevators in town said it hadn't been properly dried, so he wouldn't even let that Swede put his wheat in the elevators. He said it might contaminate all the wheat. Not that that was Cal's fault. He hadn't dried the wheat; he'd just helped the man load that wheat, which Cal thought did feel a bit damp, and helped him bring it into town.

Which is why Cal left Madelia, even though some other farmers had offered him jobs threshing oats, but the farmers who made those offers where bringing in six to eight bushels while the good, or luckier, farmers were bringing in up to fifty bushels. But a store owner let Cal sweep out his place and unload some items that came in by wagon, and he paid Cal fifty cents for his trouble and gave him a penny candy and a cup of coffee, and that was the fellow who told Cal to go up to Mankato, that that city was booming and that a fellow who wanted to work honestly could get a good job and earn a fair wage.

So Cal rode to Mankato the next day.

His horse was a fast walker, and the early September

air was cool, and Cal got an early start so he was in
Mankato by noon that day. He found a café and went
inside for some coffee and a good dinner, and asked the
fellow he had to pay if he might happen to know of
anyone hiring.

"Hiring?" The fellow checked Cal's dime and slid it
into a drawer. "For what kind of work?"

"Anything," Cal said.

"Might try Antonsen's livery," the man said, and
gave directions.

So that's where Cal went, but instead of seeing some
Dane named Antonsen, he saw someone else walk out
of the livery, leading one of the finest horses Cal had
seen in Minnesota.

And Cal couldn't stop himself from whispering the
fellow's name: "Jesse."

While Jesse James was looking up, he was also
pushing back the tails of his well-worn duster, and finding the handle of a big pistol, but his eyes showed
recognition, and also that he saw a whole lot of folks in
town, so Jesse pulled the duster back and hid that particular iron he was packing, and said, "You've made a
mistake, stranger. My name is—Jackson."

Cal wasn't an idiot. "My mistake, sir. You remind
me of my cousin, Jesse—Shufflebottom. From—umm,
Sacramento, California."

"No relation, sir," Jesse said. "I'm from—Delaware."

"Well." Cal nodded. "I'll let you be on your way.
Good day to you, sir."

"And to you."

He swung into the saddle, and rode out of town, and

Cal wondered why Jesse would be up in Minnesota. He bought a newspaper, but that didn't have any mention of Jameses or Youngers, and it wasn't until later that Cal learned of a train robbery in Missouri pulled by the James–Younger Gang had led to some arrests, and one member of the gang named names, and things had gotten hot for the outlaws, and nobody had seen them in Missouri for a while.

Instead of robbing the Mankato bank, the James–Younger Gang rode into Northfield, Minnesota—and things did not turn out well for those bold robbers on that day of September 7, 1876, when the outlaws tried to rob the First National Bank. They might have gotten away with it, except that Cal happened to ride into that town, too, because a kindly man in Mankato told him that the mill in Northfield might be hiring.

But Cal didn't get to the mill. He had just stopped in at the Dampier Hotel and asked about a room when someone outside bellowed, "Get your guns, boys! They're robbing the bank!"

And Cal had his Enfield with him, and a fellow named Manning came up to Cal and said, "Let me have that rifle, son," and didn't wait for Cal to say yes or no but jerked the rifle from his hands, and then bullets started breaking glass and splintering wood, and a frightened but brave clerk ran and tackled Cal and said, "Keep your head down. We don't want our rugs stained with blood."

And that man Manning fired once, then turned to Cal and said, "Throw me your shooting pouch," and Cal had to struggle, because the hotel clerk was still lying atop him, but he managed to slide the pouches over to that fellow, who then started shooting and reloading, shooting and reloading, and it sounded like the longest battle in the history of war. But when Cal finally crawled out from under the clerk, he realized that the shooting had stopped, but now lots of men were yelling and saying something about a posse. Cal stood up, and that man Manning handed Cal his Enfield and said, "That shoots true, son. Shoots mighty true."

And Cal took his rifle out onto the streets, and some folks clapped his back and shoulder since he was carrying a hot, smoking rifle, and Cal was too thunderstruck to say that all he had done was try to get a sweating, sobbing clerk off him.

But then he saw Clell Miller, who Cal knew rode with the Jameses and Youngers, but Clell Miller was now dead in the streets. And so was another guy, and though Cal didn't know him, the linen duster and the many pistols on his person identified him as one of the bank robbers.

Then everybody talked about getting a posse together, and Cal saw his horse, so he walked up to it and shoved the Enfield into the scabbard, and lots of men were already riding after the bank robbers, and Cal figured that he could ride out, too, and folks would think that Cal was chasing after them, too, but those folks seeking justice and revenge were riding southwest. Cal started out for Winona on the Mississippi River.

Those robbers that rode out of Northfield were bloodied and beaten; those they left behind were quite dead; and the gang decided to split up, and afterward, the

Younger brothers were captured near Madelia and pleaded guilty—so they could avoid getting convicted and hanged—and they got sent to the Minnesota pen in Stillwater, but somehow Jesse and Frank managed to get out of the state alive and had enough grit, luck, and sense to disappear for a while.

And Cal never went to Minnesota again, especially when folks started talking about a ninth man that many believed rode in with the James–Younger Gang on the Northfield raid.

CHAPTER 36

He got a job on a stern-wheeler in Winona and worked his way down to just south of Dubuque, where the *Fortune*'s boiler blew and she sank, but there were no casualties.

He landed another job, though not as good, and not on as fine a ship as the *Fortune*, at least before she burned and sank, but the *Eldorado* got Cal to St. Louis, where he ran into Captain Shufflebottom again. The reunion was brief because the captain showed Cal an item in one of the St. Louis newspapers that mentioned a dancer in Fort Worth, Texas, so Cal bought a horse and saddle and rode southwest.

The troupe had moved on, Cal was told, to Denver, someone suggested, but luck favored Cal as a trail boss came into that pool hall and said he was short two cowpokes and he needed two for a drive to, of all places, Denver.

Thirteen stampedes, two near-drownings, one broken leg, one case of bad water, and sixty-three lost steers in river crossings, mud bogs, hungry Kiowas, and a bad bee sting later, Cal arrived in Denver, collected his pay, and found out that a dancing group that might have had a gal fitting Cat's description had been here but gone down to Las Vegas, New Mexico Territory.

So Cal wound up there for a while, but then he was told to try Mesilla, down in the southern part of the territory, and that's where Cal was going when he was offered a job on a ranch in Lincoln County. And since he was out of money and didn't want to appear before Catherine Thorpe penniless, he took the job.

Which was a pretty good job until his boss, an English chap named Tunstall, got murdered by some mean hombres that worked for some rich and powerful and meaner men. In a short time, Cal was being laughed at by a skinny, ugly, bucktoothed kid called Kid, and sometimes Billy, and sometimes Billy the Kid. That kid laughed at the way Cal held a rifle or revolver, but Cal knew better than to say something mean about the boy, because the Kid was right handy with a six-shooter, and quite good at killing men who wanted to kill him. He was even good at shooting prisoners he didn't like.

Billy sort of reminded Cal of Jesse. But Jesse didn't laugh as much.

A lawyer type of guy named McSween told Billy's bunch that they were going into Lincoln to make a stand against the Dolan bunch, but then someone had brought a Santa Fe newspaper and Cal happened to read about a dancing troupe with a beautiful blonde goddess who went by the name Catherine.

Cal rode north that night. He didn't hear about the

burning of McSween's house, the deaths of lots of men on both sides, including McSween, or whatever happened to that Billy the Kid fellow because by the time Cal reached Santa Fe, those dancers had gone to Denver. Again.

And when Cal reached Denver, he learned that they had moved on to Deadwood, which was now a legal town and still booming, since Crazy Horse was dead, and Sitting Bull, living up north of the border, in Canada.

Cal rode into Deadwood, which certainly had changed, in September of 1879, but the only job he could find was working at a bakery. He was broke again, and Mrs. Ellsner was hiring, and said that Cal looked like a nice boy, and, by golly, she had never seen anyone with such beautiful eyes.

The problem with the job was that he worked when most folks were sleeping—even in a town like Deadwood, which had settled down some, but not completely, three years after Hickok's murder and the 1877 hanging in Yankton of his killer, Jack McCall.

It wasn't Cal who knocked the lantern down at two thirty in the morning, but Cal had called out his coworker's name and the fellow turned around and said, "Yeah," and it was that fellow who knocked the lantern to the floor.

The cabin was made of wood. The coal oil spread toward the wall, and the fire grew with that coal oil, then leaped up the wall with a sudden whoosh.

Neither was it Cal who had covered the wooden walls with canvas. Orange flames enveloped the first wall in a matter of seconds. Cal ran to the fellow who had knocked over the lantern and started the fire, and Cal dragged him away from the burning wall. He removed his apron and put out the fire that was burning the fellow's pants. Then he helped the fellow up, and by then, both men were choking on the smoke and could barely see. But it was Cal who got the both of them out the door.

And Cal felt the wind. It was not a light breeze. It was, well, a Dakota Territory wind and it was blowing like it meant business.

Cal found a bell and started ringing it, and the fellow who had knocked over the lantern was shouting, "Fire! Fire! Fire!"

The saloons emptied, and people came running in nightshirts, and others came fully dressed, and some prayed, and others cussed, and by then Mrs. Ellsner's Empire Bakery was destroyed. It wasn't long before the fire reached a hardware store, and that store had plenty of barrels of gunpowder. A roar and thunderous explosion sent flaming debris everywhere. And Deadwood burned and burned and burned.

It reminded Cal of a night in Chicago—eight years before.

Nobody would be dancing in Deadwood for a while, there was no Catherine Thorpe in what was left of the town, but Cal did his duty and stayed on to help rebuild, and it was in 1881 when he arrived in Tombstone, Arizona Territory, because he heard of a beautiful blonde dancing in the Oriental Saloon. And Cal found her!

But though she was a fine dancer and a beautiful woman, she was not Catherine Thorpe.

And Cal was saddling his horse and preparing to ride out of town, and was shoving his Enfield into the scabbard, when he heard a grunt and a curse and turned around to see a star and then a gun—and then stars all before him before the day turned black.

Cal was fined ten dollars and made to work a week fixing the streets for carrying a firearm in the city limits. When the judge told him he was free to leave town and the fellow who had near busted his head told him he'd be right smart if he did leave town, Cal just nodded, and went to fetch his horse from the corral, where he had to trade his Enfield to pay for all the boarding and shoeing and feeding, and as he led his horse out of the corral, he saw something that just made him mad. So he rode right back to where that fellow who had tried to crush his skull still stood smoking cigars and laughing with a pale, puny cuss who looked like he was half a step ahead of the Grim Reaper.

"Hey!" Cal was madder than a hornet. "You say it's illegal to carry firearms in this town!"

The man with the badge frowned. He looked just like that lawdog who had buffaloed Cal in Dodge City.

Cal pointed. "Well, there's a bunch of drunken cowboys near the O.K. Corral and they've got guns galore."

The thin, deathly man coughed. The mean fellow with the mustache and badge said, "Mind your own business."

"You're in cahoots with the Clantons," Cal said.

The lawman's eyes changed. "Clantons?" he said.

Cal nodded. He had played poker with Ike Clanton, who was a cheat and a bad card player.

The other fellow coughed. The man with the badge

turned and let out a shrill whistle. "Virg!" he called out. "You and Morgan, come here."

The sickly one said. "And fetch a shotgun."

And Cal, his anger appeased, turned his horse around and rode for Tucson.

He could not tell you where he went those next long months. But he was in Lawrence, Kansas, in 1882, remembering those good years—before the war, before the carnage—and visiting his mother's grave.

Cal was forty years old. Catherine would be just a few years younger, but he bet she was still beautiful. When he left the cemetery and went to his hotel, a man was waiting for him. Cal didn't recognize the man, but the man asked, "Are you *the* Calamity James?"

"Well . . ." Cal had registered under Calvin Marmaduke, knowing this close to Missouri, Kansans did not care much for anyone with James for a surname.

Then the man held out one of those flimsy blood and thunders.

CALAMITY JAMES and HIS SEARCH
FOR THE DANCING GODDESS;
OR, TRUE LOVE ON THE WESTERN FRONTIER.
By Captain Malachi J. Shufflebottom

Who Knew That Hero of America's
Wild Western Territories,
and Hopes These Words May
Lead Both Man and Woman to Happiness Forever

And the fellow just wanted to shake Cal's hand, and wish him best, and said that it sure was great to have a friend like Captain Shufflebottom, and he even let Cal keep the dime novel. But before the gent could make his way toward the stagecoach station, Cal said, "What does Captain Shufflebottom know about Catherine Thorpe?"

And the man turned and said, "Why, it's in the book. He knows where she is."

And Cal opened the book and read the last paragraph.

And my hope is that this tome will find its way to that great, wonderful, heroic young—nay, middle-aged— man I have known since he was a boy—a boy, but a man in the making. That he will cease his wanderings and go to St. Joseph, Missouri, where he will find that lovely dancer, that beautiful woman, the love of Calamity's life, for there she is, teaching dance to children of all ages and races . . . faithfully waiting for her beau to come claim her as his own.

Cal made it to St. Joseph in record time.

He asked a newspaperman, waiting at the depot to get names of any folks of note, as to the directions to the Miss—how he liked that word, *Miss*—Thorpe Dancing School. And the man told him, then asked if he might have his name and occupation.

And Cal smiled and said, "Marmaduke. No job."

He was ecstatic and took off for Lafayette Street, but he wasn't looking where he was going, he was so blinded by love that he almost knocked over a well-dressed man coming out of a haberdashery.

The man recovered, grabbing Cal's right shoulder with a firm left hand while his right hand disappeared inside his overcoat, and then Cal was staring into eyes that matched his very own.

"Jesse," Cal said, and his whisper was matched by Jesse's snarling "*You!*"

The menace died, and Jesse whispered, "What brings you here?"

Cal said, "Love."

Then Jesse did the oddest thing. He smiled. "Who'd love you?"

"I hope she loves me," Cal said as an answer, and told the address.

Jesse let go of Cal and straightened his clothes and hat, buttoned his overcoat and said, "Come on. It's right off Lafayette Street, and that's where I'm going."

They stopped at a nice frame house, painted white with green shutters, and Jesse invited Cal in.

Cal didn't want to stop for anyone until he found Catherine, but he realized that this fellow was still his brother. So they walked inside, and Jesse removed his overcoat, revealing two loaded revolvers in holsters. But his brother introduced Cal to his wife, calling him Marmaduke and saying he was a cousin from Kentucky, and even let him shake hands with his two children. The mother hurried the kids to come with her to the kitchen, and Cal took a seat in the parlor.

"You're lucky," Cal said softly.

Jesse leaned forward, his face hardening. "Lucky?" he said.

Cal waved at the house, then tilted his head toward the kitchen where Jesse's wife and children were talking in whispers.

"You got a home. A family. Me? I've been wandering most of my whole life."

Jesse pulled up a dime novel from behind a sofa cushion. It was *Calamity James and His Search for the Dancing Goddess.* "Looking for her?"

Cal swallowed, then shrugged.

"You're the lucky one, Brother," Jesse said. "You're not hounded by lawmen and murdering Pinkertons. You're not facing a hangman's noose."

He leaned toward him, and lowered his voice into a whisper. "If Ma should have disowned anyone, it shoulda been me and Frank," he said. "And you've got a good woman. Who has waited for you all those long years." He held up the dime novel again. "Have you read this, Brother?"

Cal shook his head. "Didn't even know about it till a few minutes ago."

"Well, it's a rompin' adventure. And if only half of what this Shufflebottom writes is true, you got a good woman. The way I see it, the way this captain writes about it, you two are such bad luck for everyone around you, you'd be richer than a king and queen if you were together all the time."

He pulled out a watch, checked the time.

"Nice watch," Cal said.

Jesse laughed. "Stole it from a stagecoach passenger, years back." The watch slid into a pocket. He wet his lips, then leaned forward. "That dancing place is two blocks up, then three houses down . . ."

Cal nodded.

"You'd best be on your way. I'm expecting some . . . business associates. And if they see how close our eyes match, they might make assumptions." He stood, and extended his hand.

Cal hesitated, then looked into the eyes. "You've changed, Jesse," he whispered.

"The name's Howard. Thomas Howard." He clasped his brother's hand. "Luck never lasts," Jesse said. "Good or bad. It always changes. And you make your own luck." He repeated the directions, and Jesse walked his oldest brother to the door.

Cal hit the path and saw a man coming his way. Cal pulled his hat brim down and pretended to stare at his feet but kept an eye on the stranger, who stopped, and held up his right hand.

"Excuse me, mister," the man said.

Cal stopped and raised his head.

"Frank?" the man gasped, then sighed. "Oh, no, you're not—" He cleared his throat. "I thought you were a friend of mine, Frank—uh, Smith."

"That ain't me. My name's Calam—Cal—um, Cal—ummm, Marmaduke."

"Mr. Marmaduke, is Mr. Howard home, sir? I saw you leaving his home."

Cal studied the young fellow, and he didn't look like a Pinkerton or an outlaw, but just some ordinary guy. Maybe a salesman. And he had called Jesse "Howard." And that Frank he had mistaken Cal for was a Mr.

Frank Smith. And, well, Cal really wanted to find his beloved Cat.

"He was," Cal said.

"Thank you, sir. I have something—uh, very important—to deliver him."

They walked in opposite directions, and Cal found the house, saw the sign, and practically galloped up the slight hill and then the steps, and then across the small porch, and knocked on the wood.

A woman opened the door, and Cal's face paled. This wasn't Catherine.

But the woman's face brightened. "It's you! You're— Calvin. Why, Cat has told me all about you!"

Cal's heart raced. "Is she—?"

The woman sighed. "No, she moved. Everyone in St. Joseph knows how to dance, so Catherine took off yesterday for Helena, Montana. They love to dance in Helena, Montana, these days."

She invited Cal inside, then hurried to another room, leaving Cal standing with his hat in his hand, and then she was back, and she gave Cal an envelope, and on the envelope was an address in Helena. He ripped open the side of the envelope, fingered out the letter, and read.

CAl:

If you reAd this, I'm in HelenA, MontAnA. The Address is on the envelope. I'll be wAiting for you there.

    Love you, As I've AlwAys loved you, And AlwAys will . . .

               Clumsy CAt

And Cal thanked the woman and read the address on the envelope three more times, and he stuck the envelope in a pouch and the pouch in his pocket, and forgot his hat and walked out of the house and down to Lafayette Street and then all the way to the depot.

He didn't take his eyes off the letter, reading it, kicking a dog without noticing, stepping onto the street and causing a horse to panic and take a buggy running out of control, and then he was smiling. Smiling and running toward the train station.

Someone asked, "Why are you smilin' so?"

And Cal looked at him and answered with a giant grin and bright eyes. "Because I'm the luckiest man on the face of the earth."

He was so happy, knowing he would soon be on his way to Helena, Montana, that he didn't even hear the gunshot that came from inside the house at 1318 Lafayette Street.

**TURN THE PAGE
FOR AN EXCITING PREVIEW!
JOHNSTONE COUNTRY.
GET TOUGH OR GET GHOSTED.**

**In this blazing new series
from the bestselling Johnstones,
the sole survivor of a bloody massacre
turns his rage to bounty hunting—and a new
Western legend is born. . . .**

They call him Ghost. A hard man with a hard past,
Garret "Ghost" McCoy will never forget the day
his family was brutally attacked by vicious marauders.
It forced him to grow up fast, get tough even faster,
and sharpen every skill to survive—by gun, by knife,
or by fist. A true loner and silent stalker, Ghost
is the kind of no-nonsense bounty hunter who always
gets his man. Dead or alive.
But it's only a matter of time before his reputation
catches up with him—in a dusty dead-end town
called Coyote Flats . . .

It starts with a killing.

Three murderous cattle rustlers with a bounty
on their heads reach the end of the line on the streets
of Coyote Flats—where Ghost guns them down in a
shoot-out. Impressed by the bounty hunter's gun skills,
the leader of a local outlaw gang makes Ghost an offer
he can't refuse. But Ghost refuses anyway.
Which ticks off the outlaw—and draws the attention
of *another* leader of *another* outlaw gang.
Like it or not, Ghost is stuck in the middle
of a gang war between two fierce rivals.
But there's something about the second gang
· that's different. Something *familiar* . . .

They're the marauders who killed Ghost's family.
And now they're about to get Ghosted.

NATIONAL BESTSELLING AUTHORS
WILLIAM W. JOHNSTONE
and J.A. Johnstone

THE MAN FROM BLOOD GULCH

First in a New Series!

Live Free. Read Hard.
williamjohnstone.net
Visit us at kensingtonbooks.com

On sale now, wherever Pinnacle Books are sold.

PROLOGUE

Gunshots and the wild hollering of the bandits echoed throughout the gulch, the thunder stampede of hooves not quite drowning out the screams and shouts of the terrified settlers. A dozen families lived in Parson's Gulch—forty-seven people along with chickens, hogs, dogs, cows, mules, and horses. There'd never been any trouble.

Until recently.

Twelve-year-old Garret McCoy splashed through the shallow stream, dragging along eight-year-old Mary Jane Potts, an iron grip on her thin wrist, her corn-yellow pigtails flapping in the breeze. It was like dragging along an anvil; Mary Jane fought him all the way.

McCoy reckoned he couldn't blame her. After all, most folks in their right mind wouldn't run *toward* all the shooting and screaming, which is exactly what McCoy was doing.

"I'm scared!" Mary Jane shouted.

"We've got to know what's happening." McCoy kept pulling, not willing to admit he was frightened, too.

They circled Bill Wilder's barn, squatting at the

corner to peek around and watch the chaos unfolding along the dirt road that led into and out of the gulch, houses and barns and sheds and chicken coops on either side. McCoy stared wide-eyed as two score bandits rode through the gulch, blasting away with their six-guns at anything that moved.

Doris Manning, who did the sewing for so many folks, tried to dart into the imagined safety of her clapboard home. She had made it up three of the five steps to her front porch when one of the bandits squeezed off a shot and blood bloomed wet and red between her shoulder blades. She fell forward then slipped back down the stairs.

McCoy flinched at the sound of the gunshot.

More people were killed, men and women indiscriminately.

Jasper Jenkins, the old man who whittled, down by the stream, while fishing and smoking his pipe, was shot in the face. Paul Branson, father of three, new to Parson's Gulch, chased his three children out of the way of the galloping horses only to be ridden down himself and trampled bloody into the mud. Claude Irving, the community blacksmith, came storming from his forge, rifle clutched in his meaty hands, but he never got off a shot. Three bandits peppered him with multiple blasts, spinning the big man away. Old Lady Callahan, who was always so happy to babysit the young ones, tripped and went sprawling in the mud. As she tried to get up, a horse hoof caught her in the forehead. Her eyes rolled white, and she was gone.

McCoy was terrified but found he could not turn

away from the carnage, his eyes wide with morbid fascination. A desperate bleating sound drew his attention. He turned and saw Mary Jane behind him, sitting on the ground, knees pulled up against her chest, eyes squeezed tightly shut, hands over her ears to block out the horror.

He opened his mouth to tell her—what?

That it would be okay? That he'd keep her safe?

Lies.

The marauders broke off into twos and threes, weaved in between the buildings, flushing out anyone trying to hide. Guns blazed and bodies fell over one another into the mud. Three grim riders broke off from the main body, galloping hard for the Wilder barn. McCoy's eyes went big.

He grabbed Mary Jane's wrist again, yanking her to her feet. "Come on!"

They ran around to the back side of the barn and followed the narrow footpath behind the houses until they came to Mary Jane's home, a small and rickety shack that McCoy was always surprised to see still standing. Mary Jane tried to run for the dilapidated staircase going up to her back door.

"No!" McCoy held on to her tight.

He'd seen the men kicking in doors, pulling people out of their homes. The gunfire had waned, but the screaming and shouting had increased.

"Under here!" McCoy pulled her down to her hands and knees, and then both went flat to their bellies. They wriggled under the house. McCoy kept scooting forward, inches at a time, until he was right behind the house's front steps. He glanced back often to make sure Mary Jane was still with him. She'd gone to pick berries, and McCoy's father—who was pals with Mary Jane's father—had told him to go with her, since she was too young to be wandering the woods alone.

Watch over that little girl. His father's last words to him. *She's your responsibility.*

McCoy peered through the gaps in the steps. He didn't want to be caught, but he was desperate to see what was happening. From his hiding place behind the steps, he could see his small house across the street, but that's not what firmly had McCoy's attention at the moment.

In the middle of the muddy road, McCoy's father was on his knees. One of the marauders stood behind him, a six-gun pointed at the back of his head. The marauder was a porky fellow with a greasy sneer. McCoy gasped, eyes widening with growing fear. There was blood on his father's face, at the corners of his mouth, one eye swollen closed, black-and-blue. His father didn't even look frightened, McCoy thought, just tired, head hanging, shoulders slumped.

Another stranger paced back and forth in front of his father, a sharp-featured man, thin but straight, a sneering expression on his face. McCoy had seen the man before. The patch over his left eye had made him memorable. He'd been through Parson's Gulch about a week before, and McCoy had watched him having heated words with his father, some dire dispute, although McCoy hadn't been close enough to hear the words.

Now the man was back with a bunch of marauders, roaring through the gulch to murder and terrorize. Why these men had singled out his father, McCoy couldn't guess, unless it was the fact that his father was a sort of unofficial leader in the community. A few of the folks in Parson's Gulch even called him *mayor*—half joke, half sign of respect.

"You didn't want to do this the easy way, Warren," the man in the eye patch said. "Now you see what happens. Now you see how serious my employer is about this land."

McCoy flinched at the man saying *Warren*—his father's first name. To McCoy, he was *Pa*, and to everyone else in the gulch he was *McCoy*. When McCoy's mother had been alive, she was the only one who'd called McCoy's father Warren. It seemed a cruel presumption for this nasty stranger to call McCoy's pa by his first name.

Warren McCoy spit, a mix of blood and saliva. "There ain't gold in that stream, I'm telling ya. Old Pete found a couple small nuggets, and the rest of us swarmed all over that stream, panning our hearts out. Came up with nothing, so we all just went back to our normal lives. Folks just live here now regular-like. We ain't doing nothing to nobody. Just living."

"And that's too much," said the man with the eye patch. "Bart, send him on his way."

The porky marauder lifted his six-shooter and shot Warren McCoy in the back.

People screamed.

McCoy's mouth fell open. *No.*

The world seemed to slow, his father pitching forward, eyes rolling up, until he finally landed face-first in the mud, instantly immobile like a cold slab of beef. McCoy felt dizzy, unable to rip his eyes away from the scene—like he had just witnessed something impossible, like if he just kept looking, wide-eyed and slack-jawed, his father would get up again.

Then the yelling—pure anger and hatred, words smashed together in one, long animal sound of pure fury.

It was McCoy's older brother, Danny, a fifteen-year-old walking, talking grudge against the world. He stormed down the steps of the house across the road, clutching his father's double-barrel shotgun, eyes wild with rage, face twisted.

The porky one called Bart turned and raised his gun, but he was too slow.

Danny jerked the triggers, and both barrels belched fire. Bart's head vanished in a blur of red mist. More screams. The corpse toppled onto his father's.

Danny didn't live one more second after that. The man with the eye patch along with a half dozen more of the marauders drew and blazed away at the boy.

All the onlookers kept screaming and screaming and screaming.

McCoy felt his chest tighten, his gut convulse.

Danny took a few sideways steps, lead slamming into him from every direction, fresh blooms splashing red across his chest, belly, and thighs. He took a couple more halting steps, almost like a drunken dance that would have been comical if not for the horror of it. The teen fell forward into the mud and never got up again.

McCoy tried to move without thinking—there was no reason to it, nothing that could be done, but the urge was overwhelming to crawl out from under the house and go to them.

Something kept him from moving forward.

He looked back. Mary Jane had both hands latched onto him, her thin fingers wrapped around his arm, pulling him back with everything she had. The plea in her eye couldn't have been any plainer if she'd said it out loud. *Don't go. Don't go. Don't go. Don't—*

The last words Pa had said to him floated back. *Keep watch on the girl.*

"Now, listen up, you people," the man in the eye patch shouted. "Just forget about this place. When we come back, you'd better be gone. If you're still here— well, I reckon you know what happens."

The marauders mounted their horses and rode away.

For a long moment nobody moved. The gulch had gone dead quiet save for the sniffles and sobs of the few overcome with emotion.

McCoy felt Mary Jane let go of him.

He crawled out from under the house, movements leaden, a strange dizzy feeling separating him from the rest of the world, like it was all happening behind glass. He had a vague awareness of others, folks hugging and crying, some drifting back into their homes. He had the notion somebody might be talking to him, a muted voice, like someone trying to speak to him underwater. He ignored it.

In his peripheral vision, he saw Mary Jane run into her mother's arms. Good. One less obligation to weigh him down.

He paused to look at his father and brother. They didn't look real. Just cold meat stuffed into familiar clothing now shot through with lead. He walked on and into the house, aware there were still folks calling his name.

McCoy went through the little house quickly. They didn't own much, and he barely filled the canvas sack. He grabbed the saddle and went to the small barn out back and saddled the old splotchy gelding. The animal still had a few good years in it. He mounted up. Where would he go? Kansas maybe. Hadn't his pa mentioned a sister there?

He'd figure it out one way or another.

Less than twenty minutes after his father and brother had been ruthlessly cut down in the muddy road, Garret McCoy rode out of Parson's Gulch.

And he never went back.

EIGHTEEN YEARS LATER . . .

CHAPTER 1

Eighteen years later . . .

The Colt Peacemaker felt strange on his hip.

Not bad, just new. He'd carried a Colt Navy for years, and it was a hard thing to give up something that had worked so well for so long. The Peacemaker's cartridge was bigger, and he liked that. He liked the way it bucked in his hand. Felt like power. But so far, he'd only shot tin cans and bottles with it.

Now it was time to shoot men.

The town of Black Oak was like any of a hundred others across Texas, and that meant there was at least one saloon.

The two outlaws on the saloon's front porch looked smug and overconfident. Probably because of the rifle-man in the window across the street. They'd heard he was coming for them, so they'd put a man in the window and thought it was their little secret.

But Garret McCoy had spotted him in the hotel window, second floor, all the way on the left. He'd always had good luck sniffing out men who were out to kill him, a natural instinct honed by far more practice and experience than any man should see in a lifetime. He'd joined up with a bunch of other dumb, wide-eyed Kansas boys right after Fort Sumter. They'd show those Confederates a thing or two.

The bravado had faded fast at Wilson's Creek.

Even at the raw age of eighteen, it was plain that McCoy was good at war, could ride and fight and handle guns. By Elkhorn Tavern, he had three stripes on his arm, in no small part because most of the boys he'd joined with had gotten killed.

By the Wilderness, he'd been plucked from his regiment to join a special raiding unit. He learned to ride hard and strike fast, and he was even better with a pistol than with a rifle.

And then one day the war was over, and all McCoy had learned was how to kill.

He needn't have worried, for the West always had a use for men with that exact skill. And some men were worth just as much dead as alive. McCoy didn't relish killing, but he'd seen enough death to get numb to it.

Not that he was eager for his own. He'd lived this long because he was smart and careful and patient. Patience was key. If he turned up the front steps to the saloon porch right now to face the outlaws, it would put his back to the rifleman across the street. There was no rule that said he had to face the outlaws this very minute just because they were smirking at him. He wasn't obliged to walk into their trap.

He turned abruptly to circle behind the saloon, catching the outlaws' surprised look from the side of his eye.

When he was out of sight, he touched his guns to make sure they were still there. Of course they were, but it was a fidgety habit. Two fingers on the butt of the Peacemaker on his hip, then a thumb along the hammer's cool metal of the Colt Navy in its new place, holstered under his stomach at the belt line. If he spent all the lead in the Peacemaker and still needed to shoot, he could drop it and draw the Navy crossways. It was a comfortable setup for him. He'd been too nostalgic for the Navy to give it up completely, and it was good to have the old friend ready as backup.

He entered the saloon through the back door, went down a short hall, taking it slow to give his eyes a chance to adjust. He emerged from the hallway into the front part of the saloon, a highly polished bar off to his right with an enormous oil painting depicting a woman sprawled on a divan on the wall behind it. She wasn't exactly dressed for cold weather.

The place was crowded for an afternoon, folks swilling beers and tossing back shots of whiskey, lively conversation and a few hands of poker at scattered tables. McCoy went to the bar, flagged down a harried-looking fella in a dirty apron, and asked for whiskey.

He stood there awhile, sipping from the glass, turning around to lean back against the bar and keep an eye on the front door. They'd get curious and come in soon enough.

What happened after that remained to be seen.

They entered the saloon sooner than he thought they would, stopping just inside the doors, casting about, obviously trying to spot him. A second later, they did. One elbowed the other, and they traded whispers, and in the next moment took a table across the room, backs to the wall, both watching him while McCoy watched them right back.

McCoy could just about read their minds. He hadn't stumbled into their obvious trap, and they were trying to figure what to do next. If they were smart, they'd mount up and get gone.

They were almost never smart.

The town's sheriff—a fella named Bryson Tate—was pretty good about rounding up drunks on a Saturday night and keeping the peace in a general way, but when it came to outlaw killers, he hadn't been much help. So that's when a trio of anxious men from the town council had approached McCoy. If the law couldn't rid the town of these men, then let a hired gun do it is what they figured. Tate simply didn't have the grit for it, and furthermore, it was suspected he took bribes from the outlaws to look the other way.

McCoy had put that to the test, letting it leak to Tate that he would be headed to the saloon soon to take the outlaws dead or alive. Sure enough, word got to the outlaws, and it could only have been Tate who'd tipped them off.

Now, McCoy's plan was to wait them out. They'd get impatient and make a mistake. Or the rifleman across the street would get impatient and come over to see what was going on, and then McCoy would have all three of them together. Not ideal, but better than having a sniper across the street taking potshots at him.

"Dirty" Dave Dunbar and Shane "Snake" Delany weren't the most ruthless killers McCoy had ever hunted, but they weren't model citizens by any measurement. Delany got the nickname "Snake" because he had a tattoo of a sidewinder down his shooting arm and told everyone who'd listen that he was as fast on the draw as a striking snake. Dunbar was called "Dirty" because—well, McCoy didn't know. Maybe the man didn't bathe.

By a process of elimination, that meant the man across the street with the rifle must be Larry Prince, who evidently didn't feel the need to bother with a nickname. Maybe he felt being called Prince was enough.

The saloon doors swung inward as a newcomer entered, a man hunched over in a long, gray cloak, head down and hat pulled low. There was nothing remarkable about him except the way he walked, a slow, deliberate gait, like he was weary but determined, or drunk but pretending to be sober. Nobody took much notice of him, but McCoy watched the man with curiosity as he shambled across the saloon.

When the stranger drew even with the table where Dunbar and Delany sat, he suddenly threw off his cloak, stood straight, and drew a pair of gleaming, nickel-plated Peacemakers, leveling one at each outlaw.

"Don't move," the stranger said. "Get them hands on the table."

The outlaws complied, everyone in the saloon turning to see what was happening.

McCoy realized he knew the man.

Bob Baily was another bounty hunter. He and McCoy had crossed paths before, which often happened when two hunters trailed the same prey. He wore a blue bib-front shirt and black pants with yellow stripes down the sides. A bushy mustache drooped down each side of his wide mouth.

"I like your new Peacemakers, Bob," McCoy said. "Real flashy."

Bob's eyes flashed to McCoy quickly then back to the outlaws. "That you, Garret?"

"It's me."

"Ain't seen you since Wichita."

McCoy shrugged. "I been around."

"Well, I reckon I know why you're here, and I'm just telling you to stand back," Bob told him. "I got the drop on these boys fair and square. You wanted them, you should've made a move sooner. My play, my reward."

"I guess that's about right," McCoy agreed.

"Okay, then." Bob waved his six-shooters at the two outlaws. "You two get up and head out that front door, and no funny business. I like to take my prisoners in alive—unlike some folks I could mention—but we can do it dead, if that's how you want it."

Dunbar and Delany stood slowly, hands in the air, and moved toward the front door, Bob following.

McCoy cleared his throat. "I need to warn you, Bob—"

"Warn me what?" Bob shot back. "You going to take my prisoners from me? You just stay at the bar and

enjoy your drink, and keep your hand away from that shooter on your hip."

"Dang it, Bob, you need to listen to me for your own good."

"You don't give me orders, so don't get all tough with me, Ghost McCoy." Bob licked his lips nervously.

McCoy's eyes narrowed. "I don't much fancy that nickname."

"Never mind that," Bob said. "You just mind your business, and I'll mind mine."

The outlaws left the saloon, and Bob Baily followed.

The unmistakable crack of a rifle shot split the air.

Bob flew back into the saloon, hat spinning away, fancy shooting irons drooping from his hands. He landed hard with a *wham* on the rough floorboards. Blood dripped down one side of his nose from a neat hole in the center of his forehead.

Yells, panic, curiosity, excitement, fear all mixed together from everyone in the saloon, some standing to get a better look at the show, others diving under tables for cover.

McCoy was already moving sideways from the bar, his Peacemaker flashing into his hand. Snake Delany burst back through the swinging saloon doors first, Colt Walker in his hand, blazing away where McCoy had been standing at the bar a split second ago, whiskey bottles exploding in a rain of glass and amber liquid.

McCoy fanned the hammer of his Peacemaker twice, catching Snake in the chest and knocking him back into

Dirty Dave who was trying to enter. Both men went down in a heap.

Dirty Dave recovered quickly, coming up to one knee and lifting his pistol, but he wasn't fast enough.

McCoy fired.

The shot caught Dirty Dave in the throat, and he dropped his pistol and flopped over, making a heart-breaking gurgling sound.

McCoy rushed to the front door but stood off to the side, trying to peek around the corner into the street without exposing himself to the rifleman. He took a couple of quick looks. The hotel window across the street was empty, but that didn't mean much. The shooter could have been hiding off to the side of the window just as McCoy was doing, waiting for his chance to shoot again.

Dirty Dave hadn't finished dying yet. He squirmed on the ground, kicking and twitching, both hands at his throat, blood seeping wet and red between his fingers.

McCoy took a longer look this time, but he didn't see anyone in the hotel windows, and nobody took a shot at him.

Dirty Dave stopped twitching.

McCoy heard a horse whinny, then galloping hooves. He went out the front door, stepping over the corpses of the two outlaws, and saw Larry Prince riding out of town as if the devil himself was on his tail.

McCoy put two fingers in his mouth and whistled sharp and shrill.

A boy came around the corner leading McCoy's horse by the reins. The animal was a huge black mare.

A good bit of horseflesh. The boy was a young Mexican, maybe fifteen, bucktoothed. Dark eyes. He handed McCoy the reins.

"Stayed out of sight until you whistled," the boy said. "Just like you told me."

"Good man." McCoy dipped into his vest pocket and came out with a coin. He flipped it to the boy.

McCoy mounted his horse and frowned as he saw Sheriff Tate huffing and puffing toward him, face red.

"Where do you think you're going?" Tate demanded. "You can't just shoot up my town and ride off."

"I didn't start the shooting. I finished it." McCoy pointed at the two bodies in front of the saloon. "Those are my kills, you hear? I'm coming back for my money."

Tate frowned and snarled but didn't contradict him. He didn't have his outlaws backing him up anymore.

"You'll get your bounty," Tate said. "Nobody here's going to cheat you."

"Not if they know what's good for 'em, they won't."

McCoy clicked his tongue, and the big black horse took off like a shot after Larry Prince.

Visit our website at
KensingtonBooks.com
to sign up for our newsletters, read
more from your favorite authors, see
books by series, view reading group
guides, and more!

BOOK CLUB
BETWEEN THE CHAPTERS

Become a Part of Our
Between the Chapters Book Club
Community and Join the Conversation